The Co
And The Mat

1

Dedicated to

Moira T Marshall and David W Grant.

And my three beautiful children,

James, Jenson and Robyn.

THE COMMODORE AND THE MATTERLESS MARTYR

The first of 'The Commodore' Series

Published by Book Cream

By G.D. Sills

For more on G.D Sills head over to bookcream.co.uk, where you can give feedback directly to the author, view exclusive interviews and get notifications for the next exciting release.

Chapter One – The Good Shepherd

The Good Shepherd blesses all and promises to lead us into a new era of hope, prosperity and greatness. He will lead his flock into new realms, the likes of which the Divine world has never seen. Across the planes and into the unknown he will protect us. Enlightenment and learning will be available to all with no bias or discrimination. A new dawn has befallen us. The Time-Keepers are obsolete and have retired, their interests have shifted from the greater good of the world into their own agenda. Let us stand, hand in hand, and welcome the new leader of Existence! Down with the King and up with The Good Shepherd!

The witch wept quietly in the corner of the damp dungeon. In the darkness, she pondered how long she had been in captivity. A week? A month? She wasn't sure. Her eyes strained as she tried to make out an object on the other side of the abysmal cell. The smell of an unidentified decaying cadaver, sulphur and burnt hair would make even the hardiest nauseous.

Heavy footsteps came pounding along the corridor. The witch lifted her head in curiosity as the corridor fell silent. After a brief moment, the door crashed open. The light stung the witch's eyes, she yelped and immediately shielded them with her hands.

"Please, please let me go," she croaked, still shielding her stinging eyes.

"Silence!" bellowed a beery voice from the light. "Kull, take her to the Royal Chambers."

A dish-sized hand took her roughly by the back of her neck and lifted her from the ground with ease. Kull, the giant, stood at twice the height of most men and obeyed his orders to the letter. The witch kicked and screamed but to no avail, as Kull carried her away.

The Grand Manor of The Celestial Order stood bold and proud upon its vast, immaculate grounds. Flowing greenery and floral decoration draped the landscape surrounding this magnificent building which boasted an array of different colours.

If you asked someone for directions, they'd tell you it's just past somewhere, right opposite nowhere. It can be defined as wherever you want it to be but only by invitation, courtesy of those that manage this impressive estate and the Divine world that it governs. The Celestial Order.

Beautiful it may be, but many avoid this iconic building and embrace its obscurity. Those who enter seldom leave.

Those employed at The Grand Manor were of many origins, some of the Earth and some of a different plane. With a common goal in hand, they knew the importance and essential perfection their role required. Eye contact and unnecessary interaction were met with consequences of the most unpleasant kind.

One sunny morning as the staff bustled and busied their way around The Grand Manor, a sudden panic descended as the staff rushed to the huge oak doors and opened them. They bowed in silence as the council entered. Beads of sweat gathered on the foreheads of the staff as they nervously stood to attention. The council made their way without a word, swiftly and without hesitation, to the Royal Chamber. This particular part of The Grand Manor once hosted the blue-blooded lineage that had ruled the 'Divine' world, until the dawn of their current government, The Celestial Order, long ago.

The Royal Chamber had already been prepared as the council settled into their chairs around the vast oak table. The supreme leader of the The Celestial Order and Divine, Vignis Moralis, known widely as The Good Shepherd, pondered the decorative flowers and looked momentarily frustrated as one of them had shed a petal onto the polished table. He made a mental note to reprimand the individual responsible for allowing such imperfection.

Vignis took special care in his appearance – not a single hair could ever be seen out of place, and his smart clothes were always immaculate. A stunning black suit accompanied a red rose lodged in his top pocket on this occasion. A slender, tall man, he had a charming smile that enthralled his public. A Divinian of no particular accent, his subjects gave him their unconditional faith and trust. This had been bolstered by an incredible public campaign by The Celestial Order. When the doors were closed from his adoring fans his charm became wicked, toxic and cruel.

Vignis stood waiting for the others to settle into their seats, stroking his handsome face as he considered how to tackle the main topic of the day's meeting. He had mastered the art of leadership, public relations and political affairs during his rise to power. Those that opposed him or challenged his views, he masterfully brought around to his vision. For those that he couldn't, he had them removed.

Maintaining a very modest past, it was a mystery to most where he had come from. Whenever anyone questioned his age, should they dare, he replied with "very old" and that was that. Origins and historical affiliation remained a mystery to most of the Divine community, and Vignis liked it that way.

"Are there any issues to raise before we begin the meeting?" asked Vignis calmly into the silent room.

No one gave any inclination, and silence prevailed.

"Implementation of energy as a currency has been successful. All in the Divine realm are now trading with energy, irrespective of societal placement or origin. Trading has increased and the energy tax has increased income into The Celestial Order, meaning we're on course for the final solution." Vignis smiled.

"Today we discuss a most important goal. We need to increase efficiency of energy coming into The Celestial Order, it needs to be constant, consistent and larger in volume. Only then will we have the ability to move on to the next phase of our solution." His expression became more serious as he placed his hands atop the polished table.

He looked around at the varied faces that surrounded the table. Though different in appearance, they all looked fierce, concentrated and focused on the matter at hand.

"Energy can only be harvested from the Divine and beyond, there is little to no energy to be found from Blind entities. We must continue to remain as obscure from their realm as possible. We have managed to avoid a war with the Blind for centuries. This must remain, for now at least."

Maybelle fluttered almost silently over to Vignis and whispered low enough so that others in the room couldn't hear. The room began to shuffle uncomfortably in the silence. Maybelle stood at about a foot in height, and as the only known fire fairy, she could easily be recognised. A burnt orange glow surrounded her delicate figure and outwardly friendly appearance, she had learnt much from her master. Vignis had taken it upon himself to employ her as his right-hand assistant, and he kept her nearby at all times.

Why he chose a fire fairy, nobody knew. Fairies – even fire fairies – look incredibly charming and friendly. With high levels of intelligence, they can be unpredictable and even cruel.

Vignis gave a nod of approval and gestured Maybelle away. He glanced once more at the stray petal that tarnished the immaculate table.

"Judge Humphrey, Omar Asghari. You are dismissed from the day's meeting. There is no further business that will require your attention today," Vignis ordered.

Judge Humphrey and Omar both looked at each other, slightly taken aback; they were usually included in all meetings set in place by The Celestial Order. They gathered themselves and left the room without a word in reply. This was the wisest course of action when responding to their leader.

A loud chafing and squeaking of leather echoed through the tense quiet in the grand room. Vignis shot Arteon Chubb a contemptuous look as he adjusted himself in his chair that he barely managed to fit in. Red-faced and uncomfortable, he tried to stay still and appear collected.

"Anything to add, Arteon?" Vignis snapped, clearly frustrated at his mere presence. Nervous fidgeting and sweaty palms were in abundance as Vignis scowled at Arteon. Vignis acted as though he wasn't aware of this sharp increase in atmospheric tension. The truth of the matter was that he enjoyed it. The tension played a part in his conscious effort to hold the room and control the flow of the day's events. It worked superbly.

"The Celestial Order now has the correct protocols in place to manage and oversee the income of energy. The Bank of The Celeste has now been opened and is operating on a public level and for our… other activities…" Arteon spluttered. He looked at the others as if to ask for help but, sadly, he was very much alone and certainly wouldn't receive any aid from his peers. Arteon slipped further into his chair as he waited for the focus to move away from him.

Vignis glared at Arteon for a moment, allowing a crushing silence to reign.

"I expect a written report of these activities before midday tomorrow," Vignis replied, unimpressed at his announcement.

"Yes, absolutely, consider it done," Arteon wheezed.

Arteon silently panicked and continued to perspire at an alarming rate as he considered this near-impossible task. His report wasn't entirely truthful. He had set the foundations for his task but hadn't achieved anywhere near the progress he'd reported. Vignis's suspicion had been roused and he called Arteon's bluff.

Arteon had neglected his project by delegating his tasks to those that worked for him whilst he indulged in pleasures of a mostly perverse nature.

Sitting opposite Arteon Chubb, Adelade Grey let a thin smile crack across her usually cold face. She enjoyed watching Arteon suffer for his inefficiencies. Adelade directed all management of The Celestial Order and knew full well what a task Arteon had been landed with. She looked middle-aged, always dressed formally and never spoke out of place. She knew nothing of joy, happiness or empathy, and considered them to be inefficient emotions used only by the foolish and lame.

Always looking to progress, today's meeting held great importance for her. It would be her chance to demonstrate her true capability.

Mohammed Shah, the latest addition to the governing board of The Celestial Order, sat at ease and comfort, only half paying attention to the meeting's activities. This could only be due to naivety, stupidity or both. Should Shah be challenged, he would be alone to deal with any confrontation from Vignis.

"Shah, do we have an update on our shipment?" Vignis enquired.

"The next few days at the latest," Shah replied without concern. He hadn't noticed the urgency in Vignis's voice – or he chose to ignore it.

Shah always looked his best and wore informal modern attire, such as tracksuits and leisure wear, nearly all of the time. He had obtained a place on The Celestial Orders board through an unorthodox method. The Blind could never hold a place here, but as one of the richest people in Saudi Arabia, he had managed to negotiate his way into The Celestial Order just before a terminal illness had taken him. Through Divinian magic they were able to cure his illness and bring him into the Divine world. Though money may not guarantee happiness, it can certainly provide the right connections. Nobody knew the exact details of the negotiation, but it caught the attention of Vignis, and in no time at all Shah had been offered a place on the board of The Celestial Order.

"What's the latest on our position against The Galdihar Rebellion?" Vignis asked as he flicked through some of his notes.

"They've lost all major strongholds to The Celestial Order and have been forced into hiding," Adelade Grey said with conviction. "They are all but eliminated!"

"Well, they must *all* be eliminated as soon as possible," Vignis snapped, playing down the importance of the Rebellion. "Do we know the whereabouts of The Commodore?"

"Erm…" Adelade returned to her notes and went through them wildly as Vignis glared impatiently. "He is in hiding, but we know what time line he has entered. It is only a matter of time before he is captured."

Vignis stared hard at the faces around the room.

"The continuation of time is delicate. The Commodore puts us all in jeopardy every time he travels to a different timeline," Vignis spat. "Not to mention, his escape and evasion. He is making a mockery of everything that we stand for. I want that criminal captured or – so help me – I will hold all of you responsible."

The day wore on until darkness fell over The Grand Manor. The meeting continued into the evening until the final call of business had arrived.

"Maybelle, have the witch brought to us!" barked Vignis. Maybelle fluttered out of the room without hesitation.

"Adelade, you requested to take the lead on our final matter of business," said Vignis.

He made his way across the meeting room to a darkened corner and seated himself in a wing-backed chair.

Adelade was preparing her notes when the door to the meeting room flew open, crashing against the wall. Kull entered dragging a flailing woman. She screamed and kicked, begging to be released. The giant obliged, dropping the woman in a pile on the floor. The giant left and Maybelle closed the door behind him.

"Silence!" bellowed Adelade.

The witch sobbed uncontrollably. Her hair was tangled and matted, her clothes were threadbare and filthy. It was clear that she had been held in captivity for quite some time. The witch also had another affliction that didn't stand her at any good grace. She came from the world of the Blind. The Blind are very rarely brought into the Celestial realm. The Celestial Order considered the Blind as the lowest of the low.

"You're aware as to the nature of your summoning?" questioned Adelade as she arranged her notes for the tenth time.

The witch didn't answer, but continued to sob with her head in her hands. Adelade glanced nervously towards the wing-backed chair in the corner of the room. This wasn't part of the plan, why wouldn't this simpleton conform to her questioning?

"You have been summoned to the The Grand Manor of The Celestial Order to carry out a specific task in exchange for a reduced sentence for your crimes against The Celestial Realm," Adelade asserted.

The witch sobbed louder, without looking up.

"I'm... I'm not helping you, just... just kill me now and have it over with," the witch spluttered through her tears.

"There are fates worse than death, criminal!" snapped Shah.

"Thank you," retorted Adelade, frowning at his interruption.

She paced over to the witch with her hands behind her back and a look of exaggerated empathy.

"There are two boys still in Existence, they live by Penny Meadow, currently with their aunt. It would be unfortunate for them to get tied up in your investigation," Adelade said softly.

"You wouldn't! Leave my children out of this!" screamed the witch in hysteria.

Adelade smiled, she had achieved the rise she was looking for. She continued to pace the room.

"If you do not co-operate, there will be consequences," Adelade cooed in an almost caring tone.

The witch looked up at Adelade, tired and defeated.

"What do you require of me?" the witch muttered.

"Summon Hymn," Adelade grinned.

The board members began to shift in their seats, shooting a nervous glance at each other. The name alone brought fear to all except Adelade and Vignis.

The witch remained silent for a few moments, contemplating her options… or lack thereof.

"It's not that simple. It takes time, and the process must be perfect. Many have tried and have been unsuccessful," the witch explained earnestly.

"I'm sure you'll manage just fine," said Adelade as her smile curled further. Adelade didn't smile very often and when she did, it looked sadistic and unnatural.

"I don't have the items required," the witch said, as a matter of fact. She hoped that this would abort their plans.

"Not to worry! I have had the necessary effects gathered. They're of the finest quality," Adelade enthused.

Adelade brought over a wooden box filled with the items required for the ritual. Everything she would need was present and, more to the point, the items were of a finer quality than her own.

The witch let out a sigh and began arranging the items for the ritual.

Vignis remained in the corner of the room and seemed transfixed by the witch. He knew the difficulty of her task and hadn't seen it done first hand before. He observed every motion, mentally recording the movements.

Silence reigned as the room looked at the witch, watching every move she made. She took great care in her spiritual activities and was well practiced at her craft. She damned the day she ever got involved in witchcraft. She had always practiced for advantage but had ultimately meddled in the wrong circles. Now her children were at risk.

The witch threw more logs into the open fireplace. The members of the order watched as the flames were given renewed life, lighting fiercely. She muttered an incantation and threw an assortment of concoctions into the fireplace. The flames roared and turned a deep shade of blue. She stood back and stared wide-eyed, not moving, as if ready to run.

A few moments passed by but nothing more seemed to be happening.

"Is that it?!" Adelade snorted loudly, but the witch simply gestured for her to be quiet.

Adelade scowled at the witch. No one should dare gesture to her in such a manner.

The flames began to turn back to their familiar state and shade. The witch sighed with relief and moved further away from the fireplace.

A figure began to emerge from the fireplace. Slowly, it descended from the flames and stood in front of its impromptu audience. Hymm had been summoned. The over-powering stench of rotting flesh and sulphur attacked the senses of all in attendance.

Hymm studied the room. The room looked on in awe at the other-worldly entity. An ancient, tattered Edwardian black dress flowed down to a pair of black leather boots, styled from the same era. A pair of white leather gloves accompanied the sinister attire. Above the shoulders hovered a white porcelain mask, cracked and tired with a wry smile that could bring fear and dread to the strongest of men. Behind the mask hid no face, and under the gloves were no hands. If not for the clothes, there would be no indication of a presence at all.

The room gasped and held its breath. Some considered running away, but if Hymm didn't catch them, Vignis would. All eyes were fixed on Hymm – all except Shah. He didn't seem to be particularly moved by the summoning. He watched in quite a relaxed state with a knee leant on the table, something that Vignis had noticed and held in more contempt than the offending flower petal.

Hymm. The supreme orchestrator of Oblivion, had many names. The Lord of Lament, The Final Judgement or simply, The End. Many tales are told of Hymm across all the planes and all the ages, but one remains truest of all: should you be condemned, there is no redemption.

Hymm orchestrated the punishment of all those sentenced to eternity in Oblivion. Most know very little about Oblivion, as those that are condemned never leave. Existing knowledge is mostly based on legend, centuries old.

No one spoke as Hymm turned attention to the witch. She looked back, almost fearless. What more could they do to her that she hadn't already endured?

"You have been summoned by The Celestial Order to discuss the future of Oblivion," Adelade said in a formal tone. She wavered slightly; her nerves were getting the better of her. She knew the legend of Hymm.

The other-worldly monster paid no attention to her statement.

"You summoned me mortal?" Hymm asked. The tortured voice sounded as though it hadn't uttered a sound in thousands of years.

"I did," the witch replied after a short delay.

Hymm considered the witch for a moment. It had been centuries since a mortal, witch or not, had successfully conjured Hymm.

"Like the brightest of stars, you have caught the attention of onlookers," Hymm contemplated.

The witch gave a nod.

"You have been summoned by The Celestial Order and shall answer when you are addressed!" Arteon squawked. He also knew the legend of Hymm and made an attempt to take the authoritarian role to gain some dignity from his earlier embarrassment.

Hymm turned slowly to Arteon. Fear spliced his voice, and so Hymm decided to deprive him of just that.

A swift snap of the fingers and Arteon fell to the floor with a heavy thump, completely paralysed. He began to turn blue but remained conscious. He choked quietly, unable to breathe and unable to die. A stalemate of mortality had entangled him.

The other members looked fearful and edged away from Arteon, all except the witch and Vignis. For a reason she couldn't explain, the witch felt safer in the presence of Hymm.

Hymm approached the table with curiosity and studied the flowers for a moment before reaching over. As the gloves touched them, they wilted at an accelerated rate until finally they perished.

"We, The Celestial Order, have successfully implemented a new currency across the celestial planes in the form of energy, and we understand that Oblivion has access to energy from those condemned," Adelade piped up with renewed vigour.

"I have no requirement for currency, and neither does any other resident from my plane," Hymm retorted impatiently.

"There's a new world order in place and it stretches across the entirety of the celestial planes, including yours," sneered Shah. His ignorance had finally caught up with him, exposing his inexperience and stupidity.

"And I suppose, those of the 'old world' such as myself must conform or risk being left behind in this pivotal change?" Hymm asked calmly, crossing the room slowly towards Shah. He had gained the full attention of Hymm.

"You said it yourself" grinned Shah, rising from his chair and placing his hands firmly on the table in a confrontational manner. Vignis thrived at the show from his chair. Control had become something of a speciality to Vignis, but anarchy, fear and chaos were a novelty that he thoroughly enjoyed.

Hymm looked from Shah to an old gramophone in the corner of the room. With a gentle flick of the finger, it began to whir and whine into life.

The sounds of Shah's voice echoed throughout the room.

"The Celestial Order. What a joke! They think that I have spent my life collecting enchanted items and objects of varying power. I'll use this fairy tale as a bargaining effort to gain a seat on the council and then work my way in from there!" Shah's voice arrogantly thundered from the gramophone.

The other members looked in disgust at Shah. He sat open-mouthed as the gramophone exposed him before his peers.

"I'll just keep stringing them along that I'm having them moved. Otherwise, what leverage do I have? They won't need me," Shah continued in arrogant tones.

"I'll always be one step ahead of them, what a shame age doesn't define intelligence!" he laughed.

The gramophone slowed and faded into a hard silence. Only the fireplace could be heard crackling. Meanwhile, Arteon continued to remain blue-faced and unable to move.

Shah, began to nervously adjust his collar, his hands trembling as he tried to hide his fear.

Hymm glared at him, letting Shah take a few moments to allow his exposure to settle before finally taking hold of his hand. Shah jerked violently but contact remained between them.

He shook and screamed before falling to the floor. He quickly got up and panicked, his arrogant and calculated demeanour disappeared and what remained seemed that of a frightened boy.

"I can't see, I can't see you! I can't see any of you!" Shah spluttered.

He gasped in horror as he felt his sickness returning to him. Panicking, he began flailing his arms at what he could no longer see or hear. Not only did he have no leverage to remain within The Celestial Order, he had become Blind to the Divine world once more.

Vignis beamed at this revelation from the corner of the room and marvelled at Shah as he stood panicking.

He gave a nod to Adelade and she sped to the door calling for Kull.

"Remove that man!" she shrilled to Kull. Gormless as ever, Kull made his way over to Shah.

"Please, please, I beg of you, do not remove me from the council. I have many uses! Please!" he begged as the giant took him by the scruff of the neck and led him kicking and screaming from the room.

The door slammed shut behind them. No one said a word as the muffled screams of Shah slowly disappeared down the corridor.

"The evening has been entertaining, but as I have no further business here–" Hymm began.

"Oblivion, has a high level of energy across its plane. This energy from those condemned, currently has no use across your plane. We wish to use that energy for currency across Existence, Purgatory and eventually Sanctuary," Adelade urged.

Hymm wavered in revolt for a moment at the mention of Sanctuary.

"There is nothing to negotiate, the energy is forfeit to Oblivion and this will remain," Hymm snapped impatiently and turned to leave.

"We have The Imposter's Amulet!" blurted Adelade as Hymm reached the fireplace.

Hymm paused, just shy of the mantle.

"The Imposter's Amulet has eluded even the most resourceful for centuries," said Hymm curiously, turning the harrowing mask towards Adelade.

Adelade produced the amulet from inside her immaculate purse and placed it on the table.

"This amulet allows any entity of another plane, even Oblivion, to appear as a mortal and walk unhindered," continued Adelade.

"Fool! Do you think I am unaware of its power?" snapped Hymm.

Hymm reached over, took the amulet from the table and studied it curiously. Satisfied with the amulet's authenticity, Hymm slipped it expertly away into a small pocket.

"I will arrange for any unused energy to be channelled to The Celestial Order. You are required to supply a new artefact to me, personally, every year. Should you fail, the agreement is void and your soul will reside in Oblivion where it undoubtedly belongs."

Hymm looked over at the witch one final time with curiosity, and smiled. With a snap of its fingers, Hymm vanished and the fireplace extinguished. A contract lay on the table where the amulet had been.

Arteon could be heard gasping for air, choosing to stay on the floor to recover. His rolls of fat moved hysterically as he tried to absorb as much oxygen as he could.

Adelade looked concerned, as did every other board member.

Vignis rose from his chair and took the contract from the table. He folded it neatly and placed it into his pocket.

Adelade looked a little confused at Vignis's interest in the contract.

The witch looked hopefully at the faces surrounding the table.

"Am I free?" she asked nervously.

The board looked at her distastefully and without remorse. Vignis didn't grace the witch with a reply and swiftly left the room, closely followed by Maybelle hovering behind him.

Adelade called for the giant once more.

"Take her away, put her back into isolation until further notice," Adelade ordered.

"No! Please! Let me go, I've done as you asked! What about my boys? Will they be safe?" the witch pleaded as she was led away from the Royal Chamber.

Once firmly out of earshot, Kull glanced down at the witch as he led her away.

"Name?" he growled clumsily.

"Alwin, Alwin White," the witch smiled weakly.

Chapter Two – For Richer, For Poorer

Offer me your hand and I'll promise you no solitude.
Release a further inch and you'll bequeath me your arm.
This gesture can only be accepted from you, with true
intention, dedication, in absolution. Your gesture is
represented by your ability to conform without hesitation, to
my commands dressed as requests, as this is what I desire.
As my slave, you will not perceive the transaction in this
format, but that matters little. You have cast the stone, the
act confirmed and your contract solidified. You will walk as
I tell you, but not as I practice. You will talk as I command
you, but not in my name. Heaven forbid you betray by even
a thought, for I will descend on you with the harshest of
consequence.

"I hate going home," Charlie sighed. "I wish I could stay here, on this side of the town." He kicked at a stone, as young boys do, and watched as it skipped down the dusty path.

"Why do you want to stay here? asked Billy. "It's dangerous, everyone's sick and there's… there's… these!" He held up a louse that he'd picked from his frayed jumper. "It's much nicer on your side of the village. You live in a big house, you don't get hungry and there's no crazy people screaming at night."

"What good is a big house when you don't like anyone in it?" Charlie exclaimed. He stood straight and bow-legged as he impersonated his father. "Oh, fetch the maid, I've finished on the toilet and I need help getting the stink away!"

Billy fell backwards, laughing.

"Your father isn't any fun, you're right," Billy chuckled. "We're ten years old, it's 1909, and we still don't have an automobile! We should be racing drivers!"

"How much fun that would be…" Charlie dreamed. "Winning races against the fastest in the world… everyone shouting your name from the stands… and we don't have to go to school!"

"We could take the train and leave everything behind. An adventure, just me and you against the world. We could be bandits!" replied Billy as he admired the clouds in the sky.

"The Flying Scotsman!" said Charlie. "Speeding down the line at over one-hundred miles per hour," he added as he too observed the sky. The hours passed as they talked, laughed and dreamt the day away.

"Come, it's time for you to go home," Charlie decided as he helped Billy to his feet. Billy had cerebral palsy on his right side – although it gave him disadvantages, it never got him down. "Nothing gets the better of Billy Betts," said Charlie to Billy on the most challenging of days. Most of the children considered Billy to be nothing more than lame, but Charlie wasn't one of them.

They walked back down the dusty path to the less-than-desirable area of Surrey, Blufford. They laughed and joked as they made their way at a steady pace, which was comfortable enough for Billy.

Blufford, had become infamous for dust, dirt and overcrowding, mostly due to large-scale construction projects. Factories, hotels and houses were erected in record time. Most of the construction firms were owned and operated by politicians – including Charlie's father – who ran the country. They, as often referred, lived in the wealthy neighbouring town of Lilford, reserved for the privileged. The police were paid to keep the 'peasants' out of Lilford as an unofficial rule, which was a lucrative source of income for a 'Bobby on the beat'. This ensured that the working classes of Blufford stayed down, and the Lilford house prices stayed up. The invisible division meant that the working-classes were restricted in what work they could take, and Blufford soon became a despairing area of poverty, crime and alcoholism. Those who could work had to bid for jobs. The hardest workers who requested the fewest pence on the hour were preferred.

Charlie didn't have any friends in Lilford – he hated it. Although travelling to Blufford had been strictly prohibited by his father, Charlie still went there on a regular basis and played the day to dusk in good company.

They arrived at Billy's house and said their goodbyes, summarising their day and promising to meet as early as possible the next day. Charlie made his way back to Lilford with his draw-string bag in tow, which contained the very expensive clothes that his father had bought him. This way, he could get changed before entering the familiar part of the county that he reluctantly called home.

Charlie scowled as he approached the stately home that he lived in, Kingston Abbey. Many called the estate beautiful, which indeed it was, though Charlie felt it was oppressive and boring. Kingston Abbey had a fabulously aristocratic history spanning hundreds of years. With over fifty rooms, two kitchens and fifty acres of surrounding land, it was certainly a sight to behold. Charlie approached the vast wooden door at the main entrance and tried the handle. It was locked. This meant supper had already commenced without him and, no doubt, he would be in trouble.

Charlie crept around the building to the staff entrance and tried to sneak in as quietly as he could. After dodging the staff who flurried in and out of the kitchen and dining hall, he took hold of the banister of the sweeping walnut staircase. If he could just get to the top without being noticed, he could slip away into his room. He stepped onto the first step, but a hideously loud creak exposed his presence.

"Charles Kingston!" his father roared from the great dining hall. Charlie only got referred to by his full name when he was in trouble. Without a word, Charlie walked in to the dining room and saw the faces of his family staring back at him with disappointment.

His father, Lord Chester Kingston Senior or Lord Kingston, his older brother, his senior by a few years, Chester Kingston Junior, Christopher Kingston, his younger brother, and the senior household staff were waiting for him.

"Where have you been?" his father asked furiously. His large belly, grey hair and tired face were all symptoms of a life dedicated to politics, aristocracy and business.

"He's been with the dirty peasants again!" sneered Chester. "Look at his shoes, they're filthy!" Chester nearly always looked in a constant state of disgust. He kept his nose held high and scuttled around in a rat-like fashion.

"Well, is that true?" his father spat through gritted teeth. He hated poor people and maintained they were too stupid to ever progress to anything more – though he employed many of them to help build his new hotels, offices and factories.

Charlie looked at his shoes and didn't reply.

"Why do you continue to go there when I have *specifically,* told you not to?" his father asked as he rose from his chair.

Charlie shrugged and didn't dare reply. He knew there would be no escape, and that what will be, will be.

"It's a dangerous place for you. If any of those... those... heathens, had any idea where you came from, they'd kidnap you and hold you for ransom! Just go to your room – you're grounded for the week!" his father snapped, returning to his supper.

Charlie looked deflated and opened his mouth to protest, his father looked at him and raised an eyebrow, daring him to challenge the punishment he had handed out. Charlie decided not to say anything. Instead, he turned quickly and ascended the seemingly never-ending staircase to his bedroom. Though the butlers, maids and cooks knew their place, they shook their head at Charlie as he made his way past them.

Following the routine check of his room, to make sure no one had tampered with anything, Charlie sat on his bed and tried to find one of his books he hadn't read in a while. Although his father said his story books were just ink and paper, they were a fabulous source of escapism for Charlie. He could sail the high seas and fight pirates, fly with dragons or simply be someone else for an hour or two.

After some time, a small face appeared at his doorway. "Have you come to gloat?" asked Charlie, without looking up from his book.

"You shouldn't go to Blufford; I worry that you'll go and never come back!" Christopher whispered, earnestly. "What if someone takes you away?"

"I'm okay, I'm here and I'm not hurt. It isn't as bad as father says it is. He just wants to scare us into not going. Some people there are really nice, but some smell terrible.

They break wind and don't excuse themselves. Sometimes, they encourage others to smell it too!" Charlie explained, smiling.

Christopher laughed through his hand as quietly as he could and seemed satisfied that his brother would be okay, and, with that, he made his way to his own room for the night. Charlie smiled to himself and continued reading.

Charlie tried his best to look after Christopher as he was often shunned by other members of the family. They would ridicule Christopher on a regular basis, call him an idiot and ignore his inquisitive questions, as he wasn't as smart as they were. Though Christopher wasn't as intelligent as his peers, he had a kind heart.

His older brother Chester had always been the favourite. He was clever and as sharp as a fox but he could be mean and cold to others he considered lesser than himself. Which was everyone.

As the older sibling, Chester had been taken under his father's wing to follow in his footsteps. Chester would eventually take on Kingston Abbey once his father had retired.

Charlie also received regular disapproval from the family as he was considered to be too unpredictable and poorly behaved compared to Chester. Charlie didn't mind – he liked being left alone to get on with his adventures, though he yearned for the day he could leave and discover the world. Charlie's books had given him a taste of adventure and he wanted more. He would often wonder, "Why would you stay in the same town every day? The world is vast, mysterious and curious. Adventure, excitement and learning should be the flavour of every day!"

Much later into the night, well past bedtime, Charlie took a break from his book and decided to head downstairs to get some water before going to sleep. He crept down the flowing stairs as quietly as he could so he didn't wake the staff (they would only make a fuss and want to get the water for him). Charlie didn't like to be waited on – what had he done to deserve their fuss, aside from exist? He certainly hadn't earnt it and he considered them as no less than himself – unlike his father and Chester.

As he neared the bottom of the staircase, he noticed a flickering light from the sitting room. The fireplace had been lit, and it was crackling and popping merrily. Charlie wondered why no one had extinguished it.

"Come here boy," slurred a voice from the chair. Charlie jumped as he had thought the room was empty. He moved towards the voice. His father sat in a proud leather chair in his night clothes, rather drunk. His father looked at the huge painting of his late wife and drained the whiskey from his glass. He smacked his lips and turned to Charlie.

"What do you remember of your mother?" The words rolled out of his father's mouth unsteadily. Charlie pondered the question for a few moments.

"Not much," he replied dryly.

"You must remember *something*; it wasn't too many years ago that she left us," his father replied, somewhat patiently.

"I no longer see her in my dreams or my thoughts, I try so hard but all I see is this portrait," Charlie explained. "I remember her favourite perfume, her voice and how she would laugh, but not much more." His father smiled slightly and turned back to the painting over the fireplace.

"I see," he replied. "Christopher reminds me of your mother, so I see her every day in him. You…" his father continued sadly, "remind me of myself when I was a boy. I con… constantly got into trouble and never listened to anyone. Me and my friends broke into a factory, we had stolen some matches, and shortly after, we burnt the factory

39

to the ground." Charlie stared open-mouthed. He had never heard this story before – usually his father's stories were boring, political and racist. Often in the same conversation.

"Chester is headed for greatness; you should be more like him," he slurred more as he became increasingly belligerent.

"Don't fall asleep in front of the fire, father, it's dangerous," Charlie said as the conversation had shifted to another, more familiar setting. His father could be unpredictable when he drank too much, so Charlie thought it best to end their talk and go back to bed.

The next morning, Charlie descended the stairs and entered the dining room where breakfast lay waiting. Charlie ate as speedily as he could and pulled Christopher away halfway through. They quickly got ready and made their way to school. Chester usually waited for his friends – or minions, as Charlie referred to them. They hung on every word that Chester spoke, and did as he demanded without question or hesitation. They walked the route to school, and on the way, Charlie wondered at the huge homes that lined the streets of Lilford. Christopher asked if they could stop by the paper shop, and as Charlie knew Chester would be heading there, Charlie declined without explanation.

Hills Bells Academy had inherited its name from the historic monument in the centre of the grounds. A towering steeple boasting hand-crafted singing bells centred the vast educational halls. Said to be over five-hundred years old, this private school had the reputation of making the greatest great and the weakest broken. With a strict, no-nonsense policy, students could receive the cane – or worse – for the most minor of offences. Most of the students referred to this educational machine as 'Hell's Bells Academy'. Charlie had fallen victim to the strict correctional punishments many times. The cane had descended upon Charlie's small hands for crimes as simple as reading his books at the wrong time or having a shirt slightly untucked.

Hell's Bells Academy was vast and excessively over-funded. It was meticulously maintained and cleaned to ensure the highest standards. Every teacher and student had to conform to the rules, regulations and values of the school. Charlie hated school – he didn't have any friends and mostly read his books on his knee during lessons. He found it was worth the risk of the cane.

Christopher bid Charlie a good day and raced to meet his friends.

Upon arriving at his classroom door, Charlie noticed a nervous looking boy. He had scruffy bright ginger hair and was rather chubby, his clothes weren't of the finest quality either, which was an odd occurrence for a student of Hell's Bells.

"Are you new?" asked Charlie politely.

"Yes, my name's Harry Jenkins," the boy replied nervously.

"My name's Charlie, nice to meet you," Charlie smiled. "What's that in your hand?"

"This old thing?" Harry said, holding up a carved model of a steam train. "It's a-"

"The Flying Scotsman!" Charlie cut in, excited. "Did you make it yourself?"

"Yes, I carved it out of old pieces of wood," breathed Harry, feeling much more at ease. As they started talking about their favourite locomotives, the busy hallway suddenly quietened as their teacher, Mr Gallows, made his way briskly down the corridor. His tall, thin figure and sunken features could fuel the nightmares of most children for weeks on end. Harry stood in the middle of the corridor; eyes wide with his mouth open. Charlie quickly pulled him back against the wall as was regulatory, pre-lesson.

Mr Gallows reached for the classroom door, pausing as his long, spindly fingers contacted the worn brass handle. He slowly turned his gaze to Harry and looked him up and down, making no effort to hide his disgust.

"Harry Jenkins?" Mr Gallows barked. Harry stood in horror with his mouth open. Charlie nudged him.

"Yes sir, that's… that's me," Harry stammered nervously. Mr Gallows rolled his eyes and beckoned everyone into the classroom.

"You, boy," Mr Gallows snapped. "Sit at the front."

"Who, me sir?" Harry replied nervously.

"Yes you! Who else?" said Mr Gallows angrily.

Charlie sat in his usual seat near the window in the middle of the class. He liked it there and he often sat and stared out of the window, watching the world go by – yet another cane-able offence. He had been educated on this infraction first-hand on several occasions.

The class seated themselves, without a word out of turn. Mr Gallows knew how to hold a room. No one dared to make a sound as they waited for Mr Gallows to start the lesson. He stood boldly in front of the class with his hands on his hips, scanning the room for his first victim of the day. Finally, his eyes settled on the newcomer.

"Harry, go to the shelf and find 'Essential English Poetry, Volume II', quickly," Mr Gallows hastened.

Harry squeezed out from behind his desk. A few giggles could be heard as he finally managed to free himself, but they were quickly silenced as Mr Gallows shot the class a deadly glance. Harry stood, nervously checking the shelf as everyone watched. He squinted as he read the spines of each book.

"Hurry along boy, are you simple?" barked Mr Gallows, tapping his foot impatiently. The other children laughed, all except Charlie. Mr Gallows stormed across the room, his tunic flowing behind him, located the correct book and thrust it upon Harry.

"Sit down and read the first poem for the class," growled Mr Gallows impatiently. It was clear that Mr Gallows had played this game before. He always preached to the other teachers, "Break them in as soon as you can – they are then less likely to rebel later." Harry's hands began to tremble as he got ready to read from the tired old book.

"Who p… pr… prop, thou ask… ask'st…" Harry stammered. Laughter could be heard as he tried to make his way through the timeless poem. About halfway through, Mr Gallows interrupted.

"Good heavens! Such sabotage of the English dialect – how boldly you trivialise such literary beauty. Clearly not a poet or scholar in you, boy!" Mr Gallows concluded in harsh tones. The class laughed once more as Harry's eyes began to fill. He wished to be anyone else, anywhere else.

"Take yourself to the back of the class, you will not be asked to read again… for today," Mr Gallows smiled grimly. Giggles and sniggers could be heard as Harry squeezed from behind the desk and made his way, sad and defeated, to the back of the class. He almost made it to his seat when a loud thud could be heard. Everyone looked over to see what had caused the noise and saw Harry's hand-carved locomotive on the floor – it had slipped from his pocket.

"What do we have here?" Mr Gallows sneered as he picked up the contraband from the floor. "A toy, no doubt! You should read more instead of dreaming and playing like a foolish infant!" Mr Gallows scolded. Again, stifled laughter could be heard from the other children.

"That's mine, sir," Charlie blurted. "I dropped it" The other children turned to look at Charlie. Mr Gallows looked down upon Charlie with a curious eyebrow raised.

He knew it was Harry's, but a punishment must be delivered, and it mattered little who would be the receiver.

"A punishable offence, Charles. Get to the front of the class." Mr Gallows pointed. He prepared the cane and intended to display the punishment before Charlie's very peers for the crime of humility. Charlie stood up and walked to the front of the class. He had been in this predicament on more than one occasion.

"Hold out your hands, boy!" Mr Gallows shouted. There was a sharp whip through the air and the echo of a sickening snap as the cane met its victim. Charlie winced but didn't make a sound – he refused to give his punisher the satisfaction. His hands were stinging and throbbing but he held his own against the cane and its master.

"Back to your seat. Collect your contraband from the headmaster at the end of the day. You can explain to him your reasoning for bringing this crude toy," Mr Gallows concluded.

At lunchtime, Charlie took to the quiet area of the playground and buried his head in another book. The sun beamed down, and children could be heard playing and laughing. Charlie lost himself in the book as a shadow crept over him. He looked over the top of his book and saw the headmaster's pale, deathly-looking face staring down at him. Mr Campbell. It had boggled the minds of many students, as to how someone could be a headmaster when they so clearly hated children.

Without a word, Mr Campbell held out his hand. Charlie passed the book to him and sat up straight.

"Alice in Wonderland," said Mr Campbell disapprovingly, shaking his head. "Fiction and imagination, won't help you in the real world."

Charlie didn't reply but looked at his shoes and shrugged. The headmaster scowled and looked down upon him.

"Many would give their lives for the opportunity that you have," Mr Campbell scorned. Charlie looked at him, somewhat confused. "Your father is one of the most prominent politicians in Britain, as well as a successful businessman. You could learn much from him, yet you choose to live in a world that does not aid your development."

He thrust the book upon Charlie, who remained silent. He glared upon Charlie with his hands on his hips before finally handing the confiscated toy to Charlie.

"You've no need to come to the office. Your encounter with the cane will be quite enough. Do not bring

47

your toys into school again," Mr Campbell warned. He walked away with his hands behind his back. Charlie watched as he left. As soon as he had turned the corner, he resumed his reading.

Shortly after, the lunch bell rang out, signalling everyone to move on to their next lesson. On the way across the schoolyard, Charlie heard a familiar voice screaming from between two buildings. Charlie walked over, curious as to what was causing the commotion. Upon his investigation, he found that Harry had run into trouble. Some older boys had taken hold of him and were attempting to relieve him of his lunch money.

"Hey, leave him alone, he doesn't have any money!" Charlie shouted. The boys looked at each other and laughed. They were much bigger and stronger than Charlie. The ringleader, Harvey Savoy, took Charlie by the collar. Harvey had a huge overbite and features akin to a Neanderthal; he only had a place at the school because of his family's prominence.

"What are you going to do about it?" spat Harvey. "Are you going to get your father to vote me out of the school?" Harvey then threw his head back, laughing at his seemingly incredible wit. He then dropped Charlie in a heap and turned back to Harry.

"Is that your boyfriend?" Harvey mocked. His stupid friends guffawed and laughed.

"No!" Harry retorted, crying.

"Well, if he isn't your boyfriend then hit him!" Harvey threatened. "If you don't, I'll beat you every day and take your lunch money!" Harvey shook a large, meaty fist in his face to show he meant it.

Harry looked from the boys to Charlie. Their eyes met as Charlie looked up at him from the floor. Tears stained his school shirt as he cried. Harry stepped forward and delivered a kick to Charlie hard in the chest and then to his face. The boys looked on, howling and jeering. Charlie pulled at Harry to stop as blood spilled from his swollen lip, but Harry carried on and began to smile as the other boys patted his back.

Harvey stepped forward and gave a final kick, winding Charlie. The other boys laughed and pointed as he wheezed and writhed on the floor.

"Impressive!" Harvey laughed, putting an arm around Harry. Harvey then kicked Harry so hard in the ankle that his feet gave from under him and he fell into a pile next to Charlie.

"But... I did what you said..." Harry stammered. "What do you want me to do?"

"Every day, you'll bring me a shilling, and if you don't, I'll beat you," Harvey sneered. "Dirty little peasant, you don't belong here."

Charlie could barely breathe as he struggled to his feet. Harry stayed on the floor crying and nursing a split lip. Charlie eventually stood up and staggered upright, feeling a throbbing, searing pain all over his body. He leant against the wall, removed the toy Harry had given him from his pocket and threw it back to Harry. Without another word, he walked off in search of the bathroom to get himself cleaned up so he could carry on with his day. He couldn't wait to leave school and visit Billy.

At the end of the school day, Charlie met Christopher at the gate and walked him home without a word. Christopher asked how he had cut his face. Charlie didn't reply, he just shrugged. As they arrived home, Charlie walked on so that he could visit Billy. He was supposed to be grounded but he decided to go straight over to see his friend instead of going inside and obeying his father's ruling.

Charlie did the usual walk to Blufford, getting changed, halfway there, out of his nicer school clothes, which would have clearly identified his origin.

Walking over to Billy's front door, the house seemed quieter than normal. He knocked politely and took two steps back as he waited for an answer. Billy's father, William Betts, answered. He didn't look himself – he looked more tired than usual, with his thinning ginger hair and his third-hand dusty overalls hanging off his thin frame.

"Is Billy coming out to play today?" Charlie asked politely.

"Not today, Charlie. He isn't very well. We're just waiting for the doctor to come and see him. I'll let him know that you called for him all the same," he replied.

Charlie considered the information for a moment.

"Okay, I hope he gets better soon," smiled Charlie, as politely as ever.

"As do I, Charlie. I have to get back to Billy," Mr Betts explained. Charlie gave a polite nod and walked back to the path that took him back to his familiar side of the village.

"I hope Billy is okay," Charlie thought to himself as he wandered back home.

When he reached home, he walked in and told his father he had been held back at school as he had been beaten up. It was a half-truth but thankfully it sufficed for his father.

Chapter Three – Atonement

Part I

Excuse me, I wonder if you have the time? I have wandered through the days and nights asking everyone I meet, but no one deigns to answer. They look away as if I'm mad and seem embarrassed that I ask. Heavens, every clock must be broken and that is my conclusion, as even their face turns away when I consider the unanswerable question. My apologies, where are my manners? I should have asked more formally. I wonder if you have the time? The time I lost as I grew old and my children had their own. The time that didn't wait for me or even ask my name. The time I spent as I had plenty, but now I'm running out. The time that stole my life away with no regard for want. I see you're just like all the others, not an answer or suggestion. Much obliged all the same, I'll continue my frustration.

The summer holidays had finally arrived, and Charlie couldn't have been more excited. It would be much easier to meet his best friend Billy, as Lord Kingston would be occupied with business. Chester had been put in charge of his siblings and ordered to report any misbehaviour, a responsibility he thoroughly enjoyed.

The sun shone brightly through the windows as the smell of the morning air fluttered into Charlie's bedroom, carried by a light breeze. Excited by the prospects of the day, Charlie scrambled around his room getting dressed as quickly as possible. The house wasn't as busy during the summer season, as the staff would be seeing to their own families.

Charlie slipped into the kitchen, artfully dodging the staff as he had done a hundred times before. He scanned the pantry, searching for small cakes and biscuits, stuffing them hastily into every pocket. Billy loved them. He made his way out into the corridor, scratching his face deep in thought. 'What else do I need to take with me?' he pondered. His thoughts were interrupted by a high-pitched screeching. He stopped in his tracks, frozen in fear.

"What on earth was that?" Charlie whispered aloud to himself. "Has someone broken in?"

He crept across the vast foyer; the noise seemed to be coming from the main sitting room. Slipping through the hallway, careful not to make a sound, he crouched by the door and peered inside. His eyes widened in shock at what he saw, blinking several times as if they themselves were at fault. Chester danced across the main sitting room with incredible flamboyancy and energy whilst wearing a bright red frock with matching lipstick and some badly applied make-up. He leapt and danced with gaiety and frolic, without a care for anything else. He had clearly done this before and certainly wasn't aware of anyone else in the household. Charlie watched open-mouthed at this magnificent spectacle without daring to blink, in fear of missing even a second of the performance before him. Chester jumped across the furniture, absorbed in his dance.

Giggling, Charlie came to his senses and decided to leave without alerting Chester. He couldn't wait to tell Billy, though he wasn't sure Billy would believe such a tale.

"If father saw this with his own eyes they would surely pop out of his head," thought Charlie, still giggling on the way over to Blufford. He considered telling Christopher about this incident but quickly decided against it. Christopher wasn't the best at keeping secrets.

Charlie walked across the border into Blufford and stopped in his usual secluded spot to get changed into his common clothes. He wondered if Billy would be able to come out today – he had been sick for quite some time.

"What a beautiful day, its lovely weather, it would be a shame if Billy isn't able to play today," Charlie thought. It was a fairly long walk to get to Billy's house but he didn't mind or even consider the journey as he had made it a thousand times before. As he reached the town centre and wandered into the bustling streets, a strange looking man in a black velvet top hat approached him. He looked very smart but his clothes seemed to be very old-fashioned. His attire was certainly pre-1909.

"Do you have the time, young man?" he asked. He was fabulously polite and charming.

"No sir, I'm afraid not," Charlie replied. Nobody in the street seemed to notice the well-dressed gentleman. He certainly didn't fit in with the local people, but nobody looked twice at him – an observation Charlie had made but kept to himself.

"That's quite alright, I'm clearly too early," the gentleman sighed, looking slightly disappointed. A warm smile seemed to be permanently upon him.

"Is there anything I can help you with, sir?" Charlie asked politely. He was eager to get away and get to Billy's house.

"Not yet, Charlie, not yet. But don't worry, I'm sure we will meet again," the gentleman smiled. Charlie knew the dangers of talking to strangers, especially in Blufford, but something had caught Charlie's attention.

"Who are you?" Charlie asked, as his curiosity got the better of him.

"Who I am not, would yield a more interesting answer, but shouldn't you be more concerned about who *you* are? Or who you're *going to be*?" the gentleman replied.

"Anyway, I must be going. We can't talk the entire day to dusk! Good day." The gentleman tipped his hat politely and made his way down the road. He strolled away, whistling a jolly tune as if he hadn't a care in the world or a particular place to be. Charlie watched curiously as he left, before remembering that he had to get to Billy's house. He set off as fast as he could – the faster he could get there, the more time they would have together.

Turning the corner to Billy's road, he couldn't help but smile. Everyone had come into the street to sit together in the glorious heat – children played and parents talked and drank merrily. All of the tired and tatty houses were bustling… all except Billy's house. Charlie knocked on the familiar splintered door and took two steps back with his hands behind his back, hoping that Billy would be able to play today. He waited and waited but nobody answered. He noticed a side window to one of the bedrooms was open and decided to listen in and see if anyone was home. He crouched by the window and could hear Billy's parents talking in hushed voices.

"Billy's fever won't settle," panicked Mrs Betts, as only mothers do. "I can't get his temperature down."

"As soon as I get more work, I'll buy the medicine that the doctor has recommended," Mr Betts replied, trying to hide his concern. He ran a rough, seasoned hand through his thinning hair.

"That damned foreman at Wrigley's Construction," cursed Mr Betts, "he told ten of us there wasn't any more work available, but they're still building the new offices. He said the decision came from the top."

"The Doctor says it's consumption and that if we're quick enough, he'll get better," Mrs Betts said as she stroked Billy's face. She noticed Billy's lips moving and leaned in to hear better.

"Nothing gets the best of Billy Betts…" he rasped, barely conscious.

Charlie sank against the wall of the house. Another day without his best friend. He reached into his pocket and pulled out his biscuits and cakes, popping them into a white paper bag for Billy. He posted them through the rusty letterbox and made his way home.

Charlie kept a casual pace; he wasn't in any rush to get back and he wanted to enjoy the sun. He wandered back but was soon stopped by a passing policeman on the beat. Charlie usually made a point of avoiding them, but he had been in such deep thought that he hadn't noticed him.

"What're you doing in this area, Mr Kingston?" the Constable asked. He recognised Charlie and knew he shouldn't be in Blufford.

"I came over to see a friend, but he's sick so I wasn't able to see him," Charlie confessed.

The constable rocked on his heels with his hands behind his back, wondering what to do with him.

"It's a nice day… Make your way back to where you belong and don't delay," the Constable scolded.

"Yes sir," replied Charlie. He turned to set off home when a thought occurred. "Officer, what's consumption?" Charlie asked.

"A sickness, quite common around these parts. Often spread by spitting, which is punishable by law. Let me know if you see anyone spitting, Charlie. Now, off you go."

Charlie gestured politely and rushed off home. He didn't want to get into any more trouble with the policeman. The constable had been lenient and could have easily marched him back personally for a back-hand tip. Charlie made his way back to Lilford but vowed to return to Billy's house tomorrow to check in.

As Charlie walked up the path, he noticed Christopher sitting by the front door with his head in his hands. He was looking fed up.

"What seems to be the matter?" asked Charlie, concerned.

As he approached, he noticed Christopher's eyes were swollen, and tears had left tracks down his face. Charlie inspected his younger brother closer and noticed his skin had turned an angry shade of red. It looked sore and it was stinging to the touch.

"Chester told me I had to go outside or he would feed me to the dragon in the basement. I've been here all day in the summer heat. Will you tell the dragon I mean it no harm?" Christopher sniffed sadly. Charlie beckoned Christopher back into the house.

"Go to the kitchen and get some water. I will speak to the dragon for you," Charlie smiled. Charlie watched Christopher walk to the kitchen. He waited until he was out of sight before looking for Chester.

It didn't take long before Charlie found Chester in the magnificent dining room with two of his friends. Chester sat before two of his friends like a lord before his servants. They sat smoking his father's cigars, laughing and joking as if the world was their own.

"Oh look, it's the prince of the paupers! Step back, my friends, you might catch something," Chester sneered. His friends guffawed and sniggered idiotically.

"Good one, Chester," said Ruffus, a small and rather stupid looking boy.

"You treat Christopher as though he's an animal. He didn't deserve to be left out in the sun all day," Charlie snarled. "You wouldn't have dared to treat him like that if father had been home."

"Well, he's not and I'm in charge," Chester replied coolly, leaning back in his chair and putting his feet on the table. "Run along and fetch the simpleton, Charlie. Me and my friends need a refreshing beverage. Why have staff when we have Christopher?"

His friends roared with laughter at Chester's savage demand. Charlie felt his hands curl into fists as a wicked grin spread across Chester's face. He attempted to restrain himself but the red mist had descended.

A sickening crack could be heard as Charlie landed a well-aimed blow on Chester's face, forcing him off his chair and onto the floor. Like lightning, his friends were upon Charlie and quickly pinned him to the ground – they were much stronger and larger than Charlie. Flailing and kicking, Charlie tried with all of his might to escape their grasp but they didn't give an inch.

"Hit him, Chester, hit him!" said Ruffus.

"Yeah Chester, get him!" echoed Darius.

Chester pulled himself upright, rubbing his face. He hesitated for a moment, wondering what to do. Charlie looked back angrily, still trying his best to break free without success. Chester looked around him before his eyes settled on a vase on the table. Carefully, he removed the flowers and placed them on the table. He stood over Charlie and poured the water over him until he drained the last drop. Chester watched and took satisfaction in his brother's discomfort, as Charlie gasped, coughed and spluttered.

Charlie broke one of his legs free and managed to kick Chester in the shin. Chester hopped backwards, howling with pain, before marching back to Charlie in renewed fury. He raised his boot above Charlie's face and was just about to bring it crashing down when one of the windows smashed. A split second later, Chester groaned, swayed for a moment and fell to the floor in a heap.

Chester's two friends let go of Charlie and ran from the house as fast as their legs would carry them, kicking up dust and stones along the path as they went. Charlie looked around in a state of confusion. One of the great lead-woven windows had been smashed, and pieces of glass littered the grand dining room.

Chester stirred and groaned as he regained consciousness. Just as he did, Charlie saw the offending object. He quickly swiped it up and stuffed it hastily into his pocket. The object had come through the window and hit Chester squarely in the face.

"What on earth…" Chester groaned as he came around. He looked at all of the mess in the usually pristine dining room.

"Oh no! Father won't be pleased, he left me in charge!" Chester panted frantically. He muttered incoherently as he collected the smashed glass, cutting his hands as he did so. Charlie didn't care much for the consequences. He hadn't smashed the window but he couldn't prove otherwise, and he knew for sure he would be in trouble again.

Charlie made his way to the kitchen and grabbed something to eat for Christopher, as no doubt he hadn't eaten much – if at all – that day.

"Did you get some water?" Charlie asked as he reached the top of the stairs. Christopher gave a nod and they went into the library and sat with their sandwiches. Charlie plunged his hand into his pocket, eager to study his saviour. He squinted and frowned at the object, considering it deeply. It was perfectly round and looked like a snow globe. Inside, you could make out a small island on which stood a small figure waving a yellow top hat as if greeting Charlie. There weren't any of the usual snow-like particles inside, but it was filled with water all the same.

"What's that you've got?" asked Christopher sleepily. His time in the sun had taken its toll.

"I'm not sure," replied Charlie, slowly, still inspecting the object. "I think it's a snow globe but there isn't any snow inside. It came through the window and hit Chester in the head."

"Why didn't it break?" asked Christopher.

"I'm not sure," yawned Charlie. He too had become very tired.

They heard the familiar sound of the front door opening and someone making their way inside. A frantic voice could be heard, and then a moment's silence.

"CHARLES!" bawled Lord Kingston. Christopher's eyes widened as panic began to take hold of him.

"Go to bed, Christopher," Charlie beckoned. "You won't be in any trouble; you haven't done anything wrong."

Charlie walked Christopher to his room, took a deep breath and made his way downstairs to receive his punishment.

"What on earth has happened in here!" his father raged. He looked very tired and had clearly been working long hours. Charlie explained what happened to his father to the very detail. His father listened intently, turning several shades of red until, eventually, he let out a great sigh. He took off his hat and looked at Charlie.

"Go to bed, I don't want to see you for the rest of the day," he said through gritted teeth. He cast a sideways glance at Chester and shook his head in disappointment.

Charlie made his way up the stairs without delay. He had expected a much more severe punishment for the evening's events and gratefully accepted his father's ruling.

Charlie lay in bed by his lamp, studying the foreign snow globe. The figure seemed to be smiling and jolly, almost as if it was glad to see him.

"I wonder where it came from," Charlie whispered to himself. Footsteps in the hallway snapped his concentration away and he quickly put the globe under the bed, out of sight, and extinguished his lamp. The footsteps went past the door and continued down the hallway.

"Who could be up at this time?" Charlie wondered as he adjusted himself in bed. He knew the footsteps of everyone in the household, even the staff, but these were different. They were slow and considerate.

"No doubt just the staff," Charlie said to himself comfortably, as the creaking footsteps echoed in the hall.

His eyes suddenly widened as the hairs on the back of his neck stood on end. The staff weren't home as it was the holidays. He lay still and listened intently, before finally plucking up the courage to go to the door. His palms were sweaty and his face glistened in perspiration. His heart rapped against his chest so loud he was certain the intruder would hear it.

Charlie turned the handle and opened the door slowly, peering out into the darkness. He couldn't see anything; the footsteps had stopped. He crept down the hall as lightly as possible, his heartbeat skipping at even the slightest creak. He reached Christopher's room but he was sound asleep, as was Chester and his father.

Everything seemed to be as it should, except that it was exceptionally cold in the hallway. After looking around and seeing no sign of unauthorised entry, Charlie made his way back to bed and put the evening's events to rest.

Charlie woke the next morning in a cold sweat after a particularly harrowing nightmare; one which you can't quite remember, but it leaves you with a deep feeling of sadness, despair and confusion.

At breakfast, Charlie asked if anyone else had heard footsteps in the middle of the night.

"Don't be stupid," Lord Kingston barked without looking up from his paperwork. "It's impossible to get into this house undetected."

"Maybe it's a ghost…" Chester whispered. Christopher's eyes widened as he started to sink into his chair.

"A ghost!?" Christopher gasped. "What could it possibly want?"

"You, Christopher!" Chester snarled, his eyes rolling into the back of his head in a pretend trance state. "It's coming to take you away… When you hear the footsteps in the dead of night, you'll know the ghost is coming for you…"

"Maybe, it's a girl. With red lipstick and a dress dancing through the hallway," Charlie said with exaggerated curiosity. "I wonder, do you think it likes music, Chester?"

Chester stared with his mouth agape. It opened and closed once or twice but he chose not to reply. Even his father had peered up from his paperwork at his impromptu silence.

The two brothers stared hard at each other, only Charlie had a knowing smile upon his face, daring Chester to challenge his knowledge. Chester decided against confrontation on this occasion, turning his attention to his breakfast.

"So!? Is there a ghost or not!?" cried Christopher hysterically

"No!" shouted everyone in unison at the table. Christopher looked at everyone individually for reassurance that he wasn't going to be taken away in the middle of the night, before settling back into his breakfast.

After breakfast, Charlie headed out of the house and made the familiar trip over to Blufford. He had been almost every morning, come rain or shine, to see if Billy had recovered. Each day he had received the same answer, but maybe today would be different.

Charlie made his way into the town wrapped in thought and excitement at what the day could hold for himself and Billy.

He crossed one of the busy roads in the centre of Blufford, making sure to step over the filth that had gathered by the gutter. As he got to the other side, he looked down the road and saw the polite gentleman that he had met recently, standing in a doorway. On this occasion he wasn't alone – a rather beautiful lady stood next to him, with flowing red hair and a dark leather jacket. Thoroughly disinterested, she seemed to want to be anywhere else. The gentleman smiled politely and tipped his hat. Charlie smiled and gave a brief nod of acknowledgement, as was the typical greeting in Blufford.

"I wonder what they're doing in Blufford," Charlie thought to himself. "They certainly don't belong around here, and nobody so much as looks at them!" He paused for a moment to see if anyone noticed them, but they didn't. The busy townspeople just made their way past, absorbed in their own thoughts, worries and concerns for the day. After a few moments, Charlie made his way onward to Billy's house; his excitement for the day far outweighed his curiosity in the strangers.

"You brought me all the way back here to show me a peasant boy in this filthy town?" the red-haired lady snapped.

"Don't forget your place," the gentleman said, softly. "I wanted you to see the makings of something great."

"A Blind peasant boy, no less!?" the red-haired lady laughed wickedly. She rubbed her eyes; they were dark and tired, as if she hadn't slept in years.

"It wasn't so long ago that you were of the Blind and unaware of the Divine world," the gentleman said, as a matter of fact. "Charles will be remembered, if nothing else. It's funny how the Blind change and warp." The red-haired

69

lady's eyes widened and she looked at the gentleman with a serious expression.

"Charles Kingston?" she said in disbelief.

"The very same," the gentleman replied, a smile curling in the corner of his mouth. In the blink of an eye, they were gone from the town. Not that anyone had noticed.

Part II

Charlie ran the final stretch to Billy's house, a grin spread across his face; he was totally indifferent to the onlookers that stared as he went. Something in the air felt different today – no doubt it would be the day Billy would be better!

He skidded to a halt and knocked on the door as hard and as fast as he could. He stepped back and waited patiently, but nobody came. He knocked again, and as he stepped forward, he heard someone crying from inside the house. Voices hushed and shortly after, the door opened. Billy's father, Mr Betts, stepped outside and closed the door behind him. He looked tired and concerned, as though he had the weight of the world on his shoulders.

"Is Billy coming out to play today?" asked Charlie, excitedly. He was grinning from ear to ear, hopping from one foot to the next in anticipation. Billy's father looked uncomfortable and scratched his head as if he didn't know what to say. Mr Betts sat on the doorstep in front of Charlie and let out a sigh, before looking at Charlie and smiling.

"You've been a smashing friend to Billy," Mr Betts said, smiling. "Though, I still don't know where you're bloody from or who your parents are. A man of mystery!" he laughed. "I've no doubt they are proud of you all the same."

Charlie started to suspect something was wrong. Mr Betts paused and looked at Charlie for a few moments before taking a deep breath.

"There's no easy way to tell you this... I don't think it's even hit home for me. Billy has been sick for some time, as you know, and, sadly, he passed away last night."

Charlie swayed slightly as he tried to process what Mr Betts had told him. He stared with glazed eyes before finally sitting down next to Billy's father. He looked at his shoes as he felt his world fall to pieces. A tear rolled down his nose and onto the floor. Mr Betts put an arm around him.

"What can I do to help?" Charlie asked, looking at Billy's father. He smiled back at Charlie with tears in his eyes.

"Unless you can get me a new job, there isn't anything you can do," he jested. "I'm glad that Billy had such a wonderful friend. He always talked about you. I'll go back to Wrigley's Construction tomorrow and see if they can take me back. Otherwise, Billy will have a peasant's burial. I want him to have a nice funeral, but we will see." Charlie thought hard for a moment and looked across the street.

"I want to give something to Billy; he was my best friend and surely the nicest person that I ever met!" Charlie pleaded. Mr Betts frowned slightly and leaned in to Charlie.

"You gave Billy your time, attention and patience. You were there to help him walk, play games and you even taught him how to write properly. That, little Charlie, is the greatest gift anyone could ever give."

"Time is a gift," said Charlie to himself slowly, savouring the words as he spoke. Mr Betts gave a nod of approval. They both sat in silence and watched as the local residents hustled and bustled over their daily schedule, rushing around from one place to the next in order to make ends meet.

"Anyway, you had best be going home, little Charlie," groaned Mr Betts as he rose to his feet. "It will be dark soon and you know how it can be around here." Charlie sighed and rose to his feet too. Even with this news, Charlie didn't want to go home.

"I'll see you soon," said Charlie. He embraced Mr Betts as tightly as he could. He savoured every moment and wished his own father would embrace him so. Billy's father watched as Charlie walked down the street, at the very pace he used to keep so that Billy could keep up with him.

"I wonder where he comes from?" Billy's father thought as he turned to go back indoors.

Charlie made his way back into the busy centre of Blufford. The grubby and dusty place never made an impression, he couldn't help but feel a numbness overcome him.

"Time is a gift," he thought. He watched everyone in the busy town centre, wearing their rags and hunting for riches. Charlie knew that he came from a privileged background, but began to understand the world in a different light. You could have all of the money in the world but what good would it be if you have no time left to spend it? He turned the corner and almost bumped into someone as he wiped the tears from his eyes.

"Sorry, sir," said Charlie, and started to walk past before he noticed who he'd bumped into.

"Good heavens, Charlie! We must stop meeting like this," said the well-dressed gentleman from earlier. His female friend wasn't around this time. "You look as if you've the world on your shoulders! A boy your age shouldn't have so much burdening his mind."

Charlie looked at the well-dressed man curiously. A strange man was typically something to be scared of, but Charlie wasn't. He felt oddly at ease in his presence.

"Sir, if you don't mind my asking, what's your name?" asked Charlie, curiously. "I feel it only right that I should know your name, as you know mine."

The gentleman laughed softly. His eyes glistened as he marvelled at Charlie.

"You're quite right, Charlie, where are my manners?" chuckled the gentleman. "I'm known far and wide by many names – some, even I can't remember. My name is Mr…" he paused for a moment... "Song!" he exclaimed. "Yes, Mr Song at your service."

"Good to meet you, Mr Song," replied Charlie, courteously. "My father says that asking questions of someone you've just met isn't gentlemanly-"

"I've no doubt you're going to ask anyway. You have my ear," Mr Song cut in.

"Why doesn't anybody notice you?" Charlie asked after a moment. "You're clearly not of this town yet no one stops to wonder." Mr Song smiled from ear to ear.

"You *are* observant Charlie. These… people… only see what they wish to see or, more importantly, what I want them to see." Mr Song suddenly pulled a beautiful pocket watch from his pristine coat. "My goodness, is that the time? I have some matters that require my attention. Good day to you, Mr Kingston." Mr Song tipped his hat and went to leave, before turning back to Charlie.

"Don't let Billy weigh so heavily on your mind. You've got plenty to attend to yourself!"

With that, Mr Song left Charlie standing on the corner, and disappeared into the busy centre out of sight.

Charlie made his way home and pondered Mr Song. He wasn't used to being noticed, and when he was, it usually wasn't for anything positive.

"What, on earth are you wearing?" Lord Kingston barked as Charlie walked through the door. "You look like one of those animals from Blufford!" Charlie had been consumed by the day's events and forgot to get changed on his way home.

"Is that where you've been!? Again!?" fumed his father, his face changing to a deep shade of scarlet.

"Yes father, I went to see my friend but… he isn't there anymore. I won't be going again," replied Charlie, casually seemingly unmoved by his father's rage.

"Lies, rotten lies as always!" Lord Kingston spat. Charlie remained unmoved and waited to see what the outcome would be.

"To your room, boy! Stay there for the duration of the day and you may not leave the house unless you're with Chester."

Charlie climbed the stairs, unable to think of anything else except Billy. Making his way to his bedroom, he tried to tear his thoughts away.

Charlie reached under his bed and pulled out the globe that had saved him previously. He examined the globe and wiped the dirt and dust from it. As he peered inside, a sudden wave of horror fell through him like a bucket of cold water.

The figure inside was now sitting down cross-legged, almost as if it was bored. Charlie stared, without blinking, at the globe, trying to process this occurrence. He calmed as he brought in reasonable doubt.

"The figure cannot have moved... That isn't possible. It must have always been in that position and I've only noticed it properly now. Maybe it's a trick of the light," he thought to himself.

"Christopher saw the globe," he suddenly remembered. Charlie shot down the hallway and burst into Christopher's room. His younger sibling sat humming to himself as he arranged his toy soldiers around several miniature tables. Charlie looked at them, confused.

"What have you done with your soldiers?" Charlie asked, bewildered.

"They're having a tea party, there's no war today," replied Christopher, smiling. "Would you like to join?" he asked, looking hopefully at Charlie.

"Not just now, look at this globe. Has the little man inside changed position?" Christopher reached up and studied the globe. Squinting and staring hard, with his tongue lolling to one side, he found his conclusion.

"There's no man inside," decided Christopher.

"Of course there is… Look again!" Charlie barked, frustrated.

"Is this a trick?" asked Christopher, refusing to take the globe from him and looking fearful.

Charlie looked from Christopher to the globe and checked again. Sure enough, the figure had disappeared from the globe. He dropped the globe as if it were boiling hot, and froze in renewed horror.

"Am I sick? There's a figure… I just saw it!" he thought to himself as he picked up the globe.

"Is something bad happening?" asked Christopher worriedly, as he slowly got to his feet.

"No Christopher, everything's fine, I thought I saw something inside the globe but clearly I was mistaken. There's nothing to worry about." Charlie forced a smile and made his way back to his own room.

He tried to rationalise what had just happened. Maybe there hadn't been a figure in the globe after all… A trick of the light perhaps, or too much time in the sun. Charlie put the globe on the shelf, out of sight, and climbed into bed. It had been a long, difficult day and he wanted it to end.

Charlie lay down and, before long, he fell into an uneasy sleep. He found himself on a small island surrounded by a black sea. He looked into the distance but couldn't see anything – it just went on and on. A shrill voice echoed from the distance…

"I'm here! Let me out or I'm done for,"

"Where are you?" Charlie questioned the void around him.

"Bloody… right in-front of you! Must I draw you a damned map!?"

Charlie frowned into the void, not knowing what to say. He opened his mouth to reply, before the voice cut him short.

"They're going to be here soon and I can't hide forever!" the voice urged. "I need you to wake up now… Wake up and let me out!"

Charlie suddenly felt himself falling and threw out his arms to try and steady himself. He opened his eyes and found himself in bed, soaking in sweat and breathing heavily. He looked around at the room as if to confirm he was no longer dreaming. He heard the grandfather clock in the hallway chime, signalling midnight. Charlie rubbed his eyes and sat up in bed. Pondering the nightmare he'd just experienced, he could have sworn it was real. He decided to head downstairs and get some water.

As he made his way down the stairs, he considered the events of the day and felt a deep emptiness in the pit of his stomach. He'd never see Billy again and he felt truly alone. Aside from Billy, he had no friends. Laughing, dreaming and playing the day away, he recalled some of his favourite

times and smiled as he did so. A comforting warmth began
to fill the void.

"There's a boy outside, father!" cried Billy,
slamming the front door behind him. He looked severely
shaken. Charlie had arrived before Billy got home, so he
waited with his parents. Billy's parents made their own
lemonade at home, crisp and delicious, it was both a gift
and a curse. Nothing Charlie had ever tasted felt as
refreshing as their home-made lemonade, a bittersweet
treat for gasping children. However, it became a curse, as
no other beverage on Earth compared.
"Get yourself back out there Billy, and show that
boy what-for!" Billy's father scorned. "If you don't, you
can't go out and play!" Reluctantly, Billy went back outside
as Billy's mother stood in the kitchen shaking her head.
Suddenly, Billy came back, slamming the door behind him
once again.
"Charlie, go outside and give that boy a telling!
Show Billy how it's done," Billy's father bawled as he
looked disapprovingly at Billy. Charlie left and, only
seconds later, shot back in and slammed the front door shut.
Breathing heavily, he looked terrified.
"There's a boy, outside and he's-" Charlie wheezed

"Step aside, boys, I'll see what's going on and bring this charade to a halt," announced Billy's father, standing up straight with his chest puffed, trying to look as mean as possible. Sadly, for Billy's father, he wasn't very intimidating. He was too soft and kind in nature. He marched out of the front door. Raised voices and scuffling could be heard and, suddenly, Billy's father came running back inside and slammed the front door shut. With wide eyes and holding the door, he looked at everyone in the room, silently assessing the situation.

"What's the matter?" asked Billy's mother, looking concerned. Billy's father looked at everyone in the room as though the world itself was going to end at any moment.

"There's a boy outside... he's got... he's got a huge dog poo on the end of a stick and he's chasing everyone with it!" gasped Billy's father, still catching his breath. Billy's mother broke into uncontrollable laughter and sank to her knees. Billy's father shot her a glowing stare of disapproval and looked out of the window to see if the coast was clear. Boys, girls and men ran in all directions to get away from the small boy and his smelly stick.

Charlie snapped back to reality and laughed to himself. His friend had gone, but he would always have his memories.

As Charlie turned to make his way back up the stairs, water in hand, the front door burst open and his father staggered into the hallway followed by a large group of his friends.

They weren't actually his friends but political colleagues, business partners and associates from the party that he represented. His father was considerably drunk, so he felt it best to wait in the shadows until they had disappeared into the sitting room to smoke cigars, drink brandy and laugh at distasteful jokes that weren't funny.

They staggered in one by one, laughing and shouting, each trying to pat his father on the back. He had clearly impressed his peers somehow.

"A smaller work force, yet you've accomplished more than any other construction company!" one of them cheered. Charlie waited until they all entered the sitting room before perching himself outside in the darkened hallway. His feet were splayed, ready to shoot into another hiding spot should someone come through the door.

"Maybe I can help Billy's father get another job at one of the other construction companies, so Billy can get a proper burial!" Charlie whispered to himself as he listened intently to the conversation.

His father's friends cheered and whooped as they poured brandy and lit cigars. They were clearly celebrating something big. Lord Kingston stood in front of the fireplace, a proud smile upon his face as he lapped up the admiration and praise before him. He raised a glass into the air and the group quietened down.

"Tonight, we celebrate a new dawn in business! We've passed a new law whereby labourers can opt out of the legal maximum hours and work as many as they like. Furthermore, as we've transferred them onto a salary, they'll work the same rate for less money out of our pockets!" Lord Kingston grinned drunkenly. His friends clapped and whooped as they showered him with admiration.

"How many of your workers have you got now?" asked a skinny businessman who remarkably resembled a rat.

"Two months ago, I had thirty construction workers, most of them labourers costing me a fortune every hour." Lord Kingston boasted, "I laid off ten of them, persuaded the rest to opt out of the maximum hours legislation and then put them on a salary! That means, a smaller workforce and higher rates of efficiency."

"I heard that one of them comes by almost every day asking if there's any work for him because his son is sick. Well, boo hoo!" jeered another fat businessman in a mocking tone. They all roared together and laughed. Charlie felt himself getting angry and a red mist starting to descend. They clearly had no compassion or feeling for the desperate workers of Blufford.

"Well, I don't know about that, but all I can say is thank heavens for Wrigley's Construction!" cheered Lord Kingston.

Charlie suddenly felt a wave of red-hot anger descend throughout his entire body as he realised this great truth. Had it not been for his father, Billy's father might still be employed.

The sitting room door crashed open as Charlie stormed in and stopped in front of his father.

"You! You're a murderer! It's all your fault that my best friend died!" Charlie screamed.

"I beg your pardon," started Lord Kingston.

"Shut up!" roared Charlie.

Lord Kingston looked at Charlie open-mouthed, not knowing what to say. Charlie could be a handful, but he had never seen him in this state before.

"My best friend died. He might still be alive if it wasn't for you and your horrible company!" Charlie cried. "You don't see anything but money, and mother would be *ashamed* of your behaviour." His father glanced uncomfortably at the portrait of his late wife but couldn't bring himself to look at it properly. Charlie was right, and he knew it.

Lord Kingston's friends looked awkwardly at each other. Some of them sniggered quietly and wondered what their aspirational idol would do.

"Your… your mother…" Lord Kingston slurred. "She would…"

Charlie turned and ran out of the room, dashing upstairs to his bedroom.

"Charlie!" his father called as he ran.

Slamming his bedroom door shut, he wept into his pillow, feeling devastated, angry and, most of all, guilty.

"My father killed Billy," he thought to himself over and over, torturing himself with the words. Each time he did, a new wave of dread and pain went through him. Charlie sat up in his bed. If his father would not atone for his sins, then Charlie would do it for him. Knowing that his father was still downstairs entertaining his peers, he darted down the hallway and into his father's bedroom, pulling out draws and looking under the bed. The time for worrying about consequences had long since passed – Charlie wanted more than anything to turn back time and prevent what had happened.

"Got it!" Charlie whispered to himself. He stood up triumphantly and looked at the prize. It was an old wallet that Lord Kingston kept, which always contained emergency cash. Charlie emptied the wallet and scooped up the thick wad of cash, stuffing it into his pyjamas.

"Billy will have the best burial there's ever been, just wait and see!" he thought to himself as he got dressed. It was too late to go over to Blufford, so Charlie sat with his coat on and his shoes tied, ready to head out at the first crack of dawn. Shortly after, Charlie fell asleep sat against the wall.

He found himself back on the island he had dreamt about before, only this time he had his shoes and coat with him.

"Charlie, you must get me out of here," said the voice from the void. "I'm on your shelf, I think. You must let me out."

Charlie frowned and stared into the distance. He walked forward to see if anything came into view.

"I'm very tired, I'd had enough of these nightmares and dreams that don't make any sense, I have enough to keep me busy," Charlie shouted as he walked forward cautiously.

"You're going to experience more than nightmares if you don't let me out, boy!" fumed the voice. "They can pounce on us at any moment, but I've kept you here long enough. Time for you to go home and let me out, damn it!"

Charlie felt the familiar falling sensation and woke up with a start. The sun shone through the window as the birds chirped to greet the new dawn. Charlie rubbed his eyes and looked around the room. He felt as though he'd been asleep for a few minutes, but hours had passed.

He got up and made his way across the room to the shelf and studied the globe. This time, a figure could be seen showing his hands in a 'told-you-so' kind of way. Had it been any other normal day, he would have been disturbed at the re-appearance of the figure. Recent events had numbed his senses, and he put the globe on his bedside table for later.

Charlie opened his door slowly and looked out into the hallway. The house slept soundly. Charlie took his opportunity and crept from the house, careful not to wake his family, he raced down to Blufford as quickly as he could.

People were starting their morning commute to work and stared as Charlie ran as quickly as he could, kicking up dust from the filthy walkways as he did so. Skidding around the corner onto the street where Billy's family lived, he raced up to the door and banged as hard and as fast as he could.

"Is anybody home?" he shouted at the front door, gasping for breath. The door suddenly swung open and Billy's father stood in the doorway rubbing his eyes and cursing the person that would dare wake him up early on a day of rest.

"Charlie, have you lost your mind!?" scolded Billy's father. "You nearly took the door down with that hammering and hollering! Come inside and sit down."

They both walked inside, and Charlie sat down on the old tired couch inside the house.

"Would you like something to drink, Charlie?" yawned Billy's father.

"There's something that I need to tell you, sir," Charlie began.

"Smart clothes!" Billy's father pointed at his attire. "You look really smart today, they must have cost a fortune-"

"I have something to tell you," Charlie interrupted. "My name is Charlie Kingston; my father is Lord Chester Kingston Senior and he owns-"

"Wrigley's Construction," Billy's father completed; he had a serious expression on his face.

"Yes," replied Charlie uneasily. "But-"

"Why did you lie about who you are?" Billy's father said suddenly, his fist starting to clench.

"I didn't want you to hate me," Charlie pleaded. "But look, I've brought you something..." Charlie rummaged frantically in his pockets. He pulled out a thick wad of money and presented it to Billy's father. It was a lot of money – more than Billy's father could earn in six months.

"Now you can give Billy a proper burial" Charlie pleaded earnestly. Billy's father looked at the money and then back to Charlie. He pondered for a moment and then walked over to the front door and opened it.

"Get out of my house, Charlie. We don't need your money, your lies or your pity," he spoke sternly. "I don't want to see you around here anymore; you don't belong here. Tell your father I can bury my own son."

Charlie's eyes began to fill up – he had only wanted to help. He got up from his seat and left through the open door, feeling the force of the front door as it slammed behind him. He felt a deep sinking sensation in his stomach as he started his walk back home.

"I don't know what I can do," Charlie thought as he made his way down the road. The local people had noticed Charlie's clothes and began whispering and pointing. His kind didn't belong in Blufford and they knew it. The rain began to pour down from the heavens, bouncing on the pavement, but Charlie didn't notice.

A little further up the road, he felt a hand descend on his collar and drag him into an alleyway.

"Empty your pockets! I want your money and your shoes!" That same filthy hand covered his mouth as the thief rifled through his pockets. He felt the sharp tip of a knife pressing against his neck as the thief's terrible whiskey-breath stung his eyes. He looked like he hadn't eaten in days. Unkept, greasy hair and filthy clothes hung off the thief as he continued to search him with quick, practised hands.

"Well, look at all of this!" he cackled ecstatically. The thief had found the wad of cash in his pocket and a huge smile made its way across his face. "Sorry boy, I can't have you going to the police. You'll have every copper and snooty toff looking for me." He pressed the knife closer to Charlie's neck, as Charlie closed his eyes and started to cry. A sudden thump and resounding scream could be heard as Charlie fell onto the floor in a pile. He opened his eyes and saw the thief unconscious in front of him. Blood began to flow through his hair and onto the floor. Charlie sat up next to him and gasped for air, looking around to see what – or who –had intervened.

The local police officer stood over the thief with his baton in hand.

"Mr Kingston, I thought I told you not to come around here! Not only have you disobeyed my request, but you've come dressed in clothes that no one here can afford – and you're carrying a huge wad of money!" the policeman scolded him. "I'm guessing that the money isn't yours!"

Charlie tried to regain his breath and shook his head.

"Get up, on your feet," the policeman ordered, dragging Charlie upright. "We're not going to tell your father about this incident. Do you understand?"

"Yes sir, sorry sir." Charlie coughed. He looked down at the thief as he gargled and twitched in a growing pool of blood. "What about him?"

"Forget him, people die here all the time," replied the policeman, unmoved by the slowly dying thief. He ushered Charlie out of the alleyway and marched him back home. They didn't speak as they walked back up the road to Lilford.

Chapter Four – Pastures New

Part I

If you open the door of opportunity, be sure to hold on tight. It could whip you away and take you somewhere great. It could also land you in a predicament of the most harrowing kind, there are worse fates than death. Those that frequent the door of opportunity in search of betterment, risk losing everything. Those that do not open any doors, might not get anything at all.

"Are ye waiting for the next train, son?" asked Douglas, the old railway guard. He had the softest Scottish accent and the brightest blue eyes. His tired face, though seasoned, glowed with kindness.

"No sir, I'm just watching the comings and goings. I'm waiting to see which locomotives pass through and stop at the station," Charlie replied politely. "I don't mean to cause any inconvenience. Should I leave?" Charlie prepared to vacate his seat on the bench by the platform edge. Douglas considered Charlie for a moment as he scratched his grey stubble. He seemed to be very tired.

"That's okay, you don't need to leave," Douglas replied as he sat himself next to Charlie on the bench. "Would you like a schedule, so you can see what trains will be arriving?"

"No, thank you. I'm guessing which trains will arrive and where they'll be going," Charlie replied. Douglas shivered and pulled his collar up around his ears to keep the cold out.

"It's starting to get cold now that summer has passed," Douglas observed. He looked down at Charlie and noticed him shivering. He pulled out a woolly hat and some gloves from inside his coat and handed them to Charlie.

"You can keep those; they'll keep the cold away," Douglas smiled. They silently watched hundreds of autumnal leaves tumble to the ground from the yellowing trees, the wind whipping them from the ground and whistling through the thinning branches.

"Why is it that you're here and not playing games with your friends?" Douglas asked with growing curiosity. "Surely there are better things for a young boy to be doing than sitting watching trains arrive and depart all day."

"I'm waiting," said Charlie, smiling. There was a sparkle in his eyes, reserved only for the mad and the magnificent.

"Waiting for what?" Douglas asked.

"I'm waiting for the wind to whistle my name, for the stars to reach out and guide me through the lonely nights and for my story to be written. Not a single day will be the same; each will be more exciting than the last as I solve the mysteries of life. I'll walk boldly where others dare not venture. I have so much to give, but I'm yet to be called."

Charlie watched as a train pulled into the station on the opposite platform. A crowd of passengers disembarked from the train as others waited to climb aboard. The behemoth locomotive wheezed as steam billowed out from underneath. Waiting patiently, the beast cooled and hummed as the stoker and driver prepared for the next leg of their journey.

"That sounds like a real adventure," Douglas chuckled. "I had dreams too. I wanted to be a train driver so that I could explore the nation, so I became a railway guard and awaited my calling, just as you are now. Time passed and I became old, but those dreams of adventure never faded."

Charlie and Douglas watched as the locomotive blew steam and built pressure before whooshing and huffing into life. The carriages groaned as the wheels screeched along the steel railway line. Momentum increased as the heavy beast left the station and built up speed, carrying its passengers to their next chapter.

"If your dreams never faded, why aren't you a train driver?" asked Charlie as he watched the train and carriages make their way into the distance.

"I never heard the call," Douglas sighed as he studied his wrinkled and tired hands. "The problem is, dreams never call. Not for you, not for me, not for anyone. It's up to us to make the leap into the unknown. Anyway, I must be on my way. The next train is due shortly."

Douglas slapped his hands on his knees and groaned as he got back to his feet and returned to his duties.

Charlie returned home and made his way into the welcoming warmth of the foyer. His eyes were watering from the blustering wind that he'd battled all the way home. He took off his coat and made his away across the foyer, hoping to get upstairs unnoticed.

"Charlie," Lord Kingston called from the sitting room. Charlie let out a sigh and beckoned to his father's call. He entered and allowed his eyes to wander across the various portraits of his lineage. He smiled at the new electric lights that had recently been fitted. Progression had finally come to Kingston Manor – maybe this would be the beginning of something good.

"Yes, father?" Charlie replied.

"Have you kept out of trouble?" Lord Kingston asked, with his hands on his hips.

"Yes father," Charlie replied indifferently, his eyes wandering everywhere but at his father.

"Have you made any new friends?" Lord Kingston asked awkwardly. He seemed to be struggling to find adequate conversation. Charlie finally landed his gaze upon his father.

"No, father. My only friend is still dead, I do not have any others. I would like to go for a bath, as I've had a very busy day," Charlie answered calmly and very politely.

Lord Kingston opened his mouth to reply but no words came out. He looked at Charlie, smiled and gave a nod, keen to end their exchange.

Charlie left the sitting room and went upstairs to run himself a bath. He swivelled the vast taps on the huge freestanding bath as the crashing of the water echoed throughout the huge bathroom. Charlie took a moment and pondered the bath as it slowly filled with hot water. Very few households owned even a tin bath in Blufford, but Kingston Manor had many bathrooms. They were vast, immaculate and crafted in exquisite exotic materials.

Charlie's thoughts paused on Mr Betts – was he able to take a bath this easily? In such comfort and ease? Probably not. Charlie put a hand on his chest as he waited for the bath to fill. He missed Billy and didn't ever think the void in his life would be filled.

"Best friends don't come around every day," he thought to himself. Dusk had arrived and slowly the sun set over the horizon. The wind became more ferocious and beat against the window panes. Charlie sank further into the warmth of the bath and considered the words of Douglas, the old railway guard.

"There is no calling, seek and we shall find," he whispered to himself as he lay in the water and watched the rain beat on the window.

After quite some time in the bath, he walked quietly across the landing and tried not to bring any undue attention to himself. He could hear his father entertaining Chester in the sitting room, telling stories of politics and greatness as was his usual topic of choice. He made his way into his bedroom and pondered the mysterious globe once more; the figure sat looking up, scowling at the roof of the globe. Charlie no longer felt afraid of the flippant figure and its apparent mood swings. He had settled on the assumption that no one would believe him if he told them about the figure. If he had indeed gone mad, it surely couldn't be any worse than recent events.

Charlie began to dread going to bed; the nightmares, poor quality of sleep and strange noises had plagued him since this globe had become part of his life. Once again, he fell into an uneasy sleep and found himself in the familiar wretched abyss. This time, something felt different.

He no longer heard the voice of the void – only silence reigned.

"This must be a trick," Charlie thought to himself as he stared hard into the distance. He removed his jumper and dropped it into a pile on the floor to mark where he'd been. Charlie looked up and once again began squinting into the darkness. He set off with a quick walk before breaking out into a full run. He ran as fast as he could into the endless void for what seemed an age. He gasped and huffed until he suddenly tripped over, his arms splaying as he hit his head on the floor. The pain seared and throbbed as he rolled over and held a hand to his forehead. This pain felt real, unlike any dream he'd had before. He looked around to see what he had tripped over and found his jumper to be the culprit. He looked in the direction he had been running and back where he'd come from, he couldn't see anything.

"I hate this place!" Charlie shouted into the distance in a rage. He no longer feared this strange dreamland he'd become familiar with. He stumbled to his feet and froze, not daring to move for a moment. An icy coldness had taken to his left shoulder, he felt as though he wasn't alone anymore. Turning around as quickly as he could, he gasped in horror before letting out an ear-piercing scream. A shadowy figure loomed over him, hovering above the ground. It had a pitch-black shroud for a body, while a white porcelain mask, cracked and tired, hung where its face should have been. A low growl emerged from the depths of the spectre.

Charlie turned to run but tripped over his jumper again. A cold hand gripped tightly onto his ankle and held him in the air. He turned and kicked the shroud square in the middle of the mask. The shroud dropped Charlie but he didn't hit the floor, he felt a falling sensation, just as he had done previously when his dreams concluded, and then he found himself in his bedroom.

Charlie leapt from his bed and searched frantically for the globe in the darkness of the night, with only the dim pearly moonlight assisting him. Just as he found the globe, Charlie span around and saw the shroud reaching out for him. He opened his mouth to scream, but as hard as he tried, not a sound left his mouth as the creature's hands descended around his throat. Flailing and kicking, he tried with all his might to break from the shrouded monster's grip, but to no avail. The hands began to tighten harder around his neck, Charlie choked quietly as he tried to draw breath. His eyes began to bulge and his muscles weakened as the life started to drain from him… With the last of his energy, he threw the globe in an attempt to thwart the monster, but missed.

The globe smashed, and as it did, a blinding light burst across the room. The startled monster dropped Charlie in a heap on the ground. He took a huge gulp of air and turned to see what had happened. A somewhat familiar voice could be heard shouting and cursing. Charlie's eyes began to focus as he gasped for air, nursing his throat with his hand.

The silhouette of a man was fighting the deadly shroud, they locked each other in a tight grip as they crashed around the room. The shrouded monster pinned the man to the wall to get the upper hand and gripped tightly onto his throat, relentlessly maintaining its hold. The man's eyes began to roll into the back of his head as his efforts to escape slowed. As all seemed lost, a sudden flash of light and a loud crack split the air, the two opponents fell to the ground in a heap. The shrouded monster began to burn as sparks flew, consuming all evidence of its existence. All that remained was the porcelain mask and a pile of ashes. The mysterious man lay on the floor for a moment collecting himself, an old 17th century flintlock pistol in his hand still smoking from the shot he had fired into the monster.

The mysterious man looked no older than thirty. His eyes were a beautiful shade of blue but contained all the sorrow of a man who had seen the world end ten times over. Even as the man smiled in triumph, his eyes betrayed his elation. He got to his feet, ran his hands through his thick black hair and checked his pockets for his belongings before locking eyes with Charlie, who simply stared open-mouthed at his mysterious saviour.

"Not even a thank-you?" said the man sarcastically as he continued to search his pockets. His uniform looked old and tatty; a green trench coat hung over his ancient naval uniform. Charlie opened his mouth to reply.

"Too bloody late now! I've said it for you," the man snapped. "I've been in that damn globe for weeks and weeks – it was only a matter of time before they found me."

"It was you inside the globe? Charlie stammered, still trying to process what had happened.

"Yes. It's called a woe globe and it's about the most boring place there ever was," the man replied as he looked around Charlie's room.

"What year is it?" the man asked as he inspected Charlie's books.

"1909," Charlie whispered in awe, staring at the man, not daring to blink. "What's your name?"

"Commodore James Edward Marshall, the most wanted fugitive across the four planes… but most call me 'The Commodore'." The Commodore made his way over to the door and ran his hand across the frame carefully, examining it with interest and smiling to himself.

"Mahogany doors, hand carved and dove-tailed together at the corners with absolute precision. Maple inlays, too!" The Commodore stepped back, beaming with excitement. "Very fine craftsmanship." He suddenly turned around and remembered he wasn't alone. Charlie stood still with a grin from ear to ear as he marvelled at his hero. He was certainly strange and possibly mad but, a hero nonetheless.

"I wonder…" The Commodore muttered as he made his way across the room to the pile of ash and the mask. He retrieved the mask and inspected it thoroughly. It was old and very badly worn, even before the altercation.

"You're an old one, that's for sure…" he whispered. He dropped it to the floor and ground it into pieces with the heel of his boot.

"Not one I've met before!" he concluded.

"What on earth was that thing?" asked Charlie, pointing to the smouldering remains on his bedroom floor.

"Annoying!" barked The Commodore. "They're trying to capture me and send me back to… somewhere not very pleasant."

Charlie looked confused; he opened his mouth to ask more questions but The Commodore cut in before he had the chance.

"There will be more of them soon. It's time for me to leave. We can't have your father knowing that you've been in the company of a fugitive," he explained as he pulled a battered and badly-damaged pocket watch from inside his worn uniform shirt.

"Goodness, look at the time," he said, shaking his head. "Don't tell anyone what you saw. Or do. They won't believe you anyway." The watch began to tick. The hands moved in all directions, stopping and starting as though they had a mind of their own.

Charlie felt a sadness wash through him as he watched The Commodore preparing to leave. He longed for adventure.

Lord Kingston then came skidding down the hallway to Charlie's door to see what all the commotion had been. He stared open-mouthed as a soft light began to emit from The Commodore's watch which ticked faster and faster.

"What on earth has happened in here? Who is that man?" he shouted in confusion.

Charlie looked quickly at his father and then back to The Commodore. Without a second thought, Charlie took hold of The Commodore's arm and vanished from his room, his home and 1909.

A savage wind pulled and tugged at Charlies clothes as he held onto The Commodore. He could see people moving at a pace a hundred times faster than usual, day after night flew at an accelerated rate. Not only was time shifting, they were going to a different location. Charlie could hear the whispers of voices of those that had passed long ago and those that were not even born. After a short time, which felt an age longer, time resumed its normal pace and Charlie fell to the ground.

He landed softly in a field surrounded by trees. The grass grew wildly and the land seemed unkept, much as though nobody had been there for a long time.

A hand pulled him up from the ground, he soon found himself nose to nose with The Commodore.

"Have you lost your mind!?" he shouted "Do you understand what you've done?" The Commodore released Charlie so suddenly that he fell into a pile once more. The Commodore breathed heavily and ran his hands through his thick black hair as he considered Charlie with contempt.

"I am hunted day and night by The Celestial Order… These are dangerous times, not only for me but for the four planes." The Commodore let out a sigh and looked at Charlie.

"I can't take you home, it would be too easy for them to find me." The Commodore fell back into the long, wavy grass and let out another sigh.

"It doesn't rain… but it bloody pours," he growled to himself.

Charlie looked at The Commodore as his eyes began to fill.

"I just wanted to go on an adventure," he sobbed, moving his gaze to his shoes.

"Adventure!" The Commodore shouted in disbelief. He sat up on his elbows and glowered at Charlie.

"You gave up a warm bed, a safe home and a future guaranteed by your father's success. You gave up the perfect life."

"Whose perfect life?" sniffed Charlie. "Because it certainly wasn't mine."

The Commodore shook his head as he rose to his feet. He took a final look at Charlie and stormed off through the field. Charlie felt a deep anxiety rise as he realised the severity of his actions. His heart pumped faster as he watched his hero dash across the field.

"Well, are you coming?" The Commodore called. A huge smile spread across Charlie's face as he ran to catch up.

The Commodore consulted his beaten pocket watch and mumbled to himself incoherently as they walked through the fields. Charlie looked around some more, looking for anything slightly familiar.

"Where are we?" asked Charlie.

"1342, Yorkshire somewhere," The Commodore replied, still fiddling with his watch.

"What are we looking for?" asked Charlie after some time. So far, they'd only tracked through fields and hadn't seen anyone else.

"Rohan's Reach, the capital city of the Divine world," replied The Commodore without looking up from his watch. Charlie thought to himself for a moment.

"Are you dead?" asked Charlie, rather bluntly. The Commodore looked at Charlie as they walked through the fields. The question had caught him off guard.

"Somewhat," replied The Commodore, slowly trying to gauge Charlie's reaction.

"What's it like?" asked Charlie in wonderment.

"Bloody awful," The Commodore sighed. "I'm almost dead, but not quite. I lived once, hundreds of years ago. I can't die – I've already done that. I don't feel the wind in my hair, nor the rain on my face. If I eat, it doesn't satisfy me. My thirst is unquenchable. It's just emptiness."

"Surely, you don't have anything to be scared of if you're already dead," Charlie pointed out.

"There are fates worse than simply dying. Death can be a kindness," The Commodore replied grimly.

Charlie ran his hands through the long, wavy grass as they walked. He took in the natural beauty of the untouched landscape.

"It's beautiful here," Charlie said as he admired the wilderness as they walked. Hours passed as they made their way through the trees and into the squelchy marshlands. The Commodore continued to mutter at his watch, changing direction and leading them in a path that he was almost certain was going to take them to their destination.

Part II

Charlie's legs ached and his stomach began to rumble, but he didn't make any kind of complaint. He smiled and walked with a spring in his step.

"We're not too far away now," announced The Commodore as they stopped for a break on a felled tree. He pulled some old papers from his pockets and laid them out on the decaying bark, dusting them off as he did so. "There are a thousand ways to enter the Divine world – why do they have to be so complicated?"

"What's that?" asked Charlie in wonderment. The Commodore looked up from his papers and into the direction where Charlie pointed. A golden yellow glow could be seen dancing in the bracken, forward and back as if to beckon its onlookers.

"It's a 'Will o' the wisp'," replied The Commodore dryly. "They lure the fickle-minded and light-hearted away from their paths, usually to somewhere less than pleasant."

Charlie watched in awe as the 'Will o' the wisp' danced even more beautifully.

"Get out of it! So help me, I'll bottle you up and sell you off to the nearest goblin or ghoul that pays the highest price!" The Commodore barked at the light. The playful dancing stopped almost instantly and the yellow light turned briefly to a shade of red. A smile curled in the corner of The Commodore's mouth. He removed his pistol and placed it on the tree. The Will o' the wisp danced away, turning back to its original shade of golden yellow, and it was soon out of sight.

"How do you travel through time with that watch? Does it have a map?" Charlie asked, turning his attention back to The Commodore.

"Erm, I'm not really sure, to be honest. I just think about where I need to be and move the hands. Sometimes I am nearby where I need to be and sometimes, I am far away. It's not an exact science," The Commodore thought aloud. "On the odd occasion, it doesn't work at all. Time is delicate, so I don't use it too often."

Darkness fell as the sun began to set, Charlie and The Commodore continued through the marshlands until they came to a great bog. Insects chirped into the warm night-time air, the smell of damp earth and stagnant water complemented the essentially perfect ecosystem before them.

"Here we go," beamed The Commodore with his hands on his hips. He took a ring from his pocket and placed it on his finger.

"How do I look?" came a soft voice. Charlie looked where The Commodore had been standing, but he was no longer there – instead, a beautiful young woman had taken his place. Blonde hair came down to her hips and green eyes sparkled against her natural beauty.

"Is that you!?" Charlie gasped.

"Yes, I'm in disguise. We don't want The Good Shepherd herding us in, do we?" The Commodore replied.

"Why do they want to catch you?" asked Charlie, curiously. It had just dawned on him that he had been a party to a wanted criminal, but he hadn't yet asked for the details.

"I'm a naughty boy, dear Charlie!" The Commodore laughed, darkly. "I regularly stay up past my bedtime and interrupt at the dinner table. It is most unsettling for The Good Shepherd and his Celestial Order, who simply won't tolerate this behaviour." Charlie looked around and squinted into the darkness.

"Who's The Good Shepherd?" he asked, still trying to adjust to the beautiful lady that stood before him.

"The great saviour, apparently," The Commodore spat. "He and his 'Celestial Order' promised to unite the Divine world and create a world of equality and opportunity."

"That doesn't sound so bad," Charlie inclined.

"It doesn't, does it?" The Commodore agreed. "That's how he managed to get the majority of the Divine world to support him and his minions into power. They have systematically murdered The Monarchy, The Time-Keepers, The Council of the Divine and thousands of innocent people. They do all of it in secret and portray a very different image to their public."

"So, what are they planning to do?" asked Charlie as he scratched his head, trying to make sense of everything.

"Top secret I'm afraid," whispered The Commodore with his hand on 'her' hips.

"You can tell me, I'm great at keeping secrets," Charlie pleaded, earnestly.

The beautiful lady that was The Commodore burst into laughter, though Charlie didn't find anything particularly funny.

"Trust you? That's how you get yourself killed, or tortured, or both," The Commodore explained. "There's no place for friends, trust and all of that nonsense."

"Anyway, here we go!" The Commodore beamed as he rolled up 'her' sleeves. Charlie looked hard into the puddle, trying to find the entrance.

"Where is it?" asked Charlie.

"Right here!" exclaimed The Commodore. He tied up 'her' hair and jumped into the puddle. Not so much as a splash was heard as The Commodore vanished. Charlie jumped after him/her and disappeared into darkness, falling at an ever-increasing rate. Down, down, down he fell, gathering momentum as he tumbled, reaching his hands out desperately into the darkness. A hand suddenly took hold of his own and pulled him from his descent into the startling brightness and warmth of the sun.

Charlie's eyes widened in awe at the magnificent fortress that stood before him and The Commodore. The stone walls were beautifully crafted and perfectly maintained, standing boldly as the metropolis centre of the Divine world.

At first glance, the Divine world seemed to be more akin to the medieval era of the Blind world. There wasn't any sign of electricity or technology as Charlie knew it –

this world was different. The Divine utilised enchantments, magic and alchemy rather than steam, electricity and fossil fuels. On occasion, Blind methodologies were adopted, such as weaponry and basic utensils. Charlie ran after The Commodore as he noticed 'her' walking towards the stunning entrance in the form of a marble archway. There were all kinds of fascinating creatures and entities making their way in and out of Rohan's Reach.

"Remember, Charlie, stay with me and don't talk to anyone," The Commodore ordered through his disguise.

They walked over a bridge that led to the archway. As they neared the entrance, they could see some guards on duty. The guards looked at all that came in and out very carefully, and eventually turned their attention to The Commodore and Charlie as they made their way through – but the guards didn't stop them.

Charlie could barely contain his excitement and curiosity as he marvelled at all of the different creatures; ghouls, gremlins, will o' the wisps and even a minotaur that seemed to be speaking fluent Latin to a market seller.

"I had no idea they were real," gasped Charlie, in awe of the mythical creatures. "They look different to the ones in my books."

"Stop staring at them, Charlie," The Commodore whispered. "We don't want them to find out you're a 'Blind boy'."

"I don't understand – am I Blind?" Charlie asked. He noticed some of the creatures had stopped to look at him and his unusual attire.

"It's what they call humans who refuse to acknowledge, or are unaware of, the Divine world," The Commodore whispered. "The Blind are not welcome here."

"But as I am now aware of the Divine world. Doesn't that mean I am no longer Blind?" Charlie replied defensively.

"A poor defence if you are interrogated," The Commodore jeered. "It's very rare for the Blind to wander into the Divine world, but when they do, they are dealt with quickly. Nobody ever sees them again."

Charlie looked around cautiously at the raised eyebrows and low whispers. Though alert, his spirits were not dampened.

The city had been built upon over centuries, and each era had left its mark. Higher buildings with doors for fairies seemed to reach the heavens as newer and far more polished buildings sat lower. Though mis-matched, the evidence of the times gone by stacked beautifully against each other.

As they made their way through Rohan's Reach, everyone seemed to be at peace as they laughed and conversed the day away.

"Everyone seems happy – it looks like a really nice place!" Charlie whispered to The Commodore, excited.

"That's what The Good Shepherd and his Celestial Order want you to think. They take very special care to create the illusion of grandeur and contentment, especially here in the capital," The Commodore replied, gravely. "It wouldn't be good for their image if everyone could see what they did behind closed doors. Generally, the further afield you go, the less of an illusion is in place."

Ahead, a crowd began to gather around a stage upon which stood a man with the most incredible looking black top hat and perfectly groomed moustache.

"Brethren and sistren of the Divine realm, we have come together under the guidance of the one true leader that is, The Good Shepherd!" he announced with the greatest showmanship. The crowd cheered and whooped. "For thousands of years, there has been unrest among the Divine world. Since the abdication of the monarchy, we have prospered! For we are united under The Good Shepherd's leadership. He has granted us the ability to trade energy and make our existence fruitful and peaceful, wonderful and plentiful. For The Good Shepherd!"

The crowd cheered hysterically and chanted: "Down with the King, up with The Good Shepherd! Down with the King, up with The Good Shepherd!"

"Come on, Charlie, let's go, I've had enough," The Commodore muttered, darkly.

"What happened to the King?" asked Charlie, still looking over his shoulder at the chanting crowd.

"Hundreds of years ago, King Sterling and the other monarchs were abdicated from power. That is the official statement anyway. From what I understand, he was a good man, but he listened to poor advice from his constituents," replied The Commodore scratching his chin. "He and the rest of the blue-bloods were murdered and disposed of."

Charlie looked on, and considered the bustling city once more.

"Are there other places like this?" asked Charlie.

"Oh yes, all over the world, the vast majority of them are controlled and governed by The Celestial Order," The Commodore explained. "They're enchanted, and access is usually regulated, though Rohan's Reach is the unofficial capital of the Divine world in Existence."

"If they're regulated, then how have you been getting in?" asked Charlie, quietly.

"I travel to different times, across the planes, and I use the lesser-known entrances."

"So, you're a time traveller!" Charlie said, a little too loudly. A rather large group of trolls turned to look at them.

"What're you looking at!?" The Commodore barked. "Back to your business or so help me I'll make sure you don't darken the underside of a bridge ever again!" The trolls, taken aback, returned to their conversation as they made their way further into Rohan's Reach.

"The legendary Time-Keepers have long since 'disappeared' thanks to 'The Good Shepherd'. I can travel time, yes, but I have to be careful when I do it and where I go. The Time-Keepers monitored the complicated never-ending paradox that is time, as it is very delicate. In the wrong hands, permanent damage can be done with a device like my watch. The Celestial Order can also track the energy given out by time travel – that's how they found me at your house."

The Commodore led them through the fortress, down small paths and through alleyways, leaving the joyful hustle and bustle behind. It wasn't long before they found themselves in a dark, secluded area of the town. Dirty streets, filthy clothes and a strong smell of urine were all key indicators of poverty in the area they had happened upon.

Contemptuous eyes watched from the shadows and doorways, conversations stopped, as onlookers tried to see who these outsiders were. Charlie stayed close to The Commodore – he felt safe in his company. The Commodore mumbled to himself and looked at the buildings that they passed. He was looking for something in particular and didn't seem at all concerned about the growing interest in their presence.

"You're a long way from home, Blind boy!" a voice shouted from one of the doorways. "It would be a shame if you never found your way back!" The other onlookers laughed darkly. Charlie moved in closer to The Commodore who seemed unmoved by the shouting and jeering.

"Open him up and see what he's made of!" yelled another voice. Some of them had started to follow The Commodore and Charlie. The Commodore suddenly took hold of Charlie's hand and led him down an alleyway. Some creatures were stood in their way and some had gathered behind them. They were trapped.

"Goblins," said The Commodore, grimly. "Would you believe that they used to be held in high regard?" Charlie trembled with fear but tried his best to hide it from the goblins. Their wicked amber eyes flashed in the darkness, and their sickly grey hides hung from their bones. They were undoubtedly a formidable opponent for any champion.

"And we will be again!" replied the leader. The Commodore kept his disguise, looking to anyone like a beautiful young lady with a child. Low hanging fruit for criminals, thieves or worse.

"Empty your pockets, we want all of the energy you've got – and when we have that, we'll take a little more." The goblin moved his coat aside and revealed a giant syringe and some empty glass vials. The other goblins howled and jeered at their prey. The Commodore removed a ring from his finger and revealed his true identity. The howling grew louder than ever – what a prize this would be.

"The infamous Commodore!" the leading goblin jeered. "There's boundless energy we can take from you and that fancy watch. We'll be sure to drop your body at The Celestial Order and claim our reward. We'll devour the boy." The surrounding goblins cheered and whooped in anticipation of what they were about to see.

"A wager!" The Commodore shouted. The crowd hushed to hear his proposition. "A fight against your strongest champion!" The crowd looked on to hear the leader's response. Goblins were partial to a wager.

"What do you wager?" the goblin asked curiously.

"The boy, my watch and my pistol, which you've no doubt heard about," The Commodore replied. "If you lose, you are to be demoted to the bottom of your ranks and your second is to lead your group – and you will 'give your hand'. The laughter and jeering from the crowd had stopped. It was tense and they wondered what their leader would choose. A wager had to be taken seriously. If he didn't accept the terms, then he would lose respect amongst his kin.

"I accept your terms!" the goblin lord shouted; the crowd roared their approval as the leader and The Commodore shook hands. The Commodore quickly wiped his hand on his jacket following the interaction.

"Bring Hurdimlin," howled their leader.

The champion goblin came forward, growling and thundering his huge hands across his beaten armour. An ancient sword was holstered. He looked to the crowds as he roared, and then he turned to his enemy. He looked at The Commodore and Charlie and pointed.

"Fight 'im?" Hurdimlin asked, confused.

"Not me," said The Commodore with a dark smile. "Him." The Commodore pointed at Charlie.

"What!? Me?" Charlie stammered in terror. The crowd burst into renewed laughter at such a preposterous suggestion. The leader of the goblins grinned and seemed at ease; this would be the easiest wager he'd ever placed.

"Here you go – take this sword and try not to break it, I've had it for quite some time," The Commodore prompted as he handed Charlie a tattered sword. Hurdimlin unholstered his sword and raised it into the air. The crowd roared and jeered like never before, certain that the undead sea-dog and his Blind boy would meet their conclusion.

"I don't… I can't… I don't know what I'm doing!" Charlie protested as The Commodore ushered him forwards.

"Look at it this way, Charlie, if you don't fight the goblin, we're going to die. They will steal our belongings and drain us of our energy with that giant needle they've got there. If we're still alive, they might do that first." The Commodore explained with a very serious expression. "What have you got to lose?"

They entered a small clearing in the crowd for their battle. A bell sounded and Hurdimlin wasted no time – he lunged forward, swinging his sword down over Charlie's

123

head. Charlie felt so scared, he simply closed his eyes and waited for the sword to strike him… only it never came. A clatter of metal split the air. Charlie looked up to see why he wasn't dead – or at least dying.

Charlie had deflected Hurdimlin's strike. His arm had moved without even a thought. He looked around, thoroughly confused as he deflected two more powerful blows from his opponent. A flash of concern emerged on his opponent's grubby face as he panted. Charlie felt hope spread throughout him and stood fast, ready to take on his enemy. Again, the goblin leapt forward with a howl and crossed swords with Charlie who deflected every attack with ease and perfect poise. They engaged for quite some time with neither side letting up. Charlie stepped up his technique and, shortly after, his sword founds its mark and cut deeply into Hurdimlin. The goblin recoiled and roared as blood poured from his arm. With renewed anger, he stormed forward and tried his best to thwart Charlie, but the boy managed to block every attack with ease.

The Commodore watched intently, with a dry smile upon his face. He glanced over to the leader of the goblins who looked worried – if Hurdimlin didn't win, then he would be disgraced before his very peers.

Charlie revelled in his newfound ability to swordfight. He looked over at The Commodore and saw that he was enjoying every part of this battle. The Commodore seemed to already know the outcome.

After quite some time, the goblin champion fell to the ground, exhausted. He panted and wheezed, unable to get up.

"I yield! The boy is the champion!" Hurdimlin coughed, trying to get onto his knees.

"For your cowardice and failure, you shall be sentenced to death!" screamed the goblin leader. He dragged Hurdimlin to his knees and unsheathed a fine, sharpened war axe from inside his coat. Charlie's eyes widened in horror – he had defeated the brute but had no desire to see him murdered.

"Can't you help him?" Charlie begged as he tugged at The Commodore's coat. "He has admitted defeat, why must he die?"

"There's nothing I can do, Charlie; this is their custom. Who am I to interfere?" The Commodore laughed, darkly.

"You can save him!" Charlie shrieked.

"Even if I could, I wouldn't. He tried to kill us!" The Commodore barked in reply. There was a swish through the air and Hurdimlin's head departed from the rest of his body. Blood spattered the crowd as his body fell forward. The goblin leader stood over him, panting in a rage.

"You are victorious, Commodore; I will relinquish my rank and my second will become leader," the goblin spat. He turned to walk out of the crowd.

"Ahem!" The Commodore cleared his throat. "And you will give your hand, goblin! The hand shall be passed to the new leader, lest you forget your failure as a leader." The goblin turned and stared hard at The Commodore – he seemed to have a lot of knowledge about goblin laws.

"And give my hand I shall, for I recognise my failings." The goblin placed his hand on the nearest table and drew his axe. The Commodore watched on with excitement at what was to take place. He seemed to be enjoying this sadism, taking pleasure in the pain the goblins experienced. Charlie felt horrified. He knew the goblins could have killed them, but they didn't. Charlie and The Commodore had already achieved victory – what sense was there in humiliating them further?

"You can stop this, you know," Charlie said softly to The Commodore. He ignored Charlie and watched the goblin prepare. The goblin raised the axe high above his head and brought it crashing down, separating his hand from his arm, ready to pass it on to the new leader as a mark of obedience and his failing. The goblin screeched in agony as the crowd watched on bitterly, spitting and cursing The Commodore. He watched with a sadistic smile, enjoying the carnage he had caused.

Charlie looked on, horrified and disappointed at how harsh The Commodore had been. In that moment, he seemed an entirely different person.

"You knew that was going to happen from the start, didn't you?" Charlie said accusingly, as they walked away from the goblins.

"I did," The Commodore grinned. "They had it coming. Oh, I'll need that back too." He reached over and retrieved a ring that he had stuck onto Charlie's little finger earlier without him noticing.

"Smart little prize, this ring. It contains the soul of the greatest swordsmith this side of the realm and, boy, could he fight," The Commodore beamed. "It's probably not very nice having your soul stuck in a ring, but I didn't put him there."

"You didn't have to do that to them – you could have just walked away," Charlie said, ignoring The Commodore's digression.

"They were going to steal our energy and then leave us for dead. Well, you anyway," The Commodore retorted.

"What's energy?" asked Charlie.

"It's the fibre and being of every entity – the essence of existence… your soul. It's now used as a currency, so people use it to trade," The Commodore explained.

"How do you get energy, to trade?" Charlie asked.

"The syringe that the goblin had. They remove it from anything that moves – it's a very painful process," The Commodore replied.

Charlie shivered at the thought of having his energy removed from him.

"I don't understand. It doesn't make any sense," Charlie replied, confused.

"It makes perfect sense," The Commodore replied as a matter of fact. "The Celestial Order turned energy into a currency, now everyone is fighting and stealing, which means as a society they are fragmented. If the people they govern are no longer united, they don't have to worry about an uprising."

Charlie pondered this point before coming to a final conclusion.

"I'll stick to my shillings and pounds" he stated. The Commodore laughed and patted Charlie on the shoulder.

"Ah, here we are," The Commodore announced. "Wipe your shoes before going in. They're very funny about that kind of thing."

Chapter Five – The Galdihar Rebellion

There's an obsession with blood and its density when compared to water. Many consider density to be king and of the utmost importance, whilst blindly ignoring purity. Every drop of blood will eventually rot into the earth to be forgotten, as generations pass but water will remain. Though, blood nor water create love, loyalty or bond as is often suggested. But, if you must obsess over blood and its density, also consider the fact that it contains water.

"Next!" came a shrill voice from behind the reception counter. The Commodore grumbled incoherently about the pointlessness of queueing as they moved forward. The cramped hotel-style reception room smelt heavily of damp and looked as though it hadn't been cleaned or maintained in a very long time. Charlie let his eyes wander the room before they fixed themselves upon a troll picking its nose whilst staring blankly at the wall, eventually retrieving a large gooey matter and inspecting it with delight before popping it into its mouth. Some of the others in the queue had noticed The Commodore and began whispering quietly, though The Commodore did not seem concerned.

"Who are you here to see?" droned a gravelly voice from behind the counter. Charlie gasped as he saw that the voice belonged to a rather portly winged pig in a cardigan. Her faded nametag read 'Julia'.

"Alwin White," replied The Commodore. "It's nice to see you too, Julia!"

Julia glanced up at The Commodore and gave a brief shrug.

"Is it?" she replied sarcastically. The Commodore smiled as she flicked through a large planner with experienced trotters.

"What time were you supposed to be here?" Julia asked impatiently as she searched various papers.

"Any time I please," laughed The Commodore, holding up his watch. "I'm probably late, I got held up by a rather unpleasant shroud and then found myself with an unexpected companion." He motioned to a queasy-looking Charlie. Julia looked over the counter with a raised eyebrow, a smile slowly appeared.

"Could the prophecy be true?" she asked herself. Charlie and The Commodore looked at each other confused.

"What bloody prophecy is this?" The Commodore asked as he studied Charlie.

"The prophecy of the Blind boy that will save us all," Julia snapped, impatiently.

"I'm shocked and appalled, in all honesty, Julia," The Commodore tsked, shaking his head. "You of all people should know that prophecies are nothing more than hearsay and nonsense. All of them have been proven false or been too vague to measure."

"Are you familiar with the prophecy?" Julia asked Charlie, curiously. The queue behind them became impatient and unsettled – feet tapped and heads shook.

"I'm afraid not," Charlie replied, unsure of what to say.

"The elven community in the Divine world are fond of visions and foretelling futures. A small group, known only to a few, foretold of a Blind boy that would save us all from The Celestial Order," Julia explained, keeping her voice low. "Some say that those whispers are heard from Sanctuary."

"I don't think that is me," Charlie laughed nervously as he tugged at his collar.
The Commodore studied Charlie for a moment longer before shrugging and shaking his head.

"I'd love to stay and chat," replied The Commodore impatiently, as he drummed his fingers on the counter, "but

I've got a meeting to attend." Julia continued to study Charlie before sitting back in her chair.

"Room 512b, knock twice," Julia replied irritably. "See you soon, Charlie."

"How do you know my name?" Charlie asked, curiously. Julia opened her mouth to reply, but The Commodore cut her off before she could get a word in.

"Julia is a winged, talking pig. And you're most concerned with how she knows your name?" The Commodore shook his head and muttered to himself, cursing all prophecies and winged mammals.

The Commodore beckoned to Charlie and they made their way along the tired and neglected corridor. Dust, peeling wallpaper and the over-powering stench of damp were rife throughout the building.

"What a sorry state this place has become," sighed The Commodore as he ran his hand along the wall.

"What is this place?" asked Charlie, his eyes stinging from the smell that refused to leave his nostrils.

"The Wanderer's Pass," replied The Commodore. "This enchanted portal allows folk to travel vast distances without being detected by The Celestial Order. It is certainly a lot safer than blindly travelling through time on our own. If you can find it, that is. It also offers patrons a safe place to hide out, should that be required."

"Where are we going?" asked Charlie after quite some time, as they made their way down the seemingly endless corridors.

"*I*... am going to a meeting. I'll take you to another room first and then come and get you once the meeting is finished," The Commodore explained. "Only those invited can go to the meeting." He suddenly stopped in his tracks and considered Charlie curiously.

"What's the matter?" asked Charlie, looking slightly worried. "Are we in danger?"

"Have you been here before?" The Commodore asked slowly.

"No, I don't think so," Charlie replied. The Commodore studied Charlie a moment longer as he rubbed his chin with concern.

"I don't think that our meeting was a coincidence... something isn't right. This isn't right." He began looking up and down the corridor, becoming more alarmed by the second. A moment later, he drew his pistol from his waist and pointed it at Charlie with a serious expression. Charlie looked down the barrel of the weapon and then at The Commodore.

"What have I done?" Charlie asked, undeterred by the threat of his imminent demise.

"Don't move," The Commodore ordered. He stepped forward slowly and placed a cold hand on Charlie's neck, seemingly searching for a pulse. The Commodore gave a sigh of relief and lowered his weapon.

"What strange times," he gasped as he wiped his brow. Charlie looked at The Commodore confused, unsure of what to do.

"Come along, we need to go," The Commodore ushered impatiently as he stuffed his pistol back into its holster.

After a short time, music could be heard coming from the end of the corridor. The smell of damp lingered, becoming infused with sulphur.

"Stand aside, Charlie," ordered The Commodore, as he drew his pistol once again. "I think this is the right room, but I'm not sure." Charlie stood watching with baited breath, his heart pounding against his chest. The Commodore raised a hand to knock on the tired old door, when suddenly it swung open and a pale face appeared.

"No need for that, mate!" The pale face laughed, then turned and looked at Charlie. He looked at first glance to be a bellboy, though his uniform was tattered and discoloured in places. On closer inspection, flaking porcelain and subsequent cracks could be seen on his hands and glazed face.

"Is this the Blind boy that will save us all!?" the bellboy asked, excitedly.

"Enough of this prophecy nonsense!" barked The Commodore, impatiently.

"You must be Mr Kingston?" smiled the bellboy. "I make it my business to know all of my guests."

The Commodore rolled his eyes with his arms folded, tapping his foot impatiently.

"Hello… I would prefer Charlie. Mr Kingston is typically how my father is addressed," Charlie replied politely. "What may I call you?"

"Oliver Osgood, sir. Though everyone calls me Ozzie. I'm one of the few remaining porters at the great 'Wanderer's Pass'." He answered, seemingly flustered at meeting Charlie.

"Ozzie, can you look after Charlie until I return?" The Commodore interrupted. "I have a meeting to attend."

"Certainly, come inside," Ozzie beckoned to Charlie. "There's much to be done." The Commodore pulled a pen from his pocket and scribbled onto a scrap of wallpaper he pulled from the wall.

"If I don't return in six hours, send the boy here," The Commodore said quickly as he passed the paper to Ozzie. The bellboy read the instructions with a solemn expression.

"I don't believe this will be necessary, but your request has been noted and will be adhered to, if required," Ozzie replied in a formal tone.

Charlie looked around at the tired old maintenance room that Ozzie called home. At the back, a dilapidated elevator leaned miserably to one side and looked as though it hadn't been in service for at least a century. The smell of sulphur hung in the air, emanating from the old lift.

"Welcome to my humble living quarters. As there isn't much to see in here, how about a tour of The Wanderer's Pass?" asked Ozzie with a smile.

"Yes please!" Charlie replied with excitement.

"Great! The Wanderer's Pass is a vast place – even I haven't seen every inch. But before we can go anywhere, mate, you need the right attire." Ozzie dug into his old cupboard and retrieved another bellboy hat and a visitor's badge, both of which were in remarkably good condition.

"Here, put these on. Now, prepare for the tour of a lifetime!" Ozzie exclaimed with a smile. Charlie grinned from ear to ear.

"This old elevator isn't what it used to be so it may take us some time to get around, but she hasn't failed me yet."

"It's a fine elevator, for sure!" Charlie agreed, still smiling as he lifted the large hat out of his eyes. The elevator dropped a few inches with a loud clang – the lights flickered as it slowly groaned and whined into life.

"How long have you worked here for?" asked Charlie as the elevator began its descent.

"Oh wow, I don't really know. At least, two hundred years," Ozzie replied, seemingly surprised by his own answer.

"Two hundred years!?" Charlie gasped. "Well, you must be about the oldest person I've ever met!"

"Oh, there are plenty older than me across the planes," laughed Ozzie. It wasn't very often anyone took any real interest in him.

"Across the planes?" Charlie asked, curiously.

"Yes, there are four of them," Ozzie explained. "Sanctuary is a heavenly utopia, reserved only for the purest. Only the chosen may go to Sanctuary. Oblivion is on the other end of the scale – it's a plane of torment, punishment and suffering. Once you go in, there's no coming out. Ever. Purgatory is the plane of contemplation;

138

you can be sentenced to Purgatory if your crimes are not worthy of Oblivion. Make no mistake, it's no picnic. The final plane is Existence, which is where we are now. The Blind and the Divine live side by side, in secret for the most part."

Charlie watched the dim light behind the switches illuminate the different numbers as they continued their descent.

"I'd like to go to Sanctuary. Do you think my mother will be there?" Charlie asked, earnestly. Ozzie smiled at his naivety.

"I'm sure she is… and moreover, I'm sure she is watching you proudly," Ozzie put a hand on Charlie's head and ruffled his hair.

"Ouch!" Charlie retorted.

"Oh, sorry!" Ozzie said apologetically as he removed his hand. "You'd think that I'd be used to this after just a couple hundred years." He pulled some fine sandpaper from his pocket and sanded some of the roughage from his porcelain hand.

Charlie looked from his own hands to Ozzie's with a curious frown. He had so many questions but good manners dissuaded him from asking them.

"I suppose you're wondering where these came from?" Ozzie asked with a serious expression.

Charlie didn't answer – he watched as tiny pieces fell from the tired and worn hands.

"I have served The Wanderer's Pass for a long time, but I had a life before I got to this wonderful home of mine," Ozzie recollected as he stroked the side of the elevator. "I got involved with a group that took part in summoning demons and devils from Oblivion. I got a little more than I bargained for."

Charlie listened intently and smiled as Ozzie explained. He wondered how long it had been since Ozzie had told that story to anyone.

A dull ping came from the elevator as it jerked and groaned to a stop. The elevator door whined open, Charlie shielded his eyes from the bright lights.

"After you, young sir," smiled Ozzie, as he gestured Charlie forward into the crowded room. Ragtime jazz, laughter and cigarette smoke filled the air as the duo made their way into an enormous ballroom. Art deco styling, looking not even a day old, dripped from the walls and the ceiling. Everyone seemed to be having a great time. Charlie marvelled as people from all eras laughed and danced together. The room had beautiful oak tables around the dance floor. Some people were engaged in deep conversation and some were not people at all. Ghouls, goblins and other mythical creatures were also in attendance.

Charlie remembered the advice that The Commodore had given him earlier and tried not to stare, though he didn't think he was doing very well at it. Ozzie led him through the room to the bar and they sat themselves on stools made from the finest oak and leather. He ran a hand across the mahogany bar top in wonderment –there wasn't a scratch or stain in sight, everything looked brand new.

"What'll it be?" came a thick New York accent from behind the bar. A young man stood cleaning a glass, dressed in a white shirt and black waistcoat – a classy barman, for sure.

"Nothing for me, I don't have any money," replied Charlie, as politely as ever. He licked his dry lips; he hadn't had a moment's rest so far on his adventure.

"You don't need money here," laughed the barman. "How about some cherry cola and a cheese sandwich?"

"Yes please, that would be great!" Charlie beamed. He looked closer at the barman and noticed that he had the same porcelain features as Ozzie. Charlie tried not to stare, instead, he looked around the room at the fantastic beings that surrounded him. Nobody here fought or argued – they simply enjoyed their time.

"What is everybody celebrating?" asked Charlie, as he looked around.

"Whatever they feel like. The Wanderer's Pass offers freedom and safety from The Celestial Order." He shuddered as he spoke. "There are wicked powers that be... Sadly, they appear to be winning the war."

"War?" gasped Charlie, looking around at everyone. "It doesn't look like there's a war."

"That's what The Celestial Order want you to think. They're very clever, that lot." Ozzie sighed as he looked at his chipped and tired hands. "One day, the tide will turn and we will be truly free."

The barman brought Charlie his sandwich and cherry cola. As Charlie ate, he looked down the bar and noticed a dark and lonely figure hunched over, drink in hand. Wallowing at the bottom of a bottle.

"Who is that?" asked Charlie between mouthfuls of his sandwich, his eyes clasped on the figure.

"That's a Death Shroud. They are born from the blazing furnace in Oblivion and are hired by The Celestial Order as head-hunters," said Ozzie, darky. "They don't

142

forgive and they certainly don't forget. Bloody evil things!"
Ozzie shuddered as he looked over at it.

"I've seen one before… It wasn't a very pleasant encounter. I wonder why it's here," Charlie thought aloud.

"That Shroud doesn't mean any harm. I let it drink here from time to time," defended the barman.

"Still, it would not be wise to bother it-" Ozzie turned back to where Charlie had been sitting and let out a yelp – he'd disappeared! Ozzie looked around frantically before noticing that Charlie had taken a seat next to the Shroud.

"I think you should leave it be," whispered Ozzie, nervously leaning in to Charlie, but the boy didn't reply. The Shroud continued its infinite stare at the glass, with the look of one who has the weight of the world on their shoulders. Sadness surrounded the Shroud – it felt as though all of the joy in the world had been replaced with a harrowing darkness, but this did little to deter Charlie.

"Hello," said Charlie through a smile. The Shroud turned slowly and looked at Charlie. It had a porcelain mask for a face, just like his previous attacker the night he had met The Commodore. This Shroud's mask looked much older, sported many cracks and even had a piece missing. Although not much could be determined from merely studying the Shroud, it was clear that it had seen many battles and countless years.

"My name is Charlie. What's your name?" The Shroud didn't reply, but seemed to have taken an interest in the strange child before it.

"I wouldn't bother it too much, mate," whispered Ozzie, nervously. "Nothing good ever came from a Death Shroud." Charlie looked at Ozzie, slightly disappointed at his judgement.

"And what of it?" Charlie replied through a frown. "I'm sure there's plenty that would find you terrifying."

He turned his attention back to the heavily worn face of the Shroud. Most people the Shroud encountered turned and ran away, but not Charlie. He sat with a polite smile and not a drop of fear about him – in fact, he seemed to be enjoying the company of the Shroud.

"We, are not so different, you and I," said Charlie. "We're both in a strange place where we don't really know anyone. I'm lucky that I have some company. I'm familiar with loneliness, so I can imagine how you feel."

The Shroud turned back to the glass it had been drinking from and drained it silently before holding it up for the barman to refill it, which he did.

"Charlie, we must be going. I have some other things I need to do, mate, before we head back to meet The Commodore," Ozzie said as calmly as he could, clearly very uneasy around the Shroud. Charlie smiled at the Shroud and plunged his hand into his pocket, retrieving a small figure.

"Here you go!" Charlie smiled as he presented a play-worn toy soldier to the Shroud. "This is for you; it was my brother's favourite, and he gave it me to keep me company when I felt lonely. I think that you could use it more than me."

The Shroud looked down at the figurine and picked it up cautiously, examining every corner with interest.

Charlie hopped down from his chair and made to leave with Ozzie, before a cold, heavy hand took hold of his shoulder. The Shroud took hold of Charlie in a solid grip, preventing him from leaving. As it did, the barman stepped forward, ready to engage the Shroud. Charlie looked at the Shroud and winced as it let go of him. The Shroud leant in to Charlie and handed him a tiny glass bottle.

"I'm not sure what that is, Charlie, but I think that you should take it," Ozzie eagerly advised.

"Thank you," said Charlie, as politely as ever. "I'll keep this with me."

A rattling groan came from inside the Shroud as it turned back to the figure that Charlie had given it. Ozzie quickly took Charlie back out through the main doors of the party and led him over to the elevator.

"Next stop, Maintenance!" declared Ozzie, relieved at their safe withdrawal from the party.

"You're late again," said Eamon Haste sternly from the head of the table. He sat stroking his beard, clearly discontented with the late arrival of his colleague. Haste had been reputed to be one of the most dangerous villains across the four planes – only The Commodore superseded his harrowing reputation. As a very capable mage with an incredible talent for magic, this made him a formidable enemy. Haste's eyes glinted as he stared unblinkingly at The Commodore, his modest gown hanging tiredly from his thin frame. The Commodore didn't reply, instead he chose to ignore the voice and seat himself in the last remaining chair at the table. Twenty or so participants stared The Commodore down as he took his seat, not that he had noticed.

"You can literally travel time!" Hix spat from across as the table. "Why are you even part of the Rebellion if you can't turn up on time?"

"There are many other things I'd like to do than sit here discussing our slow extinction by committee," The Commodore replied dryly. "Say, aren't you due back home soon, Hix? Oblivion is lovely this time of year, I've heard," he continued sarcastically. Hix opened his mouth to reply but changed his mind when he caught a glimpse of The Commodore's pistol. It was true, Hix came from Oblivion and, as a demon, he often faced ridicule. Hix, demonic in origin, didn't stand very tall and looked almost dragon-like. His scaly skin was of a dull orange, for those that could see him.

"Shall we continue?" Haste interrupted as he straightened his tunic. "It's good to see you, James." He gave a nod to The Commodore. The room quietened and readied itself for Haste. As the leader of The Galdihar Rebellion, he had a lot of responsibility, and his bounty almost mounted to that of The Commodore. Haste opened his mouth to begin proceedings, when The Commodore suddenly cut in.

"Where's everyone else?" asked The Commodore, looking around the room. There seemed to be fewer seated than usual.

"Presumed dead or captured, which puts us at a higher risk," Haste said indifferently.

"Walter Will has gone too?" The Commodore asked eagerly as his eyes scanned the room.

"Indeed, rumoured to have been extinguished only yesterday in Harrowfeld." Haste had an incredible knack of remaining calm and collected when delivering the most solemn of news.

"Harrowfeld, of all the places. It's a sleepy Divinian town! What an awful day!" The Commodore groaned as he planted his head in his hands. "First, I'm lumbered with unnecessary company and now I hear Walter Will has snuffed it."

Scowls and frowns rained down on The Commodore.

"Indeed, it is sad," came a soft voice from beside Haste. A beautiful lady, with the kindest eyes to ever grace a human face, interjected as she ran a hand through her soft blonde hair. Alwin White had often been described as the epitome of beauty and kindness. She loved all beings, Blind, Divine or Mythical, and hated violence, which often made the Rebellion's missions difficult.

"We have lost contact with many of our resistance contacts. The Celestial Order appears to be closing in, hence our impromptu meeting," said Alwin, sadly.

"I know we haven't gained much ground in recent times, but I had no idea it was this bad." The Commodore frowned.

"If only we had someone that could travel time and had use of a weapon that can erase any entity at the pull of a trigger," replied Hix, his comments dripping in sarcasm.

"Every member of The Galdihar Rebellion has their timeline under constant surveillance. I agreed to help the Rebellion, not lead it and commit genocide. This isn't the wild frontier!" defended The Commodore. "Oblivion had the right idea, throwing you out."

"You know nothing of Oblivion!" spat Hix, readying himself. The Commodore shook his head as a smile curled in the corner of his mouth. He pulled out a carpentry magazine from his jacket and buried himself within it. He had achieved his goal of riling Hix.

"Let's get this meeting started," Haste sighed as he sifted through some papers. "We've had word of some strange happenings that require investigation, namely mortal Blindlings who are surviving to miraculously old ages, with no explanation."

"I don't see the importance of the elderly living a bit longer than they are supposed to," The Commodore interrupted.

"Well, neither would we in any normal circumstance, but some have been alive for one hundred and fifty years, and it's raised a few eyebrows, to say the least," Haste added.

"Wouldn't this be the business of the Time-Keepers?" asked Hix.

"They're extinct. The Celestial Order has removed them entirely," Alwin replied. "The only known evidence of their existence sits in The Commodore's pocket."

"From what I've gathered, it's because they refused to bend the knee to The Good Shepherd and his herd of sheep," The Commodore replied from behind his magazine. "So, a few old-timers are refusing to snuff it on cue – what's that to do with us?"

Alwin winced slightly at The Commodore's remorseless comments.

"We believe there's a powerful entity that may be of assistance to us. Extending life isn't a common ability. We need to find out what's going on and see if they can be of assistance to our cause. These are hard times for the Rebellion. Speaking candidly, we're on the edge of losing the war," Haste said with concern. The room shifted uncomfortably.

"I can't imagine what they would do to us if we were caught," Hix said as he shivered.

"I can," Alwin added, uncomfortably. "It won't be pleasant, that's a certainty. There are fates worse than death." The room agreed uneasily, all except The Commodore, who maintained greater interest in his carpentry magazine.

"This moves us on to how we're going to tackle this issue," Haste replied, calmly. "James and Hix will investigate the elders-"

"You must be joking!? I'm not going on a mission with, that!" Hix spat as he pointed at The Commodore.

"He has a point, Haste," came The Commodore from behind his magazine. "I'll go without Hix, but I'll need to take the baggage that I've acquired."

"You'll both go. Hix has the advantage of not being seen by the Blind and he will no doubt prove to be a valuable asset on this mission," Haste replied, sternly. His calm nature remained, but he meant business. "You want to keep an eye on that 'baggage' of yours, James – you'll find him to be of more use than you think." The Commodore dropped his magazine onto the table and looked around at the room with a bewildered expression.

"Not you too, Eamon! I thought you knew better than to believe in old prophecies!" said The Commodore, disappointed. "They are never accurate. The prophecy of the Blind boy is merely hearsay and words of tired old housewives! He is a boy – I need to return him home when the time is right."

"All will become clear soon enough," smiled Alwin. The Commodore glared furiously and mumbled something about 'speaking in tongues,' but decided not to pry any further.

"Are we done here?" The Commodore asked through gritted teeth.

"Yes. The strange activity can be found at this location on this timeline." Eamon passed a small piece of paper to The Commodore, who stuck it into the back of his watch for safekeeping.

"Let's get out of here. And try to keep up," The Commodore snapped at Hix, who wisely chose not to reply. They left the room and disappeared down the hallway.

"So, what happens in this room?" asked Charlie in wonderment at the various ticks and knocks that echoed throughout.

"This is the Maintenance Room, or in other words, the heart and soul of The Wanderer's Pass," replied Ozzie, proudly. "Enchantments and other mysterious charms have been put into place to ensure the Celestial Order can't locate us."

Charlie stared open-mouthed in wonder at all of the different gauges and their different readings. Some were erratic, screeching and steaming, and others didn't move at all.

"How do you know what they all do?" asked Charlie.

"I've had a long time to learn," sighed Ozzie, again rubbing his rough hands. "I enjoy what I do, and without me this place would fall apart."

"You must be proud!" Charlie said. Ozzie beamed and nodded enthusiastically. He walked around the room with his chest thrust forward. He pulled levers and twisted some valves, and watched with joy as they ticked and screeched harder than ever.

"That should do it! Come on, it's time to get you back to The Commodore. You can keep the hat, if you like," said Ozzie.

"Oh, that would be wonderful!" Charlie beamed.

Chapter Six – Everybody's On The Run

Part I

Was it worth it? To spend the rest of your life running from yourself? Good men make bad decisions, bad men do good deeds. Life is not linear and transparent, certainly not yours. For ten mistakes we learn a thousand lessons and build resilience over time. Each push back gives you the energy to push forward. Let those mistakes be lessons and don't be concerned with running away from them. You are not alone, everybody's on the run.

"Clarence, are y'all a holy man?" asked Earl, curiously. His brash Missouri accent echoed throughout the old barn. The rain beat the old barn steadily as the wind whipped and wailed against the isolated dwelling. Earl settled himself into a large pile of straw and prepared to retire for the night after a long day.

"Hmm, I gots to be a holy man when I gots to be, but by and by I don't worry 'bout it too much. When I'm good, that's fine, and when I'm not, I'm terribly sorry and seek forgiv'ness," replied Clarence as he wandered around the old barn. Small fortunes could sometimes be found in old barns, and who'd miss the fortunes if they went missing? As far as they saw it, they were doing everyone a favour.

"See, am gon' git me a classy kinda gal and I gots no doubt she gon' be a holy one, they be the best kind," Earl dreamt as he touched his finger where the foretold wedding ring would sit.

A slight frown introduced itself across Clarence's simple face.

"Whatcha wan' know 'bout the holy kind, anyhow?" asked Clarence, curiously.

"I don' know if I believe in all o' that holy talk, I got to thinkin' it all seems pretty stupid," Earl replied slowly, considering his words as he spoke. "I ent' never seen god, or his boy Jesus, got me thinkin' they ain't nothin' but a yarn as old as time to keep us boys on the straight roads."

"Is that so?" Clarence replied as a cunning smile split his cheeks. "Reckon I can pray fo' the preddiest gal ya ever did see and she'd come down from the heavens and you'd be sent downstairs to the hottest o' hell with no supper or even a glass o' milk!"

"Hey now, don' you go bein' stupid and shakin' a hand at the holiness upstairs!" Earl propped himself up on his elbows, looking concerned.

"Come now! Y'all gon see, ya tell ya friends whatcha saw!" Clarence wandered out into the pouring rain and looked to the heavens as he raised his arms.

"Come on inside, Clarence, come now boy!" Earl shouted as he peered out from the barn door. But Clarence had other plans and had succeeded in drawing Earl's superstitions to the surface.

"Oh ya holy bein's, can ya help me fin' a perfec gal fo-" Clarence's bellows were cut short by a terrific bang and a flash of light. Earl yelled as Clarence tumbled to the ground covered in Charlie's vomit. Scrambling to his legs, his eyes darted into the darkness to see what had offended him.

"You'll get used to that, I promise," said The Commodore gruffly, as he retrieved Charlie from the sodden ground. Clarence turned a sickly shade of white as he stared in horror.

"Am sorry' I din'… I din' mean to-" stammered Clarence at the apparent holy intervention. He still hadn't noticed the half-digested sandwich that littered his overalls. His hand slowly moved to his holster as he drew a revolver, shaking as he did so.

"I wouldn't do that if I were you," The Commodore warned as he pulled Charlie behind him.

"Leave it to me," growled Hix with a wicked grin.

"No, let's see how this plays out. We need to keep a low profile," The Commodore explained

"Who ya talkin to!?" asked Clarence, frantically. "An' no lies now!"

The Commodore stared hard at Clarence and looked over to Earl, who was still cowering by the barn door. The rain poured down in sheets as they stood looking at one another. The Commodore broke the stalemate by taking a step forward. Clarence readjusted his revolver and pointed it square at The Commodore, shaking as he did so.

"I don't mean you any harm, friend," The Commodore replied after some time. "I need to get to Detroit."

"You gots a way to go, *friend*," replied Clarence. "You're in Missouri."

"Told you, we're miles away!" said Hix as a matter of fact.

"Shut it!" snapped The Commodore. Clarence looked around to see who The Commodore was speaking to.

"Are you a holy man?" asked The Commodore, noticing a tattoo of a crucifix on Clarence's neck.

"Yes sah! Monday through t'Sunday," replied Clarence, keeping a shaky draw on The Commodore.

"Well, I'm on a holy mission and I'm going to need that Hudson Hornet you've got parked alongside that barn. It looks pretty tired and all, but needs must. You wouldn't want to hinder a holy mission now, would you?" asked The Commodore, trying to sound as soft and friendly as he could.

Hix rolled his eyes and perched himself next to Charlie.

"How's I sposed to know you're a true holy man and not the devil?" asked Clarence, narrowing his eyes with suspicion.

"Well, because... Oh! I don't have time for this," said The Commodore irritably, making his way towards the barn. "I'm taking your car, I need it for a... well... mostly holy mission."

"He's going to shoot you, I reckon," Hix considered aloud.

"I'd say so too," added Charlie.

"Well, he'll get a surprise if he does," said The Commodore, not overly concerned at the increasingly jittery Clarence. A shot rang out across the field as The Commodore fell forward into the sodden earth. Wheezing and groaning, he turned slowly onto his side and rose to his feet as the wound healed at an incredible pace. A spent bullet dropped to the floor, rejected by The Commodore's body. Clarence opened his mouth to scream but nothing came out. Earl bolted from the barn, abandoning his companion, and ran as fast as he could away from the unannounced trio.

"Give me that!" The Commodore snatched Clarence's revolver away and threw it to Charlie. "You've ruined a perfectly good shirt!" He fingered the hole angrily. Clarence let out a tiny squeak and promptly passed out.

Hix couldn't stand properly for laughter, pointing at The Commodore and his ruined shirt.

"He… got you… real good!" he choked with laughter.

"What should I do with this?" asked Charlie, holding up the revolver.

"Whatever you like, try not to shoot yourself with it all the same," replied The Commodore as he walked towards the faded and corroded Hudson.

The Commodore seated himself behind the wheel and found the keys tucked behind the visor. The old Hornet turned its six cylinders over and over before finally spluttering into life. The gearbox snatched and jerked into motion, a loud ticking and tapping sounded from the engine as they shifted out onto the road.

"I've never seen a car like this before," said Charlie as he looked around from the front seat in excitement.

"There's probably quite a lot you won't be familiar with in 1964," explained The Commodore as he steered with his knees and fiddled with the watch. "Same rules as before, don't stare, and try not to bring attention to yourself."

They made their way along the Missouri country roads at a steady pace now that the rain had eased. Charlie had found some cards in the glove compartment and decided to teach Hix how to play.

They rode the deserted twilight roads for hours. The Commodore remained deep in his thoughts as Hix and Charlie gamed the night away.

"Why are we going to Detroit?" asked Charlie after the card games had been exhausted.

"Some old people won't die and the Rebellion think there's something there that could help us in the battle with The Good Shepherd," replied The Commodore, laconically.

"You can't tell him that!" shouted Hix. "You'll make him an accessory. What if he is captured!?"

"And what of it?" retorted The Commodore. "He won't be captured."

"As usual, you have all the answers, don't you," snorted Hix. "The Commodore, the saviour in our war against The Good Shepherd! I don't buy a single bit of it. No wonder your family don't bother with you."

The car screeched to a halt. Hix flew headlong into the windscreen and found himself pinned against the glass by The Commodore's pistol.

"You forget your place," The Commodore spat through gritted teeth. "Another word about my family and I'll remove you, permanently." He removed the pistol and Hix slid down into the footwell.

"I need to go for a wee," Charlie announced as he climbed over the front seat and out of the door. The velvet darkness of night draped over the trees and the country road, only broken by the yellow haze from the car's headlights and the moon. Charlie walked a little way into the forest away from the car to relieve himself in peace. He looked out into the trees and admired the stillness of the night; the rain had eased, allowing the smell of sodden earth to fill his nostrils.

"Oh, what would Billy have made of this adventure?" Charlie thought to himself as he contemplated his experiences so far. "He wouldn't believe a word of it, that's for sure. Goodness, I wish I could tell him all about it." Charlie smiled as he thought of the good times they'd had, dreaming together. His thoughts were suddenly darkened as his heart began to plummet into his stomach. Guilt rocked him to his core as he thought about Mr Betts and his unemployment, wishing all the while he could turn back time and help Billy.

"Maybe I could ask The Commodore," Charlie thought to himself as he made his way back to the car.

"No doubt you want something to eat?" The Commodore asked as he inspected the trunk of the tired Hornet. He found a pump-action shotgun and a brown leather jacket that he quickly decided to keep as payment for his ruined shirt.

"Yes please, I'm really hungry," said Charlie as politely as ever. He looked up with a slightly confused

162

expression. "Can you bring someone back from the dead?" he asked, rather bluntly.

The Commodore looked from Charlie to Hix and back again, taken aback by his bold questioning.

"Well, it's very difficult, but…" The Commodore replied uneasily.

"It can be done," Hix cut in. The Commodore shot him a scornful look.

"Why?" The Commodore asked, curiously. "It's a funny question for a boy to ask."

"Well, my best friend died. He was sick. His father couldn't help him because my father took his work away and he couldn't pay for his medication. My mother died a long time ago, maybe her too." Charlie looked hopefully from The Commodore to Hix and back again.

"Charlie," The Commodore sighed. "There's not a day that I don't wish for eternal peace. Living this half-life is excruciating." The bright, hopeful twinkle in Charlie's eyes began to fade as The Commodore went on.

"I met a lady a long time ago, very clever and incredibly charming. If you compared people to the stars, she would have shined brighter than almost all of the others, the sort of person that stays with you forever. She traded her mortal life for a cursed one, trying to help someone she loved. At first, she felt good about everything, but after a while she became sad. She cried every day and became known as The Wailing Lady of Rosemary. What an awful thing to call someone. I wish I could have helped, but our paths went in different directions." The Commodore leaned over the steering wheel and looked at the night sky as if looking for her.

"Well, we must visit her soon and see if we can help," Charlie said, hopefully.

"Sounds good to me," The Commodore smiled. "Let's get out of here."

He turned the key as the engine span. Coughing and spluttering, it lurched into gear before they set off at full pelt.

After what seemed like an eternity listening to the orchestral manoeuvres of Charlie's rumbling stomach, they arrived at an old motel that should probably have been condemned years ago. The sign that read 'vacancies' flickered in a typically creepy fashion. Needles, smashed glass and litter were plentiful and scattered across the property. The Commodore pulled in and parked the car in a dark corner of the car park away from prying eyes and the law.

"You looking for some fun?" came a gravelly, luring voice from the open window. The Commodore jumped in surprise and hit his head on the roof of the car. He hadn't seen the night worker come to the window. They all turned to see the source of the voice and were met with the brightest, reddest lipstick that ever was. It had been plastered on to a tired face in torrents.

"Oh yes please! It's been a terribly long journey and I could use lots of fun," Charlie answered, cheerfully. Hix burst into fits of choking laughter and slid down the rear seat on to the floor.

"Good evening, miss," replied The Commodore gruffly, as he rubbed his head. "Thank you for the offer but, as you can see, I have a minor with me, and that simply wouldn't be proper. Be safe and take care." The lady of the night smiled slightly. She probably meant it to be more meaningful, but as she hadn't smiled in a long time it was the best she could manage.

"I don't see the harm in having fun," grumbled Charlie.

"It's not the kind of fun you're thinking. It's well… erm… never mind what it is," The Commodore replied awkwardly. Hix burst into a renewed fit of laughter. It wasn't often that The Commodore became stuck for words.

"I don't get it. Am I missing something?" Charlie looked at The Commodore, confused. He opened his mouth, trying to find an answer for Charlie, when a scream split the night air from across the car park as the lady of the night fell onto the floor clutching her face. A fat, bearded drunkard slapped her to the ground, almost toppling himself as he did so.

"Filthy whore, try and charge me for a good time!" he slurred as he steadied himself.

"Hey, you leave her alone; she only wants to have some fun!" shouted Charlie from the car window. He turned to see where the voice was coming from, squinting into the darkness as he did so. The lady of the night struggled as she tried to stand up, but the belligerent offender delivered a brutal kick to her stomach, tossing her backwards. A sickening crack echoed across the car park as her head struck the ground.

"Fancy treating her like that. I'll sort him," smiled Hix with a wicked grin.

"No!" retorted The Commodore... but it was too late, Hix had vanished.

"Where did he go?" asked Charlie, still angry at the belligerent offender.

"To do something stupid. He could bring The Celestial Order down on us!" growled The Commodore.

"Well, let's see what Hix has planned," urged Charlie, excited to see what would unfold.

Charlie watched the drunkard intently, scanning his surroundings for Hix, but he couldn't be seen. The drunkard suddenly began to act strangely, twitching this way and that in a violent fashion.

"It's been a while since I've done this. Let's find out who the heck I am!" bawled the drunkard in a voice that clearly was not his own. His movements became erratic and his hands moved in strange motions as his eyes stared almost vacantly. He dug an uneasy hand into his wallet and pulled a driver's license from his pocket.

"It seems I'm an Earl Clementine!" he screeched ecstatically, his words coming out in forced, inconsistent pieces, almost as if they were being vomited out.

"Why, Miss, I do apologise for my behaviour! I'm just a drunkard, pathetic in every sense of the word... and my, I don't believe my briefs have been changed in many moons!" He staggered towards the lady with a fist full of dollars which he had scraped from inside his wallet. Her eyes widened in horror as she jumped to her feet and bolted away so fast that she ran out of her shoes without stopping to retrieve them. The belligerent man turned and staggered over to the car, as The Commodore shook his head in disapproval.

"Hello Charlie," he stammered. "What do you think of my makeover?"

"Hix, what are you doing inside that man? Did he eat you?" Charlie gasped.

"That's quite enough now, Hix, you're attracting attention," The Commodore explained, trying to hide a smile. Hix didn't reply – he threw a fistful of dollars into the car and gave a wobbly thumbs-up. The drunkard's eyes began to roll into the back of his head as he stumbled across the car park to the front of the motel. He began dancing the waltz as though he was a practiced professional, humming a timely tune to match. Charlie howled with laughter as he watched from the window, and even The Commodore let a low chuckle escape as he watched. Before long, some of the patrons had come out to watch the spectacle as he switched to a tango, moving with the kind of grace you'd have thought impossible for a man of his size. They jeered and laughed as he danced across the car park twisting this way and that as though nothing else in the world mattered. The Commodore and Charlie laughed so hard they had tears in their eyes, but nothing prepared them for the escalation that came. The drunkard popped the belt buckle of his tired trousers and, without a moment's hesitation, they slid down to his ankles to reveal what were probably at one time white briefs. The crowd recoiled and roared with laughter, several of the onlookers collapsed to their knees.

Soon, the drunken man slowed down before losing his balance and falling over. Just as the crowd began to gather itself, the drunkard lay on his back and vomited violently up into the air like a surfaced whale. The crowd looked on; some laughed and others shook their head in disappointment.

"That'll teach him!" Hix panted from the back seat of the old Hornet.

"How did you do that?" asked Charlie, still wiping the tears of laughter away from his eyes.

"With great effort. I haven't taken possession of anyone in a long time," he replied, still trying to gather himself.

"Come on, let's get inside and get a room for the night," said The Commodore in higher spirits. As they walked towards the entrance, the vomit-covered belligerent slowly came round and looked upon the crowd with wide, sober eyes. He saw that his pants were down and scrambled to pull them back up, escaping the crowd as fast as he could.

Part II

The Motel looked just as decrepit and tired on the inside as it did on the outside. The reception lights hung down from the ceiling, casting a dull shade of yellow across the ceiling and along the walls. Hastily repaired wiring and poor plastering repairs were plentiful across the entire reception. A questionable humming could be heard from the nicotine-stained switches on the wall. Grubby hand marks lined the door handles, but Charlie couldn't have cared any less. This was, after all, an adventure, and sacrifices of comfort and luxury must be made.

"What'll it be?" asked the unkept man behind the desk.

"One room for two," replied The Commodore.

"From outta town, huh?" asked the scruffy man with a crooked smile. Most of his teeth had departed from their rightful places, and the ones that remained looked like they didn't have much life left.

"Yep, how about that room?" said The Commodore, shortly. The man slapped a key on the desk.

"Fifteen dollars, room eleven," he coughed and pointed down the hallway. The room smelt of cigarette smoke, old alcohol and disappointment, but it was a room nonetheless, and Charlie couldn't have been happier to see a bed. The Commodore pulled a chair by the window and took a seat, pinching the drapes just enough to peek outside into the car park. The crowd had dispersed and only a pool of vomit suggested any evidence of the evening's antics. Hix took to the moth-bitten armchair at the other side of the window and quickly slipped into a deep slumber. Charlie followed suit as soon as he had finished utilising the poor excuse for a shower and slipped into bed.

"Aren't you going to get some sleep?" asked Charlie as he nestled into the sheets.

"I don't sleep," replied The Commodore, still looking out of the window.

"I wish I didn't get tired," said Charlie, thoughtfully. He considered how much more time he would have to play and go on adventures.

"It's hell," snorted The Commodore. "I'm tired, but I can't sleep, I'm hungry yet I can't eat a morsel, and no amount of water or wine quenches my thirst. There's a deep emptiness in my chest and I can't fill the void. I don't know how." The Commodore gave a long sigh. Charlie stared as he contemplated living without the basic necessities of life.

"Do you have a family?" asked Charlie, almost hesitantly. He had seen the reaction Hix had raised by merely name-dropping them earlier that day. The Commodore's head turned to Charlie with a solemn expression – his sad eyes looked deeper and more devoid than ever.

"Not any more. I had a beautiful wife and a boy not far off your age," explained The Commodore uncomfortably – it probably wasn't a subject that got raised very often. "It's funny… when I close my eyes, I can't see them anymore. As the years go by, I feel as though I know them less and less."

"Can't you travel back in time and see them?" asked Charlie.

The Commodore scowled. "No, I bloody well can't. Do you think I'd be piss-arsing about in this hole-in-the-ground if I could?" The Commodore snapped. "That's plenty for tonight. Get some sleep, we've got a long day tomorrow."

"You should call them on the telephone," yawned Charlie. "I have one at my house – you can use that when you get the chance." With that, he turned on to his side and closed his eyes.

The Commodore smiled slightly at Charlie's naivety. With a groan, he raised his tired legs onto the table and began poking and fiddling with the infamous time-piece.

Charlie woke with a start and struggled against a hand held tightly over his mouth. His eyes opened and locked with The Commodore's tired and bloodshot eyes.

"Don't speak a word," The Commodore whispered urgently; his face close to Charlie's. "They've found us".

Charlie gave a nod of acknowledgement and sat up. Hix wore a serious expression by the side of the door. Floorboards could be heard creaking in the hallway as lowered voices whispered quietly.

"Hix!" The Commodore whispered maybe a little too loudly. "Is it them?"

Hix looked back at The Commodore and gave a slow nod, his eyes wide and fearful.

"I can feel their energy, it's them alright. Two of them, I think," he replied in a hushed voice. "They're from Oblivion – I know how that energy feels," Hix spluttered, fear beginning to get the better of him. The Commodore's eyes widened.

"They're not messing around this time," said The Commodore, grimly. His eyes darted to the window. They were on the first floor and it was a fair drop down, but they could make a dash for the car. To jump time would be pointless – their hunters could track them too easily.

The Commodore drew his pistol and they made their way over to the window as quickly and quietly as possible. The door handle turned slowly and a dull thud could be heard as the lock stopped the door from opening. Silence reigned after a few attempts at the handle, before a loud smash and the splintering of wood echoed throughout the room. Charlie glimpsed the pale face of a policewoman as she moved with incredible speed towards them. She reached out to grip Charlie's face in her cold grasp, but missed as they leapt down into the car park. She tore after them as they crashed to the ground. A sickening snap and subsequent groan came from The Commodore – he had broken his leg. The policewoman darted for them but stopped just shy as The Commodore stuck his pistol in her face. Charlie helped The Commodore to his feet as the policewoman slowed her approach. As she did, a policeman moved swiftly across the car park towards them and joined his partner. They moved with incredible agility; they were almost cat-like as they closed in on their prey.

"Take another step, I dare you," The Commodore snarled, stepping backwards towards the car, his leg healing at an incredible pace. They did not reply, but moved with caution. Charlie didn't dare take his eyes away from their attackers, who stood perfectly straight and gave nothing away with their expressions, which remained glassy and almost inanimate with sinister, wry smiles. They didn't so much as blink as they considered their target. Charlie looked down at their hands – they were pale and made from porcelain. A cold shiver ran down his spine as he realised, they weren't ordinary police officers. The Commodore kept a draw on the two police officers as they continued back towards the car. If he fired a shot at one of them, the other would take him down – a fact his opponents were well aware of. Hix finally made an appearance from behind them. The policeman took particular interest in him and spoke in a language Charlie hadn't heard before. Hix responded in the foreign tongue and the policeman started laughing.

"They are offering me a reward for the boy, and freedom if I surrender you too, Commodore," Hix growled, in a low voice.

"If they offered mortality, I might even be tempted," The Commodore retorted. He didn't so much as blink as he kept his eyes on his enemy.

They bundled into the tired Hornet, fired up the engine and roared out of the car park as fast as they could. Sparks flew from under the car as it bottomed out onto the road.

"They know what timeline we're in!" Hix cried from the back of the car. "Why didn't you take them out?"

"Are you joking? We'll bring the entire Celestial Order down around us if we take even one of them down!" The Commodore replied. "This timeline will be monitored now that they've found us."

The engine screamed as The Commodore kept the gas pedal flat to the floor. He manoeuvred the huge car down the country road as best he could to get away from the strange policemen.

"Who are they?" asked Charlie, his eyes fixed on the rear-view mirror.

"Some of the nastiest mercenaries I've ever had the displeasure of meeting," The Commodore replied, grimly. "I'd rather face an army of Death Shrouds than those two. They possess almost any living entity and are masters in the art of torture. There are fates worse than death, but not much worse than being captured by those guys."

The Commodore had barely finished speaking when the rear window burst into a thousand tiny pieces. A highway patrol car roared behind them as the two smiling policemen chased them down. Another shot fired into the car and departed via the windscreen, leaving a perfect hole. The Commodore frantically returned fire with his pistol, pulling back the hammer but missing every shot. Charlie opened the armrest in the rear of the car and crept into the trunk, retrieving the loaded shotgun they had found the night before. Resting the shotgun on top of the shelf, Charlie fired a shot at the police car, the recoil throwing him backwards and on to the floor. The Commodore held Charlie down with one hand as he stomped on the brake pedal, the car lurched forward, screeching in protest as the tortured tyres did their best to hold on to the asphalt. A terrific crashing of metal and the smashing of glass could be heard as the police car ran into them with such force that the hood peeled back as though made of tin. Steam filled the air and through it came the policewoman, leaping through the shattered windscreen and onto the trunk of their car. The Commodore changed his footing and hit the accelerator, leaving the trashed police car behind them. Moving with incredible speed, the policewoman took hold of Charlie's throat and began to squeeze the life out of him. A resounding 'clunk-click' came from ahead of the policewoman and she looked up to see the shotgun in Hix's hands, the barrel aimed squarely in her face. He smiled and pulled the trigger. The deafening blast blew her back out of the rear window and into the street, pieces of porcelain littering the car. Charlie gasped and looked out of the window; the policewoman stood in the road watching them disappear into the distance as fast as their car could take them, her wry smile mysteriously still firmly in place.

"I don't like those guys," coughed Charlie. Hix laughed at his remark and The Commodore wiped his brow and breathed a sigh of relief as they sped into the distance. The rear of the old Hornet hung tragically in pieces. The fender hung down on one side and the exhaust scraped along the road.

"Detroit, here we come," murmured The Commodore, speaking to no one in particular. He held his watch in one hand as he drove; it seemed to bring him comfort.

After several hours, they arrived at a train station and left the car at the side of the road. It wouldn't be of any further use and it would draw too much attention in its poor condition.

"I love getting the train!" exclaimed Charlie, a huge grin parked on his face. "The huffing and puffing, the busy-bodying of a thousand stories boarding and departing the carriages... Oh! And the steam. I love the steam." He almost skipped into the train station and buzzed with excitement as they bought their tickets to Detroit.

"Can't say I've ever been on a train," replied Hix, thoughtfully. He screwed his face slightly as he raided his bank of memories, wondering if he had indeed been on one before. "Nope, never been on one," he concluded.

"Things have moved on, Charlie, keep that in mind," The Commodore said as he pocketed their tickets. They made their way through the station. Charlie's smile slipped slightly as he noticed the litter scattered along the platforms and beggars wandering like lost souls through the lobby. They couldn't hang around for too long before being moved on by the tired guards, who simply weren't paid enough to care for the state of the station.

"Never mind," Charlie thought to himself. The charm of the train would no doubt make up for the grubby station. After some time waiting, a train hee-hawed its way into the station as Charlie whipped his head down the track

179

to look upon the beastly locomotive. But the smile soon disappeared.

"What is that thing!?" retorted Charlie in disgust. The diesel locomotive made its way down the line slowly, lumbering along and spitting thick clouds of toxic diesel soot into the air.

"Progression," said The Commodore, indifferently.

"Where are the steam engines? The Flying Scotsman? The engines of the Great Western?" cried Charlie, watching the ugly brute pull to a stop alongside the platform. The doors opened and the saddest of faces departed as they made their way on to the next leg of their lives. They boarded the train, and Charlie felt even more disappointment as his feet stuck to the floor as he walked. Stains lined the seats and the air stank of warm urine and cigarettes. Charlie sat next to the window and looked out on to the platform, his face defeated and saddened by the terrible state of locomotive progression.

A couple of hours had passed. The Commodore's head had been buried in his carpentry magazine for quite some time, and Hix had found an old newspaper that he lay on the table to read. A cart came creaking down the gangway, pushed by an elderly man who looked as if he would rather be anywhere else.

"Anything from the cart?" he barked as he'd done a thousand times before.

"What have you got?" asked Charlie. The elderly man frowned slightly at Charlie's well-spoken words.

"Not from round here, huh?" he commented, as he collected some examples of his offerings. "I got everything you can see on here, sonny." Charlie picked some chocolate and a sandwich without paying too much attention to what it was.

"What happened to the steam trains?" asked Charlie, as he paid the elderly man.

"Hoowee, they were taken out of service quite some time ago. They cost too much to maintain, and diesel is cheaper to run long distance."

Charlie frowned again, somewhat unsatisfied with his answer. The train rattled on down the track and Charlie turned his attention back to the window. He watched the telegraph poles as they passed and tried to count them. He didn't get far before he fell into a deep sleep.

"I wonder what we're going to find in Detroit," considered Hix, as Charlie slept next to him.

"No idea," replied The Commodore from behind his magazine. "Whatever it is, I hope it's something that can help the Rebellion."

"Me too. I can't take much more of this running," Hix replied, tired. "I'd have stayed in Oblivion if I knew it would be so hard to stay alive!"

The Commodore looked over his magazine at Hix with an eyebrow raised. "What's Oblivion like?" he asked, with vague interest. Hix gave a sigh, much like the sigh a war veteran gives when he's asked how many people he's killed.

"Dark... Very dark. Full of condemned souls taking their turn in the chamber of punishment. It's like a machine of sadness and despair. On and on it goes. There's little instruction required for the slaves – they know what each cycle requires. It's not a place of knowledge. One of the first things that happens to you is that your memory becomes hazy and eventually you forget who or what you are. That in itself, is a punishment worth a thousand crimes. I don't remember how I came to exist, I just knew I did not want to stay there anymore." Hix explained it all as though it was a chore – as if he wanted to talk about anything else. The Commodore gave a nod, understanding the need to escape just as much as Hix.

"Apologies for my impromptu visitation, sir," said Adelade in her usual formal tone, her voice echoing through the vast emptiness of the sitting room. One of the many staff of The Grand Manor closed the door behind her.

"Come, sit with me," came a cold voice from the corner of the room. Vignis sat comfortably in his wing-backed chair, pondering the extinguished fireplace with wonderment, a wry smile teasing the corners of his mouth. Adelade took a seat in the neighbouring chair, sitting with her back straight and brushing imaginary dust from her immaculate skirt.

"The Commodore managed to evade capture, sir," said Adelade, almost rushing the words from her mouth. "We tracked him to existence in the 20th century. We believe he has been tasked by The Galdihar Rebellion." Vignis winced slightly at the mention of the Rebellion.

"They are all but defeated. We have eliminated the majority of the Rebellion, and the masses are mostly unaware of their plight or even the fact they exist at all. Before long, they will be destroyed, and we can move on without any further interruption to the final solution."

"Where was The Commodore sighted?" asked Vignis, laconically.

"Mid 20ᵗʰ century. We don't know why or what for, but we have him on the run. He wouldn't dare jump time as we can track him," said Adelade. A grim, satisfied smile cracked across Vignis's face.

"We have him cornered. He has nowhere else to go," smiled Vignis.

"Indeed. It won't take long to track him down, along with the boy and the demon," added Adelade. Vignis suddenly adopted a very serious expression.

"The boy? What boy?" asked Vignis. His eyes widened and he gripped the sides of his chair tighter.

"Just, a boy. I don't believe he is of any importance-" stammered Adelade.

"Fool! He has the boy, the Blind boy!" Vignis stuttered and began to turn pale. "Why didn't you tell me about the boy?"

"Sir, I'm sorry. Let me be the first to tell you we shall have them both captured as soon as we can," Adelade spluttered.

"No!" Vignis shouted. "Eliminate all three of them, immediately. They are not to leave that century alive or so help me I will have your head and the heads of the rest of this excuse for a government!" Vignis wheezed and huffed, trying to gather himself – a loss of composure represented weakness and defied his discipline.

"Release the Weeping Rift" growled Vignis as he ran his hands through his hair.

"The Weeping Rift?" repeated Adelade.

"Do I need to repeat myself?" Vignis snapped, angrily.

"No sir, right away sir," Adelade replied, before turning on her heel and leaving the room.

"Maybelle!" barked Vignis. Soundlessly, Maybelle fluttered over.

"Do you think it wise to employ the Weeping Rift?" asked Maybelle in doubtful tones. Vignis dropped himself back into his chair and gave a sigh.

"What choice do I have?" growled Vignis, his head in his hands. "The Commodore has the Blind boy, could the prophecy be true?"

"The Time-Keepers are no more, and haven't been for some time. The Commodore is an anomaly, a blip, a glitch. He is not a gift or a resurrection of any of those that we have conquered previously. Neither alive nor dead, he doesn't belong anywhere," Maybelle explained as a matter of fact. "You're going to let the words of some foolish housewives worry you?"

185

"You're quite right – there is no evidence to prove the prophecy, and once the Weeping Rift has had its way…" Vignis smiled to himself and gripped the arms of his chair in excitement.

"The Commodore is cornered and will be eliminated like the dog he is, along with the boy and the demon," declared Vignis.

Maybelle smiled with contentment at the words of her master.

Chapter Seven – No Friend of Mine

Whispers are fabulous. They can lead you to the greatest treasures, desires and vices. They prick the ears and tease the egos of even the most disciplined souls. A promise of betterment and an undermining of the risks lead many to glory or the grave, whichever the whisperer chooses. The whispers in the trees are the most lucrative and appealing, especially when the trees have whispered themselves.

"This is the place, I think," said The Commodore as he frowned at his crumpled piece of paper.

"Harry Hibbert's Home for The Elderly," Charlie read aloud from the plaque above the door. At first glance, the home looked like a modern, clean and respectable domicile for the inhabitants living out their golden years.

"It doesn't seem too bad," shrugged Charlie as they looked on.

"The doors are three inches thick in steel, the windows are barred and there's barbed wire on top of the walls. It's more secure than a prison!" said Hix, shaking his head.

The Commodore studied the vast doors, rubbing his chin in deep consideration.

"Are you getting anything from this place, Hix?" asked The Commodore without taking his eyes away from the building.

"Not a thing, all seems normal to me," replied Hix indifferently.

"Anyway!" exclaimed The Commodore in such a manner it startled Charlie. "I'm going to see what's around in this city. Hix, be a good boy, or whatever you are, and see if you can figure out how we can get inside."

"I'd love nothing more," Hix sighed, his words dripping with sarcasm. And with that, he vanished into thin air.

"Come on, let's get a newspaper and go for a coffee," said The Commodore.

"Why?" asked Charlie.

"We're going 'Eve Spotting'," smiled The Commodore.

"Eve Spotting?"

"Yes, we're going to see what Divinians are here in hiding. They won't expose themselves to the Blindlings, but there are plenty."

"It's like we're secret spies!" squealed Charlie, grinning from ear to ear.

"Exactly!"

The hustle and bustle of downtown Detroit made Charlie's head spin. His eyes widened with wonderment as he tried to take in everything at once... the clothes, the cars and the lights; the thick stench of exhaust fumes hanging in the air of the busy downtown streets; the endless honking, shouting and cursing which created an audible pandemonium, the likes of which Charlie had never seen or heard before. He noticed that passers-by were staring at him. His old-fashioned attire most likely hadn't been seen before – or at least for a long time – by the residents of this time-line.

"Hey kid, where did you get those clothes?" jeered a man with a huge afro and flared jeans. "Hey, come get a load of this!" he shouted to his friends. "This kid's clothes are far out, man!"

Charlie frowned slightly. The Commodore stopped on the sidewalk and decided to see how this would play out for his young companion.

"I'll have you know, my attire is considered to be rather complimentary in my time," said Charlie, as politely and well-spoken as ever. The man with the flares stood with his mouth slightly agape for a moment and then fell into fits of laughter.

"Compli… compl… complimentary!" he laughed as he slapped his knees. "I've seen some things in my time…!" A few more people had stopped to see what was causing all the commotion.

"Clearly, one of those things wasn't a dentist," retorted Charlie, holding his nose in disgust. The bystanders laughed heartily as the stranger with the poor oral health suddenly straightened up and made to grab Charlie, but a hand took hold of his arm in a strong, cold grip.

"Touch him, I'll touch you," growled The Commodore, nodding towards Charlie. He looked The Commodore in the eyes and lost himself in them. Something sparkled in The Commodore's eyes that he didn't like.

"Yeah, whatever man, you ain't worth it anyway," he grumbled, trying to appear as cool as possible. "Damn kids today," he mumbled to himself as he disappeared into the busy street and out of sight.

"Everyone seems so rude in the future," said Charlie, hardly moved by his encounter.

"Progression," said The Commodore grimly as he fiddled with his watch.

After a short time, they arrived at a large greasy diner and made their way inside. The Commodore positioned himself with the best view of the passers-by and left his watch perched in his hand, the face positioned skyward and looking as indifferent as always. Charlie looked at the watch and noticed it looked in a slightly worse state than when he first laid eyes upon it.

"What can I get you boys?" came a voice from behind them. The waitress made every effort to sound cheerful, but something cracked between her words. The final betrayal lay in her eyes – they looked tired and defeated.

"Coffee and a cola," replied The Commodore.

"Certainly. Will that be all?" Her voice was steady and well-practiced at hiding the ever-growing emptiness within.

"Yes, thank you."

"Thank you!" Charlie echoed politely as she left. "Why is she so sad? Everyone in the future pretends everything is okay but you can see how they hurt. I can almost feel it." He shivered slightly as he studied the diner.

"I doubt she wants to be here, working every hour under the sun for a tiny bit of money in return, but they have to survive somehow," said The Commodore, pondering the upturned watch.

"I wouldn't do something that didn't make me happy," retorted Charlie with his arms folded.

"You're from a privileged home, Charlie. You should remember that not everyone has that advantage. Some don't have family to support them or even a friend to talk to," The Commodore replied firmly. "Maybe that waitress that you're hammering on about has children that need to be fed and clothed. You should remember that not everyone has a choice." Charlie looked at The Commodore in thought, frowning slightly as he did so.

"We should pay her more," decided Charlie. "It won't make a big difference, but it's better than nothing."

"Okay, we will leave a tip," The Commodore replied, growing slightly tired of their current conversation. "Anyway, bring yourself here and I'll show you how to go 'Eve Spotting'."

Charlie shuffled his chair over and began examining the peculiar watch. Lord Kingston had quite a few pocket watches, most of which were of the highest calibre, but none of them looked quite like The Commodore's watch. There were fifteen hours upon its tired and worn face. It also seemed to note eight days, rather than seven. The glass cover over the front had shattered a long time ago, which had allowed dirt and corrosion to creep into the bevelled edge. Even in its poor state, it was clear that the watch had been crafted by the finest watchmakers that ever were.

"This, Charlie, is a fine piece of equipment, and certainly dangerous in the wrong hands. It belonged to The Time-Keepers – each one of them owned a watch just like this and they used them to travel across the planes and shift to different times. For all intents and purposes, they policed the Divine and Blind worlds, ensuring that peace stayed between the two. They were the stitching of the fabric that is the universe, a very powerful force, that's for sure," The Commodore said proudly as he admired the watch in his hand.

"Shouldn't we give this watch back to its owner?" asked Charlie, in awe of the other-worldly artifact.

"That's not possible… all of The Time-Keepers are gone. They were eliminated by The Celestial Order in the most gruesome battles in the history of… everything. I took part in one of them, it was worse than anything I had ever witnessed as a Commodore of the Royal Navy." The Commodore stared coldly past Charlie, clearly troubled by his recalling. "Anyway! 'Eve Spotting!" said The Commodore in more upbeat tones.

He readjusted the watch and placed it on the table, baring its damaged face skyward.

"If someone – or something – Divinian is nearby, the second-hand will twitch slightly. The nearer we are, the more it will twitch," The Commodore explained in a hushed voice so as not to alert the people nearby.

"It's almost like fishing!" exclaimed Charlie, excited by their task. "What are we going to do when we find someone?"

"If, we find someone – or something," corrected The Commodore, "they will no doubt be taking special care not to be recognised as anything other than a Blindling of some sort."

Charlie fixed his eyes upon the watch and tried not to blink. After a short time, his eyes began to sting, so he blinked as fast as he could so as not to miss a single beat from the watch. The Commodore, meanwhile, drank some coffee and pulled out his joinery magazine, sinking into the pages as time ticked on by.

"Why do you read those magazines?" asked Charlie after an hour or so of watching the time-piece, his head propped sleepily on his hand. The Commodore peered over the top of his magazine with an eyebrow raised.

"They are absolutely fascinating. The craftsmanship that goes into joinery and carpentry can be nothing shy of artwork!" The Commodore enthused. "They could learn a few things in here, I'll tell you that much," he added, as he turned his nose up at the poor state of the diner.

"Would your boy like anything else?" the waitress asked politely. The Commodore opened his mouth to reply, but didn't get chance to answer.

"Ticking! It ticked! It moved!" Charlie jumped up, holding the watch. The Commodore scrambled to his feet and began waving it around to get another sign of life from the watch. He thrust it in the waitress's face and then in the opposite direction.

"Got it, THIS WAY!" He jumped up and threw a fistful of dollars at the waitress before running full pelt out of the door.

"Sorry!" shouted Charlie, on his heels.

"Quickly Charlie, this way!" shouted The Commodore as he ran with his hand outstretched.

"I love Eve Spotting," laughed Charlie, as they ran across the busy sidewalk. The second hand twitched more and more as they ran. A black cat in front of them darted across the street and into an alleyway.

"Follow that cat!" shouted The Commodore, as they turned the corner and went full pelt into the alley.

The Commodore stopped halfway down and Charlie ran straight into the back of him with such force that he fell backwards. Groaning and complaining, he rose to his feet but The Commodore seemed not to notice. He stared wide-eyed at the bottom of the alleyway.

"Something isn't right," said Charlie, as he looked at a bird in the sky. It was frozen, caught in a moment of time… Everything remained still, as if time itself had taken a holiday. The Commodore looked quickly down at his watch, snapped it shut and placed it into his pocket.

"Stay with me, boy," growled The Commodore as they made their way out of the alley. Charlie gasped as they turned on to the street – everything stood still. Not a sound could be heard… not even the wind blew. They walked down the main street of downtown Detroit as The Commodore looked around. He seemed to be looking for something in particular. He ran his hands through his hair and looked around.

"I don't have time for this," he shouted into the stillness of the street.

"On the contrary," came a cool voice from the café next to them. "You have plenty of time – far more than you're entitled to! Tsk tsk." The Commodore turned and motioned for his pistol but it wasn't there.

"Hello, Mr Song," greeted Charlie, politely.

"Good to see you again, Mr Kingston!" he replied with enthusiasm, tipping his immaculate black top hat. "It's been, quite some time. Oh, James, you won't be needing this." He placed The Commodore's pistol on the table and took a sip from his cup as if he had all the time in the world.

"How do you know him?" The Commodore turned on Charlie with suspicion, his eyes cold and accusing.

"I met Mr Song in town a couple of times, he's ever so polite." Charlie smiled. "Is something wrong?"

The Commodore turned back to Mr Song. His eyes were bright and a grin split his cheeks from ear to ear.

"It has been too long, James!" declared Mr Song as he rose from his chair and joined them in the street. "Not the most pleasant of places, Detroit, but not as bad as it will be in about ten years," he chuckled.

"Where were you?" asked The Commodore through gritted teeth, his fists clenching as he trembled with anger.

"So many needlessly perished. You could have stopped it all! You could have saved The Time-Keepers from extinction. Instead, you let them die at Pepper-head Pass!"

"And miss out on all of those wicked souls?" Mr Song cut in. His charming and warm demeanour faltered as something sinister flickered momentarily in his eyes. "I'm no martyr for the putrid souls that tarnish the planes – don't confuse my agenda with your own, James."

"What do you want?" snapped The Commodore, his hands still clenched.

"I just thought I'd check in and see how you're getting on with Mr Kingston here." His cool and calm demeanour surfaced once again.

"I'm very well. Tired, a bit hungry, but I'm on the best adventure ever!" said Charlie, barely able to contain himself.

"You'll have plenty more adventures if The Commodore does what he's supposed to do," he chuckled, nonchalantly. "Anyway, back to business! The entity that you're looking for. Eliminate it with your pistol and I'll put in a good word for you with The Celestial Order."

The Commodore laughed, darkly.

"See, this is your problem. You think that anything can be bargained, but I've seen what bargaining with you

198

does to the poor souls that encounter you." The Commodore walked to the table and put the pistol back into his belt. "I'll do as I please, as per usual." The atmosphere grew tense. Charlie moved closer to The Commodore.

"You will do as you're told, James." Mr Song's smile began to fade. "I'm not an enemy you need right now."

"Well, get in line with the rest of them," smiled The Commodore.

"Don't make me-" started Mr Song.

"Don't make you what? Are you going to condemn me to Oblivion for all of eternity? No. No you are not. If you were going to do that then you would have done it already," The Commodore retorted. "So, what will it be?" He held his arms out with a wry smile upon his fearless face.

"See you again, Mr Kingston." Mr Song tipped his hat and vanished. As he did, rain began to pour from the heavens and time resumed at its normal pace.

"His name isn't really Mr Song, is it," stated Charlie, pulling his collar up around his ears to keep out the rain.

"No," said The Commodore, grimly. "That, monster, goes by lots of names, but usually 'Hymm'. The orchestrator of Oblivion itself."

Charlie shook his head in disapproval.

"Can we get out of the rain now?"

"Yes, let's go," The Commodore replied, checking that his effects were in order.

The wind whipped up the rain as Hix watched the passers-by. They didn't notice him, or the endless loneliness he kept buried in the pit of his soul. He watched on as a little girl danced and skipped through the puddles whilst holding her mother's hand. A sad smile curled in the corner of his mouth as he thought of what could never be, for the damned. A clawed hand outstretched as he summoned a flame. It flickered and danced in the rain shortly before being extinguished.

"What's up with you?" asked The Commodore as they turned the corner to where Hix had been waiting patiently.

"Six days," groaned Hix "I've been here, for six days." Charlie looked at The Commodore, confused.

"We've only been gone for a couple of hours," Charlie pleaded earnestly. "We had a coffee and a chat with

Mr Song, but he's actually called Hymm." Hix's eyes narrowed with suspicion at the mention of Hymm. He turned to The Commodore, who didn't seem particularly moved by the discrepancy in time or the mention of Hymm.

"What did the 'Craftsman of Sorrow' have to say?" asked Hix, suspiciously. He had taken special care not to encounter his previous master. Oblivion was the last place he wished to go back to.

"Not much," replied The Commodore, uninterested – he had once again turned his attention to the watch. Being unaware of the time discrepancy wasn't something that The Commodore was comfortable with. "Oh, actually!" The Commodore continued looking up at Hix. "Hymm mentioned you personally – he asked if you could go back to Oblivion and pick up some housekeeping tasks because it's getting really untidy." His words were soaked in faux eagerness.

"Very good," replied Hix, rolling his eyes.

"Hymm asked us to eliminate whatever is lurking in there," said Charlie, pointing at the vast care home.

"We are to continue our mission as planned. Hymm does not have a say over the Rebellion or us," The Commodore added firmly. "Did you find a way in?" Hix grinned so wide it seemed as though his eyes were smiling.

"I certainly have!" he enthused "They need staff –
seems there's a shortage of 'hygiene specialists' – it's the
perfect way in."

"Oh, a specialist!" Charlie clapped, encouragingly.

"He means a cleaner," sighed The Commodore. "A
decorated officer of the Royal Navy, reduced to cleaning
bedpans."

"Well you're going to fit the bill, they really need
the help," sniggered Hix, who then turned to Charlie.
"You're a visitor and here to see your grandmother, Elsie
Keen. That should get you in with few questions asked."

"We don't know what's in there, Charlie. Stay close
and don't get any fresh ideas. It could be very dangerous,"
The Commodore warned as they ascended the concrete
stairs to the main entrance. The Commodore took a deep
breath and pressed the buzzer to get entry.

"It's been hundreds of years since I went for a job
interview," he thought aloud.

"Don't be nervous," said Charlie. "You'll do great."

Arteon looked down upon Rohan's Reach from his luxury
apartment in the centre of the Divinian metropolis. As a
high-ranking official of The Celestial Order, he had many
residencies across the planes, but he preferred the safety of

Rohan's Reach. At night, you could see lights in some of the windows flickering, and if you listened closely enough, you could hear the chitter chatter of pleasant conversation. On the surface, it all seemed wonderfully peaceful. The Celestial Order had recently called for a curfew once darkness fell – they had informed the residents it was due to a rise in goblin activity. It was, in fact, placed as part of a paranoid plan to catch Rebellion partisans, as they did most of their travelling by night. Those that didn't know of the Rebellion and assumed all was at peace, shrugged and obeyed. Most of those that knew, didn't dare disobey The Good Shepherd. Guards patrolled the city, ordered to report anything even slightly out of place.

Arteon spat over the side of his balcony into the streets below, squeezing his glass as he watched to see if anyone dared to complain. No one did. His dressing gown didn't do much to complement his rotund figure – he had become even bigger and would surely have died from a heart attack if not for the medicines available in the Divine world.

"Higglesworth!" bellowed Arteon, as he scowled at his empty glass and swayed drunkenly. "I've finished this glass. Bring out the bottle and don't keep me waiting." He strained his ears, listening for the usual panic-stricken crashing and fumbling, but none came. After a few moments, he brought his glass crashing down on to the table and stormed back into his apartment away from the balcony, his silk dressing gown fluttering angrily behind him. A dense fog of body odour followed Arteon into the room. Arteon often had 'business gatherings' at the apartment, poor souls that were blackmailed into performing some of the most sickening activities the imagination could conjure for his entertainment. Those who protested were destroyed, those who talked had their families destroyed.

"What on earth are you doing?" he roared into the apartment. "Filthy offspring of a sow is what you are!" He rattled on, threatening terrible punishments as he stormed through his vast apartment and into the kitchen. He turned on Higglesworth, who stood perfectly still and didn't dare even look at Arteon. His old and tired eyes were laden with fear, and he kept his wrinkled hands on the white marble table top in plain sight, not daring to move. He had been the home assistance for Arteon for many years, not out of choice but necessity.

"What are you doing? Foolish old corpse, has your mind finally failed you? You'd better hope that it has, or you're going to regret ever crossing me!" Arteon studied Higglesworth and, as he did, the hairs on the back of his neck began to stand on end. "What are you looking at?" Higglesworth didn't answer. Arteon made his way through the kitchen and felt a wave of horror sweep over his entire body. A hooded figure sat at the dining table nursing a glass of his finest liquor.

"Good evening, Arteon. It's been quite some time since we last met," came a soft voice from under the hood. "Won't you take a seat? Oh, how I've missed you."

"Who are you and what do you want? Don't you know who I am?" spluttered Arteon, trying to stay composed. His apartment had the highest level of security, including enchantments and guards at every entrance with regular patrols. The hooded figure didn't answer but instead drained the glass and placed it gently upon the table.

"If you agree to co-operate, I'll ensure the consequences for your crimes are dealt with in the best way possible," said Arteon, trying to remain calm. He ran a hand across his eyebrows and wiped away the sweat stinging his eyes.

"*My* crimes?" laughed the hooded man softly. "Stones and glasshouses, dear boy! But, we're here to talk about you, Arteon." He lowered his hood gently and smiled at Arteon. His eyes soft and kind, his beard inevitable as ever.

"Eamon Haste," breathed Arteon, almost forcing his words out in a choked whisper. The colour drained from his face and his knees began to give from underneath him. He collapsed into a chair, opposite his enemy.

"It's been a long time since I worked alongside you, Arteon. I remember being your apprentice, though I do not remember when our paths separated," said Haste with a gentle smile. He spoke as though catching up with an old friend he hadn't seen in a long time, though they couldn't be further from friendship.

"What do you want?" said Arteon, contemptuously. His eyes flickered as his fat fists began to clench. He would be considered a hero if he could eliminate the leader of The Galdihar Rebellion. Haste smiled as he leaned back comfortably in his chair, his hands together as one would have them when content.

"I want, peace and fair treatment of all that exist across the planes. I want the abolishment of The Good Shepherd's vile decree allowing use of energy as currency, an end to this secret war and…" Eamon paused as he pondered for a moment, "a holiday in Cuba!" He chuckled warmly, irritating Arteon even more.

"You were always a thorn in my side," spat Arteon. "The old rulers had no vision for how powerful the Divine world could be."

"The Celestial Order under the leadership of The Good Shepherd will defeat The Galdihar Rebellion and rule all of the planes. We already have Purgatory and the majority of existence," Arteon sneered, his confidence slowly returning. "If your plight is so righteous, then why doesn't Sanctuary come to your aid?" A knowing smile slid across his podgy face.

"A good question," replied Haste, stroking his chin curiously. "They didn't intervene when The Celestial Order desolated the Time-Keepers or when The Good Shepherd made a half-cocked deal with Hymm for energy from Oblivion." Arteon's tiny, fat-smothered eyes narrowed. "How can he know about Hymm?" he thought to himself.

"The witch!" Arteon gasped after a few moments. "You've employed that rotten witch!" Haste retained the welcoming smile, his warm eyes almost seemed to dance but gave nothing away.

"The world will learn of The Celestial Order's plans; we will see to that." He returned to stroking his beard as he contemplated Arteon. "Higglesworth is quite the chatterbox when he gets going, too. He told me all about your plans for the energy you're harvesting. It's quite the savage tale. I had some trouble digesting it all."

Arteon turned a shade paler and began to quiver. "What did he tell you?" he spluttered.

"Enough to be getting on with," replied Haste with certainty. "I wouldn't bother with punishment, torture and your general practice of harrowing cruelty. I used to be good at removing memories. But, as time has passed, and it has, I've become out of practice. I ended up removing everything from him. He doesn't remember who he is. I wiped his mind clean of everything, silly me."

Arteon trembled so violently his rolls of fat carried waves of fury all over his body. "You will pay for your crimes," he snarled. "You cannot escape The Celestial Order."

"I admire your passion, Arteon," Haste replied with encouragement. "It's time that I left, I have plenty of work to do." He rose from the table and made his way to the balcony that Arteon had been perched upon.

"Do you remember the signal for The Galdihar Rebellion? A soaring angel across the sky?" Haste asked earnestly as he rolled up his sleeves. "I'm sure I can conjure one to mark this momentous occasion."

"No, please! The Celestial Order will think me a traitor, conspirator. I'd... I'd be punished for high treason!" Arteon began to weep as he wobbled towards Haste.

"Come now, Arteon," Eamon replied soothingly. "I'm sure you can persuade them otherwise." Without further delay, Haste threw his arms skyward and watched as a silvery figure assembled in the sky. A beautiful angel soared across the night sky for all to see. Arteon threw his sweaty hands across his eyes and dropped to his knees, squinting into the light. As his eyes adjusted, Haste vanished, leaving him with the trembling Higglesworth.

Chapter Eight – No Quarter Given

This day shall be my last, this battle final and my faith unmoved. Forward, that is the order. The fire will burn out, the dust will settle and the truth shall be enslaved by the victor and their pen. We know this day will not end in peace; the war will turn cold. My brethren, my sistren, we are the last of our kind. But what we have, that the enemy does not, is righteous intention, integrity and true purpose. Know that we did not fail, know that we are not alone and that their time will be shattered in another era. Friends, let us go forward for the last time, together!

"That's a very handsome outfit. Can I get one of those?" giggled Hix hovering behind The Commodore as he pushed a laundry bin along the spotless corridor. The clinical smell of industrial strength bleach hung in the air, ready to punish the nostrils of all that encountered it. The Commodore brushed his apron flat as he walked on, mumbling something about sending Hix back to where he came from.

"I don't feel too good," came a sickly voice from inside the laundry bin.

"Maybe next time you'll eat less of the fudge that Mrs Jackson keeps by her bedside," said The Commodore, knowingly.

"They are heavenly though…" Charlie defended, weakly. "I didn't realise I'd eaten so many."

Hix fluttered on, humming to himself, in mostly good humour as it wasn't he who had to endure. For today at least.

"I'm still not feeling anything out of the ordinary," said Hix between his orchestral humming. "I think that we've made a mistake."

"Let's see to Mr Kestler and then we'll head over to the hospital wing. That's where the oldest residents are being treated," replied The Commodore.

"MARSHALL!" boomed an oily voice from behind them. "Wait there, boy!" The Commodore gripped the handles of the laundry basket as he waited for the steps to get closer.

"What are you doing?" came an oily sneer. "You should have done the laundry an hour ago."

"My apologies Mr Stewart," replied The Commodore through gritted teeth, trying his best to sound apologetic. Mr Stewart had recently been promoted to Assistant Manager, though you would be forgiven for assuming his title was, in fact, king of the world and all that reside within. His thin, skeletal finger wagged in front of The Commodore's nose.

"You better get yourself in order, boy, there are plenty in the queue for your job. You should think yourself privileged to be employed here." Mr Stewart spat, his wrinkled face and long nose resembled that of a gremlin.

"I will do better, Mr Stewart," said The Commodore through a forced smile. His face shifted across an alarming spectrum of red.

"Do you hear him, boy?" Hix echoed, imitating Mr Stewart's oily sneer. "Give him one on the chops!"

The Commodore's eyes flickered to Hix momentarily. Luckily, only he and Charlie could hear him.

"Well, what are you waiting for? Me to do it for you? Get on with your duties or I'll write you up on a warning." Mr Stewart, now satisfied, moved on, looking for his next victim to shower in beratement.

"He isn't very nice," Charlie whispered from within the laundry bin. "He reminds me of the teachers in my school."

Charlie wondered what his brothers would be doing right now. Would they miss him? Or would life simply continue on? A smile spread across his face as he realised that they would have grown up by now and probably have a family of their own. "I wonder what their families are like," Charlie thought to himself.

"Can we go and see my brothers?" asked Charlie from under the sheets.

"Absolutely!" replied The Commodore. "If you want to send them to an insane asylum, because that's where they'll end up. Imagine their horror at seeing their brother who went missing decades previously, and he hasn't aged a single day!"

"That's a pretty basic rule of time travel" concurred Hix. "It wouldn't do us or your family well."

"Here we are," said The Commodore. "Mr Kestler's room". A torrent of swearing and profanity echoed inside the room with such consistency that they would have made the burliest of sailors blush. Charlie hopped out of the laundry bin once they were inside the room. Within the room sat a single bed, its resident scolding the very air with his presence.

"And what in the heck do you couple of backward rejects of society want?" snapped Mr Kestler. His eyes furrowed in rage, not at them in particular, but at everything that ever was, just because.

"Hello Mr Kestler," came The Commodore's unenthused voice. "How are we today?"

"YOU!" snapped Mr Kestler. "It's YOU not WE. Are you stupid, boy? Simple, even? Masquerading as a citizen of The British Empire. You're nothing more than a pillock." The Commodore raised an eyebrow, unmoved by the barrage of insults flying from Mr Kestler. He had to be at least 100 years old but every one of his marbles not only remained, but shone and sparkled. His large ears and trembling jowls looked almost comical, as if he had stolen his ears from someone much larger and kept them as his own.

"I thought I heard an accent," The Commodore eased. "Suffolk?"

"Bloody Suffolk. Sussex! Stupid boy," Mr Kestler growled.

"Have you had a bad day?" asked Charlie, as politely as ever.

"Didn't pick this one up for his intelligence did you, boy?" snorted Mr Kestler, pointing at Charlie.

"What brought you to Detroit?" asked The Commodore with a hint of interest. "Surely not the weather." Mr Kestler's eyes narrowed slightly as he contemplated dignifying The Commodore with an answer to his question.

"I came here as an apprentice engineer back when the black death could still be found under a rock." He coughed. His eyes moved from The Commodore, to Charlie and back again. "Got married like a fool, didn't I. Started a family and all that."

"Are they coming to visit you today?" Charlie interjected.

"No. They're dead," said Mr Kestler with a grin. The kind that gets satisfaction from summoning an oppressive atmosphere and trumping all in the room in measurement of tragedy. Charlie's face sank, The Commodore remained unmoved. Even Hix looked a bit awkward, he sat next to Mr Kestler and seemed to be interested in him.

"So are mine," The Commodore replied coldly as he folded the dirty laundry. "You don't see me rattling on about it though." Mr Kestler raised a curious eyebrow. The dim-witted staff at the home didn't usually dare answer so boldly.

"Well, what would you know about the hardness of life, boy," said Mr Kestler with his arms folded and an eyebrow still raised.

"More than you," The Commodore replied flatly.

"How so?"

"I am… I was, an officer of the Royal Navy." A smile curled in the corner of his mouth as he gained Mr Kestler's attention.

"Poppycock!" laughed Mr Kestler. "A bloody dreamer is what you are."

"A Commodore, the youngest Commodore ever to sail under the flag of Britannia herself." The Commodore dropped into a chair and stared coldly at Mr Kestler.

"I cut my teeth in a battle against the French, I took three of their ships as a Captain and made Commodore shortly after. What I've seen and done would make your heart stop – lord knows it did mine. The Spanish and their Armadas were well armed but used predictable tactics – they cared more about principle than victory." The Commodore took out his watch and fiddled with the lid. He didn't take his eyes off Mr Kestler.

"My grandfather was a sailor in the Navy – you cannot possibly have taken part in those battles, they were two hundred years ago." Mr Kestler spoke calmly, still processing everything being said by The Commodore. "I've heard the stories."

The Commodore smiled and pulled an old and tatty piece of neatly-folded parchment from his inside pocket. He leaned forward and showed Mr Kestler the bottom of the letter, along with the seal of the King of England.

"Stole it did you?" cackled Mr Kestler. The Commodore took Mr Kestler's hand and pressed his fingers into his own wrist and then his neck.

"There's no pulse!" Mr Kestler barked in surprise. The Commodore walked slowly to the cupboard and took a razor blade from the shelf. Hix rolled his eyes, knowing what was coming.

"I am James Edward Marshall, the youngest Commodore that ever sailed under the flag of Britannia. I won almost every battle that I ever fought, except the battle against the most formidable enemy I've ever faced," The Commodore said with pride. He looked in the mirror and attempted to fix his hair. Mr Kestler started to go pale, his eyes filled with icy fear as he watched The Commodore and the razor blade.

"And... wh... who... who was the enemy?" stammered Mr Kestler.

"Me," replied The Commodore, dryly. He led the razor across his wrist. A miniscule drop of blood left his skin – a large amount considering his heart was not functioning. The wound healed quickly as Charlie wondered if Mr Kestler would have a heart attack.

"What do you want?" Mr Kestler snapped – he seemed to have brought himself back. "I don't have any money."

"What on earth would a dead Commodore want with your useless currency?" The Commodore barked back. "I want two things from you; First, apologise to the boy for being rude in his company – he didn't deserve that. Second, there are some strange happenings going on in this armpit of a care home. So tell me, what am I missing here, Mr Kestler?" The Commodore once again dropped into the armchair.

"I'm sorry for being rude, boy" said Mr Kestler, earnestly. He looked at Charlie and gave a nod. "In the medical wing, there's a woman called Joan Elliot. She's been in this place longer than any other resident and shows no signs of departing anytime soon."

The Commodore looked at Hix with a curious eyebrow raised. Hix merely shrugged as Mr Kestler went on.

"Her room smells to high heaven of sulphur but only in the evenings. The orderlies can't figure out where the smell is coming from."

"Right, that's somewhere to start." The Commodore slapped the arms of the chair and went to get up.

"Well, hold on!" Mr Kestler said, panicked. "What happens when we die?"

"It's a long story." The Commodore groaned, unwilling to continue. "You get judged. If you've done anything vile, you ain't going to Sanctuary."

Mr Kestler thought for a moment. "I'm fine with that," he confirmed as he forced an ugly smile that seemed very out of place.

"It doesn't smell great in here," choked Hix as they entered the medical wing. His orange appearance appeared to lack its usual vibrancy. Charlie held his nose as his eyes began to water, the stench of industrial strength bleach and rotten eggs making his queasiness even worse. The medical ward seemed unusually empty. Private rooms were set to each side of the room and the lights were dim.

"It's pretty creepy in here," whined Charlie, still gripping his nose as tight as he could.

"There's something evil lurking in here," whispered Hix. "I can feel it now… we're close." The Commodore gave a nod as they walked on.

"Where are the staff?" The Commodore pondered aloud as they crept along the corridor looking for Joan Elliot's room.

An ear-splitting scream suddenly tore through the silence of the ward. Charlie jumped and moved closer to The Commodore.

"Stop screaming!" came an oily voice from one of the rooms. "This won't take long. Now be quiet!"

They peered in through the glass of the door and saw Mr Stewart bent over a patient with a pan of boiling water. He held out the old lady's hand and poured some of the water onto it. She howled and screeched in pain as he watched her burns heal within seconds.

"You're a miracle, a blessing from the heavens!" Mr Stewart raved, almost frantically.

"She's about the oldest person I have ever seen," Charlie whispered. Her hands were curled in with severe arthritis and her eyes were clouded with cataracts.

"I'd say so," The Commodore agreed. "Let's deal with Mr Stewart first." He rolled up his sleeves and removed his apron.

"Don't hurt him," Charlie pleaded under his breath.

"Are you joking?" snorted The Commodore. "Look at what he's doing to that poor lady. It's time he got a taste of his own medicine."

"We are lowering ourselves to his level," came Charlie in reply.

"I agree with The Commodore on this one, Charlie – he needs to be punished," Hix chipped in with his arms folded. Charlie frowned at The Commodore and Hix before shaking his head in disapproval.

"I'll deal with this," said Charlie finally, and he marched into the room without another word.

Mr Stewart jumped in fright as Charlie walked into the room, The Commodore and Hix following behind.

"What are you doing here?" Mr Stewart shrieked. He tried to compose himself and hide the pan of hot water.

"You are in a position of trust," said Charlie, calmly. "This poor woman does not deserve to be treated like this and I intend to report you."

"Who do you think you are?" Mr Stewart barked at Charlie, his eyes watching The Commodore. "And you, Marshall, what do you have to say for yourself? Sneaking around whilst you should be attending to your duties."

The Commodore didn't reply, and instead gave a groan of relief as he lowered himself into one of the chairs in the room. Mr Stewart motioned to leave.

"Don't move," snapped The Commodore. Mr Stewart froze and looked from The Commodore back to Charlie. "After what you did to that poor lady, Charlie would like to have a word with you. I'd rather teach you a different type of lesson." The Commodore cracked his knuckles and smiled.

"But Charlie here is opposed to violence and would like to deal with you in a more alternative and conscientious way."

"The woman, she is magical!" bleated Mr Stewart. "Her wounds heal almost instantly, and if her birth record is to be believed, she's almost one hundred and forty years old!" He looked from The Commodore back to Charlie, who remained with his arms folded and a disapproving look upon his face.

"That does not give you the right to treat this poor lady so distastefully," said Charlie, sternly. "I am going to write a complaint to the director of the home and explain what you have done. I hope you learn your lesson." Charlie nodded with conviction and folded his arms again.

"The director is my brother," laughed Mr Stewart. "You can send him as many letters as you like – who do you think he is going to believe? Me, or some strangely dressed child smuggled in by this thug."

The Commodore got to his feet and stepped towards Mr Stewart.

"No!" shouted Charlie. "I have a better idea." He looked at The Commodore who rolled his eyes and sat back in the chair, deflated.

"Hix, can you do that thing, where you take over him?" asked Charlie.

"I reckon so, but not for long. It will need to be a quick one," Hix considered, looking a confused Mr Stewart up and down.

"You're going to bring The Order down on us again," sighed The Commodore.

"I think Mr Stewart would benefit from a walk up the road in his underwear. That should be enough for him to lose his job."

"Yes sir!" Hix gave a salute and vanished. Shortly after, Mr Stewart made his way out of the room, albeit in a wobbly fashion.

"Well done, Charlie, not a scratch on him," The Commodore smiled. "Let's see what's happening here with our patient." He pulled his watch from inside his pocket and studied its face.

"I'm not getting anything here. The entity that's lurking inside the place is working very hard not to be detected. Probably why The Celestial Order hasn't already been here," The Commodore said curiously.

"She's in a lot of pain," said Charlie, observing the elderly lady.

"Not a lot gets past you, does it?" replied The Commodore, sarcastically. Charlie pretended he hadn't heard him. The Commodore gently checked the old lady's arms. She began humming a song and seemed to be a little more at ease. Charlie checked the drawers next to the old lady's bed and found some old photos.

"I wonder why her children haven't come to see her," Charlie said. "Her visitors' book hasn't been signed for over twenty-five years now."

"They're probably dead," said The Commodore, bluntly. "She is very old and should have passed a long time ago. Whoever is responsible should be ashamed."

The Commodore stood and checked his pistol, cleared the breach and cocked the firing mechanism. Let's go and see Joan Elliot. Maybe she can answer some questions for us. Charlie replaced the old photographs and kissed the old lady on the forehead. She smiled and drifted off to sleep in comfort. As they left and closed the door gently, Hix appeared looking exhausted.

"Mr Stewart will no longer be a problem," he panted as he struggled to hover steadily. "He went for a walk with no clothes on. Someone called the police, so I reckon they'll stick him on a psychiatric ward indefinitely."

Charlie beamed proudly at the news as The Commodore shrugged indifferently.

"Should have given him a beating to go along with it," he grumbled. "Anyway, let's find Joan."

Maybelle hovered anxiously outside of the boardroom door; she had never seen Vignis in such a terrible state. Humiliation wasn't something Vignis experienced very often, especially when the offender sat on his own council.

"Maybelle!" Vignis roared from inside the boardroom. Maybelle scrambled inside, slipping through the door as quick as she could. On entry, she saw two guards shaking at the boardroom table and two others reduced to a pile of still smoking dust and bones. Vignis stood with an ancient sword that seemed to be white hot. His teeth chattered with anger as he maintained a tight grip on his sword, daring the guards to make a run for it.

"Bring me Arteon," he spat through gritted teeth. Maybelle shot back out of the room without a moment's hesitation and summoned the staff to retrieve Arteon from the holding cells.

"Please, you are The Good Shepherd, we had nothing to do with The Angel in the sky," one of the remaining guards pleaded. His hands were burnt and his uniform lay in tatters across his chest.

"Filthy saboteurs, do you think me a fool?" he sneered, still trembling with anger. "You have conspired with the Rebellion to try and overthrow The Celestial Order – do not deny it, traitors."

"Please, I beg of you, do not eliminate us!" The guard wept into his stinging hands.

"I am not going to eliminate you… that would be far too easy." A sickly grin spread across his face. "You are going to Oblivion without a hearing!"

"No! Please!" The guards begged in unison. Weeping and crying, they dropped to their knees from the table. "Not Oblivion!"

"MAYBELLE!" Vignis screamed. "Take the traitors down to the holding cells and have them sent to Oblivion without a hearing! Bring. Me. Arteon." Kull, the sizeable giant, dragged a limp Arteon into the boardroom

226

and dumped him on the floor with a thud. He wept uncontrollably as he stretched his fat fingers out to touch The Good Shepherd's shoes.

"Your graciousness, plea-" he whined.

Vignis brought a heavy boot down onto Arteon's sausage fingers and ground them into the floor. Arteon wailed and screamed into the boardroom as he looked at his broken fingers.

"Stand up!" growled Vignis, pushing his face into Arteon's. As he quivered and half-rose to his feet, Vignis delivered a brutal kick to his face – the crack of his nose breaking echoed as blood flew from his round face.

"Please! No more!" Arteon spat into the floor, his round face even more swollen. "I have not had anything to do with the Rebellion, I have been a loyal member of our blessed Celestial Order."

"Do you think me a fool?" Vignis roared. "I know you have not conspired against The Celestial Order – not even you are that stupid. Our reputation has taken irreparable damage. Entities across the planes are aware that the rumours they hear of the Rebellion might actually be true. I have press conferences lined up to try and put some ease to our population's mind."

"Then what will you do with me?" Arteon whimpered. "I only ask that you do not keep me in anxious anticipation, but end me quickly."

"I do not wish to eliminate you. I could destroy you in the blink of an eye," Vignis whispered, twitching and growling as he did so. "Adelade will take over your operations and oversee the management of energy." Vignis began to calm and he paced the room, relaxing his grip on the sword – a sword that had relieved many of their lives.

"Maybelle!" shouted Vignis hoarsely – his voice had started to crack from hours of shouting and screaming. Maybelle fluttered in and waited on her master's command.

"Maybelle, Arteon is to be put on the frontline of the goblin watch outside of the gates at Rohan's Reach. Wipe his memory and send him out. Inform the captain there that he is a traitor to his people."

Maybelle gave an understanding nod and fluttered out of the room, summoning the staff to assist.

"Please, Vignis, you are The Good Shepherd – have mercy upon me!" Arteon sobbed into the ground, choking on his blood as he did so.

"There are fates worse than death, Arteon. You have argued your capability many times. Let's see how you fare against the wild goblins." Vignis sneered, disgusted by the sight of his now former colleague. He spat contemptuously and left the room as Kull dragged Arteon away. He kicked, screamed and begged as he scraped the floor on the way out.

Hix fluttered over the sleeping Joan and peered into her open mouth.

"She seems pretty normal to me. I'm not getting anything here," said Hix as he examined her from the air.

"Well, we will see, won't we," replied The Commodore, watching Joan as though she might attack them at any moment. He checked his effects. Satisfied that nothing was out of place, he continued watching Joan as she slept.

"There haven't been any visitors since forever," Charlie noted as he flicked through the visitors' book at the side of the bed. "There aren't any medical notes either."

The Commodore pointed at Joan with a satisfied grin.

"She's the one alright. Don't wake her, we don't know what or who she is," The Commodore hissed suspiciously.

"It says her name right here. Joan," replied Charlie, plainly.

"Never mind," The Commodore sighed as he rolled his eyes.

Joan's room smelt strongly of sulphur and rotten eggs, though the trio had grown used to the stench and weren't affected by it anymore. The room seemed otherwise immaculate, everything clean and properly in place – even the flowers in the vase seemed to be more vibrant than any living human in the entire establishment.

The Commodore pulled his pistol from its holster and checked it over, cocking the mechanism and aiming it squarely at Joan.

"Do you think that's necessary?" asked Charlie with a frown.

"I'm not taking any chances," replied The Commodore as a matter of fact.

"We have a problem," Hix added, fearfully. He stared at Joan, not daring to blink. "She's awake, and she can see me."

Charlie and The Commodore looked over and noticed that Joan was looking Hix in the eyes. A smile spread across her kind face as she studied him.

"You don't belong here," she said, kindly. "And neither do you, James," her eyes moved over to The Commodore.

"But you, young man, we have plenty to talk about." She winked at Charlie and moved her gaze back to The Commodore. He checked the inevitable time-piece and raised an eyebrow as it didn't show any signs of being around any Divine beings.

"We don't have time for pleasantries, Joan, or whatever you are," The Commodore cut in, impatiently. "If you don't co-operate, I'll-"

"You'll what?" Joan interrupted, politely. "Destroy me with that famous pistol of yours?" She laughed softly, not at all affected by the urgency The Commodore pressed on her.

"Death is a kindness, elimination can be... divine," she continued.

The Commodore stood up and gripped the bottom of her bed. Staring hard, his hands tightened around the metal frame.

"There are fates worse than death. Look at what you have done to the patients in here, they're suffering and cannot die," The Commodore growled.

"I have given them more time," snapped Joan. Her smile disappeared; she had clearly been agitated by The Commodore. "They are grateful for every moment extra they receive."

"No, they are old and suffering the worst pain. As they grow older, they're losing their minds and wish to die. You are not doing them a service by letting them live longer," The Commodore scorned, gripping the frame even tighter.

"There's a song in the air, James, it sings to me day and night. These Blindlings and mortals cannot hear it, but I can and it's beautiful," Joan explained, her eyes glistening.

"It is the energy in their very souls, begging to escape," replied Hix, morbidly. "I don't hear the songs of the souls any more, but when I did, it certainly was not beautiful."

"Our concepts of beauty are clearly unaligned." She waved Hix away, impatiently. "We both wish to forget our beginnings, our creator and the purpose for which we have been created."

"Hysterias," whispered The Commodore, stepping back from the bed. Hix began to move slowly from Joan, keeping his eyes on what seemed to be a kind old lady. Charlie remained indifferent and calm, choosing to remain where he was.

"That was once my name," said Joan, sadly. "I no longer associate myself with that name."

"Let that name be a curse to you," replied The Commodore, his hand trembling over his mouth as he stared on, dumfounded. "Let the damned souls you have taken, abused and tortured be associated to that name and you."

"Please, let's go," Hix cried suddenly. "I cannot bear being in the same room as, that." He too trembled.

"We did not come this far to run away," barked The Commodore. "This… filth has escaped any kind of judgement for the callous and cold crimes it has committed."

"I have repented for my crimes," pleaded Joan, beginning to sob. "I have given life to these mortals, given them more time than they were initially blessed with. I have changed, my history forgotten – this is a new era for me and I shall be recognised for it."

"We must leave," Hix repeated. "We cannot stay here. Hysterias is not a reflection of me or what I am." The Commodore turned to Hix with a serious expression.

"Indeed, Hix, you are nothing like this monster," he explained as a matter of fact.

"You do not get to decide your own fate, reconciliation or damnation," The Commodore spat, angrily, his temper rising as he spoke. "For all the lives you have destroyed and devoured, you do not deserve anyone's pity or forgiveness. I should have dealt with you at Pepper-head Pass. You're just a hired weapon that no one wants to be associated with. The Rebellion won't help you, The Celestial Order and Oblivion both have a bounty on your head."

"Then do what you need to, Commodore," she said plainly. All emotion disappeared from her face. "Give me the only salvation that remains." The Commodore looked to Hix who gave a brief nod and looked back at Joan. Slowly, he raised his pistol and took aim at Joan, cocking the trigger as he did so.

"I still remember the order that went out across our lines," said The Commodore, filling with grief. "'No quarter given'. We stood fast as you and your comrades charged the barricade. Our allies fell like flies as we were crushed and the last of The Time-Keepers were destroyed. You broke our backs; you broke our enchantments, but you didn't break our belief in what was right."

The Commodore stopped suddenly, staring through Joan as though she wasn't there. Hix also paused, motionless, in an almost comedic manner.

"What's wrong with them?" asked Charlie, a little more confrontationally than could be expected from him.

"Nothing, they are a frozen in a moment of time," said Joan with a wearisome sigh. She turned to Charlie and smiled, lifting her head from the pillow.

"You are an important young man, Mr Kingston. The Commodore does not know how important you are; indeed, it is essential that he does not."

"I don't feel very important. I am merely enjoying an adventure – the greatest of adventures, I might add," Charlie confessed. Joan laughed softly and took a moment to admire Charlie.

"My boy, you have barely even started. Would you like to understand more of The Commodore? What made him great, what made him fall and what made him infamous?"

Charlie thought for a moment as he studied The Commodore.

"I would not want to offend The Commodore; he has done me more of a service than anyone before him," he replied, feeling guilty for even contemplating the notion of betraying his champion.

"I can tell you his story, that is all. I can take you through timelines of his memories so that you can understand his pain, motivation and purpose," Joan whispered, confidently. "He would not know anything of it, it would be between you and I."

"But there is such a thing as 'knowing too much'," Charlie objected, politely.

"There is also knowing nothing at all. He who seeks shall find... he who does not, shrouds himself in ignorance," Joan countered with a cheeky smile. She raised a withered hand to Charlie, holding it out to him.

"Take my hand. Let me show you what most will not see. If nothing else, I promise you wisdom." Her voice was calm and confident.

Charlie studied her hand and frowned slightly, he looked to The Commodore and smiled.

"It's what you would do, Commodore," he thought aloud and took Joan's hand.

Chapter Nine – Beaufort, Bamford and Bum

Part I

Tread those beneath you as though they do not exist. You might find it difficult at first but greatness will never be achieved without sacrifice, why must it be yours? Eventually it will become instinctual, carried out without even the slightest thought. Pride, possession and progression are the key principles of our existence and you must lead with a hard hand, make an example of those below you to truly seal oppression. Ensure that you pick your battles, ensure that you are certain to win by staggering odds, if you are uncertain, use those below you and observe.

Charlie recoiled as the blinding light gave way to the imagery of a busy waterfront town. He shaded his eyes, eager to take in his surroundings. Horses, clipped and clopped pulling their tired carts behind them, passers-by walked briskly about their day. Fishermen, sailors, businessmen and meager peasants beat the streets without the usual segregation of class Charlie had been familiar with. He noticed they were by the sea – behemoth merchant ships and naval vessels dotting the horizon as far as the eye could see. Charlie smiled as he considered the view, which looked like many of the paintings he gazed upon at home. Kingston Abbey sported hundreds of hand-painted artworks, Charlie often pondered them and considered them to be a window into a period of time long since passed.

"Can they see me?" he asked as he waved at one particularly worried looking citizen.

"No, they cannot. Nor can they hear you or feel your touch. You are a phantom and are merely spectating," came a familiar voice, but it sounded much younger. Charlie looked to see Joan by his side, only she couldn't be more than twenty years old. As beautiful as she looked, there remained a formidable presence within her.

"Where are we?" asked Charlie.

"This is Portsmouth, 1723 by the Blindling calendar," she said with a sneer. "A disgusting location, by any measure."

"A familiar face?" asked Joan as she gave a nod towards a passing gentleman.

"I don't believe it is," replied Charlie, looking hard at the man. "The Commodore!" gasped Charlie as he drew nearer. He walked casually, taking his time on his route. His eyes were gentle and warm, a far-cry from the cold sadness that dwelt within them now. For someone who would come to gain the ability to manipulate time itself, he seemed not to concern himself with any urgency. Charlie studied his modest working clothes and followed the whistling Commodore.

"Before his infamy and legend, he was known simply as James. Remember, he cannot see or hear you. This is merely a mirage, a collection of memories past. Keep that in mind," Joan warned as she followed in tow.

James made his way into a large workshop just off the busy walkway at the front. Charlie and Joan followed.

"Marshall, I need a word," said Arthur, the owner of the workshop.

"Certainly, though I warn you the morning will make fools of us both if I do not start the window frames," James jested cheerfully. James seemed almost a stranger to Charlie in every way. His clean appearance and chipper disposition were alien to all that Charlie knew about him.

"I've got somethin' you need to know." Arthur went on. He sat himself down on a chair and sighed as one does when they reach a certain age. A burly man and a master of his trade, Arthur had always been good to those in his employment. His rough hands rested on his thighs as his battered work boots tapped uneasily.

"This little workshop has turned out same incredible carpentry over the years, and your hand has helped in recent times," said Arthur, smiling nostalgically. "You will have noticed, I'm sure, that we've been very quiet recently." Arthur cleared his throat and looked around the workshop awkwardly. The smell of sawdust and hard work lingered pleasantly in the air, Arthur noticed it for the first time in a while and savoured it for a moment.

"We have been quiet, quite right," replied James, brightly, "but we have the contract for the Merchant Navy, which will take us right up to capacity." His optimism faltered slightly as he noticed the severe and worried look on Arthur's face.

"The contract has gone to Thorne and West," said Arthur, gruffly. James looked dumbfounded for a moment, before shaking his head in disbelief.

"Is that so?" James retorted. "Our work is superior and I am doubtless we can save the crown a coin or three!"

Arthur looked around the workshop, as though he hadn't heard James.

"Marshall, many will tell you that knowledge and intellect is king. You could be forgiven for believing every word of that." Arthur stared with his hands on his hips away from James. "A favoured acquaintance and a word in the right ear will always supersede knowledge and intellect." James listened intently, hanging on to every word.

"As we do not have the contract from the Merchant Navy, I have no choice but to end your employment. I understand you have obligations to your family and would not take it personally for you to seek work with our competitor," said Arthur distantly, his eyes staring past James.

"I could do no such thing," retorted James, appalled. "I pledged my loyalty to you and this establishment; I cannot forget the blessing when I first came here and had no employment." Arthur put a hand on his shoulder in such a way that it clearly indicated there wasn't any other outcome to be had from their conversation.

"You have turned out some fine work, James," Arthur smiled. "If anything should change, I will let you know by way of mouth, not letter. It will be my priority.

Without any improvement, I will be closing this shop at the end of the season."

James made his way home, his hands in his pockets, swallowed by his own troubled thoughts to such a degree that the world seemed not to be of any importance. As he approached his family's humble home, he placed a hand upon the door and took a deep sigh of relief. They had managed to scrape by solely on his small income as an apprentice.

"Hello Mary-" James started.

"Father!" Henry shouted; glee spread across his small face as he ran to greet him. "I've had an amazing day today; I drew pictures and we even walked by the school house. Can I go to the school house soon?" Henry's face beamed with excitement as he stood with bated breath, waiting for his father's response. He had inherited his father's thick black hair and bright blue eyes, but his smile belonged to his mother. James simply smiled, knelt forward and embraced Henry as only a father can do to his son.

"Ready yourself for dinner, Henry," came a thick Edinburgh accent from the other side of the room. "Come now, give your father time to enter the room."

Their humble home consisted of only two rooms, and the few pieces of worn furniture they owned seemed to be stretched to hide the sheer bareness within. James removed his flat cap and held it to his chest, his eyes purposely averting his wife's curious glance. Mary had that rarely attributed effortless grace. She seemingly never exerted a fleeting movement and simply flowed calmly whenever she moved. Though very clever, Mary hadn't even the slightest inheritance of any coin that her wealthy family had in Scotland. Abandonment of the family crest, values and loyalty had resulted in expulsion.

"There has been a complication, where my apprenticeship is – or was – concerned," James stammered, nervously. He began to perspirate, fearing not his wife's fury or scolding, but her disappointment.

Mary raised her eyebrow even higher, and struggled with all of her might to hide a cheeky smirk at her husband's feverish discomfort.

"Arthur has, erm, had some financial difficulties in recent times, but we had secured a new contract with iron certainty." James fiddled with his hat as his palms began to moisten. "Only, the security of the contract wasn't quite… erm…"

"Iron?" Mary finished softly. James lifted his gaze and met Mary's, her attempts at hiding a smile collapsed and a grin began to spread across her beautiful face.

"I now find myself, regrettably, not quite…" James procrastinated.

"Employed?" Mary smiled. James gave a solemn nod and gave a sigh as he dropped his hat to the floor and flopped into his usual chair.

"Did you count the bells from the clock tower?" asked Mary as she sat herself neatly on the arm of the James's chair.

"Three, just as I approached the door," replied James, deflated, his head in his hands.

"The day isn't done, I'm sure that the next opportunity is right around the corner," smiled Mary, encouragingly. She always had the ability to see the best in a poor situation. Her smile faded slightly as she began to fidget with her wedding ring awkwardly.

"We're behind on the rent again."

James looked up at Mary suddenly.

"Did Jenkins come banging on the door in a drunken stupor again?" James asked, urgently. Mary nodded, gravely.

"I simply told him that you weren't home, it took some persuading to make him leave, but he did after a little bit of negotiation."

James clenched a fist as he shook in anger.

"Please don't get into any trouble James!" Mary pleaded, but it was too late. James had already snapped up his hat from the floor and left.

He stormed round to the public house, his fists clenched and eyes bulging in rage. Smashed glass, garbage and human waste littered the cobbled alleyways and entries. James didn't notice them anymore and stormed forward with only a single thought in mind, to find Jenkins. Whispering eyes followed him curiously as he approached the notorious drinking-hole of the town. The door of the public house swung open with a crash but no one appeared to notice. James slipped through the over-crowded public house, searching for Jenkins. The smell of stale ale and poor hygiene stung the nostrils of the unfamiliar, James continued on his blinkered search. Eventually, James sighted Jenkins sitting at a small table in a secluded nook, talking intensively to two young ladies for hire.

"And so, I killed the two thieves with my bare hands and got a pardon from the Crown, on a count of doing the country a service," Jenkins's beery voice boomed at the two women. His breath could have peeled the paint from the walls but they didn't seem to notice or chose to ignore the stench, a sign that business was slow and they were keen to get his.

"Such a big, strong man, and handsome too!" Clarabelle swooned at Jenkins, stroking his arm as she did so.

"I told you he was a hero, didn't I?" soothed Catherine, as she pondered him dreamily. A dangerous intuition flashed in both of their eyes, though Jenkins remained ignorant to their motive.

James watched on unnoticed by the occupied Jenkins as he considered his surroundings.

"Excuse me, where are the coat pegs?" James asked the landlady politely. She pointed a grubby, filthy finger to around the corner and shot him a scowl as she turned to continue cleaning a pitcher. He tipped his hat and searched quickly through the coats, found Jenkins's and ransacked the pockets with practiced hands. As he retrieved Jenkins's purse, he looked up and saw Clarabelle staring right at him. His heart skipped a beat as he panicked for a moment. She slowly raised her head and looked to expose James for his crime. James raised a finger to his lips. He took two coins from within the purse and placed them on the bar underneath a piece of paper, mouthing 'for you' to Clarabelle. She smiled and gave him a wink. With a sigh of relief, he wiped his brow and walked over to Jenkins.

"Jenkins, apologies for the rent being late, but here it is, with a tad extra for the inconvenience." He dropped the coins into Jenkins's hand and made to leave. A tug of his coat almost tipped him over, Jenkins had taken hold of him.

"I should think so! You are damned lucky I don't evict you and your peasant family for the trouble you cause me." Jenkins spat and slurred drunkenly. James clenched his fists once again and envisioned taking a swing for his fat jaw, but soon thought better of it.

"I understand, *sir,*" James replied, his words dripping in exaggerated sarcasm. Clarabelle sat back with a surprised expression. She had the sense that it would have escalated into violence and she was usually right about things like that. James tipped his hat to both of the ladies and winked at Clarabelle. On his way out, he stopped by the biggest, burliest shipyard docker in the entire establishment and approached him.

"Good evening," James began politely, his hat in his hands.

"Yeah?" he snapped, annoyed by James's interruption.

"A handsome man, such as yourself, could not possibly have been born from a brother and sister." James looked him up and down thoughtfully, as the man rose from his chair in an aggressive manner.

"A simpleton, are you? You dare to make such assumptions about me?" he shouted in a rage, his heavy body towering over James.

"Oh dear, not me, sir," James replied in exaggerated earnest. "Quite frankly, I have been informed that you are the product of an incestual relationship by two siblings from a man at the other end of the bar – the fat man called Jenkins." James pointed at Jenkins who had once again fallen into deep conversation with his company.

"Move!" roared the burly docker, and he charged over to Jenkins. James smiled to himself. As he reached the door, heavy commotion raged behind him, along with the unmistakable sound of a glass being smashed over someone's head. Probably Jenkins's...

James disappeared out of the public house and into the street to continue his search for employment. The rain poured heavily, prompting him to pull the collar of his dusty coat up around his ears. Knocking from door to door, it became apparent that most of the reputable companies weren't taking on any new employees. After some time, James dropped on to a bench and looked out onto the seafront. The shipyard always seemed busy, but without any prior fishing experience or the like, it would be a non-starter.

"Enjoying the weather, dear boy?" came a beery, raspy laugh. "Heavens, you have surely not dropped to my level of accommodation, or lack thereof?" Franky Fender, the local vagrant of the seafront came and sat by James. Never without a bottle in hand, his alcoholism had led him to the streets and there he had stayed. His matted and filthy overcoat draped over the side of the bench as he leaned to James with a rotten grin.

"Not quite, though I fear that I am not far behind," James sighed. "Work has dried up, it appears."

"Not at all, you're just looking in the wrong places," Franky retorted. "Spare me half a crown and I may be inclined to give you direction on where you can find employment."

"Franky, I know where there is work. But not work that suits me or my experiences. Legal ones, at least," said James dismissively, but still half interested in what Franky might know of.

"Considering your rudeness and disbelief in my knowing, better make it a half-crown AND a bottle of rum." Franky slurred drunkenly, his smile bearing all of the rotten teeth still remaining in his mouth.

"I appreciate the gesture, but I do not have half a crown to spare. If I had any rum, I would probably drink it in one and bury my sorrows, for a day," sighed James, leaning back.

"Well, if you're not interested in working for the King, Country and Crown, I better be on my way." Franky rose from his bench and went to leave as a hand tugged his coat.

"The Crown?" James repeated, his curiosity getting the better of him.

"The Crown," confirmed Franky, pulling his coat out of James's grip and making to leave. "You clearly don't have any interest; I will see you and yours in the street next to me, I suspect."

"A crown if your information leads to employment," James promised. "I give you, my word."

"A man, any man, every man… their word means nothing to me anymore," Franky laughed, taking a long pull from his bottle.

"What is yours worth?" James enquired, eagerly.

250

"Quite simply priceless," he retorted, almost offended at being questioned on his word.

"I will give you my wedding band, as collateral," James pleaded, holding out his tin wedding band. "It's not worth anything to anyone but me." Franky considered the ring with a suspicious eye, before looking through the ring at James.

"Consider it done. I want a crown if you are employed and I want a crown if you are not employed." Franky spat into his hand and held it to James, who repeated the ritualistic handshake, and they shook.

"The Royal Navy are taking applications, English only," Franky smiled. James sat himself back down in renewed deflation.

"I do not have the relevant experience to get work with the Royal Navy," he barked, angrily. He began to consider other methods of retrieving his wedding band from the vagrant that were less pleasurable.

"You don't need any. All hands are needed, they are heading out further over the horizon than ever before," Franky slurred, almost falling as he spoke.

"Then why don't you get work yourself?" James asked, suspiciously.

"Sea-sick," shrugged Franky before he burst into a fit of drunken laughter. James stared blankly, unsure of the validity in Franky's answer.

"Anyway," James continued, standing from the bench, "I will see you here tomorrow, a crown in either eventuality." With that, James made his way to the office of 'The New Royal Navy'.

James approached the office of 'The New Royal Navy'. As he touched the heavy door, his sodden shoes slipped on the marble floor, sending the door crashing wide open. The many faces that worked inside turned to see what had offended their ears on such a dismal day. James removed his hat and walked on with it pressed against his chest, apologising here and there awkwardly as he made his way forward.

"Do you have business here?" came a stern, militarian voice from behind the counter.

"No, sir, but I wish to." James gave a damp smile to the man behind counter, in awe of his immaculately-pressed uniform.

"No time for smart mouths or jokes here, boy," he retorted sharply, but without any personal prejudice. "So I ask, what is the nature of your visit?"

"Work, sir, a… well… friend, I suppose, informed me that 'The New Royal Navy' are offering employment." James replied as politely as he could, clasping his hat even tighter to his chest. One of the office employees gave a loud tut as she noticed the rather large puddle that had gathered underneath the impromptu visitor.

The man behind the desk sat back, pushing his spectacles further down his nose and looking James up and down.

"I have work available, but only as a loader for the ships. The pay is fair, but hard work it most certainly is."

James opened his mouth to reply, but the man behind the desk cut him off.

"No criminals, scum, troublemakers or thieves may apply. Your name will be run by the Crown and it is an offence to put forward an application with an attempt to hide any such conviction. Is that understood?"

James gave an earnest nod as the man slapped an application form onto the desk.

Part II

"Have you ever seen such a sad sight?" sneered Beaufort from the back of the office. He held his head high and nose even higher at all that were below him. He brushed imaginary dust from his tidy uniform as he watched James, well out of earshot.

"Indeed," Bamford sniggered. "I cannot bare the sight of such filth; does he dare apply for 'The New Royal Navy?' Bamford disagreed with all that did not agree with Beaufort, more out of fear than anything else.

"Sur… surely… he is not going to apply to be an officer?" spat Bum from between mouthfuls of pastry. His short, fat body wiggled and jiggled with glee at every mouthful. Beaufort examined his piggish resemblance in disgust.

"You fat idiot!" Beaufort shouted suddenly. "You've got pastry on my new uniform!" He raised a hand and slapped Bum across the face. Bum squealed in pig-like fashion and did so again as Bamford delivered another slap to his other side.

Beaufort, Bamford and Bum were, without any compromise, lucky. Their fathers, grandfathers and great-grandfathers had all been top-tier officers in the Navy and, as such, they found themselves Captains regardless of their capability. Though immaculate and intelligent (with the exception of Bum), they were hideously cruel to those beneath them. Sadly, that was most.

"That sopping tramp does not deserve even the lowest position in the Navy," Beaufort exclaimed, still wiping away the greasy pastry. "Bum, remove his application form when he departs," he ordered.

"You, you... d... do it," stammered Bum in weak protest. "I hold the same rank as you." Bamford backed away as Beaufort rounded on him.

"You malignant blob of faecal disappointment!" snorted Beaufort, his nose held high and his eyes closed. "My father put you in place as a favour to your family. I am certain he hates me, burdening me with your lumpy hide." His face reddened as he removed a silk glove and struck Bum with the back of his hand. Bum let out a squeal for the third time that hour and fell onto the writing desk. Weeping, he slid slowly down in a dramatic fashion.

"I heard your father drinks that much, he's forgotten how to write!" jeered Bamford, glancing at Beaufort for his approval.

"Wouldn't be a surprise," sneered Beaufort. He watched as James left the office. Narrowing his eyes, he summoned Bamford.

"Remove his application," he directed. Bamford didn't dare delay for even a moment and shot out. Bamford approached the desk and demanded the application form that the 'peasant' had just submitted. The man behind the desk looked at Bamford and frowned slightly, once again sliding his spectacles down his nose to get a better look at him.

"Captain Bamford... *sir*," he exaggerated, displeased at Bamford's presence. "That 'peasant' gave the best application out of all that have applied today. I would urge you to re-consider-"

"I am Captain Bamford of the King's Royal Navy!" snapped Bamford, his head held high and his eyes closed. The clerk rolled his eyes, but Bamford didn't notice.

"Hand me that man's application, or I will have no choice but to issue disciplinary action!" He raised an arm skyward with such force that a button popped from his collar and unravelled itself onto the floor. Beaufort shook his head as he watched Bamford from the back of the vast office. Bamford snatched the button from the floor and looked around. Everyone had stopped to watch him. He stared back, daring a single person to laugh at him, but no one did.

"*Sir*, Captain Bamford, *sir…*" he replied. "You should not get your beautiful hands dirty on a piece of paper that a mere peasant has handled. Allow me to unburden you and dispose of it for you, as per your orders."

A smug smile spread slowly across his face. Bamford gave a nod and walked away, stuffing his collar back on hastily.

James sat by the fire in an attempt to dry himself. He shivered and shook as he sat with his hands outstretched.

"Do you miss home?" asked James, staring into the fire. It crackled and popped merrily as the flames lit the room from corner to corner. Mary looked up from her book.

"Every day," replied Mary, softly. "Is there a reason for your questioning?"

James continued to ponder the flames of the fire and gave a heavy sigh.

"We have nothing, living in borderline poverty in this disease-ridden cesspit," James grumbled. "The grim scenery of Portsmouth does not compare to the rolling hills of the Highlands, the Grand Stag Manor or your family's heritage, to which you are no longer entitled. They are rich and could have given you anything you ever wanted." Mary smiled as she looked upon James in admiration.

"I can't help feeling as though you gave up everything for nothing," James continued, grumpily. Mary stood from her chair and stroked James softly on the face before gently kissing him on the cheek.

"I'll make us some tea," said Mary, encouragingly.

Charlie watched James and his family with the most extreme eagerness, careful not to miss a single detail. He reached out for James to touch him, but his hand went straight through.

"This is all wrong," thought Charlie out loud. He shook his head and covered his mouth with a hand. His stomach began to knot while he observed.

"How so?" asked Joan with interest. She pondered Charlie, much as James had pondered the fire.

"The Commodore thinks that he has nothing, but he has in fact…"

"Everything?" added Joan. Charlie looked at Joan, his eyes starting to fill. He nodded gravely.

"But Charlie, they have not a penny to call their own. You, come from a privileged family and have access to luxuries most will only dream of."

Charlie watched on, and once again shook his head.

"I would trade everything for what The Commodore has."

"Had," corrected Joan.

As dawn broke the night sky, two Navy officers made their way down the darkened road to the Marshall residence.

"Are you certain this is the place?" said the larger officer to the other.

"Quite," replied the other, impatiently. The large officer looked doubtfully around them. Smashed bottles and even a drunkard littered the depressing road. He turned back to the door and rapped so hard that even the previously unconscious drunken man opened a curious eye and looked for the source of his disturbance. James cursed and swore as he made his way to the door, hastily stuffing his shirt into his pants.

"What is the meaning of this racket?" he growled angrily as he opened the door. James looked from one officer to the other, rubbing his eyes as though they might be an illusion.

"James Marshall?" piped the smaller of the officers. James looked from one to the other again, his pulse increased slightly as his mind raced. Had he been informed on for stealing Jenkins's money, he wondered to himself. Jenkins knew a lot of people, but surely not anybody in the Navy.

"I am indeed James Marshall," he replied slowly. "Am I to be summoned for a crime?"

The smaller officer raised an eyebrow slightly, glancing to his colleague.

"I do not know the reason for your summoning, only that you are to be summoned," he replied impatiently. "Three minutes, or you will be taken in… whatever you call this… attire." He pointed with mild disgust.

"Very well." James slammed the door shut and prepared for the day as quickly as he could. The larger of the officers turned and noticed that the drunkard had risen unsteadily to his feet, considering them suspiciously.

"Keep your distance, citizen, or you'll end up face down without a hope of getting up again."

Without a word, he stumbled off as quickly as he could into the alleyway and out of sight.

After a short time, James came out and accompanied the silent naval officers to their headquarters.

They said nothing, but gave the occasional eyeroll and quiet click of the tongue in disappointment. As they arrived, the smaller of the officers pushed James inside.

"Sit down. Your name will be called. Do not move." With that, the officers left to continue their day.

James looked around the immaculate office that he had entered only the day before, only now there weren't many in attendance. Just some other solemn faces – although they all looked to be nervous, there was a distinct difference between them. The other nervous candidates all came from money. Expensive shoes, hats and outfits were in abundance, aside from James, whose clothes were tired and probably third hand before they found their way into his ownership.

By and by, the candidates became fewer and fewer as they were shouted forward.

"This mustn't be a criminal hearing," James thought to himself, becoming a bit more at ease. He could get up and leave, as there seemed to be nobody guarding the entrance. On that premise, he stayed put and waited to see how the situation would unfold.

"Marshall!" came a shrill voice. James rose and walked in to the small room where the summons had come from. He sat himself down at a broad oak desk littered with quills, ink and endless pieces of paper in a neat chaos. Three men sat behind the desk, none of whom seemed to acknowledge his presence at first. The spectacled man from yesterday sat among the trio.

"You have applied for the position of Naval Officer's Apprentice. A very prestigious role indeed. Especially for your… demographic," said a well-spoken officer from the desk. A poorly hidden sneer poured through his words.

"Sir, I think there has been some kind of-" James began, as the spectacled man gave a subtle shake of the head and rose a finger to his lips out of sight of the other two officers.

"You were saying?" spoke the third officer, looking up from his papers.

"Nothing, sir. My apologies, please continue," James replied quickly. His eyes darted to the spectacled man who smiled slightly and gave a subtle wink.

"This position has a high rate of failure. Tardiness, disobedience and anything short of total dedication to the crown will not be tolerated," spoke the third officer almost mechanically. It was clear he had spoken the same words time and time again.

"This programme is relatively new and still in the trial period, so there is a lot that could change at short notice. Do you have any criminal convictions, spent or otherwise? Please consider your answer carefully as if you do not answer truthfully, the punishment will certainly be incarceration."

"No, sir," replied James with certainty.

"Are you associated with or related to a convict?"

"I don't know, sir," James replied, pulling at his collar and nervously glancing sideways. "I was orphaned as a boy; I do not know of any blood relatives."

"A simple 'no' would have been fine," was the impatient response. "You are to complete a test to measure intellect and comprehension. There is a high rate of failure and only five percent achieve a pass, so do read it carefully." The officer held out a stack of papers and waved them impatiently. James took them clumsily, almost dropping them.

"Complete the test at a desk of your choosing in the main office. Do not sit within three seats of another candidate, or both of your tests will be void."

"Thank you, sir," James wheezed, struggling to keep up with what was happening. His head span as he tried to make sense of it all. He hadn't applied for a position such as this, and if he were found to be a fraud he could be in trouble. He wandered out into the main office and seated himself to complete the test. After a quick look, he got started.

"How did a man such as that come to apply for this position?" asked the third officer from inside the small office.

"This trial procurement of apprentice officers is new. There are no formal entry requirements, aside from background checks. The New Royal Navy is expanding at a healthy rate, and with the French and Spanish constantly at our heels, it seems to be a good way to procure talent," replied the spectacled man, coolly. The other two officers looked at each other and then to the spectacled man.

"There is a certain level of... majesty in the Royal Navy," replied the second officer. "Surely that must count for something?" The spectacled man carried on with his paperwork and gave an indifferent shrug as he left to return to the reception desk. He glanced over at James who had his head down and his quill shuffling at great speed. He smiled to himself as he sat down.

"Bloody toffs," he muttered, low enough for only himself to hear.

After completing the test, James made his way over to the spectacled man and handed in his paperwork.

"There has been some mistake!" James whispered earnestly to the spectacled man. The latter looked up from his paperwork and narrowed his eyes as he looked at James.

"A mistake?" he replied, clearly peeved by James's short-sightedness. "I would call it an opportunity, wouldn't you?"

James studied the man in the spectacles, almost expecting a punchline, a joke or a great reveal to this mysterious calling. James opened his mouth to reply, but no words came out.

"Better get yourself away. I will process your test. You will receive an answer by tomorrow at four o'clock if you have been successful. You are dismissed." He waved impatiently at James

"But-"

"Dismissed," snapped the spectacled man. James turned sharply and left as quickly as he could, still processing what had happened. The spectacled man smiled again as he watched James leave.

Charlie glanced sideways at Joan as he contemplated for a moment.

"Is there anything blessed in the Divine realm?" Charlie asked.

Joan gave a sneer and growled at the mere mention of anything related to Sanctuary.

"There is," Joan replied, shortly. "Lies, manipulation and restriction," she spat vehemently.

"Sounds like The Celestial Order, from what I've heard," replied Charlie, insightfully.

"At least they seek greatness and power, however flawed they are," Joan snapped, getting more annoyed.

A spring came to James's step as he began to feel the buzz of excitement. Could he really be accepted into the New Royal Navy? As an apprentice officer, at that? He smiled as he walked, barely noticing the ice cold wind that had picked up. He looked out at the ships that came in and out, by and by. They carried some men to the grave and others to victory. They were iconic and an essential staple in the British empire and the discovery of the new world. Excitement he had not felt in a long time began to buzz through him, an officer of the New Royal Navy, he repeated to himself time and time again. His family would be proud of him and he could finally feel worthy of them.

"This man looks to be a man who has found employment. The unemployed do not smile in such a manner," came a familiar beery voice.

"Not quite. I have submitted an application," replied James, unable to stop smiling. "I have a crown though, Franky." James dug a hand into his worn pocket and gave him the last coin he had to his name. As promised, Franky gave him the wedding band, albeit a little grubbier than it once was. James placed it upon his finger, feeling a little bit more complete.

"Do you ever look at the stars, Franky?" James asked, looking out across the sea.

"Often," replied Franky with a puzzled look upon his face. "Why do you enquire as to my frequenting of the night sky?"

"Some stars burn brighter than others, and on occasion we come across people that shine slightly brighter than others. They are special people, and we recognise them by the fact that they are utterly unforgettable. A lynchpin in our souls, the tide in our ocean, the pages in our books." James turned to Franky. "You are one of those people."

"I shine brighter than other people?" Franky asked, intrigued by James and his philosophical conversation.

"Well, maybe after a good wash."

Franky looked at James with a serious expression for a moment, and then burst into laughter. They both laughed together for what seemed an eternity.

"I owe you a bottle of rum," James noted as he walked on from Franky, who remained in a fit of laughter.

"The Commodore is a great man," Charlie admired.

"Good or bad, they are black and white, while greatness is an even shade of grey. Greatness is not biased to the good or bad intentions of an individual. Yes, The Commodore is certainly great," Joan replied, knowingly. A wicked smile teased the corners of her mouth and a dangerous light flickered in her eyes, but only for a moment.

After an eternity of waiting, a letter finally slid under the door. Henry dropped his book to the floor and raced to retrieve it. Mary clicked her tongue disapprovingly as she picked up the book and carefully ironed out the pages. Such books were expensive and hard to come by.

"A letter, mother!" Henry announced, grinning from ear to ear. "It's a special letter too." He ran a hand across the smooth creamy envelope and admired the handwritten name, *James Marshall*. Turning it over, he narrowed his eyes to view the wax seal in more detail. *By order of the New Royal Navy*. He gasped, as the importance of the letter began to dawn on him.

"Where is father?" he asked, his eyes almost bulging from their sockets.

"What's all of this commotion and skulduggery?" James asked as he walked in from the neighbouring room semi-dressed. Henry handed the letter to his father, rocking on his heels in excitement, waiting for him to open it. Mary folded her arms curiously and raised an eyebrow slightly, wondering what the contents would be. Her husband had failed to inform her of his recent application.

James considered the letter; his heart began to beat faster as he imagined the possibilities of its contents. Was it an approval for his application or a summons to court for his uninvited application of a majestic role? James broke the seal and read the letter. Henry had now escalated to jumping whilst tugging on his father's shirt to get a glimpse of the contents of the envelope.

"Well?" asked Henry, buzzing with excitement. "Father, what does it say? I fear I might die if you do not tell me what the special letter says!"

James looked down at Henry and sank into his chair, dropping the letter as he did so. A smile broke across his face as he beamed at his wife and son with pride, for himself – for the first time in a long time.

"I did it." He breathed, barely able to get his words out. "I did it!"

"What did you do?" asked Mary, falling victim to his contagious smile. "May I read the letter?"

"You certainly may," he spluttered as he scooped up the letter and handed it over. "I have been accepted as an apprentice officer for the New Royal Navy! A real salary, uniform and a career ahead of us. It will be hard work, but I shall give it all that I have."

Mary's smile faltered for a moment.

"You will surely be away from us for extended periods at a time," she explained calmly, not wanting to dampen his spirits.

"It will all work out. Imagine the life we are going to have!" James half-shouted, running his hands through his thick hair.

"Father, are you going to be a Captain?" Henry asked.

"Almost certainly!" James replied as excited as Henry, swinging his son into the air. "I'll be fighting pirates and savages, sailing the free world in the name of Britannia herself!"

Henry's eyes sparkled with delight as the most dangerous and exciting tales of adventure ran through his mind.

Joan placed a hand on Charlie's shoulder. He jumped slightly, so engrossed had he become in this living memory, he had forgotten his companion for a moment.

"Let me show you what greatness can be, and how quickly it can all be taken away," said Joan, keen to move away from this memory.

"The Commodore, he really had everything and didn't even know it," smiled Charlie, admiring the celebrations in their dingy home. The cracked and splintered walls around them signalled depression, hopelessness and failure. But in that moment, not a place in the world could have compared to the positive energy and light that emitted from the little family. It resonated across every wall with such purity and grace you could almost touch it.

Chapter Ten – The Crushing Depths

Part I

We preach to the veterans, don't we? "Oh man, you're home and safe. You're lucky!" we say. The truth is they aren't lucky at all. Most will never see a good night's sleep for as long as they live. Is that what we're going to call it? Living? The truth is, no veteran ever survived. They all fell in battle, even the ones that made it back. They can never retrieve what they left behind on the battlefield. What they saw cannot be unseen, cannot be unfelt, cannot be forgotten.

Vignis frowned heavily as he looked upon the mammoth steel monster, his hands firmly on his hips, rocking impatiently. Purple steam rolled out from underneath and atop the machine, it almost seemed as though the beast had woken from a deep slumber.

"What do you call this?" Vignis snapped, impatiently.

"It's a locomotive, sir," replied Ernst, nervously. He pulled feverishly at the filthy collar of his dirty overalls as his eyes did their best to avoid Vignis's burning gaze. Ernst had been recruited only a few weeks ago to pull together an entire transport infrastructure. He enjoyed a mostly quiet life as an educated goblin and did his best to avoid any government interference. As this request had come from Vignis himself, it would not have been wise to decline.

"And?" snapped Vignis, growing more impatient by the second. "What does the bloody thing do?"

"It enables travel, along the railroad that we are in the process of completing to other areas of the Divine world." Ernst tripped over his words as he spoke, whilst wiping his clammy hands on his overalls. "From Velmar to Karis and all the major cities in between."

"It does not require water or coal as you would require on a standard locomotive from the Blind world," he continued.

Vignis turned sharply to Ernst at the mere mention of the Blind.

"You have brought a primitive contraption from the Blind world to our serene and Divine lands?" he asked in a sharp, dangerous tone. It would most certainly have been the end of him if he concurred.

"No sir, we have taken a design from that world and improved it beyond measure. The simple Blindlings could not possibly have created a machine as fine as this. It has even been enchanted to travel without a driver when required," he explained, almost pleading as he did so. "At one hundred miles per hour, it has the ability to split through the Blind world undetected, reaching destinations across the Divine realm in only minutes.

Vignis's eyes flickered over to his bodyguards and a rather bored-looking Maybelle. She looked upon the locomotive unimpressed with her arms folded, hovering indifferently.

"It's faster than any form of teleportation and offers group travel, rather than individual travel," Ernst added, desperately. He noticed Vignis's glance and considered all of the rumours that had gone around as to the many different torture methods The Celestial Order were experts in.

Vignis considered the vast locomotive and its fine hand-crafted coaches once more with a raised eyebrow.

"How long until the railroad is finished?" he asked directly, not taking his gaze away from the locomotive.

"Two months," Ernst lied, confidently. It would take at least twice that, but it might just save him on this occasion.

"That's too long, I want it completed in half of that at the most," he ordered as he turned to leave. Ernst stifled a sigh of relief when Vignis turned to look at him once more. Their eyes met awkwardly and his entire life began to flash before his eyes as he thought, 'This is it, I'm done,' over and over again.

"What do you call this 'locomotive'?" Vignis asked, slowly. Ernst thought his heart might explode; he hadn't even thought of a name. "Well? I haven't got all day!"

"The Celestial Flight," Ernst blurted, feeling momentarily impressed he'd managed to think of the name in such a short time. Vignis looked from Ernst to the train and gave a brief nod of approval. After Vignis and his company had left, his knees gave way and he held on to the locomotive for support.

"Damn the day that I agreed to do this project. Surely Oblivion would be easier to deal with," he mumbled to himself, finally getting stability over his legs.

The familiar blinding light stung Charlie's eyes as he and Joan moved to a different segment of the memory. Watery details assembled and clarified together. Charlie glanced up at Joan for a moment. She seemed different. She was smiling intently, deliberately, thirstily. With her new-found engagement she looked around, soaking in every tiny detail down to the very atmosphere itself. Charlie looked away feeling slightly uneasy.

"You will see, boy, that greatness is not bound by binary choices or mere intent. It is as grey as the very clouds that surround us." Her voice rattled with anticipation at what would be told. A dull anxiety filled the very air around them. That which Charlie found unsettling seemed to be fuelling Joan.

"I'm not sure that I wish to see-" Charlie started.

"You do not have a choice!" she laughed, darkly "We will return when I say so. Knowledge is what you sought, isn't it!?"

Charlie felt a void in his stomach as his eyes teased his face with tears. He quickly moved them away and focused on his surroundings.

The wind blew wildly around them, pushing the thick, dark clouds overhead into what would doubtlessly become a storm. The crew of the ship busied themselves on the orders of the officers, altering the vast sails to better take advantage of the wind. They rattled and whipped as the sea crashed angrily against the side of the ship, rising and falling with the waves in a rhythmic motion.

"Sir, we should drop the sails and move with the tide. These are dangerous waters even without the bad weather!" shouted a sailor as he shielded his eyes from the wind and ocean spray.

"Commodore Marshall has taken command of HMS Fury; his orders are to proceed as fast as the winds can carry us," Lieutenant Dalton shouted in return; he held his tricorne hat down on his head as it tried to escape into the wind.

"This is madness!" yelled the sailor after a moment's contemplation. His eyes filled with fear of what may come.

"Yes, it is, but Commodore Marshall isn't known for his orthodoxy. Don't let the Captain or Commodore hear you talking that way, it may be taken as mutiny!" Dalton warned.

Elias Dalton had attended the same officer school as Commodore Marshall and knew him very well. They often played cards together when the other crewmen had retired for the evening. It wasn't good to show favour to a lower ranking officer in front of the other officers, it could be interpreted as weakness.

A huge wave crashed into the side of the ship, forcing Lieutenant Dalton to take hold of the barrier with both hands, which allowed his hat to escape into the wind.

"Damn and blast!" he cursed, shaking his fist at the sky. The sailor laughed hysterically, pointing at his hat as it flew into the distance.

"Get me another hat!" Lieutenant Dalton barked at the sailor. His laughter disappeared as quickly as it had arrived.

"But… but what if there aren't any?" he replied, scratching his head nervously.

"Then bloody well make one, you fool!" Lieutenant Dalton snapped.

Without another moment's hesitation, the sailor bolted down into the depths of the ship away from the deck, hoping that Lieutenant Dalton would fall overboard.

Dalton looked around as the crew became agitated, a crew that talked under their breath could be dangerous. Hushed voices and accusing eyes were plenty amongst them.

"I heard that he's a madman," muttered a gunman to the cook. They stood under the eaves of the door to the Captain's quarters, trying unsuccessfully to avoid the rain as it descended in torrents, growing heavier by the minute.

"We are in uncharted waters, in bad weather with very few supplies remaining. He is, without doubt, a madman." The cook agreed, rubbing his hands together in an attempt to warm them.

Dalton made his way towards the Captain's quarters briskly, cursing the weather for stealing his hat. The gunman and the cook looked at each other for a moment and then to the approaching Lieutenant.

"Surely he didn't hear us from all the way over there," the gunman whispered desperately. The cook didn't reply, but turned a sickly shade of white as Dalton approached.

"What on earth are you two doing?" he barked, angrily. Their mouths opened but not a sound came out. "Wittering the day away like a pair of old housewives!"

The gunman opened his mouth again and raised a weak finger to the cook who began to turn another shade of white.

"Get on with your work, or I'll have you both on a charge!" he snapped finally, slamming the door to the

Captain's quarters behind him. He shook his head as he wrung some of the rain from his royal blue coat. They had been at sea for a long time without any stoppage for supplies or trade. The reasons as to why they sailed for so long were hazy and changed each week without rhyme or reason. Dalton made his way through the heavier doors after a sufficient wringing and found himself presented by a rather annoyed-looking Commodore Marshall and Captain Blunt.

"Good evening, sir," Dalton saluted, half-heartedly.

"Anything to report?" The Commodore asked, a little bit more formally than usual. He glanced sideways at Captain Blunt before raising a suggestive eyebrow at Dalton.

"Yes sir, I need to report on my inspection of the crew's uniforms as you requested earlier today," he lied coolly. He stood straight and looked past The Commodore in proper military fashion.

Captain Blunt looked from Dalton to The Commodore curiously, scratching at his weeks' worth of white stubble.

"Yes, 'Commodore'," he started, his words dripping with an aristocratic air. "If you don't mind, I will retire to my quarters and leave you to your duties."

Captain Blunt never referred to The Commodore as 'sir,' even though he held a superior rank. In actual fact, he found it ridiculous that a young man could have acquired such prestige without any well-placed connections or internal referral. That said, he knew better than to make enemies of superiors.

"Very well, Captain," he replied, giving a brief nod. Captain Blunt gathered his belongings and gave Dalton a sneering look before leaving. As the door closed behind him, The Commodore leaned back into his chair and gave a sigh of relief.

"I thought he would never leave!" he slurred slightly. Dalton looked closer and noticed that The Commodore's eyes were glassy and blood-shot. Dalton pretended not to notice as he seated himself. The table had become a mess of maps, star charts, calculations and counter calculations, with notes scribbled in hasty handwriting.

"Cards?" Dalton yawned as he stretched. The Commodore gave a nod as he emptied the contents of his teacup in one go, before topping it up to the brim with rum. Dalton pretended not to notice and refused an outstretched bottle from The Commodore.

The pair played for several hours, mostly in silence, as The Commodore became more and more intoxicated. The ship groaned and creaked as it rode the waves of the storm. Occasionally, distressed voices could be heard from the decks, but The Commodore and Lieutenant Dalton ignored them.

"There's a lot of... unrest... on the ship, James," said Dalton slowly, without lifting his eyes from the cards.

"Is that so?" he replied uninterested, his tongue poking from the corner of his mouth as he squinted at the cards. "It had better be an impressive mutiny, they know the consequences of treason if they fail."

Dalton looked upon The Commodore in stunned silence for a moment, waiting for some kind of reaction. As none came, he slapped his cards on the table.

"How can you be so obtuse?" Dalton snapped, forgetting momentarily his rank aboard HMS Fury.

"Well I can see your bloody cards now!" shouted the drunken Commodore. "Ruined the game you have. I hope you're happy, Dalton!"

"You could end up with a mutiny, James!" Dalton barked in return.

"I run my ships my way," The Commodore said, carelessly waiving Dalton's comments.

"Ships? You mean 'Ship.' We lost HMS Saint and HMS Lorde. No one knows where they are," Dalton explained as you would to a simpleton. The Commodore stared with a stupid expression at Dalton, slowly registering the information.

"They are in formation!" he shouted. The Commodore stumbled to the window at the rear of the ship and cupped his hands to the glass to see better.

"I saw them only an hour ago!" The Commodore snapped; his face glued to the window panes.

"We lost them three days ago," Dalton spat furiously through gritted teeth. The Commodore kept his face to the window panes, straining his bloodshot eyes, hoping for them to appear.

A wave crashed into the side of their ship with such ferocity that they both lost their footing and fell onto the mahogany furniture.

"Drop the sails, for goodness sake… drop the sails!" wheezed Dalton, trying to gather his breath. The Commodore searched frantically on hands and knees for his bottle of rum, muttering and cursing as he did so. Dalton remained where he was for a moment to see if the ocean would follow up on the previous assault.

Charlie hadn't spoken a word in a considerable amount of time. He watched intently as The Commodore scrambled around the Captain's quarters without a care for anything else.

"Quite a sight, isn't it?" sneered Joan as she watched on. "The Commodore, at the bottom of a bottle without a hope in the world." She rubbed her hands together as a wicked smile curled in the corner of her mouth.

"I cannot understand why anyone – or anything – would take joy in the sorrows of another," snapped Charlie, breaking his silence. He clenched a fist as his temper rose.

"Such a linear and single-sighted attitude, especially for one destined for greatness!" Joan scolded as one would a belligerent child. She seemed to be enjoying his dishevelment somewhat as she smirked and laughed to herself.

"There's a letter on the floor over there," Joan pointed, her smirk remaining firmly in place. "It might give you some, insight."

Charlie narrowed his eyes suspiciously at Joan but, as usual, curiosity had got the better of him. The yellow paper shone beautifully in the candlelight, doubtlessly the finest quality of the time. The handwriting almost felt taboo to look upon with its breathtaking cursive perfection.

Commodore Marshall,

It is with great regret and the sincerest of condolences that I write this letter, but it would simply be improper to allow you to return to the Empire before hearing the news.

It has been reported that your family home on the edge of Oxfordshire has been subject to a robbery in the middle of the night on the 22ⁿᵈ of August. Your wife and son sadly passed away at the hands of those responsible for the intentional trespassing. Although it doubtlessly offers no comfort, the reports indicate they were killed instantly and were not subject to any additional abuse as these criminals are often capable of afflicting.

You are granted a month's leave upon return to England to be spent however you choose. I would recommend seeking an audience with your village priest for comfort and to give you the time to mourn this tragic loss.

It is not often that I write these letters; they are often to the families of our honourable officers and of standard form. I know these words are probably fruitless and empty in light

*of any consolation – all the same, I would like to thank you
on behalf of myself and The British Empire for the sacrifice
you have personally made by conducting impressive and
effective service to The New Royal Navy.*

*I have sent three identical letters to ensure a timely receipt
and to set your expectations on your return.*

*As the youngest Commodore ever to sail under the flag of
Britannia, I would also like to remind you of the incredible
progress you have made in the five years of your service.
You have achieved much, but there is more to be done.*

*I look forward to meeting you after your leave for a briefing
of this year's expeditions across charted waters.*

Sincerest regards,

Admiral A. Foresythe

Charlie looked from the letter to The Commodore, who now
sat drinking from his bottle as though nothing else mattered.
Dalton rose to his feet unsteadily and adjusted his uniform.

"Why do you bother with that thing?" slurred The Commodore as he pointed a wobbly finger at Dalton's wig. He laughed drunkenly as Dalton shot him a scowl and threw the wig at The Commodore.

"He seems to be taking this news rather badly," Charlie observed, worriedly.

"That is putting it mildly," Joan added. "But, from sadness, sorrow and anger can come incredible passion, direction and great achievements." Her excitement began to return, similar to a child on Christmas Eve.

The door crashed open as a gunman came stumbling into the quarters. He lost his footing and fell into the mahogany desk. A sickening crack echoed as blood and teeth scattered across the floor.

"Sir!" the gunman spluttered through a mixture of blood and broken teeth, "a ship with black sails has been sighted!" His eyes were wide as he trembled in fear. The Commodore did not raise even an eyebrow, he simply looked to Dalton.

"Go and confirm this report, Dalton, I am sure it is merely an illusion of the ocean." He shrugged indifferently. "We have all worked hard these past few weeks – the tide does strange things to a fatigued man."

Dalton scowled at The Commodore, momentarily forgetting his duty as Lieutenant, and opened his mouth to retaliate. His eyes glanced to the gunman who stood staring at Dalton, almost totally unaware of his own mangled mouth.

"Yes sir," he blurted and turned on a heel to leave.

The weather had taken a turn for the worse, rain descended from the heavens in sheets, stirring the ocean into colossal waves that roared and crashed into the ship. Dalton made his way through the chaos that reigned across the decks. The crew panicked, shouting and pointing into the darkness.

"Front and centre!" Dalton roared into the rain. Only a few of the crew heard him, but that was enough – when they stood to attention the rest followed. Soldiers, officers and sailors fell in. Rain poured down their necks as they shivered, frozen to the bone, though none of them noticed. All attention fell upon Dalton.

"Where has this ship been sighted?" he bellowed.

"Starboard side, 45 degrees north by north east," a keen young sailor shouted. His immaculate uniform contrasted against those of his filthy colleagues. He trembled more than the others and had turned a shade of green. Dalton gave a brief nod and made his way to the starboard side where he looked across the raging ocean, straining his eyes to catch a glimpse of the ship with black sails. He scanned the horizon for a couple of minutes and almost resigned before catching sight of the ship in the distance. His heart skipped several beats as adrenaline began to surge through his veins. He remembered his training and did his best to stifle the fear and remain calm. The crew were wise and saw through his attempts to shroud his reaction.

"Piracy as well we all know is coming to an end. Its day is done and they know better than to cross swords with the British Empire," he stated loudly, his voice cracking once or twice as the colour drained from him. It was true that piracy had been on the decline over the past few decades but they were savages, capable of the most heinous acts that were unthinkable to most.

"My advice to The Commodore will be to let it pass. We have our own mission that does not include any skirmishes with pirates." He tried to come across as calm as possible.

"Oh yeah? What mission is that?" came a disgruntled voice from the back of the crew.

"The one where you follow orders without question – or face the consequences!" Dalton roared back at the crew; his eyes darted across the many faces as he looked for the offending individual.

"We're sick of following that madman! Commodore Marshall has led us from bad to worse. Starved, unwashed and unpaid, we have followed orders. For what?" came the voice. Dalton scanned the faces of those at attention and noted how many of them seemed unmoved by the speaker, which meant they agreed.

"You will do as you are ordered, or face the consequences. Let it be known that you have been warned. TO STATIONS!" he roared finally, and marched back to the Captain's quarters. As he entered, he noticed The Commodore picking up the gunman's teeth and handing them over to him, talking casually about the advances of dental work in the modern era.

"You are dismissed," Dalton snapped to the gunman. He looked from Dalton to The Commodore, hesitating. He hadn't found all of his teeth yet.

"Have you taken leave of your senses, man? Off you go, report to your station!" Dalton shouted, red-faced.

"I don't think you had to speak to him like that!" slurred The Commodore as the gunman left. He had clearly continued drinking since Dalton had last been in the quarters. He scowled at The Commodore once again.

"There is a ship with black sails, sir." The Commodore sobered almost instantly. His eyes widened and his pupils dilated as a wicked smile split the corner of his mouth.

"Piracy has been declining for decades; we can avoid conflict if we adjust our course slightly," Dalton continued.

"Shut up Dalton," came a severe growl from The Commodore as he collected his effects and straightened his uniform. "You will do as you are ordered and nothing more. They will regret the day they crossed The Commodore." A crazed look flashed through his eyes for a moment.

"Sir, I beg you to reconsider," Dalton pleaded.

"Another word and you will face court martial," barked The Commodore as he made his way out on to the deck. Some of the crew turned in surprise – many of them hadn't seen The Commodore in days, they had only heard rumours of drunkenness and cruelty.

"Guns ready starboard side, set the sails to catch that ship!" he yelled across the deck. "All hands to weapons and be ready to engage the enemy!"

The many tired faces of the crew hesitated for a moment, their eyes just as bloodshot and sleep-deprived as The Commodore's.

"Do I need to repeat myself?!" He bellowed.

At once they began to run from station to station, in and out of the hull and into the breach, preparing small arms and the cannons. Dalton stood the regulatory distance behind The Commodore, hiding his trembling hand behind his back. Whenever they were approaching an enemy his hand shook violently, a side effect of adrenaline as it took hold of him.

"All crew to me, ignore this drunkard and his rogue agenda!" a voice shouted from the helm. The Commodore turned around to see who dared counter a superior's order. Captain Blunt stood in full battle uniform at the helm with a serious expression. He made his way down to the raging Commodore as he stood, fists clenched, outraged at the sheer audacity of the geriatric officer. It only took one or two of the crewmembers to stop and take attention for the rest to follow shortly after. Silence fell across them and nothing but the roar of the ocean, beat of the rain and groaning of the ship could be heard.

"You dare to counter my order, Blunt?" sneered The Commodore, jabbing Blunt in the chest with a pointed finger. "Arrest this man and take him to the stocks!" The Commodore shouted over his shoulder, but no one moved. They stood, watching, waiting for the outcome. They had discussed mutiny between them several times recently, but no one dared move one way or the other. Eyes shifted between each other as some examined their boots and others their hands.

"You will find that you are no longer in control here, *'Commodore',*" Blunt explained through his aristocratic naval cavity. "Your crew have had enough of you and your fickle orders. It is safer for us to avoid piracy as we are not equipped for battle. I am hereby commandeering this ship, and you will be taken into custody." He closed his eyes and raised his nose above The Commodore as his type often did.

The Commodore looked out across the crew without a word. Dalton kept his regulatory distance from him and rested an uneasy hand on the grip of his pistol. He knew that Blunt was right but he had settled on the side of The Commodore, irrespective of the outcome. Dalton could never sail under the command of Blunt at any rate. He watched The Commodore wondering what step he would take next. The crew remained deadly silent – they had moved their gaze from their shoes to The Commodore, staring hard at him. His time had come. He felt in his chest that control of the situation was slipping from his grasp with every timed beat of each individual raindrop.

Charlie looked on at the spectacle, his breath held in suspense of what would come. Joan, meanwhile, rocked on her heels and rapped a hand against her leg, apparently unable to stay still from anticipation of what would be.

Part II

"The Commodore, what can he do?" Charlie whispered desperately, and rather pointlessly. Joan did not answer but seemed to be annoyed by the interruption of her entertainment. A swift nod towards The Commodore was enough for Charlie to take the hint and keep quiet. He raised his hands nervously to his mouth as what seemed to be an eternity passed.

The Commodore looked from Dalton to the rest of the crew, nodding with a submissive expression. As he turned, his hand flew to his holster – he drew his pistol, snapped back the hammer and took aim at Blunt. He hesitated for a moment as Dalton's mouth dropped in horror. He knew that The Commodore would need to do something radical but not this. A single shot echoed across the ocean. Dalton jumped and fell over in surprise as the crew recoiled and some younger colleagues screamed. Blunt swayed for a moment, clutching his face before dropping to his knees. He gargled as the blood spilled heavily into the streams of rainwater across the deck and he fell forward as

dead as the very masonry on which they stood. Smoke
licked and teased the end of the gun's barrel; The
Commodore let a slight sigh of relief escape. It could easily
have misfired or not fired at all due to the heavy rainfall.

"Let this be a lesson to anyone else that thinks it
wise to oppose an officer and consider mutiny for even a
moment!" The Commodore shouted angrily at the crew. His
eyes bulged as he raged. He had lost all control of his
emotions and the crazy look in his eyes remained, unmoved,
revealing. The madness had taken him and there was
nothing that could be done – The Commodore felt
invincible.

"Throw this coward's body overboard and set the
sails – chase that ship! I want their Captain alive and the
rest thrown to the depths!" he yelled to the crew. Without a
second's hesitation, they jumped into action and ran to their
stations, taking their orders as though their lives depended
on them. From what they saw, they probably did. Dalton
took a step or two back from The Commodore. This man
was a friend, comrade and colleague, but now there stood a
stranger in his place. He didn't dare approach him, and
instead continued with his duties, taking special care to
make sure that all of the weapons were loaded and battle-
ready.

The Commodore stood on the bow, breathing deeply as his teeth ground together in raw fury. His eyes were wide and accusing, electric almost. He searched for the ship, hoping with every fibre of his being that it would appear in the distance. HMS Fury was reputed to be one of the quickest vessels in the entire British Navy and had been built with this purpose in mind. The rain came down even heavier, spoiling his view through the brass spyglass. Unmoving, he remained with it welded to his eye.

His thoughts wandered to his wife and son. Anger and rage surged even harder through his veins, pulsing and beating with adrenaline. What had they done to deserve such behaviour? Life is nothing more than an accident, we are not special, just lucky to grace the Earth with our presence. There is no God – what God would allow such atrocities to occur to those that are so undeserving? If there is a god or higher being, they must be held to account for their part in the inaction that allowed his family to suffer.

He tried to remember them – their faces, their voices and even their scents, but he only conjured faces contorted in agonising pain as he imagined their demise. His heart sank and twisted painfully as a tear ran down his face, hidden by the rain and the ocean spray. What did it matter if they pursued the enemy vessel or not? An empty void grew inside his chest as he felt that nothing really mattered anymore.

He dropped the spyglass to the floor and fell on to the side of the bow, he considered the different meanings and interpretations of 'inevitable' as he stared hard at the stunning craftsmanship that was HMS Fury. He thought about his time as a carpenter's apprentice – the smell of the sawdust, the hammering and sawing. All that remained was principle, he thought to himself. The principle of knowing what you are and your duty, should it apply. It comforted him slightly to understand he had at least the Royal Navy and his duty of service.

After some time, The Commodore rose to his feet and collected his spyglass. He turned to head towards the Captain's quarters when he decided to have a final look through the spyglass. Just as he concluded that nothing would appear in the distance, his heart gave a leap as he saw a flag fluttering manically in the stormy weather. He only just made it out, but there it was.

The filth, treachery and villainy of those that conformed to piracy sickened The Commodore far more than most. Stealing from those that have little, taking what you can and giving nothing back to the people.

A broad smile split across his menacing face as he bolted for the helm.

"Dalton, to the helm with me!" he shouted as he ran.

Another look through the spyglass and he adjusted their course slightly, grinning crazily as he did so.

"Sir?" came Dalton, formally addressing the terrifying superior.

"Look, there they are, the filthy dogs!" he pointed, hopping in sheer excitement. "They are not far away and surely cannot match HMS Fury for outright speed behind the wind!"

He thrust the spyglass under Dalton's nose for him to look for himself. Dalton said nothing as he felt his heart sink – the black sail could clearly be seen from the ship ahead of them.

"That looks to be a rather large ship," Dalton considered, slowly. "I wonder where they managed to get that from?"

"It won't be very large when we have finished with it," The Commodore cackled, rubbing his hands together.

"I think The Commodore has lost his mind," Charlie mumbled to nobody in particular.

"Oh, come now," jeered Joan. "He has found his full potential! All of that power and dedication, you would be a fool not to admire that!"

Charlie shook his head disapprovingly as they watched on.

"We are not to capture their ship or take any prisoners. They are to sink to the depths, aside from their Captain. I have special plans for him…" The Commodore ordered. "Oh, and my dear Dalton. You have been promoted for this voyage to Captain."

Dalton looked from The Commodore to the ship in the distance. His shoulders fell and he turned a regretful face to The Commodore.

"I decline the promotion; I am a Lieutenant of the Royal Navy and had been appointed before our voyage. I will not be party to your personal crusade of piracy. However, I will follow your orders because that is what I am positioned to do," Dalton spoke as a matter of fact, in perfect form. The Commodore considered him for a moment with a raised eyebrow.

"Fetch me some rum, Lieutenant. I think I left some in the Captain's quarters." He sneered disrespectfully, waving him away as he spoke.

Dalton fulfilled his orders and made his way onto the hull of the ship. The crew looked uneasy as they whispered frantically between each other. They suddenly fell silent as Dalton entered, standing to attention in true Naval fashion.

"Are the guns ready to engage the enemy?" he asked informally as he unbuttoned his collar and untucked his shirt.

"Aye, sir!" they shouted in unison. Dalton gave a nod of approval and opened a bottle of whiskey that he had been hiding in his personal quarters for the entire voyage. It had been reserved for special occasions, and he had decided that this occasion warranted the consumption of the treasured alcohol. He looked around at the curious faces and took a long pull from the bottle before passing it to his nearest colleague, a rather nervous-looking soldier, a little older than was usual.

"Take a drink and pass it to the next man, make sure each has a taste. It's incredibly good quality and very expensive." Dalton held the bottle out to the man who looked bewildered and slightly frightened by his unorthodox and improper behaviour.

"Take the bottle or you'll wear it, man!" he snapped, shaking the bottle angrily. Without a second's delay, the solider took the bottle, greeted it with his lips and passed it to the next man. Dalton groaned as he sat on a pile of cannonballs and inspected his pistol. He cleaned the barrel, cocked it and replaced it, confident that it would not let him down in his time of need.

The voices from the top deck grew louder and more frantic. Dalton looked from the starboard side porthole and gasped as he saw the size of the enemy ship. It sailed at a third larger than HMS Fury and doubtlessly had a larger crew aboard. He noticed a faded emblem on the rear, he strained his eyes to see what they had attempted to remove. He made out 'East India Trading Company'. He recoiled slightly as his head began to spin – how had they managed to steal a ship from the 'East India Trading Company'? he thought to himself.

Dalton made his way back up to The Commodore, considering their enemy as he did so.

"They have stolen that ship from the 'East India Trading Company'," Dalton explained formally to The Commodore, who looked as though he might explode with excitement.

"So what? Are they going to battle us with stolen herbs and spices?" he laughed mockingly.

"The 'East India Trading Company' are usually heavily armed; we are carrying only forty percent capacity of ammunition and powder," Dalton reeled out, almost robotically. The Commodore didn't seem to hear him or the devastating news, his eyes were fixed on the enemy ship whose crew looked rather unimpressed by HMS Fury.

The storm beat down upon the two vessels with renewed vigour. Hammering and howling, the wind teased the sails as they whipped and snapped angrily. Both crews stood by, awaiting their orders.

Charlie stared open-mouthed at the stolen vessel; it was larger than HMS Fury by quite a margin. The damned crew looked down upon The Commodore and his crew with haggard and scarred faces, their clothes filthy, weapons in hand. Their swords were drawn and pistols stuffed hastily into the front of their belts, ready to engage yet another enemy with fearless brutality. Dalton looked sideways at The Commodore and then back to the stolen ship. The Captain of the enemy ship joined his crew and looked upon HMS Fury. His eyes scanned his enemy for The Commodore. As they landed upon him, his face contorted into what was meant to be a smile. He removed his hat and curtsied before bursting into a beery laugh.

"They do not wish to engage us," Dalton explained almost desperately, his hand trembling worse than ever. "We could sail straight past-"

"Dalton," The Commodore snapped. "We have a duty to king and country. They are thieves, murderers and plunderers. They must be dealt with!" His bloodshot eyes met with his enemy's. For a moment, it seemed as though they had an understanding. The Commodore pulled his sword from his side and gripped it tightly.

"All men to battle stations! Man the cannons and prepare the ammunition! Dalton, with me," he bellowed.

The enemy ship became a flurry of action just as quickly, running to prepare for the battle with HMS Fury. The pirate captain shook his head disapprovingly before he himself barked orders to the condemned crew.

Charlie looked on in horror, unable to take his eyes away from what was happening.

"They are outnumbered, outgunned and there's a storm," said Charlie, helplessly.

"We will see what your 'precious' Commodore has planned for his enemy," snorted Joan as she folded her arms.

Charlie shuddered at her words as they pierced his concentration on the unfolding events.

"The Commodore... he will win. He... must win," Charlie whispered, mostly to himself.

The enemy ship fired the first shots from their cannons. Most of them fell short, a clear sign that they were unfamiliar with their equipment. The Commodore stood by his gunners, waiting for the prime moment to fire into the storm. Dalton stood by, unusually calm and collected. His face remained expressionless as he stared past The Commodore, wrapped in his own thoughts.

As the storm raged on, the ships rose and fell in the harsh waves, which groaned and crashed against them. The crew waited eagerly for instructions, their anxiety increasing by the very second as they waited for the order to fire at their enemy. The Commodore kept waiting. A new salvo of cannon-fire crashed into the side of HMS Fury, killing and maiming some of the gunners as masonry and metal exploded into splintered fragments of shrapnel. The Commodore didn't take any notice and instead waited.

"Fire!" roared Dalton suddenly from aside him. Each cannon roared as a tongue of flame spat from the barrel and launched the heavy cannonballs at their enemy. Almost all of them hit the enemy ship with devastating effect.

"Load the guns!" he roared again. "Use the light ammunition – leave the heavy ones until they are closer to us!"

The Commodore puffed out his chest and opened his mouth, ready to shower Dalton in abuse for his insubordination.

"Fire!" roared Dalton in full swing, his pistol drawn as the enemy ship drew closer through the storm.

"Load the heavy ammunition!" he bellowed as they came closer. Seconds later they received a renewed battering from the enemy guns. Dalton dropped to the floor and screwed his eyes against the rain and ocean spray that intruded.

The Commodore looked out at their enemy as they drew closer – heavy damage had been inflicted on both vessels. The ships crashed against the waves as the storm grew heavier and angrier than ever before. He looked at Dalton as he scrambled to his feet and ran to the top deck. The crew ran in all directions, firing small arms at the enemy without success. He drew his sword and hacked away at one of the ropes securing the starboard mast. It snapped and sprung away, taking the mast with it as the ship groaned and leaned almost at a perfect 45-degree angle. Another salvo from the enemy ship crashed into the faltering HMS Fury with a deafening roar. The Commodore slipped and fell down the stairs into the hull, hitting his head as he did so.

He stirred and opened his eyes to see that almost all of the cannons had been destroyed and most of his gunners were dead. Dalton sat perfectly straight in one of the chairs, oblivious to the carnage that surrounded them.

"There are no more gunners to command, sir," Dalton shrugged as a matter of fact. The Commodore looked at him. He had become perfectly sober. How long had he been at battle? An hour, six hours? He couldn't remember. He pulled off his ruined coat and ran to the nearest cannon, loading and firing as fast as he could. A dying gunner lay by his side, holding his wounded midriff tightly and breathing heavily.

"We should have thrown you overboard!" he wheezed as the life slowly drained from him. The Commodore glanced over; the gunner couldn't have been older than eighteen at the most. The Commodore fired a final shot downward towards the enemy running gear in an attempt to disable the enemy ship, but failed miserably. Abandoning the cannon, he made his way back to the top deck.

The enemy had boarded the ruined HMS Fury and engaged his crew in a brutal skirmish. They fought savagely as screams and shouts could be heard alongside the cracking of small arms fire. The Captain of the stolen vessel simply looked on, confident of victory. The Commodore drew his sword and fought the savages alongside his crew. A giant of a man took hold of him by the coat and threw him to the ground. He raised a giant axe and began to bring it down, as The Commodore fired a shot from his pistol into his enemy's face. The man roared and bellowed in agony as he flailed his arms before finally crashing forward upon the deck, lifeless.

The skirmish continued as The Commodore fought with all his might against the wretched enemy. Seconds became minutes, as minutes became hours – how long they fought for, he wasn't sure.

Dalton fired a shot from his musket, which missed as his opponent descended upon him. A cold blade sank into his chest, forcing a searing pain throughout his body. He screamed as he fell, his mind racing as he lay shivering. The cold rain washed his hot blood away from him. His heart beat faster as life began to slip away from him. He looked up to see The Commodore fighting valiantly against his enemy, a strange feeling of contentment and warmth began to wash over him. No longer would he have to endure the responsibility of the crew, The Commodore's increasingly fickle orders and his discontentment at sea. It would all be over in a few short minutes, Dalton smiled weakly as he watched his enemies and comrades fall around him. The screaming grew quieter until he could hear only the storm, the whipping of the wind and the hammering rain. Slowly, they too quietened, until Dalton heard nothing at all.

The Commodore wiped his face with a bloodied hand, smearing it even more with a mixture of filth, blood and water. Panting, he withdrew his sword and stepped back from his opponent, watching as he slid to the ground, groaning. The pirate's hand made for a pistol, but The Commodore kicked it away from him and sank his blade fatally into his back. The deafening sound of battle became quiet, and cheering could be heard. The Commodore dropped his shoulders in relief and smiled. He turned on a heel to congratulate his comrades on their victory, but instead he found the enemy crew cheering. All of them except their Captain, who stood with his sword in hand, his ripped coat flapping in the wind as the rain washed over his scarred face.

"What do we do now, sir?" asked an officer gasping for breath – he had been badly maimed. Only four others and The Commodore had survived. Everyone else had perished. HMS Fury lay in tatters, splinters of shattered wood were everywhere and a small fire had started somewhere on the hull.

"Lay down your weapons," The Commodore ordered. The few survivors did as he asked, without hesitation. The condemned pirate crew watched on silently, awaiting their Captain's orders. The Captain stepped towards The Commodore, a scorning look upon his scarred and battle-hardened face.

"Why?" he growled in a low, husky voice. The Commodore stood to attention, looking past the Captain. Expressionless and defeated, he said nothing.

"Why?" repeated the Captain, growing more annoyed. He delivered a blow to The Commodore's abdomen and watched as he doubled over in pain, coughing and wheezing.

"You could have sailed on, but instead you decided to battle an enemy that you clearly under-estimated." The Captain took a blade from his belt and held it to The Commodore's face.

"What difference does it make? You may have been victorious today, but your kind face extinction. Every country in the civilised world has your card marked."

The Commodore spat viciously at The Captain. His face was full of hatred and bitterness, the kind that is eternal, damning and incurable. The Captain snorted at The Commodore's remark.

"As the modern world evolves, so does ours. Those that have perished did so because of their refusal to adapt, learn and observe." The Captain growled as he cut into The Commodore's face with the knife. He yelled as his crew laughed and jeered.

"Let me demonstrate," said the Captain, mockingly, "to those that are defeated, as you can see, your ship is destroyed and the battle is lost. You may join my crew or sink to the depths with the rest of your dead comrades! I will find work for you with my crew based on the skills that you attained from the Royal Navy or whatever swine-ridden organisation cast you out to sea."

The Commodore studied the captain for a moment, confused. Those that engaged in piracy weren't usually this well-spoken – he must have had an education.

The survivors looked awkwardly to each other and then to The Commodore. His eyes darted to each of them.

"Remember the oath you took – your obligation to The British Empire!" the Commodore shouted, hysterically. The enemy crew burst into renewed laughter, mocking the statement of pointless principle. Even the Captain laughed at his desperate remarks.

"Commodore, save your breath!" he jeered in his husky voice. He ran his hands curiously through his jagged beard as he studied him. "My crew are a collection of people from different countries, religions and classes. I have soldiers from the Spanish Armada, the Hungarian army and even the Royal Navy. Warriors, educated men and adventurers. I adapted my crew to the challenges that I face year on year. Heck, I even took a ship from The East India Trading Company without so much as a shot fired." His crew beat their chests as they whooped together in unison.

"I have destroyed many of your kind, just for the fun of it!" The Commodore choked.

"I am aware. You have made quite a reputation for yourself across the seas, and it's almost a shame to send you to the depths," the Captain growled. "Now, who's behind the times? Who's almost extinct? You thought yourself a pioneer of the ocean but, my boy, how wrong you are." The Captain struck him with the butt of his knife, sending The Commodore howling to the floor.

"Take this fool and strap him to a cannon!" the Captain shouted. The crew howled and whooped as they dragged him down the steps onto the hull, where they tied him to the cannon. The Commodore wriggled and writhed, trying to free himself from their grip, but they didn't budge an inch.

"He must escape!" Charlie shouted. "He must make this right!"

"He mustn't do anything, boy!" Joan jeered back at him. "I think he's been pretty darn brilliant! Sank his entire crew and destroyed his reputation for the sake of his principle." She laughed as she watched eagerly. The finale loomed and she had no desire for an encore. The main attraction satisfied her greatly.

"Commodore, as you have probably figured, there is no escape. The adventure stops here. Are there any last words before we send you to the depths?" the Captain leered in his husky tone.

"Rule Britannia!" he yelled savagely, almost foaming at the mouth. His bloodshot eyes darted in every direction in sensational anger.

"Send him to the depths!" the Captain shouted. "And sink this ship! I don't want the Royal Navy finding this wreck and coming after us."

With that, The Commodore felt the cannon being tipped over the side of ship, granting him one last glance of the destroyed vessel. His stomach turned as he plummeted to the ocean. The wind whistled around him as he gained speed before the icy water consumed him and the cannon. He looked up as he sank, darkness gathering around him as he fell into the depths. He closed his eyes and tried to remember his wife and his son. As hard as he tried, he could not summon an image of them. Guilt, bitterness and sadness surged throughout his body. The depths of the ocean crushed down upon him, squeezing what little air remained in his lungs out of his chest. He wheezed and choked, kicked and wriggled, until nothing else remained... and the spark of his life slowly extinguished.

"The Commodore can't die..." whispered Charlie as his eyes began to fill up.

"Is the evidence before you not enough?" Joan snorted. "He is no hero – only a monster that led his entire crew to their deaths. And for what? Principle?"

"I want to go back now," Charlie wheezed; he held a hand to his stomach as it tangled itself in knots.

"As you wish," replied Joan, rolling her eyes. She snapped her fingers and they were whisked back to the overpowering stench of clinical bleach and over-cooked cabbage.

Chapter Eleven – The Incredible Bullet-Catching Stranger

Part I

Evolution does not take time. That is a statement of fact, not opinion. What can evolution, possibly take from time? Time is neither yes or no, black or white, right or wrong. It does not aid or obstruct, give or take, love or hate. Any association to these references is metaphorical, subjective or make-believe. Time serves only to measure that which passes, inevitably, without end. If you fail to evolve, alongside the movement of time, you are condemned to obsoletion through your own ignorance.

Vignis strolled along the side of the canal that led to the centre of Rohan's Reach. Beautiful communal gardens and sleepy store fronts were in abundance along the scenic route. Due to the steadily increasing rate of violence, it was unwise to deviate too far from the centre of Rohan's Reach. He had decided to take a calculated risk and head out for some exercise, he watched the residents of the beautiful city go about their daily business. The Divine world had changed dramatically since the introduction of energy as a currency. Those that previously begrudged each other merged reluctantly, for the sake of survival. It was true that open disputes between species and entities had declined, but it was also true that the crime rate had spiralled out of control. Murder, theft and poverty now thrived as minorities battled for survival, doing whatever they could to obtain energy.

The townspeople gasped when they noticed Vignis walking in deep contemplation, his personal bodyguards only a few metres behind him. Even those that had heard the rumours of their cold war with The Galdihar Rebellion greeted him enthusiastically, though Vignis ignored them. He paused as he looked into the canal and saw the corpse of a 'Hermosa Elf' face down in the water. It drifted slowly past, though it looked to have been there for some time. A large hole at the back of her neck signified she had been drained of her energy and discarded. He considered the corpse for a little while, though he had no compassion for the loss of life. Vignis had witnessed and inflicted far worse punishment himself.

"There are worse fates than death," said one of his humongous iron-clad bodyguards gravely. Vignis shot her a furious glance. He hated that saying – he felt that it trivialised his ideas of punishment and torture. To him, it was considered an art, and an artist he was.

"Have the Hermosa Elf removed from the canal," he snapped, bluntly. "It's getting close to the centre of Rohan's Reach."

Hermosa Elves were considered to be of high authority amongst their kind, often from their own form of aristocracy. To see one cut down so publicly and in cold blood was a sign of the times.

"Maybelle!" barked Vignis impatiently as he looked around to make sure they were out of earshot.

"Yes master?" she asked politely.

"Summon Omar Asghari and Judge Humphrey for a meeting in one hour, I'll have their heads if they are late by even a minute," he snapped.

"Yes master, right away." She paused for a moment and considered Vignis. He seemed flustered and agitated.

"Master, may I be so bold as to ask the nature of the summoning?" came Maybelle, sweetly. She sounded almost motherly. Vignis looked her in the eye as she hovered in front of him. He trusted her more than any other entity that existed across the planes. Had it been anyone else that had questioned his motives, they would certainly be dealt with in the harshest manner.

"The final solution that we are working towards, we are to bring the schedule forward. Confidential information has been compromised thanks to Arteon and his ridiculous servant." Vignis turned to consider the canal once more, his eyes moving to the beautiful landscape beyond Rohan's Reach. As he looked across the rolling hills, he saw everything… but nothing at all. His mind raced as he considered different scenarios and challenges irrespective of their likeliness, slowly becoming a slave to his own mind.

"Do you think that would be a wise move?" Maybelle questioned, politely.

"We have little choice now, Maybelle," muttered Vignis. "So much has changed in such little time. We must stay ahead of our enemies."

"Master, we have one opportunity to fulfil the final solution. Failure to sec-"

"That is enough," said Vignis, sternly. He shot a contemptuous look at her. Maybelle gave a quick nod and disappeared as quickly as she had arrived. His thoughts began to question Maybelle and her motives and the possibility of her being compromised. Paranoia raged throughout him. Though they had a special bond and had been a duo for a long time, she had never questioned his motives in this manner before.

"Do you see your *hero* in a new light?" asked Joan, who had returned to her aged form.

"I do. Those memories were secret. I have betrayed his trust," mumbled Charlie. He stared at his frozen comrades as guilt poured from his heart.

"You have much to learn," sighed Joan as she shook her head disapprovingly. She then leaned forward and snapped her fingers. Time resumed at a normal pace.

The Commodore looked from Charlie to Joan and back to Charlie. His eyes narrowed suspiciously as he examined them and then finally himself. He wiped dust from his sleeve and consulted his ruined time-travelling pocket watch.

He opened his mouth to confront Joan, a knowing smile paraded mockingly on her aged face. He then looked to Charlie who had resigned to inspecting his shoes, awkwardly avoiding his hero's gaze.

"You wish for me to end you, Hysterias?" The Commodore leered.

"More than you can possibly imagine," she replied, hungrily.

"For your crimes, punishment and cruelty you should be condemned-" he started…

"To Extinction," she interjected, still smiling. Charlie observed as Hix looked out of the window. He seemed to be looking for something.

"How old are you?" The Commodore asked all of a sudden.

"My existence cannot be measured by your primitive 'Time'," she spat, insulted. "I am older than any language, but not quite as old as your 'Time'."

"Something's not right… It feels like we've been here forever," muttered Hix, staring out of the window. His eyes were wide and he had a worried expression on his face. The Commodore ignored him, focusing only on Hysterias and how to deal with the dangerous beast.

"You are reputed to be one of the most dangerous entities ever to have existed," said The Commodore, slowly. "Undefeated and flawless in battle."

"Oh stop, you're making me blush," she smiled.

The Commodore's expression was serious, but he was slightly confused. He tugged at his shirt as he considered what to do.

"The Giving Tree," started Joan, beginning to look worried. "I know where The Giving Tree is located. I will tell you its location, if you promise to bring me to my final conclusion. It would be an honour and doubtlessly a legendary achievement to add to your legacy," she said hurriedly, almost pleading.

"What's 'The Giving Tree'? asked Charlie. His eyes seemed colder than usual.

"It's a myth," The Commodore sneered, keeping his eyes fixed on Hysterias.

"It is no myth!" she barked impatiently, keen to bring a close to the negotiation.

"The Giving Tree, looks like a blossom tree but it never sheds all of its purple bloom. It has the power to grant the wildest dreams and greatest desires of any individual, so long as they are worthy. If they are not, they are condemned to incurable madness or permanent elimination," The Commodore explained to Charlie. "That is the legend, but nobody has ever confirmed its existence."

"The legend is true; I know where it is," Hysterias explained, feverishly. She leaned over and took a pen and paper, scribbling as quickly as she could the location of the tree.

"Here!" she started. "Take it!" Charlie looked at the paper but could make no sense of the writing – it appeared to be in a different language.

"Throw that garbage away," The Commodore laughed darkly as he rose from his chair. Charlie folded it neatly and slotted it into his pocket, ignoring The Commodore's instructions. He tightened his grip on the infamous pistol and readjusted his aim at Hysterias. She smiled and closed her eyes, accepting her demise. In a second it would all be over; never again would she feel the pain of existence. The Commodore pulled back the hammer. The sound of the click resonated as silence prevailed. She waited for the final shot to be fired, but it never came. A chair scraped the floor as footsteps sounded.

"Charlie, Hix, let's go. We should report our findings to the Rebellion." He stuffed his pistol hastily into his coat, and made to leave.

"Wait! Where are you going? Don't leave me here!" Joan screamed angrily. "We had a deal, we had an accord, you know what I am capable of!"

The Commodore paused as they reached the door. He turned back to Joan with a knowing look.

"I do," he agreed. "And so do The Celestial Order. Maybe they will take mercy upon you – though I doubt it."

Joan screamed in fury as the ground began to tremble. Charlie covered his ears with his hands as the lights flickered. The Commodore laughed grimly as he held out his watch, its face towards Joan.

"This is for The Time-Keepers!" he said, as a blinding light consumed the room. A loud bang echoed as they jumped through time.

Charlie vomited once again as they arrived in their new era. His eyes were stinging as he looked around to familiarise himself with his surroundings.

"I just can't get used to that," Charlie choked, wobbling to his feet. Hix looked around, still unsettled.

"Do you think they will find Hysterias?" asked Hix, earnestly.

"Without a doubt," replied The Commodore, confidently.

"There isn't much here… Where are we?" Charlie groaned.

"Missouri, 1835. I think," The Commodore replied as they looked around. The night air was humid and warm. He strained his eyes as he looked through the darkness trying to get a bearing. The soft and peaceful flowing of the Mississippi River could be heard close by, joined in tandem by the night-time insects as they clicked and buzzed.

"We need to get a move on – once The Celestial Order have found Hysterias, they'll be on to us as quick as a flash," The Commodore explained as they walked alongside the great river.

"Halley's Comet," Hix observed as he looked to the sky. "November 30th."

"I must have missed it," The Commodore replied, disappointed, scanning the sky eagerly as they stumbled along.

A makeshift raft teased the surface of the peaceful river, tied to the shore with an amateur knot. The Commodore quickly looked around, unhooked it and ushered his company aboard.

"Where are we going?" asked Charlie as they drifted downstream.

"I have no idea. Let's see if we can find a town on our route," replied The Commodore, scratching his chin. "Hopefully, the owner of the raft doesn't see us."

"I'm sure they won't mind us borrowing it for our adventure," Hix added.

Charlie considered their adventure so far as he lay looking skyward. The stars were brighter than he had ever seen them. He remembered the books he had read about the stars, and set about trying to find the constellations. The raft bobbed gently along the river as a cool breeze swept through the reeds and tall grass. The Commodore considered Charlie, scratching his chin curiously with a peaceful expression. Charlie noticed him looking, and suddenly noticed the substantial differences between the memories he saw and the present day. The Commodore's eyes were cold, empty and lonely. Although only young when he left his mortal state, his time as a fugitive had taken its toll on him.

"What did Hysterias show you?" The Commodore asked as he rubbed his eyes.

"Nothing, we were with him," Hix butted in, defending Charlie. The Commodore stared hard at Hix.

"We were paused in a segment of time for at least two years, maybe even three!" The Commodore barked at Hix.

"Years!? But we were only gone for a couple of hours at the most!" Charlie blurted before he could stop himself.

Hix narrowed his eyes suspiciously, totally unaware they had been paused for even a moment.

"So, what did that foul beast show you?" The Commodore asked again, a little more agitated. Charlie turned his gaze to his shoes; a guilty feeling ate into him.

He knew that those memories were private and belonged to The Commodore.

"You," Charlie mumbled to his shoes.

"Yes, well I figured as much," The Commodore laughed, easing the tension slightly. "What about me?"

Charlie remained silent; his bottom lip began to tremble as his guilt turned to disappointment in himself.

"Entities such as Hysterias are wholly malignant and wicked. They do not feel guilt, shame or compassion. Whatever it has shown you was for a reason. You are lucky that you didn't come to any harm," The Commodore explained patiently. Charlie's eyes began to fill.

"Joan, Hysterias… or whatever its name was… showed me you, when you were an apprentice," Charlie explained trying to fight his tears back. The Commodore gave an understanding nod as Hix stared open-mouthed as prior events were unravelled.

"And, surely that's not all?" The Commodore encouraged.

"HMS… HMS Fury," Charlie stammered through his tears. He felt as small as a mouse, embarrassed and ashamed. The Commodore sat back, his mouth becoming a stern line as he remembered the stormy night that led him to his demise.

"Which part, of my voyage did you see?" The Commodore asked, a growl creeping into his words.

"The storm, the mutiny and the final battle," Charlie continued. The Commodore returned to his thoughts, scratching his chin.

"I also saw Dalton and your letter-"

The Commodore quickly held up a hand.

"That's quite enough," he concluded sharply, trying not to cause any further upset. "Aside from my meager beginnings and my timely demise, what else did you see?"

"Nothing. That's all. I promise," Charlie pleaded.

The Commodore frowned and then turned to Hix who looked perplexed. The Commodore and his past were a mystery to almost all. Only his name bore the legend of a man condemned and a hostile fugitive. His name, as events were displaying, seemed to be more of a curse.

"Bloody cretin missed out the best bits!" he snorted. "You have been shown those events for a reason, Charlie. I have done some wicked things, that much is true."

"But they were not intentional," Charlie added.

"No, not on that occasion, at least. But what does it matter to those that lost their lives? Not a thing. A lot of detail has been missed out – I'm still not entirely sure why you were shown those particular dates other than to discredit me, but that seems to be too petty." The Commodore ran his hands through his hair.

Charlie once again returned to examining his shoes as he choked and gasped in tears. The Commodore lay down next to Charlie and tapped the raft next to him, they both looked up at the stars together. Even Hix joined in.

"Not a day goes by that I don't think about that storm," The Commodore explained, uneasily. "I wish that I could change those events, but sadly that cannot be done."

"But you have your watch," said Charlie as a matter of fact.

"It would be too easy for The Celestial Order to find me along my own timeline. I cannot return to any of it. Even if I could, they are pivotal events in my history. It is impossible for me to change them; I am an anomaly. Neither dead nor alive, I don't really exist anymore. Nor does my timeline. Technically. It's all very complicated."

Charlie looked sad as he examined the sky and the stars. The Commodore noticed and turned back to the stars.

"I had many great adventures, before and after that night on HMS Fury," The Commodore explained, cheerfully. It wasn't often that Hix or Charlie ever heard The Commodore in such good spirits.

"There were three Naval officers, from some toff-nosed line of inbred upper-class purity, that tried everything they could to make my life a misery and get me to resign from the Navy. Beaufort, Bamford and-"

"Bum!" Charlie finished ecstatically. All three laughed together as they sailed down-river.

"Yes, that's right!" The Commodore laughed. "What dirty tricks they played, simply because I wasn't up to 'their' standard of what officers should be. It wasn't even their decision! They got their places because of their family ties."

"Surely, that's not right," said Charlie, wiping away a tear from laughter, this time.

"Right or not, that's the way it is. It's not what you know but who you know that sets people ahead a lot of the time," he explained as though he had all of the time in the world.

Hix listened eagerly as they observed the sky. As he wasn't of the Blind world, he found these insights fascinating and felt understanding of his suffering, achievements and motives. He never spoke of his feelings or understandings. As a product of Oblivion, it was widely believed that he was an evil entity that could never comprehend the emotions of benign entities, such as love, ambition and happiness. 'Only bad things came from Oblivion,' they would say when in the company of strangers.

"I entered the Navy as a mere officer's apprentice, got approved and we set sail only weeks after. I saved three men from drowning when their small boat sprung a leak and tipped over – the fools couldn't even swim. Fancy joining the Navy unable to swim," he reminisced, smiling. "That annoyed the three jackals and put me on their radar for good. They would have got me out too if one of the old Admirals hadn't stuck up for me. Admiral Foresythe was my mentor – a tough man who never gave compliments. But he saw something in me that most didn't, and for the most part I excelled, even with those three buffoons trying to trip me everywhere I went."

The trio continued to smile and enjoy the twilight as they moved on. The Commodore started laughing, his belly in stiches as the laughter came from his stomach. Charlie and Hix looked at him as though he were a stranger – he never laughed like this.

"Beaufort Bamford and Bum were given an award for… something ridiculous. I can't remember what the award was for. When the ceremony started, I paid several children to catapult manure at them as they arrived on stage.

The smell stayed with them for weeks!" The Commodore gasped for air as tears streamed down his face. Charlie and Hix fell away from each other, howling and bawling as they too laughed and teared up in joy.

"But, really, they won in the end," The Commodore said as his laughing began to subside. He looked out on to the bank, still smiling. He ran his hand through the water as they moved.

"How did they win?" asked Charlie, curious, still trying to curb his laughter.

"It's not important, but I gave all three of them the runaround for a long time," The Commodore concluded. From his tone, Charlie knew not to pry any further.

Part II

The Grand Manor became alive all of a sudden as news travelled that Vignis would arrive at any moment for an impromptu meeting. The staff that managed the building scattered and scrambled to arrange everything to as near to perfection as possible. Should it not be, Vignis would no doubt seek someone to make an example of.

The boardroom fireplace had been lit, and it crackled merrily as the flames lit the room, assisted by the various lamps throughout. The long oak table shimmered and shined, polished to within an inch of perfection, reflecting the long flames from the fireplace as they danced.

Maybelle arrived first, which was quite usual. She didn't utter a word to anyone as she fluttered into the building as composed as ever. The staff stood by and watched as she arranged documents, muttering and murmuring as she did so. Fairies, aren't considered to be extremely dangerous. They have led many to their ultimate conclusion over the years, but with the right training and knowledge it's quite simple to overcome them. Kull watched as she fluttered to and fro, arranging and preparing. Giants aren't particularly intelligent, fast-moving or aware of personal hygiene for the most part, but even they knew how much energy a fairy contained and what that energy would be worth on the open market. He breathed through his mouth as his dopey expression contorted this way and that while he considered different methods of overcoming Maybelle. Most of these methods involved a club.

A Dunn Elf – mostly referred to as a common elf – stood by and watched the giant with interest. Her green skin and black eyes looked terrifying to the unfamiliar, but were commonplace around the Divine realm. Her long black hair shone tidily alongside her immaculate uniform. She raised an eyebrow at the giant, wondering what he was pondering, her expression became quite severe when she noticed him watching Maybelle like a hawk.

"Hey… psst!" she hissed not quite loud enough. "Hey, don't even think about it!"

Kull turned his gaze lazily to the Dunn Elf, his gormless expression full of confusion.

"I know what you are thinking!" she accused, wagging her finger at him. "Don't you dare go near Maybelle. If you touch her, we'll all be reprimanded and no doubt executed! I can see the wheels of your mind slowly turning. Don't even think about it!"

Kull turned away from the Dunn Elf with a frown, certainly not intimidated, but the point had been made. The Dunn Elf regressed into her own thoughts, cursing and damning the day that she had sought employment with The Celestial Order. It wasn't a position that you could walk away from. If you did, you typically walked away from existing on any plane, except maybe Oblivion.

"Name," boomed a voice so suddenly it made her jump. For a moment, she thought she had been caught cursing The Celestial Order in her own head. She noticed Kull staring at her, open-mouthed and slightly vacant.

"San," she whispered hesitantly. Giants weren't renowned for conversational etiquette.

"San," repeated Kull, in a booming voice. "Sanguine?"

"Yes, that's right. It's short for Sanguine," she replied, suspicious of this smarter-than-usual giant. Kull thought for what seemed an eternity, his face contorting so much that it seemed that the consideration brought him pain.

"Will I die?" he asked bluntly.

San looked pityingly at him; ignorance had been blissful for the giant, but even he now felt the anxiety of working at The Celestial Order. She looked into the boardroom from where they stood and almost perished at the sight of Maybelle staring straight at her. She took a moment to collect herself before rushing to the door of the boardroom.

"Can I help you, Miss?" she enquired politely, her mind racing as the thought 'please don't kill me' over and over. Maybelle did not reply immediately and an awkward silence fell between them. San felt for sure that Maybelle could read her mind. Maybelle smiled, very aware of the crushing silence between them.

"Is there an issue with the giant?" Maybelle enquired, softly. San glanced over at the giant who had resorted to scratching in between his legs, a brief satisfactory smile spreading over his face. San thought for a moment. 'Can she read my mind? Has Maybelle heard the conversation? Am I being tested?' And then 'damn the day I agreed to work here' raced and repeated through her mind.

"No, Miss," San replied, earnestly. "Giants aren't the most intelli-"

"That will be all," Maybelle interrupted, as she returned to preparing the meeting. San looked at Maybelle, her mouth hanging open slightly. She gave a brief nod and returned to her place near Kull.

"Friends?" he asked, with a finger alarmingly deep into his nostril.

"Why not?" she sighed, her shoulders dropping disappointingly. A sense of responsibility for Kull and keeping him out of trouble washed over her, joining the endless sea of other worries that she considered throughout most days.

The front doors of The Grand Manor flew open as Vignis arrived along with Omar Asghari and Judge Humphrey. They moved swiftly through the foyer and into the boardroom without a word for each other or the attending staff. San watched Kull as his eyes followed the trio into the boardroom with interest, the wheels of his mind once again at work. San felt an anxiety as she worried about what he was thinking. Even the slightest error could result in punishment, and the consequences often stretched to colleagues.

"Bad man?" he bellowed unintentionally as the boardroom doors closed. San felt a wave of horror descend as her eyes flashed to the other colleagues that were standing by. They glanced at him awkwardly, some even stepping away from him as if to rid themselves of any attribution to his condemning words.

"No," whispered San, desperately. "The Good Shepherd." Kull looked confused once more, and returned to his thoughts. San looked at her colleagues as they glared at her. She smiled awkwardly and shook her head dismissively.

They seated themselves around the immaculate table. Vignis glanced around the room to check for any imperfections that he could chastise his staff for, but he didn't see anything out of place. No matter, he would doubtlessly find something.

His audience looked at him expectantly. This meeting had been pulled together at short notice which meant that it must be important. Vignis looked flustered, dishevelled and slightly scruffy, which were alarming traits to those that knew him well.

"The final solution – our plans – may have been compromised," Vignis exclaimed to his colleagues. They were aware that Arteon Chubb had been removed from his position, but no one knew why, aside from Maybelle. Vignis looked around at the attendees. His eyes widened slightly as he ran a nervous hand through his messy hair.

"Maybelle, summon Adelade," he said hastily, and she flew out of the room as quickly as she could. He could feel the eyes of those in attendance, the odd raised eyebrow, as they took his appearance into account. Would they question his integrity, his methods or authority?

'I could crush them like beetles if they dared to challenge me,' he thought to himself. He snapped back to the meeting, noticing that he had left them for a few moments whilst he observed his thoughts.

"We have potential obstacles; the plans may have been compromised by The Galdihar Rebellion," he began with a sigh. "Specifically, that we are gathering and storing energy." He looked around at his colleagues and considered them.

"Do they know about the final stage?" Omar asked, eagerly.

Vignis paused, considering Omar thoughtfully.

"Although it is not likely, I cannot say for certain," said Vignis, slowly. "What I can say for certain, is that our plans will go ahead. The final solution must, and will, be carried out."

Omar opened his mouth to question further, but Vignis held up a hand.

"We are not to discuss the final stage; we do not know who else may have been compromised." Vignis turned to look out of the window.

"I suppose that you have lost trust in us, too?" Judge Humphrey asked. A solid deafening silence filled the room as Vignis did not respond immediately. Omar glanced sideways at Judge Humphrey, cursing him for his boldness.

"You would not have the privilege of engaging me in this conversation if I had any doubts about your integrity," Vignis growled, still looking towards the window, his back turned. He certainly didn't trust his colleagues, but knew that they feared him more than anything else. That was enough to trust they would not betray him.

"Judge Humphrey!" came a jolly voice from the door. They had all been so engaged that nobody saw the door open. "It has been quite some time! We have some arrangements that need to be discussed and concluded!" Hymm walked over and placed a gentle hand upon Judge Humphrey's shoulder. His immaculate 19th century business attire gleamed along with his shoes that shone like mirrors, his top hat leaning at a jaunty angle. Every particle of his appearance had been carefully considered; the magic of The Imposter's Amulet worked beautifully.

"Another time," Judge Humphrey grumbled quietly.

"Not very confidence-inspiring, are you?" Hymm laughed as he walked towards Vignis. He had turned to see who dared interrupt his meeting.

"This amulet, is working an absolute treat!" he chuckled happily.

Vignis raised a curious eyebrow, wondering what business he had here.

"Omar, good to see you as always," Hymm smiled, tipping his hat.

Omar scowled at Hymm; his arms folded as he snubbed him contemptuously.

"Do not patronise me, Hymm," said Omar in a low tone.

"Not the welcome I was hoping for!" Hymm jested. "Have you let any more of your residents escape in recent years?"

"You are of the same authority as me!" Omar shouted angrily. He stood fast, slamming his hands on the table angrily. "You are no better, parading Existence as though you own the entire plane. You make me sick!" He spat.

Hymm let his jovial and jolly demeanour slip for a moment.

"Letting residents escape your plane and bargaining for want of more power, and you dare to compare yourself with me?" Hymm spoke softly, his words dripping in threat.

"It was one!" Omar yelled. "One resident that escaped!"

"He's doing a ton of damage, I'm sure you'd agree!" Hymm laughed, his jovial air returning.

"Judge Humphrey should have sentenced the resident to a harsher punishment – then none of this would have happened!" Omar snorted.

"We've discussed this. It was the right judgement at the time!" Judge Humphrey defended.

"Well, nobody escapes Oblivion." Hymm smiled mockingly, concluding the discussion.

Vignis considered Hymm carefully. He didn't make visits without reason.

"What can we do for you, Hymm?" Vignis asked almost politely.

"What can you do for me? What a question." Hymm considered, as he walked around the table. "Very open, that's for sure. You, Vignis, promised me more of these enchanted jewels, but so far I have received nothing."

His smile could probably be interpreted as considerate and gentle to anyone who didn't know what he was capable of.

"We have had difficulty in locating them, that much is true," Vignis started.

"But you have not made it a priority!" Hymm replied, still smiling. "Bargaining with me is not something to be taken lightly." He looked around at the many faces and considered them, as a red-faced Adelade entered the room. She stopped for a moment as she noticed Hymm, before taking a seat at the table.

"Ahh, the signee of our little contract! This is someone who would not want to break our terms, I have no doubt," Hymm continued.

"I have made discovering the jewels my business-"

"I do not care for your business," Hymm snapped, interrupting Vignis with a polarised attitude. "Only my own."

Omar rolled his eyes and folded his arms. Hymm whipped his head around and considered Omar deeply.

"We have found Hysterias," Adelade piped up suddenly. The other attendees turned their heads to Adelade at the mention of Hysterias. "The Weeping Rift has been dispatched to retrieve The Commodore and the boy. We know where they are."

Vignis smiled broadly, his shoulders dropping slightly as he felt some relief.

"How did we find Hysterias?" he enquired.

"The Commodore. He jumped time with the boy and a demonic being. We tracked them to the timeline a while ago, though weren't certain of the location until he made that move," Adelade blurted quickly, attempting to diffuse the situation.

"Good work, Adelade," Vignis breathed. He looked around and saw those in attendance look at him differently, almost as though they saw him as an equal. Vignis stood up straight and cleared his throat.

"Your enchanted items, they will be with you as soon possible-"

"Those are vague and open estimations, Vignis," Hymm warned with a plain expression. "Should you not deliver, I will be concluding our contract early."

Hymm shot a sinister wink at Adelade, who quickly averted her eyes and re-arranged her papers for the fifth or sixth time. Vignis noticed the exchange and returned his focus to the matters at hand. Adelade had become irreplaceable – if she came to any adverse conclusion, the final solution would simply stall and fall apart, he had no doubt The Celestial Order would shortly follow.

"As a goodwill gesture, I will deliver Hysterias to Oblivion for you to deal with. I only ask that the energy from Hysterias is sent back as part of our agreement," Vignis explained, trying to sound polite, but missing the mark dreadfully.

Hymm rolled his tongue thoughtfully, considering the benefits of Hysterias and what such power could be used for.

"Very well." Hymm gave a brief nod, smiled politely and vanished into thin air. Nobody in the room spoke. They looked at each other, unsure if he had actually left the room or not.

"The Commodore and The Galdihar Rebellion must be thwarted as soon as possible. Any further shortcomings will be reviewed by me personally," Vignis explained severely. "Dismissed!"

Orange light began to split the night sky as the sun rose over the horizon. The clicking and singing of the insects subsided as they prepared for the day. The Commodore roped their stolen raft to an awning at the side of a small village, only a short walk from the Mississippi river. The trio climbed onto the embankment and made their way into town.

"Where are we?" yawned Charlie as he rubbed his tired eyes with balled fists.

"No idea, don't really care," replied The Commodore, shortly. "We just need to keep a low profile before we can jump to another timeline."

"What's wrong with this one?" asked Charlie.

"Polio, filthy water, obscure diseases, famine, violence… amongst other things," Hix answered, cheerfully.

"I didn't think either of you would have to worry about that," Charlie returned.

The Commodore and Hix looked at each other and then to Charlie.

"We don't," they replied in unison.

"Ah, of course you don't," Charlie laughed, nervously.

The small waterside town felt eerily quiet as only a few of the townspeople were up, tending to their livelihoods. They trudged the town as raised eyebrows followed the outsiders – outsiders not only to their town but also to their time. The Commodore spotted a public bench and seated himself. Charlie and Hix followed suit as The Commodore retrieved his watch and placed it looking skyward.

"Eve Spotting?" Charlie enquired, a smile across his face.

"Yep, there will doubtlessly be some kind of Divine network that we can connect with around here." He watched the passers-by suspiciously and then looked down at the second hand to see if it twitched.

"There's something here. Something big," Hix piped up with a concerned expression.

"Good, we can hopefully get some supplies," The Commodore muttered as he watched his time-piece like a hawk, his tongue slightly sticking out.

"Whatever it is, it's not something that I have encountered before," Hix warned.

"Stop your belly-aching, you're always so fearful," The Commodore jeered.

He suddenly became aware that the busying townspeople were plenty, and many of them had taken notice of the strange man apparently talking to himself.

"S'cuse me, son," came a deep Missouri accent near Charlie. "Are you in any kinda trouble?"

An elderly man had been watching The Commodore with growing concern. His straw hat was almost in ruins, as were his sack cloth pants and darned shirt.

"No, I am quite alright, thank you," Charlie replied with perfectly polite etiquette.

The elderly man almost bowled over at the sound of his accent.

"Your kind have some cheek showin' ya faces around here since we gained our independence," he half-joked to Charlie. "Come now, let me take you away from this strange gentleman." He leaned over to take Charlie by the shoulder, but the boy recoiled from the stranger's withered hand.

"Listen, old-timer. Touch the boy and you are finished," The Commodore snapped impatiently, still glancing down at his skyward-facing watch. More townspeople stopped by to see what the commotion was. They pointed at their clothes, and giggled and whispered to each other.

"Where's the Sheriff?" The Commodore demanded.

"Over there!" pointed a lady, who had stopped to see what was happening. Charlie followed her finger and saw a corpse slumped in a doorway with an empty bottle of whiskey in his hand. He had been there for at least a week.

"Let's settle this like men, without the law. I can draw quicker than anyone this side of the Mississippi!" bawled the elderly man from beside him suddenly. His arm shook as he retrieved a revolver from his holster and held it in the air.

"Well, that escalated quickly," chuckled Hix. Charlie gave a nod in agreement.

"I don't have time for this. I won't be here at sundown, or whenever you propose we should partake in your barbaric activities," The Commodore dismissed without looking at him.

"No time like the present," replied the elderly man, cocking back the hammer on his pistol. "If you don't, it's off to prison for you!"

"Oh no! Not prison! I guess your Sheriff will lock me up. Oh, wait…" The Commodore replied sarcastically. He looked around at the townspeople and met faces unamused and rather serious expressions. His sarcasm had missed the mark and made no impression.

"Fine!" huffed The Commodore as he snapped his watch shut. "Let's get this over with."

Charlie turned to a distracted Hix, he seemed to be looking for something, whispering incoherently as he did so.

"What is it?" Charlie asked as they joined the growing crowd that surrounded the two champions.

"I don't... know," muttered Hix as he sniffed the air. "Whatever it is, it isn't good."

Charlie turned to watch the duel take place as both combatants presented their weapons. The old man displayed his revolver to the owner of the local saloon who was acting as a referee and standard setter.

"Very good," he nodded.

The Commodore displayed his ancient pistol. The townspeople craned their necks, looked at the weapon and then at The Commodore. They fell into laughter, screaming and crying at The Commodore and his weaponry. He simply rolled his eyes and continued on. Only the elderly gentlemen, his opponent, didn't laugh.

"Twenty paces and not a step more or less. Weapons holstered, and may the best man win," the saloon owner called before turning to join the crowd. The elderly gentleman stood, one eye squinting with his fingers splayed, ready to draw and fire fast. The Commodore stood to the side, his left foot forward with a disinterested expression. Their eyes met as they held each other's gaze. The Commodore gave a wink and blew his opponent a kiss. The elderly man spat and shot him a disgusted look in return. Charlie watched with his arms folded and an eyebrow raised, curious as to what the outcome would be.

"Aren't you going to help?" Charlie whispered to Hix, expectantly. He turned slowly to Charlie, annoyed.

"What am I? His guardian?" he retorted. "Let him figure this out himself."

Hix returned to looking across the crowd, for whatever seemed to be unsettling him.

"Draw!" shouted the elderly man. A split second later, he drew his pistol and fired at The Commodore. The Commodore threw out his hand and stumbled backwards, very much alive. The elderly gentleman considered him with amazement. He checked his gun and looked back at The Commodore as he walked towards him. The Commodore held out his hand and passed the spent bullet to the elderly gentlemen.

"You missed," said The Commodore in patronising tones.

The elderly gentleman looked at him in complete confusion, his mouth agape without a sound escaping.

"Again," The Commodore added as he walked back to his position, resuming his duel ready stance. The elderly gentlemen resumed his stance too, studying his opponent with a worried look. Charlie smiled as he considered the adults around him.

"I know him!" he beamed as he pointed at The Commodore.

"Draw!" yelled the elderly gentleman, pointing and firing his pistol with considerable speed and poise. Once again, The Commodore didn't fire – he stumbled backwards and fell to the ground. The elderly gentleman smiled, but it didn't last long, as The Commodore stood once again and made his way over to the elderly gentleman. The crowd gasped, sure that he had been fatally wounded.

"I caught this for you," The Commodore choked as he brought a spent bullet from his mouth and handed it to the elderly gentleman.

"How did-" he started, but The Commodore about-turned and prepared for another round.

The townspeople uttered not a single sound as they watched, eyes bulging at the incredible bullet-catching stranger.

"Draw!" screamed the elderly gentleman, fear spread across his face. The Commodore brought his arm around, but not faster than his opponent. His pistol fired and hit The Commodore squarely in the chest. He stumbled back a few steps, his face contorted in pain, then he gargled slightly as he coughed blood onto the floor and collapsed.

The elderly man looked almost as though he couldn't believe his luck! He had finally ended the bullet-catching stranger.

"You backed the wrong horse, kid," said a burly toothless yokel from behind Charlie. A large grin spread across his face.

"It appears so," replied Charlie with a smile. The elderly gentleman strolled over to The Commodore – he had to be sure of victory before any celebration. He leaned over The Commodore, peering at him curiously before tapping him with the toe of his shoe. He smiled, certain of victory, before The Commodore's eyes sprang open and he hopped to his feet.

"Another hole in my bloody shirt!" he bawled angrily.

The elderly gentleman almost jumped his height in horror as the colour drained from every bit of his face, his mouth agape and eyes wide with fear.

"You shoulda… died!" he stammered.

"I sort of, already have…" whispered The Commodore.

The elderly gentleman gasped, inhaling deeper and deeper. Charlie thought for certain he'd burst. Charlie prepared for the elderly gentleman to scream, but he clutched his chest instead. Agonising pain shot through his body before he fell face down in the dirt, as dead as the week-old corpse that used to be their sheriff. The townspeople looked from the elderly gentleman to The Commodore, mouths open in amazement. The owner of the saloon raised The Commodore's hand high in the air.

"The incredible bullet-catching traveller!" he shouted.

A volley of cheers, whistles and screams erupted from the crowd, congratulating The Commodore on his victory. They patted The Commodore, brought him flowers and even made him food that he naturally passed to Charlie. The boy had forgotten how hungry he was and ate as though he had never eaten before. He stuffed cake and chicken into his mouth at the same time as fast as he could, disregarding all of the table etiquette that he had been taught. It was glorious.

Charlie and The Commodore were treated like kings by the townspeople over the coming days, and everyone greeted them with smiles and waves. Hix watched quietly as housewives made them food and store owners gave them wears at no cost, hanging from their every word, the very definition of heroes. Hix felt a void in his chest, an emptiness that bred sadness and sorrow.

"Why can't I be..." Hix whispered to himself, "human." Nobody heard him, but he wished that they could. He hated what he was – a product of a plane so vile that nobody in any state wanted to visit. As he had no capacity for evil or hatred, he had no business in Oblivion either. He decided that he belonged nowhere, no way, no how.

Chapter Twelve – The Jilted and Jaded, Wilted and Faded

You can save a dozen souls, by concluding the life of only one. Heinous, yes, but necessary. The other dozen souls must live on! Could you murder an innocent with your own two hands, to save half a dozen from torture, pain and death? The innocent one weeps and begs, seated before you, bound and blinded as they tremble in uncertainty. End them and save three other souls from a gritty conclusion. What are you waiting for? It is logical perfection! End one, save two. It's still a great deal, no negotiation required, right? Sacrifice one for the freedom of many. Only, it is you that is seated, bound and blinded, trembling in uncertainty. How do those odds stack now? Perspective is everything.

The Commodore paced the room with a cigar in his mouth, dropping ash carelessly onto his rather expensive smoking jacket.

"This is the life; it's been a long time since I've had these luxuries." He puffed happily as he paced. Charlie peered from under the peak of his huge cowboy hat, it slipped down over his eyes but that didn't deter him from sporting the incredible headwear.

Even Hix, as distracted as he had been, adopted a beautiful yellow top hat. Charlie laughed as he made his way around the room.

"What are you laughing at, boy?" Hix asked, smirking at Charlie.

"Look!" Charlie pointed. Hix turned and looked in the mirror, he had no reflection but the top hat hovered eerily. To any unsuspecting witness, it would doubtlessly have raised several questions.

The room smelt of old, untreated timber, a hint of dry rot completed the scent. The Commodore looked across the wooden beams above him, both considering and condemning them at the same time. He shook his head and muttered to himself as he worked out his method, as opposed to those that had built their residence. For the first time in days, Charlie maintained a full stomach and had experienced some real sleep. He tried to work out how long he had gone without several of life's necessities, but gave up after using up both his fingers and toes. He turned and saw that Hix had removed his striking yellow top hat from his head. He stared longingly into the mirror, a sorrowful expression on his face. He moved the hat up and down as he considered his reflection, or lack thereof. Charlie knew something wasn't right and approached him in his usual polite manner.

"Are you okay, Hix?" Charlie asked, warmly.

"Oh, erm, yes. Fine. Never better." Hix coughed awkwardly as he moved away from the mirror. He seemed almost guilty for his thoughts.

Charlie put an arm around Hix and looked back into the mirror, they both laughed at how ridiculous they looked. The Commodore watched Hix with interest from a chair in the corner of the room. For centuries, The Commodore had travelled mostly alone in his evasion of The Celestial Order, with only very small periods of company. He strained his mind as he rolled the cigar around his mouth, watching the smoke rise to the ceiling. He tried to conjure memories of the centuries he had been on the run, but for an inexplicable reason struggled to do so.

Darkness fell over the sleepy town, the still warm air felt sticky, humid and uncomfortable. The Commodore sat on the porch of the old house staring out into the night, the inevitable time-piece lying on his knee as he swayed the rocking chair.

"I can't sleep," yawned Charlie as he took a seat next to him. The Commodore didn't answer, but continued to stare into the abyss, frowning heavily as he did so.

"I like it here," Hix chirped from above them. He sat merrily on the awning over the porch.

"You've brightened up," The Commodore snorted sarcastically. "What happened to 'something's not right, we're all going to die'" He waved his hands in a dramatic fashion. Hix chose not to answer but continued to smile, though it looked somewhat forced.

"I know what you're trying to do," said Hix, knowingly.

"I'm not trying to do anything," The Commodore replied a pinch too innocently. "But you clearly haven't noticed."

"Noticed what?" asked Hix and Charlie in unison.

"The time," The Commodore replied, laconically.

"What of it?" snapped Hix, becoming more agitated.

"The sun went down tonight, three hours early. It should still be daytime," The Commodore replied with a serious expression. Charlie looked down and noticed The Commodore's hand tightly gripping his pistol. Hix looked about him as though the very air itself might be plotting against him.

"What's more interesting is that none of our wonderful neighbours seem to have noticed," added The Commodore.

After a few moments of staring into the eerie darkness, The Commodore rose from his chair and calmly made his way inside. Charlie and Hix followed him closely.

"Is it Hymm?" Charlie asked, thoughtfully.

The Commodore shook his head as he poured some milk from a jug into a beaten tankard. The pungent stench of turned milk emanated from the tankard, but The Commodore seemed to have his thoughts elsewhere.

"Something, wicked is here," said The Commodore slowly as he looked at Hix.

"Why is the milk bad?" interjected Charlie.

"Concentrated hatred can turn even the purest," Hix explained, solemnly.

He glanced over to the mirror in the corner of the room once more. Charlie opened his mouth to ask a question, but a loud knock at the door cut him short.

The Commodore looked at Hix and Charlie for a moment, before making his way over and holding the handle.

"Who may I ask is calling?" The Commodore enquired in a formal tone.

"Ask my brother," came a tortured voice from beyond the door.

Hix swooped down onto a chair and began to tremble uncontrollably. His eyes had lost their fiery brightness – they were dull, deep and fearful.

"The Weeping Rift," he spluttered quietly.

"Is that your brother?" asked Charlie, politely.

"That is no brother of mine," Hix stammered, severely.

"Come now," rattled the voice from behind the door. "Must we quarrel after such a long time?"

The Commodore opened the door and stepped back in horror at what stood before him. The rotten corpse of the local Sheriff stood proud and tall. His decaying face drooped on one side as two amber eyes stared at The Commodore. Those bottomless amber eyes were bright and menacing. If you contemplated them for long enough, the weeping of a thousand tortured souls could be heard.

The Commodore aimed his pistol at the corpse and pulled the trigger. The shot echoed across the hills as the corpse swayed slightly before steadying himself. The corpse looked upon The Commodore with disapproval before making his way inside. Hix trembled with fear as he looked upon the infamous Weeping Rift.

"Who are you?" asked Charlie politely, mostly unmoved by what stood before him. The Sheriff studied Charlie for a moment as a smile began to crack on the functioning side of his face.

"Who am I, brother?" the Sheriff rasped. His neck clicked and cracked as he looked to the demon.

"The Weeping Rift," replied Hix, disgusted. "You are a destroyer of worlds, devourer of souls and a torturer so masterful, even Hymm cast you from Oblivion."

"Hmm," growled the Sheriff thoughtfully. "Father was most difficult to please."

A solemn expression took place upon the decayed face.

"Father?" spat Hix. "We were not born or raised. We were forged in the fiercest flames of hatred, fuelled by the pain and anguish of those condemned."

The Sheriff considered Hix curiously before shifting his gaze back to Charlie. He looked upon the boy and noted the absence of fear and loathing.

"You do not fear me, boy?" The Sheriff rattled as he scratched at his decaying face. A chunk of rotten flesh fell to the floor, but the Sheriff didn't seem to notice.

"I do not," replied Charlie, bluntly.

"We are not so different, you and I; our stars are closely aligned in what will be," the Sheriff explained.

"Enough of these games-" The Commodore began.

"You will speak when I decide!" bellowed the Sheriff.

He snapped his fingers and The Commodore fell to the floor semi-conscious. Charlie gasped as The Commodore's eyes rolled into the back of his head. Although unable to move, the inevitable time-piece remained in his grasp.

Charlie made to protest, but as he did, a loud knocking echoed from the door.

"Don't open it!" Hix shouted.

As the words left his mouth, the Sheriff cast him into the air and through the dry wall with an effortless wave of the hand.

"It's for you," smiled the Sheriff in a sickly-sweet voice.

Charlie looked on fearlessly and stormed to the door. He placed a hand on the door handle and looked back defiantly at the Sheriff, keen not to show fear. He shot a final scowl before he opened the door and gasped. He blinked several times and felt dizzy from trying to process what stood before him. A familiar smile met him – as did the outstretched hands of Billy Betts. Charlie took a moment to gather himself before falling into his warm embrace. Charlie's smile stretched from ear to ear as he gasped and laughed with joy, hopping from one foot to the other.

"You could have helped me, Charlie," wheezed Billy.

"I'm sorry, I just wanted to be a good friend," Charlie replied as he squeezed Billy even tighter. Charlie felt warmth begin to disappear from Billy. He swayed slightly as Charlie tried to balance him. Billy began to cough and fell to his knees, wheezing and spluttering as he did so.

"Someone help!" Charlie shouted as he watched the colour drain from Billy's face. The Sheriff remained where he was, thoroughly enjoying the events unfolding as The Commodore and Hix remained immobile.

Billy lay down in front of Charlie, his coughing started to ease as his eyes became glazed and unforgiving.

"Please don't go!" Charlie wept as he held his best friend.

Billy's eyes rolled into the back of his head as he became motionless and the steady rising and falling of his chest slowed to a standstill. Charlie watched on open-mouthed as tears fell from his eyes. He began crying uncontrollably as he rocked the corpse back and forth.

"It's not real," spluttered Hix from beneath the smashed dry wall.

The Sheriff brought Hix into sight with a mere flick of his rotten wrist. He hovered momentarily before crashing onto the floor. With what energy he had left, Hix lifted his head to look at the Sheriff. The endless amber stare met his own as he felt himself slip into a world not entirely his own. A deep void opened from the depths of his soul, as all that he had learnt about being human slowly slipped away. A conscious change absorbed him entirely, transforming him back to being the monster he was crafted to be. That which Hix feared most, had been realised.

The Sheriff smiled as Hix rose from the ground and took flight towards Charlie. The demon watched on with pleasure as Charlie wept over the corpse of his best friend. A wide smile of joy and ecstasy entangled Hix as he fed from the sadness that emanated from Charlie. The Commodore coughed and wheezed into vague consciousness; his hand still tightly wrapped around the inevitable time-piece. He opened one eye and groaned as he witnessed the harrowing scene of Charlie, Billy and Hix.

"Turning tricks for The Celestial Order?" spluttered The Commodore, defiantly. "How you have conformed!"

The Sheriff turned to The Commodore before rising from the chair and standing over the infamous felon.

"I conform to no one!" barked the Sheriff as more flesh slipped from his jaw.

"Cheap talk, cheap tricks. This is child's play." The Commodore laughed mockingly. The deep night sky began to advance through into a new dawn as the Sheriff raised an arm skyward.

"You'll have to try harder than that," snapped the Sheriff.

He looked down at The Commodore's deflated expression and smiled as the dawn wound back to the twilight hours. The Commodore had attempted to advance time as the Sheriff had drawn it back again.

"This is my realm now and only *I* decide what happens here," the Sheriff spat.

"Charlie, listen to me. This isn't real!" The Commodore shouted.

Charlie didn't hear anything aside from the sobbing sounds of his own anguish and sadness. The Commodore observed the smell of the twilight air and untreated timber. He listened to the cries and uncontrollable sobbing of

Charlie and saw nothing aside from the bitter end they seemed to be heading towards. A warm hand upon his shoulder took him by surprise. He lay flat to see who had approached him and felt tears flood his eyesight almost immediately. Rubbing his eyes frantically, he stared again to confirm what he saw. Henry stood over his father with the familiar warm smile and deep eyes of his mother.

"Hello, son," The Commodore whispered. "It's been quite some time, hasn't it?"

"Yes, father," replied Henry with a gentle smile as he embraced his father.

The Commodore wished and willed, more than anyone had before, that he could remain in this moment for the rest of eternity. No more pain, no more sadness or guilt. Just the sheer pleasure and serenity that comes from holding a loved one dearly.

"I am sorry that I…" The Commodore choked. "…you are…"

He tried to talk, but instead resorted to holding back the tears as they attempted to force their way forward.

The Sheriff, meanwhile, enjoyed the unfolding misery and began dissecting the very timeline that surrounded Charlie, The Commodore and Hix. The stars began to dim against the perfect velvet sky, the wind slowed to a dead stop as the small town ground to a bewildered silence. The Sheriff marvelled at those in his presence, taking a moment to enjoy the beauty of their sadness, if there ever was such a thing. A thunderous snap of the fingers signalled the beginning of their annihilation as a black hole expanded into the middle of the house. Screams and groans could be heard echoing from inside the infinite hole as it slowly drew objects close and devoured them, never to be seen again. The void served only to feed The Weeping Rift and sustain its unquenchable thirst for sadness, pain and torture.

An orange light flashed as three guardsmen of The Celestial Order appeared. They stood fast with weapons drawn as they studied the room, before finally laying eyes on the Sheriff.

"Poor timing as always," the Sheriff sneered. "Can't you see that I am busy?"

"We tracked The Commodore to this location; unauthorised use of time travel had been detected," the first guard reported. His eyes were wide as he watched the infinite hole digest the timeline.

"And now you can leave!" snapped the Sheriff.

"We are here to retrieve The Commodore," shouted the second guard.

The Commodore looked over to the quarrelling foursome through a lemon-haze of confusion, his watch remained clasped tightly in his hand. He stroked the bezel of the seasoned time-piece as he studied the room slowly. Charlie continued to wail uncontrollably as Hix watched on with delight.

"Look at me, father," urged Henry, pulling The Commodore's face towards him.

"You... you aren't real," whispered The Commodore as a small window of clarity began to present itself.

"I am real!" screamed Henry "I am here, father!"

In an instant, The Commodore darted for Charlie and Hix. He gripped them both tightly as the Sheriff raised his arm skyward once more. The Commodore swept the hour hand of his beaten watch with his thumb in an attempt to move time forward. The Sheriff countered the movement of time with all his might as he tried to move time backwards. Endless thunder shook the earth as the wooden dwelling began to tremble and shake. Just as the Sheriff thought he had the edge, The Commodore smiled and moved his thumb in the opposite direction, shifting the hour hand in the other direction. A white flash and subsequent bang shot the trio from sight and away from 1835.

The trio landed hard in darkness. It felt cold but safe and, more importantly, real. The Commodore lay with an arm outstretched. He looked at Charlie and Hix – they were alive but unconscious. He looked around at their surroundings – a disused building that apparently hadn't seen any life or love for a very long time. The Commodore tried to stand but fell forward. He had no more strength left and quickly passed out.

"No one survives The Weeping Rift," a voice echoed in the darkness – it sounded miles away.

"The Commodore isn't just anyone," came a contradictory voice as a matter of fact. It was soft and soothing. The Commodore tried to open his eyes but couldn't muster the strength. Whoever they were, they were of no threat.

Haste stood in the disused room with The Commodore, Charlie and Hix. He considered them with a worried expression, his arms folded as he considered what to do. They had been moved onto an old bed. It was split, springs were exposed and it smelt of damp, but it was better than the floor. Haste turned on a heel and marched through to another room.

"How long have they been unconscious?" asked Alwin White, concerned.

"Three days," Haste replied, uneasily. "We can't stay here; he used the watch to get here so it's only a matter of time until The Celestial Order come knocking."

"We need to proceed with the plan," said Alwin, calmly.

"There aren't enough members. We have lost many in recent months alone. Our numbers stand at around fifty in total," Ozzie piped up from the corner of the room. He sanded his uncomfortable porcelain hands, wincing as he did so.

"Fifty million wouldn't be enough," Haste laughed, darkly. "The odds are stacked against us. We need awareness of the people across the planes, but Blindlings must be kept unaware."

"There are fates worse than death," Ozzie nodded, darkly.

"We need to move them to the Wanderer's Pass," Haste decided. "We have waited long enough now."

Alwin opened her mouth to speak as the two derelict doors blew off their hinges, shattering into a thousand pieces. The air became thick with dust and debris. Haste wafted the dusty air in front of him standing fast.

"Cut the head off the serpent, that's all we need to do," came a soft voice. Maybelle fluttered into the room, accompanied by at least twenty guardsmen that were stood ready to engage at a moment's notice. Their armour shone beautifully, immaculate and polished to perfection. Helmets were drawn over their faces – only accusing and energetic eyes could be seen through the darkness.

"Here without your master?" Haste mocked. "I wasn't aware that you were allowed out of town without permission!"

"You have been blessed with a smart mouth," Maybelle snorted. "We will see how smart you are when we cut out your tongue. We have ways of dealing with your kind, don't we, witch?"

Maybelle turned her gaze to Alwin, who stared right back at her, hatred of the purest kind in her eyes.

"You placed an enchantment on your children. I found them. I touched their hair and the skin on their face. How beautiful they would look with porcelain," Maybelle spat.

"Stay away from my children!" Alwin shrieked.

"I have agents working every day to break your enchantments. I will personally ensure they take a trip to

Oblivion after we have our way," Maybelle snarled in return.

"And look! They have recruited a bellboy!" she laughed, pointing at Ozzie. Looking down she saw his hands and their porcelain state.

"A brush with Oblivion too. I am impressed."

"Yet here I am," he replied, unafraid.

A hollow bang came from the bedroom next door, followed swiftly by a smashing of glass. The guardsmen took a tighter grip of their weapons and re-asserted their stance as the door crashed open. The Commodore stumbled into the room, barely conscious. He looked around at everyone, his hand gripping his pistol. He drew deep breaths and leaned against the wall, taking everything in. His shirt flapped about him, untucked. He looked all but defeated.

"Commodore Marshall reporting in," he wheezed, while raising a hand in an attempt to salute Haste. "Our mission was not successful. The elder we encountered in Detroit was Hysterias. Not an elder that would have been any use to us, so I threw it to the dogs." He gave a nod towards Maybelle.

"It cannot be," Maybelle gasped. "The Weeping Rift... nobody escapes The Weeping Rift!"

"Nobody escapes Purgatory, nobody evades The Celestial Order and nobody survives The Weeping Rift," sneered The Commodore, weakly. "I corrupted an entire hour of the timeline in 1835. The Weeping Rift, your stupid guardsmen and the population of that small town are condemned forever."

The Commodore smiled smugly as he held his chest, a searing pain burning throughout his body.

"Charlie!" The Commodore shouted, gasping for air as he did so. Shortly after Charlie joined them, rubbing his eyes. He looked around at everyone, confused, before his eyes settled on Maybelle. She stared back, open-mouthed in disbelief.

"Hello, my name is Charlie," he yawned.

The Commodore laughed again, choking and coughing as he did so. He reached into his pocket and retrieved his watch.

"Make another move and all of you are finished," Maybelle barked, suddenly finding herself. "Come with us peacefully and you will experience an easier journey."

The Commodore blew a raspberry and gave a thumbs-down. He fired a shot at Maybelle but missed, hitting one of the guards squarely in the face. The latter fell down silently before burning up and becoming nothing more than a smouldering mound of ashes.

"Get them!" Maybelle shrieked. The Commodore leapt into action, taking Charlie by the scruff of the neck and diving headfirst back into the bedroom. Wood, concrete and bricks smashed and splintered around them, The Commodore fired several shots into the room, taking down two more guards. Hix appeared from thin air and engaged another. Haste, Alwin and Ozzie had already disappeared, leaving Maybelle and the remaining guards to close in.

"Hix, we need to go now!" The Commodore yelled, ready to leap, his watch in hand.

All he needed to do was grab Hix and they could jump time together.

"I am staying. Take Charlie!" Hix shouted back as he clawed the head of a guard, savagely. Maybelle flew at incredible speed towards Charlie, her only objective being to kill the boy and end the prophecy.

"No, we can't leave him!" screamed Charlie as The Commodore took his hand – and once again, they leapt to another timeline, leaving only a flash and bang behind them.

Chapter Thirteen – 25 hours A Day

Part I

Do you ever get that feeling? Where you feel as though time has stopped? It's usually somewhere between being conscious and unconscious, though not quite subconscious. The birds fall silent, the sun and the moon disappear and the Earth seems to have stopped on its axis. Everything becomes perfectly distorted and yet immaculate. Peacefully out of control. This is the 25th hour.

Charlie and The Commodore arrived at their destination, only this time, it was The Commodore who fell to the ground. He scrambled to his feet, feeling slightly embarrassed. Charlie stood steadily, his eyes glazed with disappointment and sadness.

"Hix… We must go back and get him," Charlie pleaded, tugging at The Commodore's coat. "We just left him behind to die."

The Commodore began searching his pockets frantically, but stopped rather suddenly when he noticed their surroundings. He waved Charlie to be quiet.

"But we must get Hix!" Charlie continued.

"Shut up!" snapped The Commodore. "We won't be able to get him if we're captured, will we?" he asked rhetorically.

Charlie obliged and quietened. They observed their surroundings as The Commodore began searching his pockets again.

"They're gone," whispered The Commodore, rather worried. "The watch, my pistol. They're gone!"

A dead silence surrounded them – only The Commodore and Charlie were making a sound. The black sky had no moon or stars, no clouds or wind. Just stillness. Although it was dark, they could see piles of old clothes, broken household items, books, magazines and many more everyday items. A thick layer of dust covered everything, as though nothing had so much as moved in decades.

"There's not a tree, blade of grass or any evidence of anything alive," The Commodore muttered to himself as they walked through the unorganised mess.

"It's the inside, outside," said Charlie, looking skyward.

"Seems that way," replied The Commodore, scratching his head. "Don't touch anything, it could be dangerous."

"Is it true what you said?" asked Charlie after a short while.

"What?" retorted The Commodore.

"What we did to the timeline in 1835," Charlie continued. "Are they really stuck there, all those people?"

"Indeed, they are," The Commodore replied, indifferently. "Had I not made that choice, we wouldn't be having this discussion."

Charlie's brow furrowed as he considered this moral dilemma. Innocent lives had been trapped in that hour of 1835, condemned only to repeat that hour forever.

"Can we go back and help them?" Charlie pleaded.

"No," snapped The Commodore. "They are done. Needs must, for the greater good."

A frosty silence surrounded the duo, only interrupted by their own footsteps.

They walked on for what seemed to be hours, looking for a sign of anything that would give them a clue as to their location.

"Is this the end of the world?" asked Charlie, unafraid.

"No," said The Commodore, checking his pockets for the one-hundredth time that hour. "I've seen the end of the world; it has a lot less garbage."

"What was it like?" Charlie replied.

"The world, but the end," The Commodore responded shortly. "I arrived there by accident; I didn't hang around for too long, as you can probably imagine."

"I'd have stayed for a while," Charlie contemplated, as he imagined the end of the world.

"It's the end of the world," snapped The Commodore, impatiently. "There wasn't exactly much left."

Vignis walked swiftly up the steps into The Grand Manor, his face pale with rage. Maybelle had already arrived and sat patiently in the boardroom, alone. The door swung open as Vignis stormed in. He pointed a finger at Maybelle before turning and noticing the staff watching from the foyer.

"Get back to work!" he yelled frantically, "or so help me, I will have each and every one of you sent to Oblivion without a second's notice!"

They scuttled at break-neck speed like cockroaches into every other part of The Grand Manor, leaving anywhere near the foyer barren and empty. Vignis closed the door behind him and stood over Maybelle with his hands on his hips.

She sat in one of the chairs, her wings still and drooping, looking at the floor in shame. "I am-" she began.

"Shut your mouth!" he spat through gritted teeth, his chest rising and falling as anger coursed through him. "Thirty guardsmen you took, without my permission."

Maybelle said nothing – she did not dare meet his gaze.

"How many returned?" he snapped.

"Well, we have…"

"HOW MANY!?"

"Three" Maybelle muttered.

Vignis howled like a wounded animal as his face changed to a deep shade of red in fury.

"We are on the verge of war and you decided to take *my* guardsmen on a day trip, returning only three of them?" he raged, trying to understand her incomprehensible strategy.

"There wasn't any time to alert you, I found a secret meeting place that the Rebellion were using and decided that we should strike – eliminate them while we had the chance. The Commodore, the boy and the other leaders of the Rebellion were present. There aren't many of them left," Maybelle reported, almost robotically.

"Did you *eliminate* any of them?" Vignis snorted, already knowing what the answer would be.

"No. But we did take a prisoner."

"The Commodore?" he asked, hopefully.

"No. A demon. He defected to The Galdihar Rebellion," Maybelle added.

Vignis studied Maybelle for a moment. He considered eliminating her. It would be simple and no one would ever question him. Different methods ran through his mind at lightning speed, but he could not bring himself to do it. Compassion had not been something that he practiced regularly – he saw any level of heartfelt kindness as weakness.

He walked to the other side of the room and sat in one of the wing-backed chairs with a weary sigh.

"The Galdihar Rebellion are not a joke," he growled as he looked towards the window and out onto the hills. "They are very dangerous, especially Haste and The Commodore. You could have been eliminated or even captured, then we would all have been at risk."

"I am here to serve you; I only did what I thought to be the best move," Maybelle pleaded.

"What is wrong with you?" he snapped back quite suddenly. "You have never been disobedient, but now you do as you please with such boldness. What has changed?"

Maybelle made her way over to the window, demonstrating yet another brazen move. Most would not dare to move when being interrogated by Vignis.

"Our world is evolving faster and faster each day," said Maybelle, philosophically. "I want to evolve with it – I do not wish to be left behind."

Vignis narrowed his eyes, unsure of what to make of Maybelle's sudden interest in self-preservation.

"I imagine that we will be-," she started.

"Well, we are not here to waste the day imagining, are we?" sneered Vignis, impatiently. "Simply do as you are asked. Your independent judgement cannot be trusted!"

Vignis stood and walked to the window to get a better view of the beautiful rolling hills.

"You captured a demon, you say?" Vignis asked without looking at her.

"Yes," Maybelle responded, without hesitation.

"Have it taken to the interrogation room. I have a few questions," he snapped.

Maybelle flew to the door.

"Oh, and your presence during the interrogation will not be necessary," Vignis snorted, still looking out of the window. Maybelle gave a brief nod and left without delay.

The Commodore stopped for a moment and strained an ear. Charlie turned to see why he had stopped. They had walked in silence for quite some time.

"What is it?" asked Charlie.

"I can hear music, I think," The Commodore replied quietly.

Charlie strained his ears but heard only the growling of a hungry stomach – not his own.

"Is that you?" Charlie asked, looking at The Commodore's stomach.

"Yes, I'm really hungry," The Commodore replied.

He jumped at the realisation and put his hands on his stomach. "Charlie, I'm hungry…!" The Commodore stared for a moment, trying to make sense of what was happening. He hadn't eaten a morsel in centuries. He moved his hand to his wrist and held his breath as he pressed into the pressure point.

"I have a pulse, too!" he gasped.

He touched his confused face as he tried to make sense of what was happening. Charlie watched, unsure of whether to celebrate or be afraid. They both turned simultaneously and raised their noses, sniffing heavily again and again, trying to confirm what their senses informed them.

"Can you smell….?" The Commodore started…

"Food!" Charlie shouted, happily.

They looked at each other and ran in the direction of where the delicious scent seemed to be emanating from. They tripped and stumbled over each other, stopping every now and then to sniff the air, reconfirming their direction.

"There it is!" yelled The Commodore, excited.

A bright silver highway diner sat in a clearing amongst the piles of old items. It looked brand new. The neon lights illuminated the clearing as the sound of chatting diners and the clinking of plates could be heard from inside. They burst in through the door and stopped, their mouths open as they tried to make sense of what they saw. Immaculate tables and spotless chairs lined the diner, and the smell of fresh food wafted sweetly throughout. The chitter-chatter was loud and the sound of plates and cutlery could be heard as though it was packed to capacity. Only it wasn't. It was empty. Not a single sign of life could be seen, only heard.

"Stay with me, Charlie," The Commodore whispered.

"A table for two?" said a voice from thin air.

Most would have screamed and ran for their lives, but they had become accustomed to strange happenings. The Commodore frowned and slowly put a hand out towards where the voice came from.

"Yes, please," Charlie chirped, happily.

"Fabulous," came the eerie voice. "Will this booth be suitable?"

A chair slid out from a booth only a few tables down. The Commodore was hesitant, but Charlie seemed to appreciate the pleasantry and promptly sat down. The Commodore followed and seated himself opposite Charlie.

"Would you both like a menu?" said the voice.

"Where are you?" asked The Commodore.

The voice didn't reply, an awkward silence prevailed.

"Would you both like a menu?" said the voice once more, though slightly agitated. "We are very busy this evening."

"Yes, please," piped Charlie once again.

Out of nowhere, two menus appeared.

"Drinks?" came the voice.

"A coke and a coffee please," replied Charlie, as politely as ever.

"Coming right up. I'll be back shortly with your drinks," the voice concluded.

The Commodore looked around, bewildered, his mouth open slightly as he tried to make sense of what was happening.

"This is new to me," muttered The Commodore, turning in his seat as he examined the empty diner.

"We don't need to know everything," Charlie retorted from his seat. "Some things just are."

The Commodore examined him with suspicious eyes and searched his pockets once again.

"And some are not," he replied as a matter of fact. "I did not survive this long by accepting everything at face value."

"You didn't survive," said Charlie, bluntly. He wasn't being rude, just literal.

The Commodore scowled at him and thought for a moment, before he decided that Charlie was in fact, quite accurate. He opened his mouth to reply, when a cup of coffee and a glass of coke were thrust in front of them.

"Yay!" Charlie celebrated, and drained half of the glass at an alarming rate.

The Commodore sniffed at his coffee, gave a nod of approval and drank some. It tasted fantastic, so much so that his mouth began watering uncontrollably. He put a hand over it, conscious of those that may be watching.

"So, what will it be?" asked the voice a little more cheerfully.

"Steak, medium rare, new potatoes and a side of buttered asparagus," the Commodore reeled. He hadn't even looked at the menu.

"Very good," replied the voice, curtly. "And you?"

"A hamburger and fries. Can I get a chocolate sundae, too?" he asked.

"Certainly," the voice replied, cheerfully. "I'll be back shortly."

The Commodore stood from his chair and looked around suspiciously. There wasn't a dirty dish or used dishcloth in sight.

"I wonder where Hix is," Charlie pondered, concerned.

"Don't worry about Hix," the Commodore replied, shortly.

The Commodore also considered Hix – he felt guilty for leaving him behind, but what choice did he have? The boy could not be put at risk for the sake of a demon.

"Do you have many friends?" Charlie asked.

The question caught The Commodore somewhat off-guard. He looked at Charlie, giving him his full attention.

"Erm… no. Not really," The Commodore replied slowly. "I had friends, but they are gone now."

"I don't understand," Charlie replied.

"Well, times change and we meet new people. We don't see the old ones as much anymore. My time changes a lot," The Commodore explained.

Charlie raised an eyebrow. Even he saw through The Commodore's terrible explanation.

"No, Charlie, I don't. I don't have time for friends and all they do is slow me down and die," he returned, agitated that he had been deciphered by a small boy.

"I'm your friend though, right?" Charlie asked, yearning for his approval.

"I suppose," The Commodore smiled, defeated.

Two plates, cutlery and a chocolate sundae slid on to the table. Charlie and The Commodore both looked at each other and then to the void where the voice seemed to be coming from.

"Bon appetit, boys," the voice said politely.

And with that, they began eating as though they hadn't eaten for years. For one of them, this was true.

Charlie and The Commodore left the diner and headed back to the strange darkness they had managed to land themselves in. Charlie rummaged through a pile of odds and ends looking to see what he could find.

"What are you looking for?" asked The Commodore.

"This!" Charlie held a compass under his nose.

"You searched the pile, looking for a compass that you did not know was there, and you found a compass?" The Commodore asked, bewildered.

"Yes, that's right," Charlie replied as a matter of fact.

"I'll give that a try," said The Commodore. "I need a torch."

He rummaged through the nearest pile of items as Charlie watched on. The Commodore suddenly jumped back with a yelp waving his hand in every direction. A pair of tired wind-up teeth had bitten him sorely on the thumb.

He cursed and swore as he released the item and kicked it into the distance.

Charlie fell to the floor, unable to control himself for laughter.

"Was that you?" snapped The Commodore accusingly.

Charlie gave a faint nod as streams of tears rolled down his cheeks.

"So you can get what you want, but I get bitten?" The Commodore barked, still disgruntled.

"Shall we head north?" wheezed Charlie through his laughter.

"That's as good a direction as any around here," The Commodore sighed.

They navigated through the piles of items, every so often they would stop and search to see if they could find anything of use.

"I've found something!" Charlie shouted, half-submerged in a pile of old kitchenware. "I'm not sure what it is though."

The Commodore followed and looked into the pile with him. His eyes widened as he jerked Charlie away from his find. Charlie scowled at him. "I found it, let me get it!" Charlie shouted.

"It's a corpse!" The Commodore snapped.

Charlie froze with a panic-stricken expression and began to quickly wipe his hands on anything he could find nearby. The Commodore wasn't moved in the slightest.

"At least, that's what I think it is," he continued curiously. He shrugged and took the corpse by the boot, pulling it from the pile.

"He looks familiar," The Commodore rambled to nobody in particular. "I'm not even sure if he's dead."

"CAN YOU HEAR US!?" Charlie yelled into the ear of the corpse. It didn't move an inch.

The Commodore glared at him, scornfully.

"Can't you ask him any louder?" The Commodore replied sarcastically.

Charlie drew in a deep breath, ready to shout even louder.

"That won't be necessary," The Commodore concluded before Charlie had the chance to try and wake the dead.

"He has red cheeks, he's warm but he doesn't breathe or have a pulse. Stuck in time, seemingly." The Commodore scratched his head as he observed him.

The not-quite-dead corpse wore an incredible brown blazer with darned elbows and a bow-tie, bright red. He looked young with greaser-style hair.

"There's another one over here!" Charlie yelled from another pile. He pulled a lady out from the pile; The Commodore made his way over. She also looked young and sported a very formal appearance – hair tied up and formal business clothes from what seemed to be the 17th century.

"Clara Skye," The Commodore said with certainty. "One of the Time-Keepers, erased from existence and beyond, sadly. I met her once, very kind and clever."

"Do I know the Time-Keepers?" asked Charlie.

"No, why?" The Commodore replied as he stroked her face.

"I feel as though I should," said Charlie, somewhat confused. Something in the depths of his mind triggered, déjà vu almost, but before the event had occurred.

"I wouldn't worry about that," said The Commodore.

"Why?" Charlie replied.

"This place isn't real, you are not real, I am not real. This is a simulation of what once was, has been, but not what can be. Because it hasn't happened yet," said The Commodore, severely.

Charlie's head began to spin as he tried to comprehend what The Commodore had said.

"I am real, I know I am real," Charlie decided after some time.

"Your consciousness is real, but we are not. We are seeing, what someone – or something – wants us to see." The Commodore seemed a little more at ease with their location. "This is the 25th hour. I've never been here before, I've only heard about it."

"There are only 24 hours in a day… where does the 25th hour come from?" Charlie asked, somewhat puzzled.

"There are more than just the standard 24 hours, but this is a cheap trick," The Commodore sneered as he looked out across the items.

Charlie opened his mouth to reply, but a bright light and resounding bang cut him short.

"Cheap trick? I say! How very dare you!" A scolding voice came from behind them.

Charlie and The Commodore turned to see the source of the voice and were met with hands on hips, a scowl and one of the prettiest faces that either of them had ever seen. They both felt that she was familiar – something, somewhere in the deepest recesses of their mind triggered.

A distant memory evaded them, no matter how hard they tried to draw it forward.

"How dare I?" smiled The Commodore. "This place, it's a dump. If you're going to create a synthetic area for our consciousness, why not include a little luxury?"

Her mouth opened and then slammed shut again with only a 'hmmph' escaping from her. She shook angrily, but as angry as she was, neither The Commodore or Charlie felt intimidated. Instead, they were curious. Why wouldn't you be?

"Where are we, if our consciousness is here?" Charlie piped up.

"A fantastic question!" concurred The Commodore, slightly embarrassed that he hadn't asked the same question sooner.

"Don't worry about that, you are here, in mind at least. The rest of you, for what that is worth, is safe." She yawned, waiving the question away. Her flowing Victorian dress and black wavy hair contrasted against each other heavily. She attempted to brush away the masses of dust from her dress but gave up shortly after. She tied up her hair hastily and rolled up her sleeves, before looking from The Commodore to Charlie and back again.

"My name is Charlie, what is your name?" the boy asked perfectly politely.

She considered him for a moment, and then a smile slowly spread across her face.

"Domina Tempore," she curtsied politely.

"Lady Time?" scoffed The Commodore, rudely.

Domina winced slightly at his confrontational tone but maintained her smile, hands placed gently on her hips.

"Domina. Tempore," she reiterated. "What is your name?" she asked The Commodore.

He opened his mouth to reply, before Domina cut back in again.

"Oh wait, you're dead. No one cares what your name is," she interrupted. "Follow me, let's go." She turned on her heel and snapped her fingers as though her new-found company were dogs. The Commodore muttered and complained under his breath but Charlie and Domina ignored him.

Part II

After a short walk, they arrived at a small house. It was a peculiar building that looked as though it had been lifted from a pleasant suburban neighbourhood. Domina beckoned them inside the house, that seemed to be already sat indoors.

"Wait! Shoes off at the door!" Domina demanded, though she kept her own shoes on.

Charlie and The Commodore looked sideways at each other, then obliged. She smiled with satisfaction as they acquiesced to her request. She beamed, looking from one to the other, both of them looking mildly puzzled.

"Tea!" she proclaimed.

Domina snapped her fingers and a pot of tea suddenly appeared on the table by their side. She snapped her fingers again and the tea began to pour itself. There would have been a time that Charlie would have been amazed by such a display, but he merely smiled, mildly impressed.

"It's not rubbish!" she snapped suddenly, her expression becoming very serious. She clenched her fists, and as she did, a ticking noise emanated from Domina as she raged.

"Nobody said-" The Commodore started.

"You didn't have to!" she replied quickly. "I can read your thoughts; I know you more than you know yourselves. It's hard, being me. Watching, listening, wanting, missing."

Domina began to look upset and weep, but quickly became happy again when she noticed the teapot and helped herself to a fresh cup. Charlie looked from Domina to the door and began calculating how long it would take him to escape, should he need to. The Commodore seemed to be very interested in Domina and not at all alarmed by her swift change of mood.

The Commodore took his teacup and looked around the room. He noticed glass cabinets filled with trinkets, odds and ends.

"Memories," she explained, as The Commodore looked across the items.

"Are they memories out there too?" he asked politely.

"Some of them. Others are for safe-keeping," she explained, her eyes beginning to fill. The items meant a lot to her.

"Clara Skye," The Commodore began.

"She is no concern of yours. Her consciousness resides with me for safe-keeping," Domina retorted.

The Commodore smiled and looked back to the cabinet. He made to take a sip of tea from his cup when he froze. His hand began to tremble as he dropped the teacup to the floor, which smashed into a thousand pieces. Very slowly, he opened the cabinet door and took hold of a spinning top. It was worn and well used, covered in dust and dirt.

"Where did you get this?" he whispered, inspecting the old toy carefully with trembling hands.

"What do you care?" she asked bluntly. "You left it behind."

"It was not yours to take," whispered The Commodore.

"Now that you are here, you can stay!" she smiled, clasping her hands together. "How I admire you, James, and how I will come to admire you, Charlie. I have not had visitors for a long, long time. Those that I have invited have declined, usually politely." She made her way to a chair by the window and leaned on her hand, staring out into the distance. The ticking noise became more prominent once again.

"I have witnessed the most fabulous sights and been partnered with the bravest companions across the planes, across centuries and millennia, I am the last of my kind."

Domina looked longingly at The Commodore, she reached out from her chair and held his hand gently, as a single tear dropped soundlessly to the floor.

"But you are my favourite so far. I cannot promise that it will remain that way. You break the laws of time and conform to only what you decide is right. That is admirable, certainly."

Her hand fell from his as she returned to looking out of the window.

"They told me that I should cease to be, for the good of the future, time and stability of the planes. I refused, and here we are, the Past, the Present and the Future. We are to do great things, for there is much to be done."

"You should probably get a cleaner, too," Charlie interrupted. His face was serious and calculated. A penny had dropped with the resounding certainty of a hammer being brought down upon the head of a nail.

"There is much to do, but you can't do much with that mess out there. It's time for a clean." He gave a condescending look to Domina. She smiled, as she knew what he knew.

Kull stood straighter than usual, by the main doors of The Grand Manor. He felt more aware, his eyes narrowed slightly and his mouth moved silently as he actively thought to himself. San watched him with growing curiosity and, against her better judgement, compassion.

"How long have you been here?" asked San from the sweeping staircase she was cleaning, as she slowly descended.

He screwed up his face in deep contemplation as he attempted to access the deepest recesses of his memory.

"Long," he droned finally.

"Ever the conversationist," San sighed, mostly to herself, as she cleaned the staircase spindles.

"Why... are... you... here," Kull asked slowly.

"I needed work, at very short notice. I thought that it would be a noble and intellectual pursuit, but I was wrong," she replied.

"You are good. I am good," he added, his speech getting faster.

"I don't know about that; we witness endless cruelty and punishment mostly to those that don't deserve it, yet we don't intervene. I hardly think we are good," she explained, continuing to clean.

"We can change it," Kull boomed.

San looked around them quickly to see if anyone else had heard Kull. Nobody had. They were busy with their own duties.

"If anyone hears us, we are going to be destroyed," San pleaded to Kull, quietly.

Kull looked unmoved by San's anxiety of others hearing their conversation.

"We must be good!" he replied passionately.

San looked at him bewildered – where had he gained this mindset, she wondered to herself. This must be the only giant consciously aware of the actions and implications of those around them. She scratched her head and pondered the giant as he returned to the depths of his mind. His huge dinner plate-sized hands hung by his sides as he stared hard at nothing in particular.

Vignis descended the very stairs that San had been cleaning only moments earlier. He took his time, his hand holding the polished banister as he too stared into the abyss.

"Good morning," smiled San, cheerfully.

Vignis paused and looked across at San, her smile beginning to fade as fear took its place. 'Why did I greet

401

him?' she thought to herself. 'Great job, San, you're certainly going to be erased,' her consciousness screamed.

"Good morning," replied Vignis, his eyebrows furrowing slightly as he tried to recall her name. He picked most of the staff himself – only a few predated his tenure in leadership.

Kull stared hard at Vignis, his fingers curled into balled fists as he began to scowl at The Good Shepherd.

"I wasn't aware of your attendance today, sir," San continued, her smile now renewed. "Is there anything that I can do for you?"

Vignis stared at her for a few moments before slowly shaking his head.

"No, I do not require assistance. Unless you know where I can find the leaders of The Galdihar Rebellion?" He sighed as he completed his descent and made his way over to San. Her mouth hung in shock, not knowing what to say. Everyone on the staff knew of the Rebellion, but nobody dared to talk about them, even to each other.

"I do not know who they are," she stammered.

"Of course you do. Everyone in here does," he replied, in a friendly manner that only made their transaction even more terrifying. "I was joking. But we all need to be vigilant."

Vignis turned and noticed Kull glaring at him. His face contorted as the wheels of his mind turned. Although nobody could possibly know what he was thinking, you could not mistake his clear disdain for Vignis.

"Dangerous beasts, giants. I took him myself from his pack some years ago. They would not conform, so they were eliminated," Vignis explained to San. "They can be trained to a certain degree, but they aren't very clever."

Kull looked away from Vignis and relaxed his hands, his face becoming more at peace than it had been.

"Anyway, there's plenty to be done. Keep up the good work" He smiled, patted her on the shoulder and then turned and disappeared down the long corridor.

San waited until he was out of sight before collapsing into a nearby chair. She gasped and held her hands to her face. Vignis had never so much as acknowledged her existence before, let alone engaged her in conversation. She looked over at Kull who continued to stare into the abyss.

"I will destroy him," Kull boomed.

San gave a nod and waved her hand as she tried to catch her breath.

"Of course, you will," she replied sarcastically. "You'll get us killed first, I've no doubt."

Vignis made his way down the long corridor and took a sharp left down the cold stone steps into what was formerly a dungeon. It had since been converted into a torture chamber – iron chairs, chains and various weaponry lined the walls.

Hix, sat in a chair in the middle of the vast room, a black sack over his head. The room was cold, dark and damp and solidly maintained the atmosphere of despair and hopelessness. Vignis allowed the heavy door to slam behind him as he entered – prisoners always jumped and panicked at this point. Everyone except Hix. Vignis raised a curious eyebrow at Hix. Could he be a worthy adversary? One could test his skillset in interrogation and torture? He always hoped for a challenge but found most to be a disappointment. Maybe Hix would be different.

"It isn't often that I have demonic entities in this room," Vignis explained calmly to Hix.

Hix didn't reply. His claws tightened onto the arms of the chair.

"Oblivion," Vignis began as he paced the room with his arms behind his back. "A plane that strikes fear into even the most hardened creatures by its mere mentioning. I do not fear Oblivion, I plan to conquer it. I have the entire plane and Hymm in the palm of my hand. A most useful tool."

"You have nothing of the sort," Hix growled from under the sack. "You cannot possibly imagine what Oblivion contains. No imagination can capture even a tiny percentage of what happens in that wicked place."

A grim smile curled at the corners of his mouth as he continued to pace the room. He was making progress already.

"I have never graced Oblivion with my presence, that is true. There is no requirement for me to do so. Hymm is the orchestrator, and all I need to do is have him by my side," said Vignis as he grinned. His steps echoed throughout the room as he paced, purposefully, deliberately and intentionally. "Myself and Hymm, we aren't so different. I have what he needs and we have reached an agreement which bolsters the ultimate plan that The Celestial Order have employed.

"Not on your life," snorted Hix. "You are delusional and foolish. You are unravelling at the seams and losing your grip on the empire you have cruelly snatched from innocent lives."

The smile on Vignis's face disappeared as quickly as it had arrived. He marched to one of the tables and picked up a handgun. He always started with weaponry of the Blind world. Though he hated the Blindlings and their world, their innovation could be put to good use. Vignis held the gun to Hix's kneecap and fired. Hix screamed from under the sack, which muffled his wailing slightly. Vignis smiled and laughed at his pain, but recoiled away from Hix, his mouth agape, as the wails turned to laughter. Hix cackled mockingly at him.

"You need to do better than that!" he laughed heartily, his words echoing in a patronising manner, something Vignis was not familiar with. He watched the sack on his victim's head bob up and down with the laughter. His fists shook with anger but he contained himself. Vignis firmly believed that loss of composure displayed weakness. He made his way over to one of the tables and picked up a jewellery box. He ran a hand along the polished rosewood lid, admiring the hand-crafted box of vanity. He took a chair and sat himself opposite Hix, who had calmed from laughing and now listened eagerly, wondering what would be next.

"Do you know what the 'Sisters Whisper' is?" asked Vignis quietly. He leaned forward, removed the sack from Hix and looked him in the eyes. They were deep, orange and endless. Hix held his own for a few moments before looking away. He knew full well what the 'Sisters Whisper' was. A deep dread began to fill his chest as he gripped the sides of the chair once more.

"What's the matter?" Vignis asked through a sickly grin. "No more smart remarks?"

He waited to hear what the reply would be, but none came. Vignis held the box out towards Hix, as though showing off its beauty.

"Many think that the 'Sisters Whisper' originated in Oblivion, but in fact, it came from Sanctuary. The great, mysterious, blessed land." Vignis spat on the floor at the mention of Sanctuary. "Tobias the Great created it to help him meditate and learn from his mistakes, a kind of living hindsight. He mistook its potency, and eventually it drove him mad. Instead of allowing him to replay his chosen memories, it replayed those that troubled him the most. Again. And again. Until he went mad. The lords of Sanctuary banished him to existence as a Blindling. He lived a peasant and died a peasant."

He considered the jewellery box once more, smiling as he did so. Hix braced himself as Vignis prepared to open the box.

"It isn't real. It isn't real. It isn't real…" said Hix over and over again as he closed his eyes. Vignis opened the box nearer Hix, a beautiful figure inside began to rotate slowly as a pretty jingle played. Before long, the room filled with many whispering voices. Hix screamed at the top of his voice as Vignis laughed…

Chapter Fourteen – Condemnation, Redemption and The
Gregorian

Part I

*There is something human in the darkness that surrounds
my world. I wish that I could be human. Though the mortal
mind would be slowly twisted and warped into something
abysmal where sanity has no place. I am not of the mortal
world; I am consciousness defined. Ah, to live, to love. I
mask my envy in the guise of aspiration, but how can I
aspire to that which I cannot be? Rather than be me, should
I instead cease to be? My beloved masters scorned me so. I
am not like the others. I am Domina Tempus, The Lady of
Time.*

The Commodore contemplated Domina with curiosity as
she hummed the most fabulous of melodies. She stared

expectantly out of the window, as though waiting for company to arrive. Her long, flowing dress, old as it may be, perfectly captured her figure and represented an era long forgotten.

"You still haven't figured it out, have you?" Charlie interrupted.

"Indeed, I have not," The Commodore replied, mostly absent from their conversation as he looked upon Domina. "Who is she?"

"Lady time," Charlie replied as a matter of fact.

"Domina Tempura!" Domina shrilled, overhearing their conversation.

"I'm sure that you will figure it out," Charlie smiled cheekily.

The Commodore rolled his eyes and brought his attention back to the spinning top in his hand. He pondered it once more, examining each side, smiling as he did so.

"How the simple joys made you happy," The Commodore whispered to the spinning top.

He looked over the spinning top and noticed Charlie looking at him with a curious eyebrow raised.

"Do you know how to use one of these?" asked The Commodore, rather more severely than was required.

Charlie shook his head whilst maintaining a bead on the spinning top.

"Would you like me to show you?" The Commodore asked. Charlie gave an excited nod in acceptance before they dropped to their knees and played with the spinning top. Hours passed as they wound the spinning top time and time again, testing its capability on a variety of different surfaces. Domina watched on with joy as they played, laughed and joked. An inconsolable yearning beat from within her as she studied the pair. She considered her own hands for a few moments, imagining what it would be like to be mortal.

"My son adored this spinning top. He had little time for anything else." The Commodore smiled as he held the toy to the light, observing and appreciating every scratch and imperfection upon the perfect relic of his past.

Charlie smiled and listened to The Commodore's remembrance. He never spoke of his family, Charlie felt honoured that he chose to share his memories with the current company.

"To some you are a hero and to others you are a heretic," said Domina darkly. "I have witnessed every event that has contributed to your legend. The question is, where do you see yourself?"

"We have been together for so long, James. Many memories, certainly. I enjoy hearing you talk of the times I did not have the fortune to witness."

"I have been alone for centuries, with only brief companionship in between," replied The Commodore politely.

He stood straight and spoke properly, complimenting Domina and her over-rehearsed etiquette.

"The Fury," said Charlie, firmly involving himself in the current conversation.

His bold words cut the atmosphere and drew every bit of The Commodore's attention. He glared at Charlie, his lips pursed and eyes narrowed as he stood with his hands behind his back in perfect military fashion.

"What happened, after HMS Fury?" Charlie added.

"Everything," Domina answered, in place of The Commodore. "What fun that time was."

"Fun never came into it. You cannot possibly know of the struggles I endured after sinking to the depths," The Commodore retorted, maintaining his composure but clearly irritated.

"We should show Charlie what happened following your… untimely demise," said Domina with excitement.

"Relive memories that haunt me to the present day?" The Commodore asked rhetorically.

Domina considered The Commodore with a severe expression, polarising her demeanour once more.

"Well, this is *my* domain and you cannot leave without my say-so." She folded her arms and turned up her nose to The Commodore. "We can educate Charlie, or you can spend the rest of eternity here. What will it be? I have lived amongst my artifacts for longer than you can comprehend, it is of no detriment to me." She spoke boldly, with intention and commitment. The Commodore looked from Domina to Charlie.

"I need my watch and my pistol," he growled.

"You may not negotiate with me, James," she scorned with her arms folded. "Your weapon will return when I decide. And the watch, well it's closer than you think."

Charlie sniggered into his hand, failing fabulously at any attempt to hide his amusement.

"Very well," snapped The Commodore.

"Excellent!" Domina exclaimed, clapping her hands together. "I must get my coat!"

Domina disappeared to a different part of the house, leaving The Commodore and Charlie together.

"So, where is it that you think we are?" asked The Commodore sarcastically.

"I do not *think* I know where we are. I *know* where we are and I'm disappointed that you have not figured it out," Charlie replied, his words dripping in condescension.

"As you clearly don't know," he continued, "we are-"

"I can figure it out myself!" retorted The Commodore. "When did children become so entitled?"

Charlie opened his mouth to argue but decided against it when Domina returned in a coat with a sun umbrella, happily leaning against her shoulder.

"Shall we?" she asked with excitement as she took The Commodore and Charlie in arm.

Before they could answer, the familiar flash and resounding boom echoed around them as they tore into one of The Commodore's memories.

Charlie screwed his eyes as the blurry memory began to focus and define, each detail dropping into view as it became as clear as the day the event occurred. The Commodore stood straight with a serious expression, he made it clear that he disapproved of the viewing of his memories. Domina rocked on her heels, barely able to contain her excitement.

Charlie looked around in awe at the vast and seemingly endless hallway, the most beautiful architecture stood as proud as the day it was made, without a single blemish. White marble floors reflected the hand-painted scenes of beauty on the ceiling. The stunning images of children laughing and playing ran the length of the ceiling in serene beauty, as the huge mahogany doors contrasted the décor in what can only be described as, perfectly. It seemed rather quiet in the hallway. Only the occasional person would walk swiftly by. It felt peaceful in the vast hallway, a halfway house of contentment.

A light made its way quite slowly down the hallway towards them, almost like the will o' the wisp, but it shone a bright white rather than the usual yellow.

"That is a soul destined for Sanctuary," explained Domina as she leant down to Charlie.

"I haven't seen one before. It's rather beautiful," Charlie admired.

"In times gone by, you could see them quite regularly in the Divine world. Since The Celestial Order came into power, they are rarely seen. Especially on the premise of their value in terms of energy," The Commodore added darkly.

"A sad state of affairs," Domina stated, rather plainly. "It's about time for your judgement, *Commodore*," she smiled cheekily.

The Commodore rolled his eyes as they made their way down the vast hall together.

"Here we are!" Domina chimed.

They made their way through one of the huge mahogany doors, Charlie gasped at the vast and busy courtroom. Benches were lined across the walls, with seven or so rows and a chair in the middle. The feeling of contentment began to shift more to intention. There was an undeniable intensity of the courtroom, especially with so many in attendance.

"This has to be one of the busiest courtrooms for a judgement," said Domina, rather impressed. "Usually there's only a handful."

Those in attendance sat patiently on their benches, whispering and muttering to each other as they waited.

"Judgement. That is what each Blinding and Divinian will face when they pass from their mortal state. Usually, a judgement is done without your attendance, if it's clear-cut. If not, you are subject to a court," The Commodore explained.

"Do you think I will have to attend a judgement?" asked Charlie after a moment's thought.

"After accompanying a known fugitive? I would say definitely," said Domina, softly. She smiled gently as she delivered the grim news. Charlie gulped and quickly shifted his attention to the unfolding events.

The huge door slammed shut as Judge Humphrey entered swiftly, his long black gown flapping behind him. A collection of notes and books were under his arm and a rather interesting looking wig was perched perfectly upon his crown. Judge Humphrey never smiled or laughed. He made his way to the judge's panel and sat in the middle of four other judges, one of which was a goblin. Silence reigned as the room waited for the subject to enter. The door opened once more as two large guards dropped a man into the stand – he seemed to be semi-conscious. The room remained silent as only the drips and drops of water could be heard, hitting the floor around the semi-conscious man in the chair.

"This judgement has been brought to my attention; the accused stands against potential subjection to Oblivion for all of eternity. Murder, callous disregard for life, selfish intent, theft, dereliction of duty, abandonment and many other offences," Judge Humphrey boomed. "Does the accused have a representative?"

The room remained silent. The semi-conscious man looked up at Judge Humphrey. He wiped water from his face and laughed as he looked around.

"Representative?" he laughed, coughing as he did so. "I've been at the bottom of the ocean."

"We are quite aware," Judge Humphrey snapped irritably as he flicked through his notes.

Charlie looked at the soaking man and noticed that it was in fact The Commodore. He turned to his hero, who looked disapprovingly back at Charlie and shook his head at the scenario being played out before them.

"HMS Fury, a vessel that sailed for the New Royal Navy. It was destroyed and sent to the depths of the ocean after you lost in battle," Judge Humphrey read aloud. "It could have been prevented, but your selfish actions and callous disregard for the lives – ultimately in your care – are what you stand accused of."

"I did my duty!" coughed The Commodore loudly.

"You did what you wanted, and as far as I can see, there is no reason that you should not be sentenced to Oblivion," Judge Humphrey snorted.

"Send me wherever you damn well please, I have lost everything that was dear to me," he shouted, slumping further into the chair.

His uniform lay in tatters, stained and ruined from his time at the bottom of the ocean. The room buzzed with whispering as they discussed his fate.

Charlie looked at each of the judges, it was clear that their decision is what would condemn The Commodore.

"Expand on your point – what did you lose?" the goblin judge asked, rather abruptly.

Judge Humphrey looked at him with a raised eyebrow, he was hoping for an open and shut case so that he could get back to other matters of personal importance.

"Everything. My family were murdered by trespassers at our family home." The Commodore choked, his hands tightening on the arms of the chair. "So, what do I care for your condemnation?"

The judges looked sideways at each other awkwardly – all except Judge Humphrey who didn't seem concerned at The Commodore's statement.

"What were their names?" snapped Judge Humphrey impatiently.

"Henry Marshall, Mary Marshall," The Commodore reeled, his voice cracking in pain.

The judges flicked through their notes with well-practised hands as The Commodore looked curiously at the faces around the room.

"They are indeed deceased," Judge Humphrey boomed once again.

The Commodore looked up at him contemptuously as he gripped the chair even tighter.

"Henry and Mary passed in normal circumstances. Some years following your disastrous voyage," the goblin judge explained with a distinct lack of empathy or understanding.

The Commodore looked up suddenly and rose from his chair, his eyes darting from one to the other as a rather large penny began to drop. He made to walk to them but chains around his ankles prevented him from moving.

"They were alive?" The Commodore asked, bewildered.

"Indeed, they were. They now reside in Sanctuary where they belong. Unlike yourself," Judge Humphrey added.

"How can that be, I only died mere hours ago?" The Commodore pleaded.

"Time is not what it seems. We had quite some preparation to do for this case before we brought you forward," said Judge Humphrey.

"But I had a letter, from Admiral Foresythe himself," The Commodore stammered, trying to grasp and absorb the information he was being given. His eyes filled as he tasted almost every emotion possible.

"You had a letter," said the goblin judge with a knowing look.

"It cannot be," whispered The Commodore. "Beaufort, Bamford and Bum. They faked a letter about my family." He gasped and dropped into the chair. He considered the judges and began to laugh, a laugh which echoed throughout the chambers and hit a pitch only the insane are capable of reaching. Those in attendance looked down upon their subject, without remorse, but with disapproval. His laughter turned abruptly to painful tears, as he sank into the chair and wept.

"I told you, they had the last laugh," said The Commodore, grimly.

Charlie looked at The Commodore and smiled a knowing, forgiving smile as Domina reached out and held his hand. It was cold. Although she smiled, her eyes seemed empty, unblinking and synthetic.

"It was a different time, James," said Domina, attempting to be cheerful.

The Commodore looked down at her hand holding his, slightly awkwardly. He considered the joining of their hands for a moment and then turned back to his memory.

"I do not understand why we are holding hands," said Domina. "But I rather enjoy it-"

"Domina," interrupted The Commodore, "you're ruining the moment. Let it be."

Hix slumped miserably to one side in the chair, beaten, bruised and burnt. Muttering incoherently to himself in a multitude of languages, he stared at the cold stone floor. Vignis considered him through tired eyes, his sleeves rolled up and sweat pouring from his forehead. A variety of items lay scattered around them, enchanted weapons, Blindling weapons, otherworldly cursed items that seemed to any other to be a normal day-to-day item. Take, for example, a normal-looking belt – to the naked eye it seemed to represent no threat to anyone, except maybe for short drops with sudden stops. Once the wearer fastened the belt, it would tighten very slowly, inch by inch, until the very life had been squeezed from out of them. Only then, would it return to being a normal belt. It was an item created and enchanted by some of the most wicked sadists that had ever existed, but not from Oblivion, as most would assume. No, they had the habit of being far more creative in their methods of subtle torment.

"The Rebellion, where will they be meeting next?" Vignis snarled and spat through his teeth. "You do not have the capacity to take much more of this."

"How long?" whispered Hix.

"What are you drivelling on about? Answer the damned questions!" Vignis bawled in return.

"How long, have I endured?" Hix whispered, still looking at the stone floor.

"Two days," Vignis snapped quickly.

In fact, it had been six days, one of the longest continuous meetings of this kind Vignis had ever conducted, though he would never tell Hix that.

"Then, bring me day three, four and five," Hix coughed. He raised his gaze to Vignis's and smiled mockingly, using every bit of strength he had remaining.

"You will not see another hour! I can promise you that! Oblivion, that is where you are destined for!" Vignis roared into his face.

He raised an ancient sword in perfect warrior stance and prepared to bring Hix to his final conclusion. Hix chuckled to himself as his amusement steadily increased to an outburst of laughter. It hurt to breathe, let alone laugh, but he was determined to do so at any cost to himself.

"Oblivion?" he winced between laughter. "So, you are to send me home?"

Vignis let his arms drop by his side, he looked at the demon, flabbergasted. His mouth opened but not a sound came out. Hix was right, the threat of Oblivion would be of no consequence or be anything other than familiar to Hix, Undesirable, yes, but tolerable.

"Master?" came a quiet voice from the door. "I did knock, but you did not hear me."

Maybelle fluttered over to Vignis. He turned to Maybelle, breathing deeply as though he might explode at any moment. Maybelle considered their guest with disgust and hatred. Hix looked up and their gaze met. He smirked for a moment.

"Maybelle, the legend, the survivor, the rejected," he smirked and dropped his head down to look at the floor.

"You reference my leaving of Oblivion, demon?" she sneered, her words poisonous and intently malicious.

"Leav... leaving?" he stammered. "You mean, expulsion?"

"Expulsion?" Vignis retorted.

"For... for conspiring to overthrow a Prince of Oblivion. Oh, and her real name is *Mirelle*."

"Mirelle?" Vignis shouted. "You were, expelled from Oblivion? For conspiracy? I have never heard of anything like it!" he stammered, his composure beginning to fray and split at the seams.

"Do not listen to this filth!" Maybelle squawked, her face full of panic. "He is trying to manipulate you; this is all a trick!"

Vignis looked from Maybelle to the all-but-dead Hix, his eyes filled with suspicion and paranoia. He tightened his grip on the sword as he studied Maybelle closely. Her eyes begged for mercy, although she dared not ask for it verbally. Mercy displayed guilt, weakness and inability to Vignis.

"How can I know the truth?" Vignis pleaded, more to himself than anyone else in the room, the sword slowly rising as he continued to keep a bead on Maybelle.

"You can't!" laughed Hix loudly. "You... yo... you will never... know."

Hix began to fade in and out of consciousness as Vignis kept his gaze fixed on Maybelle.

"I came to tell you that the yearly celestial party is a mere six hours away," she whispered, holding back tears.

She wondered if this would be the final conversation she would have with her master, and as the moments slipped by, it almost certainly seemed that it would be.

"We must prepare – your people demand the attendance of 'The Good Shepherd'."

Vignis dropped the sword to the floor and fell into an empty seat nearby. He considered Maybelle as he seethed, unsure of what to do.

"You swore allegiance to me," he muttered. "I saved you."

"There is no truth to what this filthy demon, has told you. It is nothing more than a tale to drive a rift between us," Maybelle explained calmly.

Vignis turned to Hix, who had fallen into a state of unconsciousness. He spat at the demon and turned back to Maybelle. He considered her as his thoughts drew back to a distant memory.

"I once held the rank of 'Captain' in the Myriad Army. The greatest force that ever was," he explained, looking through Maybelle, into his past. She listened intently; his past was a mystery to most, including her.

"We were trained to kill, destroy and plunder from an early age. Devastating armies of elves, goblins and Blindlings, often before they knew what was happening. We didn't lose a battle in over one hundred and fifty years. We knew only savage victory. That was until we were ambushed by 'Blindling Crusaders' who had somehow learnt to use our own tactics against us. Arrows flew from all sides as they advanced and eliminated us in a deadly skirmish. Everyone in that division perished, except me." Vignis shifted uncomfortably as he remembered the day vividly. "They pulled me, wounded and beaten, from the cadavers of my comrades, and beat me until there was almost nothing left. I saw that two of our own lieutenants had defected days before our arrival, which gave them the upper hand," Vignis croaked. He threw a mug across the room and spat vehemently at the demon. "They let me go with the only purpose of telling Emperor Rodius how we had been defeated. I walked for one hundred days alone, until I found you."

Maybelle squeaked with pride as she remembered the day.

"We walked for ten more days, together," Maybelle added. "You promised that we would never taste defeat and we would rise to dominate all planes of the known world." She savoured each word she spoke, recalling the day they met fondly.

"Why did you save me?" asked Maybelle, boldly.

"You and I had met the same fate. We had been defeated and cast to the lowest point an entity can find themselves in. I, from the battle that we lost, and you from the inner circles of Oblivion."

Vignis smiled weakly as he looked around the room.

"I still have my enchanted armour in this very building. I keep it close, to remind me of what defeat, embarrassment and shame feels like.

"Our union has been tested; but we have only strengthened our bond as we have celebrated each victory," said Maybelle proudly.

Vignis stood from the chair and gave a nod to Maybelle.

"Get my wardrobe in order, arrange 'The Great Hall of Valmir' and ensure that we have the right security in place. Handpick each of them yourself and ensure they have been checked for any single sign of deference to The Galdihar Rebellion," he ordered. "The Great Hall of Valmir hasn't been used for over a century. I think this momentous occasion should be celebrated accordingly."

"Yes master, thank you, master," she replied adoringly, and then fluttered as fast as she could out of the room. Once again, she had endured her master's scorn with her head still on her shoulders – something that no other entity on any plane had ever managed to achieve.

Part II

The hammer came down repeatedly, offending the ears of all in attendance as the voices in the room slowly quietened.

"Order, order! I will have order in my courtroom!" Judge Humphrey boomed. "We have deliberated and considered for many hours; it is time to bring this session to a close."

He stood from his seat, the other four judges by his side looked on at the sodden Commodore. Silence finally prevailed in its entirety as the witnesses eagerly watched on to hear what the outcome would be.

"For his heinous disregard for life and subsequent failure to embrace responsibility for his crimes, I recommend that Commodore James Edward Marshall should be exiled to the wretched plane of Oblivion, which by default, carries an eternal sentence." Judge Humphrey looked around the courtroom and gave a definitive nod before seating himself. The room became alive with whispering as they considered the recommended sentence.

It seemed harsh, given the circumstances, but it was expected.

"I ask my honourable colleagues how they cast their vote. For those in favour of the recommended sentence, raise your hand," he boomed once more. Silence fell again as no one dared even to blink, out of fear of missing the judgement first hand.

The Commodore looked at the floor, his eyes red and swollen from weeping. He muttered to himself, totally detached from the room.

One judge on the right raised a hand, and shortly after another judge raised a hand on the left side of Judge Humphrey.

Judge Humphrey rolled his eyes at the outcome. He had been hoping for a 'full house' so that he could send this cretin to the world below and get on with his day. A special wine he had acquired sat on his table at home, and Judge Humphrey wanted to get home to taste it.

"As we have a tie, what is the recommendation in place of what we have already put forward?" he asked his colleagues with a raised eyebrow that seemed to be asking why they had decided to keep him from his wine, rather than why they had not agreed with him. As one of the judges opened his mouth to make a suggestion, a man stood from one of the far benches and bellowed across the court.

"I would like to put forward a recommendation of character to be considered before he is sentenced," the voice shouted. Those in attendance craned their necks and strained their bodies to get a look at the man that had interrupted an official court with such unorthodoxy.

Judge Humphrey quickly decided that the wine could wait for another time and that today must be dealt with.

"Who, may I ask, is putting forward this recommendation?" the goblin judge asked, using his hand as a visor and squinting his eyes to focus on the disrupter.

"Captain Elias Dalton, of the New Royal Navy of Great Britain," the voice called in return.

The Commodore looked up at the mention of his former colleague and friend, his face bewildered. The judges leaned in together to discuss the matter between themselves, whispering feverishly at the unorthodox method of providing a reference. They looked at The Commodore from time to time and then back to themselves, before finally giving a nod of agreement.

"You may step down and give a reference for the defendant," Judge Humphrey called, lacking as much interest as everyone else in attendance. He had condemned many entities of all kinds and heard every story imaginable over centuries. Although unorthodox, it wasn't anything that he thought would go down in the history books. Dalton weaved between the seated attendees as they eagerly moved out of his way, keen to see how the rest of the case would unfold. He made his way to The Commodore and stood by his side, his hands behind his back in perfectly correct naval fashion. Although many of the attendees were not familiar with the Blind world, they respected traditions and formalities of the Blindlings, especially in circumstances such as these.

"Captain?" said The Commodore, smiling weakly. "You turned down my proposal for promotion, Lieutenant."

"I decided that I would take you up on the offer as I lay dying on the decks of 'The Fury'," Dalton replied, curtly. "I hope you don't mind, Jim?"

"Not at all," replied The Commodore, gratefully.

Nobody had called him Jim for as long as he could remember. Only his closest friends and treasured family called him Jim. He felt that Dalton had forgiven him and, moreover, he didn't feel alone anymore.

"What is your statement, Captain Dalton?" asked Judge Humphrey.

"Commodore Marshall has always displayed exemplary military conduct during his time in the New Royal Navy," Dalton began.

"It doesn't seem that way, from what transpired upon the condemned vessel," called out one of the judges on the right.

"Commodore Marshall," Dalton continued, as though he hadn't heard the judge. "Holds the record of the youngest Commodore ever to sail under the flag of Britannia, rising through the ranks in an incredibly short amount of time. His study, dedication and proven leadership will go down in the history books and serve as an incredible inspiration to aspiring Naval officers, maybe even outside of Great Britain. Commodore Marshall is also a dear friend – we went through officers' school together and studied together. His dedication, sincerity and loyalty to the crown served as a reminder that there are, indeed, great people to be found in what you would call, the Blind world."

"He sank an entire ship of innocent souls, displaying none of these characteristics that you have attributed to him." Judge Humphrey snapped, impatiently. "We do not have time for wallowing and revelling in fond memories that bear no relevance to the sentence we have proposed."

Dalton looked from Judge Humphrey to The Commodore and smirked. The Commodore looked back at him blankly, convinced there wasn't anything to smirk about.

"You cannot convict Commodore Marshall based on one outstanding incident," Dalton proclaimed.

Judge Humphrey changed to a shade of red hitherto unknown to any colour chart in existence. He opened his mouth to reply, but Dalton continued.

"Conviction based only on one event during one's lifetime is not moral, reasonable or acceptable. If you applied the same ruling to every case that landed in these vast, honourable walls, then you would no doubt have sent every defendant to Oblivion." Dalton held out his hands and tilted his head slightly. The smirk returned. The four judges sitting either side of Judge Humphrey considered Dalton's words.

"You forget your place!" Judge Humphrey howled. "I have never been spoken to with such disrespect and disregard. If you have finished, you may return to your seat."

Charlie jumped slightly, as Dalton looked round and seemed to fix his gaze upon him. He froze as the hairs on his neck stood on end, reducing his breathing to almost nothing.

"Can he see me?" whispered Charlie, thoroughly caught off-guard.

"No," said The Commodore as he watched on. "This is a memory; all of this has already happened. It's impossible."

Dalton smirked towards Charlie and shifted his gaze away. Domina smiled as she held onto The Commodore's arm, she had become totally invested in the memory. Though she knew the outcome, knew the story and the conviction, she remained enthralled and encapsulated in only the events unfolding in front of them.

"I have not finished," replied Dalton quickly, bordering on rudeness. Some of those in attendance gasped, their eyes almost popping out of their skulls as they hung from every word this madman had to say. "I ask that you extend your consideration only to Commodore Marshall's service during his time in the New Royal Navy and his dedication to his family. I ask of you; how many lives were spared when The Commodore seized five ships from the Spanish Armada. Not a single life lost, not a single shot fired. All prisoners were treated respectfully and were processed correctly. During one of the largest pirate raids in the history of Port Royal, The Commodore intervened and led his men bravely to victory with minimal losses. After an extensive battle with the Dutch, where we crippled most of their ships, he assigned two British vessels to escort them back to their own waters so that they would not be intercepted by pirates. In actual fact, this was, and still is, against regulation and can carry the death penalty for bordering on treason."

Dalton looked around at the court before finally settling on the panel of judges.

"His family-" Dalton started.

"They were not lost!" Judge Humphrey roared.

"Commodore Marshall has lost everything. Including his family," Dalton replied finally. "I only ask that you take this statement into consideration for the passing-down of Commodore Marshall's conviction."

Dalton gave a nod and made his way back to his seat high in the benches, safe in the mind he had done his best to assist his friend and colleague.

"Before we cast a vote, those not in agreement will pass their recommendation on what the outcome should be." Judge Humphrey sat himself down as the goblin judge stood and read from his papers.

"We believe Commodore Marshall should be sentenced to eternity in the barren lands of Purgatory without parole and will be exiled from Existence." He reeled the sentence without any feeling, just as he had a thousand times before.

The Commodore remained slumped in his chair, his eyes staring and unmoved at the reading of the two sentences that both presented themselves as possibilities for his future.

"We will discuss these matters and then cast another vote," the goblin judge finalised before reseating himself.

"What happened to Dalton?" asked Charlie

"I do not know. I never saw him again," The Commodore replied. The Commodore felt shame and regret. He watched the memory steadily and with strength, but inwardly he felt empty.

"I ask the panel once more to cast your vote. For those in favour of condemnation to Purgatory?" Judge Humphrey boomed, he had calmed significantly now that he expected to leave soon. Two judges on the left raised their arms, another on the right side raised also, creating a majority.

"Very well, Commodore Marshall. You are hereby sentenced to Purgatory for eternity without possibility of parole." Judge Humphrey closed his book and looked down upon The Commodore who still looked to the floor. "You should take the time to appreciate the statement given from your former friend, who sadly passed when you could have prevented it. It satisfies me to know that you will *never* be in that position of responsibility again. Dismissed!"

Judge Humphrey brought his hammer down with a crack and collected his belongings, eager to leave.

The room began to clear as two guards came to escort The Commodore to his next destination and complete the hearing.

"I never did see that kind of responsibility again," The Commodore muttered to himself.

Charlie heard him and considered his words. He knew that he missed the responsibility of leadership and the task of developing his colleagues and fellow officers.

"Oh James, why don't we head over to when we first met?" asked Domina, lovingly.

"Forgive me, I do not remember the first time we met," replied The Commodore, slowly.

He shifted uncomfortably, feeling a deep sense of guilt as one would when forgetting someone's name.

"Then let me refresh your memory!" said Domina, cheerfully.

Charlie clapped, excited to see the next chapter of what made The Commodore, and started the legend that would pass the hearts, minds and lips of many amongst the Divine world.

Part III

The memory faded as another took its place, the familiar blur becoming as clear as the day it first occurred. The sky became dark, without stars but with two moons. They contrasted the black sky in a dull amber orange, a rather sinister sight to behold. The land was mostly barren, thick sand dunes rolled across the landscape endlessly into the distance. A low wind whipped the sand from the top of the dunes and carried the tiny sand stones across the plane. Lifeless, hopeless and empty. The barren lands of Purgatory offered the perfect place for contemplation of one's wrongdoings and regrets to the point of insanity, which was the usual route for most condemned to the plane.

"This is a horrible place," said Charlie, a cold shiver making its way down his spine.

"I quite agree. Time slows to a crawl amongst the dunes," Domina explained, sullenly.

"Time is plenty, may your heart stay empty, as you search the sands for your redemption," The Commodore chimed. "That statement was drilled into us from day one and became the law of our existence, if you could call it that. Many souls are lost amongst the sand dunes and they are incredibly frightening to happen across."

The trio looked across the dunes and saw a familiar figure making his way towards them. A tatty old top hat was perched on his head at a jaunty angle, while an old rag tied over his mouth and nose stopped the sand from choking him. A reclaimed pair of welder's goggles sat firmly over his eyes; his skin had been irritated by them but it was worth the pain to keep the sand away from the eyes.

The Commodore looked at himself approaching, and the memories rolled into his mind as he replayed his time in Purgatory. Memories that he himself thought he had forgotten. They watched as the convicted Commodore kicked at the sand. He stared for a moment, then produced a trenching spade and began to dig feverishly.

"I have lost count of the holes I have dug in the sands of Purgatory," said The Commodore, darkly. "Two-hundred and seventy years I spent here. I know it was a lot, but it felt like a thousand years. We had to dig and find artifacts to take back to the masters of Purgatory. We were told that there wasn't anything special to be found here, and they were right almost all of the time. Just junk that finds its way here one way or another."

"Ahem," coughed Domina, who looked offended. "Only junk?"

She raised an eyebrow in The Commodore's direction, he looked awkwardly away from her gaze.

"You still haven't figured it out yet, have you?" asked Charlie, failing to hide a wry smile.

"Of course, I have," lied The Commodore.

"All will be revealed," said Domina, rolling her eyes and folding her arms.

The digging suddenly stopped as The Commodore removed his welding goggles. He looked down into the hole he had been digging and pulled out what looked to be a piece of circular scrap metal. He considered it and ran his hands along the top before placing it carefully in his pocket and walking back along the dunes. He walked for hours before a building finally came into view. The tall building looked as though it had been abandoned for at least a century. It lay in ruin and seemed to be crumbling into the very sand it stood upon.

As The Commodore approached the building, he entered the main door into a holding cage in the middle. The smell of blood and sweat stung the nose and brought tears to the eyes of all, even those that had been accustomed to it for a long time.

"Anything to declare?" asked an ancient, wicked-looking elf from the other side of the cage.

"Sadly not. I did not find anything in the sands and I will continue to dig until I find my redemption," The Commodore reeled as he had a thousand times before. The elf narrowed his eyes and grinned in a sickly manner.

"You shall be searched *before* entry," said the elf, clearly suspicious of The Commodore's answer. The punishment for trying to sneak any contraband or undeclared items in would be an extension of the sentence by the masters of Purgatory, and would also result in no recommendation for release.

"I am on my way to see Master Leech," replied The Commodore, coldly. "He sent me to a particular location to search, but my searching was indeed fruitless. I am to report to him immediately and without delay. I do not think he would look kindly on your conduct, especially concerning a special mission." The Commodore folded his arms and leaned coolly against the bars of the holding cage. He had made his point, his cards held against his chest tightly, daring the ancient elf to call his bluff. Silence stood between them. Only the wind could be heard outside as they stared at each other without blinking.

"Very well," said the ancient elf, disappointed.

He had the choice to call The Commodore, but opted to fold instead. The elf had spent centuries in Purgatory and had an instinctual ability to sniff out those that were guilty. The Commodore had a narrow escape, that was for sure. A bell screamed as the cage opened and he made his way inside the building. He removed his top hat and coat, shaking them down to remove the sand he had accumulated. Deep in thought, he made his way to the stairs, before a huge greasy hand took hold of him. The Commodore turned angrily to see who had intercepted him, raising a fist as he did so. A foul-smelling beast, half troll, half giant towered over him. His matted fur had accumulated dirt and filth over many decades and most were doubtful he had ever bathed. His huge jaw exposed black, rotten teeth with breath so potently grim it was said it could strip the very flesh from your bones.

"Marshall, how much time have you served of your sentence?" the Gregorian leered, his eyes flashing to his three peers who were watching avidly. Two goblins and an imp followed the Gregorian at his heels, sticking by him as much as they could to ward off any interference from others.

"A little over half," The Commodore replied, impatiently.

"I don't like your attitude, Blindling!" the Gregorian spat.

Although a giant-troll hybrid, two species typically of lesser intelligence, the Gregorian had a reputation for being very cunning and clever. Most wondered how the sadistic beast had managed to avoid being sentenced to Oblivion.

The Commodore winced at the stench of the Gregorian's breath – as his vision hazed, he considered the possibility of his poor hygiene being intentional.

"What do you want?" The Commodore asked bluntly while slowly brushing his pocket with the back of his hand to make sure that his find from the dunes hadn't fallen out. The Gregorian noticed his movement and narrowed his eyes with suspicion.

"I want what you have in your pocket, human," the Gregorian smiled, pulling The Commodore closer. He recoiled once more from the stench of his breath. The Commodore stared into the Gregorian's eyes for a few moments – he then exhaled, defeated, and gave a brief nod.

The Gregorian grinned triumphantly as The Commodore reached into his pocket. A second later, the Gregorian screamed and dropped The Commodore to the floor. He had indeed reached into his pocket, but did not retrieve his find. Instead, he took a fistful of sand and threw it into the monster's eyes. One of his followers attempted to stop The Commodore but he delivered a kick worthy of a star football player and sent the goblin hurtling through the air, a high-pitched squeal emanating from the beast as it disappeared down the corridor. The Commodore turned and ran at full pelt to get away from the Gregorian and his cretinous comrades. He ran without stopping, taking swift turns and doubling back to ensure they couldn't locate him. Some of the prisoners popped their heads out from their dormitory to see what was causing the commotion. The Commodore slowed down and took a moment to check if they had managed to follow him. He leaned on the wall and caught his breath but no one came. It would be too dangerous to head to his dormitory just yet, so he made his way to the Master's quarters instead.

The prison plane of Purgatory had many unwritten laws, largely upheld by the other prisoners. Illegal trade, extortion and banishment to the endless sand dunes were rife. The Commodore refused to conform to any law, unofficial or otherwise, unless it held personal interest to himself. As a result, The Commodore had few allies.

Master Leech was one of five masters of Purgatory, all of which reported to Omar Asghari. The orchestrator and leader of the barren plane. Master Leech was a stout, small man with a thin beard who always looked annoyed. He had the reputation of being one of the worst masters of Purgatory, but the truth was, if you were of use, you would have an easier time during your sentence.

The Commodore approached the splintered door of his office and knocked three times, taking a step back from the door to await his summons. None came, so he took a seat by the door and waited. As he did so, he pulled his find from his pocket and considered it. It was a lump of circular metal, covered in sand and dirt. He rubbed as much of it away as he could and found it be a pocket watch, the very one that would make him one of the most infamous beings across the planes. He cleaned it obsessively, and eventually revealed the watch in all of its beauty. Damaged, but beautiful.

Domina looked sideways at the modern-day Commodore and smirked. He looked at her blankly, the penny still far from being dropped. Charlie shook his head in disapproval. The Commodore frowned at him and returned to watching the memory, very much engrossed.

The door to the Master's office opened and Omar Asghari came out. The Commodore looked up at him and then looked away, it was best not to speak to the Masters unless spoken to.

"Have you found anything of interest in the dunes?" Omar rasped, with an air of authority.

"No sir, not yet. But I remain optimistic," The Commodore replied formally.

"Very good, maybe you will find your redemption." Omar smiled thinly. He studied The Commodore for a moment and then disappeared swiftly down the corridor.

"Come inside," barked Master Leech, sounding chronically annoyed.

The Commodore made his way inside and stood in front of the Master's desk – the Master took a seat and waved to a chair. The Commodore seated himself – you had to wait to be asked to sit by the Masters.

"What did you find in the deserts today, James?" asked Master Leech from behind his desk. His hands were folded and leant against his pursed lips, perfectly complementing his narrowed eyes. He considered Master Leech for a moment, calculating the risks of being dishonest in his answer. He quickly decided against it – the Masters were highly skilled in unmasking deception. The Master watched as he dipped a hand into his pocket and placed the watch on his desk.

"You found this today?" asked The Master with a raised eyebrow.

The Commodore gave a brief nod. The Master slowly retrieved the watch and studied it before looking back at The Commodore.

"Do you know what this is?" asked The Master, inquisitively.

"Broken," he replied as a matter of fact.

The Master shot him a scornful look over the top of the watch. He didn't approve of sarcasm or attempts at wit.

"It's a Time-Keepers Watch," said The Master slowly. "They are… obsolete. The Celestial Order have taken over most of their duties. I am surprised they haven't been replaced already."

He snapped the watch shut, and a piece of broken glass fell from the watch onto the table.

"The barren land of Purgatory is an interesting place; evidence of times gone by appear occasionally. More interestingly, relics of the future also find a place here. Perhaps this is what you have found today," he pondered aloud, a grim smile widening as he considered the relic a sign of The Time-Keepers' obsoletion.

He looked down at the watch once again and then back at The Commodore – an expression of contemplation now took place. After a few moments, he leaned into a draw attached to his desk and retrieved an ancient-looking pistol, equally filthy and neglected.

"I acquired this piece of treasure a very long time ago. As you know, time moves at a slower pace in Purgatory. It's a pistol that also belonged to The Time-Keepers. It is a mere ornament now, its power and enchantments have long-since decayed and depleted."

"Is it just a pistol?" asked The Commodore as he looked at the ancient relic. He had read about the Time-Keepers and knew of their legend.

"It is now, but it once had the power to erase any entity, mortal or otherwise. They would simply cease to be. A formidable weapon, certainly." The Commodore retrieved the pistol and squeezed the trigger, but it had seized and wouldn't budge.

"Anyway, we must be getting on. Place both of these items on the shelf before you leave, there is much to be done," Master Leech concluded as he turned his attention to some paperwork on his desk.

"Very well, master," The Commodore gave a nod, put his chair carefully back in its place and walked over to the vast shelf filled with all kinds of odds and trinkets. A fleeting sense of attachment swept over him as he stretched his hand out to the shelf. The Commodore glanced sideways and saw that Master Leech remained buried in his paperwork. A split-second decision later and The Commodore slipped the watch up his sleeve and dropped the pistol on the shelf.

He considered the watch as he walked, digging the dirt out of the beautifully crafted grooves and patterns. As he navigated the corridors, he bumped into something.

"Sorry," The Commodore started as he looked down.

He froze as he noticed it was one of the Gregorian's followers, a tired and rather disgusting goblin.

"The Gregorian, he will destroy you!" he croaked, rattling a pointed finger in his face.

The Commodore slipped the watch away – he saw the goblin's eyes follow his hands and, without a second's delay, he picked up the goblin and locked him in a disused utility cupboard.

"Hey! Hey let me out!" the goblin squeaked.

The Commodore looked around to see if anyone else had noticed him, but they hadn't and so he decided to make a swift dart for his quarters. There weren't meant to be any benefits in Purgatory – it was bleak, dull and hopeless. One advantage was that each inmate had their own room and could enjoy time alone when not on duty in the sand dunes. The Commodore made his way inside – the cracked and damaged walls were grey and oppressive, intimidating almost. He had made some comforts, a makeshift bookcase with mostly forbidden books to educate him on the Divine world outside of Purgatory, and other trinkets, odds and ends he had acquired and not submitted to the powers above.

The Commodore sat for hours, cleaning and reviving the ancient watch. The case was badly damaged and the clockwork seemed mostly destroyed or missing. He disassembled the parts carefully and lovingly, and every so often he searched boxes of trinkets to find some other clockwork pieces that might fit into the watch.

"It all seems hopeless, looking at it from this angle," Domina admired as she watched the memory of The Commodore. "I remember the curious feeling as you worked away, though I did not know who you were."

The Commodore looked at Domina rather bewildered and confused, but again, conscious of appearing rude, he tried to hide it.

"Were you in Purgatory, in this room with me?" he asked with hesitancy.

"Quite," Domina replied conclusively. "I remember as the weeks became months and months became years. I just sat, watching and waiting."

"Were you an inmate?" The Commodore asked, rather accusingly.

"In a manner of speaking," she concluded, now rather agitated at his interrupting of her viewing pleasure. He looked awkwardly to Charlie who shook his head once again and then went back to the memory.

Many years passed as The Commodore managed to get pieces to fit into the watch and bring it back to some kind of functioning state. He came across the Gregorian on occasion, sometimes avoiding a beating, but other times he was unable to escape. Whatever the outcome, he never informed the authorities but instead grew stronger, more resilient and more capable for their next encounter.

Charlie watched the memory and thought about his own encounters with trouble. A growing sense of relation grew as he began to understand The Commodore and his journey.

One evening, the weather was particularly adverse. It never rained, but on occasion the wind would blow the dunes into a sandstorm which meant certain doom if you were to try and venture out into the abysmal conditions. On order of the Masters, they were given a day's rest – or at least until the storm ended. The Commodore naturally took to his watch and began finalising his repairs. His tongue ebbed from one corner of his mouth to the other as he steadied his hand, placing the final screw onto the makeshift mechanism he had created for the watch. Although he had polished it to the best of his ability, it still had severe dents and scratches as well as still having smashed glass over the top of the face. He took a deep breath as he placed two fingers delicately on the winder. He turned it slowly and the resistance began to build from the winder, which was a good sign. Wind it tight, but not too tight. Overtightening would lead to catastrophic failure. The Commodore released the winding mechanism and held his breath.

Nothing happened. The watch did not tick or tock. It did not sweep or swipe and it showed no sign of life whatsoever. The Commodore smiled to himself, closed the watch and placed it neatly into his pocket where it would stay, close to his heart for over a year.

"All that hard work and for nothing," Domina smiled, knowingly.

"That's right, why didn't you get angry?" Charlie asked "You get angry at much smaller inconveniences."

"Oh, do I?" retorted The Commodore. "Like what?"

"You were positively furious at Worcester sauce flavoured crisps in Detroit. You said that they had doubtlessly never seen Worcester sauce and declared them a fraud." Charlie looked at him with a blank expression.

"How petty," concluded Domina, turning back to the memory.

"It wasn't for nothing," The Commodore sighed. "The watch gave me an objective, something to carry on for. It kept me from insanity."

Domina smiled as though she already knew what The Commodore had told her.

"Let us see a legend be born," said Domina cheerfully. "We need to get back soon. I can't have you hovering around in my conscious space for too long. Also, I don't remember where I left you both. Sorry about that. I'm sure you're fine though."

The memory advanced once more to The Commodore sitting at his desk reading through The Celestial Times. It was a newspaper that was usually thoroughly out of date by the time it arrived in Purgatory. He read the articles and compared what they claimed as truth to the history books and found most of it was fabricated – propaganda by The Celestial Order to keep its readers in fear and to help maintain order. He collected a handful of newspapers and made his way to Master Leech's office to find some answers.

"We have watched decades pass," said Charlie slowly. "But everything stays the same here."

"Torture," added The Commodore.

"There's more to this plane than everyone thinks," chirped Domina.

"And what is that?" said The Commodore and Charlie simultaneously.

Domina looked at them both and shook her head, but declined to answer them.

The Commodore knocked the regulatory three times and took a step away from the door.

"Come inside," snapped a particularly peeved voice. "Don't sit down. What do you want?"

Master Leech looked flustered, and regarded The Commodore as a rather troublesome inconvenience.

"I wondered if you could enlighten me further on The Celestial World and, more importantly, The Celestial Order," The Commodore asked extra politely, as he had noticed the Master's poor mood.

The Master studied him with distaste and inferiority.

"You collect your trinkets; you read your books and carry out your duties almost as well as the other creatures I have to endure here," the Master stood from his seat and approached The Commodore.

"And what for? To escape the feelings of guilt for leading your comrades to their doom? Or for abandoning your family?" The Master smiled provocatively, willing The Commodore to respond.

The Commodore shook with anger, his fists clenched as his face contorted this way and that. He did not reply, but stormed from the room, slamming the door behind him. The Master chuckled with satisfaction. His sadistic attack had landed right where he wanted it to. Why should an inmate have a better day than he?

The Commodore walked along the corridors, his hands in his pockets as he looked at the floor. He lifted his head after some hours and noticed he was in an unfamiliar part of the building.

"James," growled a voice from behind him.

The Commodore turned and recoiled at the stench of the Gregorian. He was alone, which was unusual.

"I followed you down here," he smiled. "A final meeting between us. There are fates worse than death, James. I'm going to crush you and leave you inside one of the containers here for the rest of time. Only you and your thoughts."

The Commodore glanced to his left and took hold of a bar, but the Gregorian had already considered the move and took hold of it, shaking The Commodore off with ease. The Gregorian roared as he brought the bar down with a crash, The Commodore leapt aside just in time and scrambled to his feet. He ran as fast as he could, but the Gregorian was on his heels as he did. The corridor narrowed to a single door; he took hold of the handle but it was locked. He turned and considered the Gregorian; a giant, hairy hand squashed his head against the door.

"Let's see what you have in your pockets, James. What treasures are you hiding?" He growled as he rifled his pockets. A loud ticking began to sound as the Gregorian searched.

"It was a hard decision to intervene, but I couldn't leave you to the hands of that monster," explained Domina.

"Intervene? I was alone…" The Commodore stopped and realised who 'Lady Time' was.

"You are the watch?" He stammered; thousands of questions swarmed together in his mind as he took hold of her arm.

"Not now, James!" smiled Domina. "We're getting to the best part."

"I figured that out ages ago," beamed Charlie proudly.

The Commodore hardly heard him as he watched Domina with renewed awe and interest.

"What's that ticking noise?" snarled the Gregorian. He pulled the watch from his pocket with one hand whilst crushing The Commodore's skull with the other. A blinding light filled the entire corridor, the Gregorian dropped the watch and roared, loosening his grip on The Commodore. He saw an opportunity and leapt for the watch. Every fibre of his being fought to save the watch from harm, though he could not explain why. The Gregorian recovered and made for the battered Commodore. The Commodore looked at his watch as though it may be for the last time. He thought of somewhere safe and noticed the winder move unassisted. A bright light and resounding boom echoed as The Commodore vanished from sight. The Gregorian reeled in rage; his bulging eyes looked everywhere but there was no trace of him. Another blinding light and resounding bang cut through the corridor as The Commodore re-appeared with the very bar the Gregorian had been wielding only moments earlier. He ran towards The Commodore, howling with rage. A giant, hairy fist made its way at lightning speed towards The Commodore's face but it never found its intended destination. The Commodore vanished once again.

The Gregorian backed himself against the wall, panting wildly as his eyes darted in all directions. Another light shone, the bang sounded once more… and that is all the Gregorian remembered. The Commodore stood over his opponent, blood dripping from the bar in his hand. The watch ticked happily, measuring time perfectly as though it had never done anything else. The Commodore stood over the Gregorian, breathing deeply as he considered the incredible time-piece. The bar slipped from his hands as he felt renewed hope, power and purpose sweep through him.

"It's time, to make things right," The Commodore whispered to the watch. He smiled for a moment, but the smile quickly faded as official voices could be heard down the corridor.

Omar Asghari appeared and looked The Commodore dead in the eyes as he approached. The Commodore smiled knowingly and vanished.

"Where... where has he gone?" Omar stammered. Nobody had ever escaped Purgatory in recorded history.

The Commodore appeared in the Master's quarters. He raided the trinket shelf and found the pistol he had inspected many years prior. Squeezing the grip tightly, he felt a gentle warmth connect him to the weapon. Although still battered, the moving parts unseized and presented themselves ready for action.

"It's not too late, James," came a warning voice at the doorway. "You might get away with a simple extension of your sentence."

The Commodore turned and took aim at Master Leech. He was accompanied by several official agents of The Celestial Order. News had travelled fast of the unauthorised use of his powers.

"Hand me the watch and the pistol. What was meant for the Time-Keepers certainly wasn't meant for a mere mortal," Master Leech reasoned.

He had no concern for The Commodore, only himself. Should word get out that he had allowed an inmate to escape, he would certainly face The Good Shepherd personally. Something he had managed to avoid so far.

"It's time for me to leave, *Master*," The Commodore laughed. His eyes danced with excitement and joy.

"They will call you 'The Villain of Purgatory'," Master Leech warned.

"The Commodore… that will do just fine," smiled The Commodore, conclusively.

The Master threw out his arm and released a Death Shroud, which roared through the air to its target. The Commodore fired a shot into the Shroud and vanished into thin air, leaving only the remaining company and a smouldering pile of ashes where the Death Shroud once was.

Chapter Fifteen – Live by The Blade…

Arrows, blades and bullets never ended a single life. Not in all of history. The taught bow, wielder of the blade and the finger on the trigger. Those are the ones responsible. We are conditioned to believe that life is the most precious gift of all. Priceless. Though war, genocide and racial cleansing disagree. Human life is one of the most commonly spent commodities across the planet. What if the soldiers lay down their arms and simply said no. Not today. Not another day. What if?

Vignis considered himself in the full-length mirror of his bedroom. His elegant black dinner suit and rather alluring mask looked as though they had been made for him personally. And they had been – he wore bespoke designs created by the finest seamstress the Divine world had ever seen. Once every century, the 'Great Celestial Ball' took place, hosted by Vignis himself. It had been orchestrated with the purpose of enticing the most powerful and influential guests from all over the world. It's no secret that

464

having great connections can open many more doors on the corridor of opportunity, and Vignis wanted to open as many of them as he could.

"The guests will be arriving in a couple of hours," said Maybelle meekly from the door.

"Very well," said Vignis. "Do we have any updates on the Rebellion and what their plans might be?"

"No, not since our last altercation. The demon is still in the interrogation room, he has not relinquished any further information," Maybelle replied.

"He is certainly more resilient than I first expected," he admitted reluctantly. "I will ensure that he is destroyed once we have concluded the ball."

Vignis returned to his mirror and considered himself once again, removing imaginary specks of dust from his suit.

"We are not far from the final solution," he said thoughtfully. "Adelade has been working hard to ensure we are on time, more so since the removal of Arteon."

Maybelle listened intently to her master, not daring to take her attention away, especially since their recent altercation.

"I do wonder if she can be trusted. It is a great responsibility to be contracted in any situation, but with Hymm, it makes the matter more severe," Vignis pondered.

"Should we have her removed?" Maybelle asked, hopefully. She didn't care much for Adelade and considered her presence unnecessary.

"No. We can consider this again at another time. I must prepare for the ball."

"Yes master!" Maybelle chimed and fluttered away.

The Commodore sat himself in a chair and helped himself to some tea from the table. It was still piping hot, even though they had been absent from Domina's home for quite some time. Charlie opened his mouth to ask how that was possible, but decided in the grand scheme of his adventure, it mattered very little and simply accepted it for what it was.

"I had no idea that my watch contained any kind of consciousness," The Commodore explained as he took a sip from his cup. He recoiled slightly, underestimating how hot it actually was.

"Your watch?" Domina scoffed, she folder her arms and narrowed her eyes as her head tilted slightly to one side. "I belong to no one. I am not a pet or possession. Not even The Time-Keepers dared to consider me so obtusely."

The Commodore looked blankly at Domina, unintentional as his comments may have been, they had still landed on a particularly sensitive nerve.

"Why me?" asked The Commodore in an attempt to guide the conversation into less confrontational tones.

"Why not?" replied Domina, indifferently.

She seated herself opposite The Commodore and returned to gazing out of the window. They watched as Charlie kicked a football between the endless stacks of Domina's keepsakes, darting in and out of them with skill and precision. He kicked the ball high into the air, it disappeared into the darkness as Charlie waited with arms wide to catch it, but it never back came down. Disappointed, he came back into the house and seated himself by Domina. A pleasant silence descended between the trio as each considered their own thoughts for a while. There is something tranquil, contented and beautiful about sitting and enjoying pleasant company. Even when nobody speaks a word.

"Goodness! I almost forgot!" Domina suddenly jumped from her chair, knocking the teapot to the floor. It smashed to pieces, sending hot tea everywhere –but that was of little concern.

"The Grand Celestial Ball!" she shouted.

"What of it?" replied The Commodore, taking another sip of tea from his cup, he shook his head at the smashed teapot as he spoke.

"Why, everyone will be there. I think that you and Charlie should attend."

"Have you lost your mind?"

"Well, I never really had one to begin with," replied Domina, cheekily.

"Very good," The Commodore replied as he rolled his eyes. "The Celestial Order will be there; I don't know if you've noticed but I am the most wanted fugitive across the planes, and Charlie probably has a bounty on him by now."

"A bounty?" Charlie gasped. "On my head?"

"And the rest of your body," Domina added severely.

"Like a real bandit?" he said, his eyes glowing with excitement.

"Very much so," The Commodore warned.

"The Commodore? A coward?" laughed Domina. "If I had known you were yellow-bellied, I would surely not have chosen you as my champion!"

"Coward!?" The Commodore choked, halfway through a sip of tea.

He rose from his chair flustered, offended and with minor scolding.

"Charlie! Get your coat. Coward indeed! I'll show you coward," The Commodore barked

"I don't have a coat" Charlie replied, confused.

"Don't answer back!" The Commodore snapped.

Charlie shook his head and chose not to reply.

"The Grand Celestial Ball," said Domina, dreamily. "A masquerade party no less. Oh, how I would love to attend. Dancing, laughing and making friends. I can get you inside, mostly undetected. You'll have to be careful."

The Commodore stopped as he approached the front door of the strange house. He turned and considered Domina for a moment, his eyes moving uncomfortably away from her as he shuffled his feet awkwardly.

"Is there any chance we will meet in this form again?" asked The Commodore sheepishly.

"Maybe, but probably not. I might, I'm not sure. Heavens, what a question to ask!" Domina replied in a state of total confusion.

"Nothing is straightforward in the Divine world," said Charlie with a sigh.

The Commodore raised his eyebrows in agreement.

"Right, let's get you down to the Grand Celestial Ball," said Domina, conclusively.

"Wait, why are we going to the ball?" The Commodore asked all of a sudden. "Surely it would make more sense to meet the Rebellion elsewhere."

"Hix," said Charlie, rather seriously.

"You should take more notice of Charlie," Domina laughed, pointing a thumb at him. "Greatness in the making."

Charlie smiled from ear to ear as the familiar light flashed and a resounding boom echoed around them.

The Commodore frowned at Charlie as they stood squashed together in what appeared to be a wardrobe. The smell of mothballs and neglect filled their nostrils. The Commodore peered through the crack between the doors to check for anyone in the bedroom, but they appeared to be alone. Very slowly, he opened the door and went to step out, but fell with a thud to the ground, Charlie landed on top of him.

"It's okay, I'm fine," whispered Charlie reassuringly as The Commodore winced. The small boy's knee had gone into the small of his back. The huge bedroom was rather minimalist. The tall ceiling sported the most beautiful hand-wrought plaster work, expertly painted in

Georgian fashion. The pale pink walls indicated it to be the room of a lady, who clearly hadn't been there for quite some time. There wasn't any make-up and the bed had been made perfectly, though slightly dusty from lack of use.

The Commodore crept over to the large window that measured almost to the ceiling. He peered outside taking special care not to be noticed. The rolling hills seemed to go on forever into the distance, there weren't any cars, bikes or signs of normal day-to-day Blindling living. The Commodore suddenly dropped to the floor as a great epiphanic realisation dawned upon him.

"We're at The Grand Manor," he whispered quietly. "She's dumped us right in the lion's den!"

His watch ticked quietly from inside his pocket, a sign that Domina had heard his comment and didn't seem overly pleased.

"What is The Grand Manor?" asked Charlie, confused.

"The enchanted headquarters of those that govern the Divine realm. Well, most of it," he replied.

"The Celestial Order?" gasped Charlie.

The Commodore nodded gravely as they both looked at each other. Charlie crept back to the wardrobe and opened some of the drawers.

"What are you doing?" asked The Commodore. He had his pistol drawn ready for action should it be required.

"Look!" said Charlie, a little too loud for The Commodore's liking. "We can wear these, it's a masquerade party after all."

Charlie held up some clothes that were perfectly fitting for the event. The Commodore shook his head and let out a low sigh.

After a very quiet exchange of clothes, The Commodore stood with a black velvet coat, a matching black mask and a complimentary bush style hat with a long peacock feather sticking out from the side.

"You look great," whispered Charlie in admiration. He looked down at his own attire, rather less impressed.

"If anyone asks, you're a high elf, a lady at that," The Commodore explained as he stuffed his pistol into his belt and popped the inevitable time-piece into his top pocket.

"I look rather silly," said Charlie with a sigh, as he popped on a floral hat and adjusted his magnolia mask. "That said, I could take this home to my older brother. I'm quite sure he'd find it rather fitting."

"Your brother?" asked The Commodore, bewildered.

"Never mind, it's a long story," giggled Charlie as he remembered his brother and his secret pastime fondly.

"Can't we just kill The Good Shepherd?" asked Charlie, rather bluntly.

The Commodore observed him with a rather disappointed look; he had become accustomed to his companion's more compassionate traits.

"I'm afraid it isn't quite as simple as that. If we remove him, one of his colleagues will simply take his place, and on it goes," said The Commodore, darkly. "Let's try and find Hix, they might have already dealt with him."

"You must call me Master at all times; it keeps things simple," The Commodore explained as he made a final check of his attire. "And I'll call you…"

"Lady Tempus," Charlie finished with a smile. The watch could be heard ticking merrily from The Commodore's pocket. He gave a nod of understanding and they made their way to the bedroom door. The Commodore drew his pistol and dropped the hammer back as he slowly cracked the door open and peered outside. The hustle and bustle of guests entering the party through the foyer could be heard as he peered into the darkened corridor. He motioned to Charlie and they crept through, keeping low. They were no doubt in a restricted area and needed to join the guests in order to get an idea of where Hix might be held. The Commodore leaned against a door as he peered towards the balcony edge that overlooked the main entrance. A slight click came from the door, and a second later it swung open with a bang. A maid opened her mouth to scream but The Commodore brought the handle of his pistol down on her head. She slid to the floor soundlessly as The Commodore bound and gagged her before stuffing her into the wardrobe of the room.

"Sorry!" whispered Charlie into the wardrobe as they left and continued on down the corridor. A few well-placed steps later and they slipped into the mainstream of guests walking into the building. Charlie tried his best to maintain his composure as he looked around, mesmerised by the variety of costumes, masks and entities that were in attendance.

"Excuse me, have you brought a child with you?" came a very deep French accent from behind The Commodore. He turned, slightly startled and opened his mouth to reply. The Frenchman had attire of the finest quality and a mask to complement, seeming to be almost completely human aside from a large tribal marking across the left side of his face.

"How very dare you!" Charlie replied in a terrible attempt at a lady's voice. "I am a lady of great importance! A child! Indeed!"

The Frenchman turned a shade of red and looked around awkwardly to see if anyone had noticed his error. Some had.

"My apologies, I did not mean to offend a lady such as yourself," he stammered

"Lady Tempus!" Charlie shrilled once again. "Master, take me away from this heinous excuse of a... whatever he is!"

The Commodore looked around and saw that some of the guests had stopped to see what was causing the commotion. Charlie took his arm and they continued their way into the Great Hall of Valmir.

The Grand Manor had been lavishly decorated, with every detail attended to with absolute precision. The chandeliers lit the room in a warm light and complemented the vast oak dance hall perfectly. A band played slow ballroom music for their guests. Charlie pondered The Grand Manor as they made their way through, considering the décor and styling. From what he knew of The Celestial Order, the building certainly didn't reflect their reputation. The Grand Manor felt warm, inviting and homely.

Charlie and The Commodore made their way in, taking care not to draw any unnecessary attention to themselves.

The variety of the masks worn by the guests made Charlie's head spin as he looked around open-mouthed. People of all ages and origins danced, talked and laughed the hours by.

The Commodore observed the vast room and noted the doors, wondering which could lead them to Hix, if he was indeed still in the building.

"Would you like to dance?" asked Charlie in his terrible attempt at a feminine voice. The Commodore rolled his eyes as they took to the dance floor.

"I'm sure there are some moral implications to our activity here," muttered The Commodore under his breath. His eyes scanned the room as he looked for some sign of where Hix might be. He turned just in time to see Maybelle fly out of a door and close it carefully behind her. She looked around quickly before rejoining the guests.

"Let's go," said The Commodore, excited to finally find a lead. They turned to leave the dance floor but noticed the guests turned their attention.

The Commodore's eyes widened as the lights became brighter and the guests stopped and turned towards the band. He went for his pistol when Charlie took his arm and stopped him. They turned and saw Vignis, The Good Shepherd, walking on to the floor to speak to his audience. A light and consistent clapping came from the guests, The Commodore and Charlie quickly joined in.

"Thank you, it's great to see all of you this evening!" The Good Shepherd smiled as he bore his hands towards the audience, he knew exactly how to pander to his guests. The applause subsided as The Good Shepherd prepared to speak.

"The Divine realm is heading towards a new dawn, a new time, a fair time," The Good Shepherd explained. A warm round of applause complimented his words. "Many of you have benefited greatly from the changes The Celestial Order have implemented since our establishment over the old system." A few of the guests gave a knowing laugh as they winked cheekily at each other. It was no secret that the implementation of energy as a currency had been very lucrative for the privileged few.

"There are plans in motion to align the four planes. Accessibility, free travel and exclusivity are key points for the near future. Your support has been pivotal in helping to drive our mission," said Vignis, as he looked around at the many masks surrounding him. They were in his pocket, perfectly aligned to support his endeavours.

"My friends, enjoy the party. Take today for yourselves, I look forward to greeting each of you over the course of the evening." Vignis smiled and gave a small bow to his audience. The warm applause returned as the lights grew dim once again and the music began to play, a little more upbeat this time.

"Come on, Charlie, let's get away from him. He's the last person we need to speak to just now!" said The Commodore as he pulled Charlie away eagerly. They made their way over to the door that Maybelle had come out from and darted inside, quick enough to not be noticed by the other guests. The brightly lit corridor had a polite notice hung over a rope: 'No Unauthorised Access'. The Commodore considered this poor attempt at security with a raised eyebrow. He poked the sign with his pistol wondering if it could be rigged. As nothing happened, he gave a loud tut and pushed it out of the way and drew his pistol, looking for some indication of where Hix might be.

"Master, might I steal your attention for just a moment?" asked Maybelle, politely.

Vignis turned, smiling, but clearly annoyed at the interruption. He looked back at the guests he had been conversing with – two high elves from one of the most affluent families in the entire Divine world.

"Please excuse me, for just a moment," Vignis smiled as he retreated from them with Maybelle. The two guests looked at each other confused and then back at the retreating Vignis.

"This better be important!" he snapped angrily, but quiet enough so that others could not hear.

"We have a problem," she whispered, earnestly.

"And what is that?" he snorted.

"Two of our guards are missing," Maybelle stammered.

"How could you let this happen?" he spat through gritted teeth. "I told you to pick each one yourself!"

"I did," she replied. "Two of them have not reported back from their routine checks."

"Have you alerted the other guards?" asked Vignis in patronising tones.

"No," Maybelle admitted.

Vignis didn't reply. He folded his arms and raised his eyebrows. Maybelle gawped at him for a moment and then fluttered off at full speed, almost knocking a waiter over as she did so. He shook his head and returned to speaking to his guests. Some of them had heard the rumours of The Galdihar Rebellion and the growing discontent amongst the citizens across the Divine world. The upper classes and elitist types that attended these kinds of events lived securely away from the common entities of the realm and typically dismissed the claims of oppression and tyranny. After all, they benefited most from the changes that he had implemented.

The Commodore tried what felt like the one thousandth handle along the seemingly endless corridor. He turned to Charlie with a hopeless expression.

"I can only assume that Hix has been, erm…" his eyes darted awkwardly, "…moved to another place?"

He scratched the back of his head uncomfortably, but as usual Charlie saw right through his attempt at glossing the truth.

"He might be dead," said Charlie, rather forwardly.

"Technically, he wasn't even alive," The Commodore replied, trying to find a positive angle.

"Let's keep looking," sighed Charlie, rolling his eyes at The Commodore.

Charlie gripped the next door handle and gave it a turn. It swung open but the room was dark. They squinted their eyes as they peered inside and eventually tip-toed further in. Voices could be heard from down the corridor; The Commodore lurched forward and closed the door plunging them into darkness. He checked that Charlie was by his side and pressed his ear to the door.

"The demon has been dealt with, but he's still in the interrogation room. All but expired, I heard," a voice squeaked.

"We have much bigger problems to deal with," boomed a much deeper voice. "We have two guards missing. That means intruders."

Charlie looked at The Commodore, confused. The Commodore looked back and shrugged, just as bewildered as Charlie.

"We didn't interfere with any of the security," whispered The Commodore, mostly to himself. They waited intently for the voices to disappear up the corridor. As the voices faded into the distance, both The Commodore and Charlie opened the door and re-joined the corridor. The Commodore wiped a bead of sweat from his forehead and turned to Charlie.

A cracking sound split the air as an electric blue flash lit the walls. The Commodore dropped to the floor as Charlie let out a scream. He looked around, trying to work out what had happened. The Commodore had been paralysed and lay totally still, only able to move his eyes.

"Don't move," snapped a high-pitched voice.

Charlie turned to see a wicked-looking lady approach them. She gave them both a sneering look as she kicked The Commodore, checking he had been sufficiently paralysed. The lady in question, had been the head of The Celestial Home Guard for a long time. Trinsis The Bold. At modest height, she didn't appear to be any more formidable than others of her stature, a fact that often worked in her favour. Many centuries ago, she fought alongside some of the best warriors known to the Divine world. Eventually, she retired, but found the simple life to be too bland and instead took employment with The Celestial Order. She was a warrior through and through, but cruel and unforgiving.

"Thought you would sabotage the 'Grand Ball,' did you?" she cackled again. "I expected more from the Rebellion than this pathetic stunt. We'll take you down to the interrogation room… I'm sure that The Good Shepherd will be pleased to see you"

The Commodore couldn't speak, but instead tried to mouth the most foul and potent curse words imaginable.

"Boy – walk two metres in front. Try to run and I'll cut you down like a pig," she snapped. Trinsis took The Commodore by the collar and dragged him with incredible ease down the hall. Charlie didn't say a word, but complied with her demands.

The door of the interrogation room swung open; Charlie tumbled across the stone floor thanks to a boot in the small of his back. The Commodore grunted angrily as he too was thrown into the room. Charlie looked up and saw a limp and mostly unconscious Hix restrained in a chair. He smiled inwardly at the discovery of their companion. Trinsis pulled up two chairs and restrained both The Commodore and Charlie next to the demon, returning The Commodore to a normal state once she had double-checked his restraints. A long string of foul words came from The Commodore for minutes on end – without a single repetition!

"The Galdihar Rebellion is on its knees," Trinsis spat in reply to The Commodore's abuse. "I look forward to crippling what remains of your pathetic band of criminals."

The Commodore looked up into her face without remorse or fear. Charlie looked around the room hoping for some miracle to help them, but not a shred of inspiration hit him. She raised her hand to strike The Commodore but span around to face the door, where San stood. Open-mouthed, she observed The Commodore, Charlie and Hix. She had heard the rumours of the Rebellion, but seeing them in person made it all the more real. No longer were they a myth.

"What do you want, elf?" snapped Trinsis, rudely.

"Is there anything I can help you with, ma'am?" she blurted after a couple of moments' silence.

"Yes, actually. Inform Maybelle and The Good Shepherd that we have captured the intruders and that they are restrained," she ordered, proudly. Her hands were placed firmly on her hips – she was triumphant over her catch. San took a last look, her eyes hungrily taking in every detail of the prisoners, before giving a nod and darting off down the corridor.

Trinsis turned and inspected the gruesome torture devices that The Good Shepherd had used on Hix. They were still covered in his thick black blood. She observed each one, nodding, clearly impressed that Hix had made it this far without arriving at his final conclusion. Regardless of what side of the fence she was, at heart she remained a warrior and she respected his resilience.

"The demon, where did it come from?" she asked without turning to either Charlie or The Commodore. She heard no reply as her prisoners remained silent.

"I have battled beasts of all kinds, many of which couldn't have lasted more than a tenth of what that demon has endured." Her words cut the air, and only her hobnailed boots against the cold stone floor made a sound. She replaced the weapons as though they hadn't been interfered with, as excited voices could be heard coming down the corridor. Smiling, she rounded on her prisoners.

"I would love to tell you that the end is near, though it probably isn't. There are fates worse than death," she cackled wickedly. Charlie remained silent, unmoved and without fear. The Commodore turned and looked at him apologetically. He had intended to protect Charlie from the evils of this strange world and return him home once they had found a safe time to do so. Charlie returned a smile to The Commodore. The boy was forgiving, understanding and not for a moment regretful.

The voices became louder as they approached the doorway, The Commodore gave a sigh and prepared himself for the worst, his concern aimed entirely around the child he had failed to protect. He thought of his own son, and felt the familiar void and shame condemning him...

Chapter Sixteen - ...Die by the Blade

Part I

Take the fight forward. Bear arms and soldier on fighting for what is right. When your ability and reputation grow, you have the choice to pillage, plunder and steal. As your needs become wants and your iron becomes gold, be aware of those around you. Friends and allies can quickly become jackals and hyenas if the right opportunity presents itself. Live by the blade. Die by the blade.

The Celestial Flight billowed vast clouds of purple steam from beneath. The formidable locomotive hissed and whistled gently, ready for its maiden journey across the brand-new rail network. The immaculate silver and black paintwork shimmered and shined; the brass pipework contrasted the incredible craftsmanship beautifully.

Ernst stook back with his hands on his hips, admiring the vast steam and enchantment-powered hybrid locomotive.

He let his shoulders fall as he removed his frayed and dusty cap, finally feeling the crushing burden of time constraint and imminent arrest lift. The locomotive and its railroad had been completed and at double time. Though the line between improbable and impossible had been blurred significantly, he and his team had been triumphant.

"Are there going to be more of these locomotives?" asked a rather interested old lady in passing.

"Erm, I think so," said Ernst uncertainly. "This is the first of its kind. The track runs throughout most of the Divine world but has the ability to speed through time at 100mph."

"Interesting," said the lady, slowly. "And what do you call it?"

"The Celestial Flight," beamed Ernst, proudly.

The Lady looked back at Ernst with a blank expression, her hands on her hips.

"Does it fly then?" she asked.

Ernst frowned at the lady and cursed her something rotten inwardly, but kept his thoughts to himself.

"No, it doesn't. It's a locomotive. They don't fly," he replied, irritated.

"Bit of a fraud then, isn't it?" she retorted.

Ernst considered her with the utmost contempt. It was on the very tip of his tongue to tell her of the stress and anxiety that had befallen him. Ernst and his team had achieved a tremendously difficult task in getting the machine ready in time. But instead, Ernst scowled.

"Hardly a fraud," he snorted, before she had chance to question him further. "I have other tasks to attend to ma'am, have a great day."

Ernst jumped into the cab, adjusted the pressure and released the brakes. The steel monster huffed and hawed slowly as he moved the locomotive and its luxury carriages into the yard away from the main line. The line had been adjusted by request of The Good Shepherd himself – he had requested that a station be built at the end of the line inside the Bank of The Celeste. Another organisation built hastily to accommodate their new-found 'currency'.

Although it added even more pressure to the deadline, Ernst and his team were able to complete it.

Across the line, the locomotive would travel across a beautiful stone viaduct sporting what can only be described as prime viewing pleasure over Rohan's Reach.

Not many of the citizens from across the celestial world had taken much interest in the locomotive. Those that had never seen one before considered it ugly, and those that had, considered it to be old fashioned and a bit pointless. In the grand scheme of things, that mattered very little to Ernst so long as The Good Shepherd approved of it. He had a feeling that The Good Shepherd would be commandeering the luxury locomotive for his own personal use rather than the wider use of the public for which it was intended.

Adelade wheezed as she ran to The Grand Manor, her shoes in hand and hair almost finished. She stopped to catch her breath and noticed a puddle on the floor. She looked into the reflection and began finishing her make-up and adjusting her hair. Another face appeared alongside her own in the water – she jumped up and let out a small scream. She turned and noticed a fantastic smile and warm, welcoming eyes.

"Adelade, it has been too long!" said Hymm in a fabulously welcoming tone. He held out his arms in a welcoming fashion. His top hat and formal dress shone as immaculately as ever.

"I did not expect you, apologies for my unorthodox appearance," she stammered, trying to remain professional and calm.

"That's perfectly alright my dear! Most don't expect me," he chuckled, patting her on the shoulder. "Here for the party, I assume?"

"Indeed," she nodded nervously.

"Why, you seem out of sorts, my girl, is everything alright?" Hymm asked.

The illusion of humility and care had taken Hymm centuries to perfect, he seemed to be the very definition of genuine, though his intentions had a motive that included neither care nor humility. He knew that their contract was in play and still the terms had not been met. It was her head on the contract, and so he had to visit his contractee from time to time.

"Yes, thank you for asking. I have, erm, got to go inside and meet the guests," she pointed and stammered, eager to get away from Hymm.

Hymm studied her with fascination, as she stuttered and stammered her way through the conversation. He resembled a cat with a cornered mouse, simply toying with his subject.

"Well, before you go off inside and enjoy your evening of gaiety and frolic, might I make a suggestion?" he asked politely.

"Yes, of course," Adelade replied quickly, her eyes flashing over to the building. She had already arrived late and desired nothing more than to part company with Hymm.

"Consider your contract," he said, rather to-the-point. The warm joy had gone from his eyes and he looked far more serious. "We agreed a set of expectations for the completion of our contract, and I expect them to be adhered to by the very letter."

Adelade studied Hymm for a moment and considered her words carefully.

"As far as I understand, you cannot find the enchanted treasures that you wish for me to seek," Adelade replied politely but with intention.

Hymm gave a dark, hollow laugh and studied Adelade, marginally impressed.

"You have thirty days to deliver on your contract. Don't make me find you," Hymm snapped.

Adelade recoiled and looked fearfully at The Grand Manor for a moment. When she returned her gaze, Hymm had vanished from sight.

Charlie closed his eyes as the voices grew louder, their steps echoing down the corridor as they approached. He considered his adventure without regret or sadness. He felt a warm smile spread across his face as he grew excited. Excited to see his mother again after such a long absence – there are fates worse than death but maybe there would be a positive. He kept his eyes closed as the door crashed open. The room became alive with violence and destruction, he opened his eyes against his better judgement and saw Kull, San, Haste and Alwin in the room. The Commodore jeered and whooped as Kull tightened his huge hands around Trinsis's throat and squeezed. Her eyes bulged as she choked, her tongue lolling from the corner of her mouth as her eyes began to roll into the back of her head. Kull drove her head into the table with incredible force and released her. Her limp body collapsed into a pile on the floor where she remained motionless. Kull stood back, panting and grunting as his arms fell by his side. Years of anger, frustration and suppressed rage had been released upon the unsuspecting Trinsis.

"Good show!" laughed The Commodore. "Get us out of here so we can escape!"

"What an evening!" exclaimed Haste, leaning in to release the prisoners.

Charlie looked at Haste's arms and noticed they were severely injured – his face looked swollen and beaten too.

"It's just a scratch," Haste smiled. "We came across a rather capable mage."

"We must leave – hurry!" said Alwin feverishly, she looked around frantically, expecting the entire Celestial Order to pile down on them at any moment.

"Thank you," smiled The Commodore, patting Kull on his vast shoulders. He hadn't quite settled from his rage but managed a small nod of acknowledgement.

"We need to leave; The Celestial Order are readying themselves to launch the 'final solution'," Haste explained quickly.

"Ahem," came a small voice from behind them.

San looked at the many curious faces of The Galdihar Rebellion rather sheepishly.

"We, can't stay here," said San, nervously. "We are sure to be dealt with by The Celestial Order."

"What's your name?" asked The Commodore, impatiently.

"Sanguine, or San for short," she replied politely.

Kull remained tense and seemed to be absent from their conversation.

"Well, it's great to meet you, San, but we had better be going. Good luck with The Celestial Order." He gave a lazy salute and turned away from her.

"We couldn't have rescued you three without San and Kull," retorted Alwin with her arms folded.

"Ah, I see," said The Commodore, feeling a little bit embarrassed. "As you've probably heard, we're down on members just now. Welcome aboard The Galdihar Rebellion. We have bounties on all of our heads, a small child and a devout dislike for The Celestial Order."

San smiled and opened her mouth to reply, but the sound of angry voices and crashing in the corridor had cut her short. The Commodore took hold of Charlie and swung the barely conscious Hix over his shoulder.

Haste darted to the doorway and peered his head around. A movement from his arms and a bright light flew down at the approaching guards.

"Quickly!" he shouted to his comrades. They filed out of the room as quickly as they could, only to find the guards surrounding them, weapons drawn.

"Surrender yourselves! You are under arrest for treason against The Celestial Order and the Divine world!" a guard bawled at them from under his helmet.

Vignis ran down the corridor to see what was causing the commotion.

"Stop them!" he shouted as he ran. "Do not let them escape or I'll have all of your heads!"

The Commodore looked Vignis dead in the face and gave a cheeky wink as he teleported the Rebellion away from The Grand Manor with a flash and a bang.

The Rebellion dropped into a large damp field with a soggy thump. San vomited violently on her knees as, strangely, Kull seemed unmoved.

"You'll get used to that," said Charlie, cheerfully.

"Where are we?" she choked.

"Some part of the Holy Roman Empire, 1404. It should take them a while to catch up with us here," The Commodore replied without looking up from his watch. "Don't speak to the locals. They're probably simple."

Haste and Alwin were tending to Hix who had come around somewhat since their escape, though he still looked far worse for wear.

"We have good news," stated Alwin to The Commodore, with her usual pleasant tones.

"It's been a while since I've heard any good news," The Commodore replied. "What is it?"

"We discovered three sky-sailors," she explained, rather excited.

"I thought they were all destroyed," said The Commodore, "along with the Time-Keepers, if I remember correctly."

"That's what we assumed also," said Alwin.

"So, where did you find them?" asked The Commodore, curiously.

"Won them in a game of cards," laughed Haste as he scratched his chin. "Some aristocrat boasted about them after a few too many drinks."

"What's a 'sky-sailor'?" asked Charlie, as inquisitively as ever.

"A vast ship made from the finest materials, designed to sail the skies rather than the seas."

Charlie stood with his mouth agape as his mind conjured images of the majestic vessels sailing the skies.

"We have uncovered the plans for the final solution, in every grim detail," said Haste, severely. "Would you lead the Rebellion and sail the sky-sailors against The Celestial Order, James?"

The Commodore looked around at the expectant faces, considering what he was being asked. To sail once again and command a collection of vessels... His knowledge, passion and blood yearned for the opportunity.

"I cannot," he replied bluntly. "I have not commanded a vessel for centuries and my last expedition didn't end well." He fumbled with his watch which began to tick rather violently.

"Oh, you can shut up as well," he snapped at the watch, which promptly became still.

"We must strike now. The plans for the final solution are underway. All will be lost if we do not act now," Haste explained calmly.

"Things have changed, Haste," The Commodore retorted. "I must return the boy; I have taken part in the Rebellion's partisan activities for long enough."

The members of the Rebellion looked from one to the other, confused, bewildered and disappointed.

"We have to defeat The Celestial Order," Charlie urged.

"I need to get you home, Charlie," The Commodore replied, scornfully. "You have no business being here, it is a dangerous and hostile place. I should never have let you come this far; I must take you home."

"Charlie, is very important," Alwin explained.

"He is just a boy!" The Commodore yelled. "He must get home; it isn't safe here."

"The prophecy," Haste stated calmly.

"To hell with the prophecy!" The Commodore bawled. "What a lot of nonsense. I've heard a thousand prophecies and at best they're half-truths, based mostly on coincidence."

"True or not," said Haste, calmly. "The Celestial Order have a bounty on Charlie. How long do you think it will be before they find him at home?"

The Commodore studied Haste with his mouth slightly agape, his mind racing over the point he had not considered previously. He sat himself down on the floor and scowled, looking away from the gaze of 'the Rebellion.'

"To take a boy into battle?" The Commodore muttered. "That is madness, insanity and nonsense."

"James, The Celestial Order have a bounty on Charlie because they are scared of him. They see him as a threat. His presence in battle would be hugely beneficial, we can protect him," Haste urged. "Look at what we have been through over the years, we are not defeated yet."

The Commodore looked at the surrounding faces, stuck between trying to do the right thing and being talked into what would ultimately be the right thing. We are often presented with the right and wrong decisions in life, but seldom the right and the right.

"We must get Charlie home after the battle," said The Commodore finally after quite some time. The Rebellion breathed a sigh of relief.

"What is your opinion on necromancy?" smiled Haste as he gave The Commodore a pat on the back.

"Filthy magic, that should have been forgotten before it even existed," spat The Commodore.

"Well, we're going to need it. Let's go," laughed Haste. "Let's get over to The Valley of The Dead. That's where the sky-sailors are."

Haste preferred to teleport with traditional magic rather than enchanted devices – it was harder for The Celestial Order to track them, but not impossible.

Shortly after, they teleported to The Valley of the Dead, an obscure part of the Divine world that very few ever grace with their presence. Charlie shielded his eyes from the burning sun they had appeared under, he looked around at the vast cemetery. He gasped as he looked into the distance and noticed that it seemed to go on forever. Headstone after headstone, most of which were rotten. A sweet, sickly smell lingered in the air.

"What is this place?" asked Alwin, feeling rather queasy.

"The Valley of the Dead," said Haste, rather cheerfully.

"What makes this place so special?" asked Charlie.

"The Valley of the Dead harbours those that have been forgotten. No one places any tribute to the residents here and so they are collected in this place," Haste explained, still rather cheerful. "It's the perfect place to store a few stolen sky-sailors."

The Rebellion set off in a line, following their leader without question. San and Kull walked silently together, wondering where their next chapter would take them. They did not know any of the members of the Rebellion, but they felt safe, wanted and valued – something that The Celestial Order could never offer. They weaved their way through the endless crumbling gravestones. As they did, Charlie tried to read the names and dates on them but most were worn away. The Commodore looked over into an adjacent field, though most of the grass was thin, balding and brown. He looked hard at them as though trying to find something in particular.

"What are they?" asked Charlie after following his gaze. In the distance were what seemed to be oil pumps that turned slowly and rhythmically. Seemingly infinite, they were scattered as far as the eye could see. Some of them looked almost new, whereas others were rusty, tired and dilapidated. A selection had completely stopped working and lay still, rotting into the ground they sat upon. The entire area had a very melancholy atmosphere along with the bizarre sense of trespassing.

"They are life-lungers," The Commodore explained, grimly. "Each one represents the life force of every living individual across the planet. The ones that look new are for healthy entities, in their prime. The poor condition ones suggest they are nearing the end of their life, and the ones that aren't working at all… well, you can probably guess."

Charlie considered the life-lungers as they walked towards their destination, turning and pumping slowly and indifferently.

"How can something so lifeless reflect the beauty of living and life?" asked Charlie to no one in particular. Haste, Alwin and The Commodore looked around at Charlie and pondered him with interest, though no one responded to his question.

"Bad men will fall," droned Kull to San. She smiled as they walked, although he had real intention behind his words, San often found them humorously mistimed.

"I never thought that we would be part of the Rebellion," said San through a smile. "But I feel free, and that is something that I have not felt for, well, ever."

"Freedom," Kull boomed slowly, as though considering the concept of their topic.

"That's right," San replied. "Freedom. I'd rather taste freedom for a year, than live for one-hundred in the service of The Celestial Order."

Kull didn't reply – his face contorted as he withdrew into his own thoughts, keeping pace automatically with his new peers.

Many of the Rebellion, Charlie included, gasped at the sight of the sky-sailors. Beautifully crafted, they looked like any other 18th century vessels that The Commodore had commanded previously except they sailed atop the very breeze, instead of cutting through the sea. The sky-sailors looked far worse for wear and displayed a level of neglect from their time stored away. The sails were split, frayed and patched, while a lot of the masonry had faded and various parts were damaged or missing.

"You want us to engage The Celestial Order with these?" asked The Commodore, rather unimpressed. "They're falling to pieces; they'll crumble before we even get there!"

Haste considered the magnificent enchanted vessels with an adoring smile. One of the few remaining beauties of how the Divine world used to be, before The Celestial Order.

"They are incredible," said Charlie in awe. He approached one of the ships and noticed each had a rope ladder hanging down. He took hold of the ladder and began his ascension into the huge sky-sailor as the others followed suit.

Hix sat on the deck and stared out into the distance – he hadn't said much to any of his comrades since his rescue. His face was badly scarred, although on the mend. An aura of anger and bitterness seemed to be eating into him as he tried not to engage anyone in conversation.

"It's going to be a new world, Hix," said Charlie, cheerfully. He patted his friend on the shoulder and smiled a friendly smile. Hix smiled in return as they looked out into the distance together.

"Damn Oblivion," cursed Hix suddenly. "Damn that rotten place, why did I have to originate from there? It has been endless cruelty and third-class treatment from every corner. My kin treat me as though I am a coward and a failure and the other world treats me as a monster."

Charlie listened intently to Hix and felt a resonance with his own feelings of outcastery.

"I would personally like to thank Oblivion," replied Charlie, still smiling.
Hix seemed to be waiting for a punchline of some sort, his face contorted into a mixture of sneering disgust and confusion.

"I would like to thank them for creating someone as kind, generous and selfless as you are, Hix," Charlie explained. "Our adventure would have been far more difficult and very boring without you. Your help, sacrifice and loyalty have taken The Galdihar Rebellion from strength to strength, so far as I can see."

Hix looked into Charlie's eyes and saw that every word he spoke came from the heart and reflected his friend's true thoughts.

"So, if you are going to blame Oblivion, you must blame it for everything. Not just the bad, but the good too. You're my best friend, after all." Charlie maintained an incredible balance of speaking from the heart but without sounding arrogant or condescending, often a difficult skill to master.

Hix stared at Charlie in stunned silence, not knowing what to say.

"Thank you," he blurted after a few moments. "A best friend... I have never had one of those before."

"You're most welcome," replied Charlie curtly, and with that, he scurried off to check out the rest of the huge vessel. Although there were three, they all congregated on the deck of just one of the boats. Around twenty of them were present when they first arrived, but now there were around sixty. Almost every member of The Galdihar Rebellion was present and had been summoned specially for the mission. Haste had a particular flair for illusion magic. He sent a faded Angel as a calling sign for the members of the Rebellion that only they could see.

Haste called for silence. The crowd turned to face him, and those that were in the lower decks came to the top to see what the fuss was about. Haste looked out across his comrades, a ragtag mixture of entities that had one common goal: to topple The Celestial Order and restore equality to the realm. They looked back at him with absolution in their eyes and alignment in their hearts.

"My friends, we are about to embark on the mission that we have spoken about since the dawn of The Galdihar Rebellion. We have lost many brave members and their sacrifice will not be in vain. Today, we take the battle to The Celestial Order and thaw out this cold war. The people will hear about us from far and wide – their eyes will be opened and the curtain of illusion will be raised," said Haste, confidently. He stood straight and with intention. He had waited for this day for a long time. "The Celestial Order have five hundred times our strength; they control the realm for the most part and dismiss our very existence as a myth to their public. Today is the day it ends. Some of us may not return from the battle, if anyone would like to reconsider, they can leave and return to their daily lives. There will be no ridicule or embarrassment in doing so."

Haste looked across the crowd and saw that not a single attendee moved. They stood fast and ready to engage their enemy.

"Some of you may have heard of 'The Final Solution' that The Celestial Order are currently finalising. I can tell you that it is no rumour and that the consequences of such a plan are nothing shy of heinous. Today, I can confirm those plans," said Haste.

"They have converted energy to a currency and, as you know, energy is the very foundation of our existence. They are collecting and harvesting energy from their new-found economy to power an army of a thousand invincible soldiers. They are powered by the energy of deceased or spent entities. I cannot imagine that is a painless process."

The crowd gasped in horror at the sinister plans Haste shared with them.

"These soldiers will be highly skilled and forged for the purpose of invasion into Sanctuary, Oblivion and eventually the Blind world. 'The *Bank* of The Celeste' is a front for their wicked plan. The soldiers are crafted in the building and are no doubt part of other sadistic rituals. Once they have complete control, they will be able to do as they please with little interruption from anyone else. The final stage will be to 'cleanse' entities across the world and create a new world order for the selected few. I, for one, say no!" Haste roared, throwing a fist into the air.

The crowd yelled and cheered in agreement with Haste. They jumped and waved their weapons, jeering and chanting.

"Some of you were warriors once – you will be captained in allocated groups. As we are utilising the sky-sailors for battle, The Commodore will lead us," shouted Haste.

The crowd whooped and cheered, a response that The Commodore was not expecting. He looked around in amazement. Not only would he lead, but they wanted him to orchestrate the mission.

The Commodore approached Haste and put a hand on his shoulder, a smile on his face.

"We're going to need more than sixty people to properly man these vessels," said The Commodore as a matter of fact.

"How many do you need?" asked Haste, cheerfully.

"At least double our figure."

"Done!" said Haste has he clapped his hands together. "I'll be back shortly."

The Commodore watched with a raised eyebrow as he disappeared off into the crowd, wondering how he was going to double the Rebellion's already reduced figure.

Part II

Vignis paced the meeting room with his hands behind his back. The entire board of The Celestial Order were present.

Omar Asghari noticed Vignis's shirt was untucked and his sleeves had unbuttoned, a sight that no one ever saw publicly, if at all. Adelade sat and stared past Vignis, her inevitable notebooks parked perfectly on her knee. Judge Humphrey tried to look calm, collected and innocent. He was innocent, but the more he tried, the more he looked out of place.

Vignis stopped and looked across the meeting room at the empty seats. Many of the board had been lost, mostly due to Vignis removing them from their position. Maybelle stayed away from the main table, looking sheepish as she hovered in the corner near the door. Adelade wondered if Maybelle had planned an escape route if the meeting went sour – doubtlessly she had.

"The Rebellion," Vignis began, atomising the silence, "attended our event this evening. They were able to enter, retrieve their Demon and leave."

He allowed the silence to reign once more as he looked across the many faces, most of which were averting from his gaze.

"We have no choice but to begin the first phase of the final solution in the next few days, or we risk years of hard work and planning," Vignis stated.

"May I just say-" stuttered Judge Humphrey, raising his hand.

"No, you may not," snapped Vignis.

Judge Humphrey looked around awkwardly at his peers. They looked away and shifted uncomfortably as though the embarrassment might be infectious.

"Hymm requires an action on our bargain for more enchanted items that he would find of use," blurted Adelade from her chair. Her face turned a deep shade of red as Vignis's eyes narrowed upon her, forcing her eyes to the floor.

"*Our* bargain?" scoffed Vignis. "*Your* bargain. It is your responsibility to source the items."

"But I have not had time, with all of our planning and scheduling," she pleaded.

"Your own management of time is NOT my concern!" barked Vignis, concluding their brief conversation.

Vignis breathed deeply as he considered his peers. Together, they had the knowledge and power to overthrow Vignis, but none of them dared. They dared not even consider treason against The Good Shepherd.

"What should we do about the demon?" asked Maybelle, once again breaking the intermittent silence.

"Let them have the demon. He is of no use to us anymore. Increase the bounty ten-fold on all of their heads. I am sure there are mercenaries that will pick them up eventually," Vignis said, finally.

"Our public, the Divine world, must not know of our plans. They are to be conducted in the guise of a foreign entity. This way, we can deny any involvement. Should our people understand what we are proposing, it will lead to certain unrest and take us back hundreds of years," Vignis said calmly, collecting himself.

"You are all dismissed," Vignis barked and left the room. Leaving his colleagues still seated as they tried to make sense of what they had discussed.

The Commodore had chosen his vessel and began familiarising himself with every corner. Settling in to a new vessel was important; to understand the ship meant that you understood every capability and weakness. They had cannons on board as well as various small arms – some of them were enchanted but most of them looked to be standard Blindling weapons.

"If we lose the battle, will I die?" asked Charlie from behind The Commodore. He asked in a rather casual manner and seemed rather at peace with the concept of no longer existing in mortal form.

"Lose? Are you kidding?" The Commodore laughed. "The odds are not only stacked in our favour, but victory and achievement of our goal is guaranteed from the first shot fired. I promise you that."

Charlie stared hard, frowning as the inner circles of his mind contemplated their victory.

"Can I have a sword?" he asked suddenly, rather excited.

The Commodore studied Charlie for a moment, a little deflated and disappointed. The innocence and naivety that all children are naturally born with, were slowly fading away, and in their place a survivor would rise.

"Charlie, there is no pride or joy to be found in killing. When you cross swords, there is no other option but to kill, or be killed," The Commodore explained with a warm smile. "I have a far more important job for you, Charlie."

Charlie's eyes lit up with excitement as he considered his hero, a huge grin spreading involuntarily.

"I am The Commodore, which means that I will command this ship and the other two. But I need a captain under me here, to relay my orders and ensure they are carried out properly."

The Commodore crouched down to Charlie, reached into his pocket and removed the inevitable time-piece. It ticked and tocked merrily in his hand.

"Would you like to be captain of this fine vessel?" asked The Commodore.

"Yes, Commodore!" beamed Charlie, proudly saluting as he did so.

"Very well," grinned The Commodore. "We have much to do!"

Charlie buzzed with excitement as he scrambled around the deck of the ship, familiarising himself with as much as he could. His enthusiasm increased more than anyone could have thought possible when he found a tattered old captain's tricorn. He dusted it down and looked as though he might explode at any moment.

The Commodore stopped for a moment as they heard rumbling from the hills. The air came alive with a noise, but they couldn't quite make out what it was. The members of the Rebellion looked out to see if they could identify it. Haste came running towards them as quickly as he could, a whopping smile of pride smeared upon his face.

"Your crewmembers are coming," he wheezed to The Commodore.

Alwin shook her head, with her hands folded in disappointment.

"A witch, afraid of a little necromancy?" he jeered, which only seemed to annoy her further.

"It is dark magic and has been outlawed for a long time," she muttered.

"I seem to remember that you cut your teeth with dark magic a long time ago," teased Haste, his prideful smile remaining.

"That *was* a long time ago," she snapped. "I may be a witch, but I have bettered myself since then."

"And a very fine witch you are," added Haste, still beaming.

The Commodore frowned heavily as he looked out across the horizon. The noise had been getting steadily louder as the source came into view. Some of the Rebellion screamed as they looked out upon the nearing crowd. Charlie's eyes widened as he removed his hat, his mouth gaping.

"Let's go and, erm, greet them," said The Commodore, gruffly.

"Are they dead?" asked Charlie from behind The Commodore.

"Sort of. Mostly. Undead, is probably the best description," replied The Commodore, rather unsure himself.

"Are *you* undead?" Charlie asked.

"Let's not get into that," concluded The Commodore, not wishing to open that particular can of worms.

A sea of undead stood before them, groaning and swaying slightly. Some of them were in terrible shape.

"So, what now?" asked The Commodore, scratching his head.

"Command them," said Haste, simply.

The Commodore looked across them and eventually settled his eyes on one of the undead soldiers nearest to him. He considered the undead subject with narrowed eyes; he seemed to have been an older gentleman at some point. His flesh hung tragically from his face and his eyes were glassy. His stare seemed to look through The Commodore, rather than at him.

"You there!" ordered The Commodore. "Stand to attention!"

The undead man snapped his heels together and made to salute, but caught his swinging jaw, causing it to fall off entirely. Charlie jumped back and began to heave.

Haste picked up the jawbone that had abandoned its owner and placed it rather terribly back into the poor fellow's skull.

"Good as new," he beamed.

The Commodore looked at Alwin – she seemed to be able to read his mind as the thought 'Haste must be a madman beyond all relative comprehension' crossed both of their thoughts.

The Commodore gave a sigh and threw out several orders to the crowd before him. They delayed for a few moments and tiredly pulled themselves into three columns, standing to attention.

The Commodore gave a satisfied nod and ordered the three columns to their respective ships. Alwin followed Haste away, heavily disapproving of the entire ordeal.

Charlie studied their new-found numbers with interest, though keeping a safe distance from them. Some of them moaned, others were silent, each with their own glassy stare as though they weren't consciously present.

"Prepare the weapons!" ordered The Commodore. The order was echoed by Charlie, who shouted at the top of his lungs with such force it sounded as though his throat might split open. Haste echoed the order to his crew on the second ship and Hix to the third ship.

Final checks, hasty repairs and equipment checks were carried out from the timely orders The Commodore gave. He beamed inwardly, excited to be back in the position of a Commodore once more. His face told another story of focus, drive and intent. As a Commodore, you could not smile and jest with your crew. It simply wasn't proper.

"Drop the sails, and set a course for 15 degrees north by north west in formation," The Commodore shouted. Charlie echoed the order, as did Haste and Hix once more. Some of the members of the Rebellion felt uneasy with their undead comrades, and kept themselves distanced.

Charlie stood in awe, excitement gripping him as butterflies exploded in his stomach. He felt the vessel begin to move and cut through the air at a steady pace. To be in battle – with friends and comrades – for a cause more worthy than almost any other.

"Commodore Marshall," Charlie addressed, from The Commodore's side.

"Captain Kingston?" he replied formally, without looking at Charlie.

"What is our destination?" Charlie asked.

"Rohan's Reach. We will take the fight to The Celestial Order. Today we give them everything that we've got. They will remember the day they crossed The Commodore," said The Commodore, darkly. He snapped his watch shut and focused on watching the crew. They shifted from one area to the next carrying out their duties and preparing their vessel further.

"A day and a night at this pace should see us at Rohan's Reach," said The Commodore, satisfied.

"We will be sighted before our arrival. The Celestial Order will be prepared and waiting for us," Hix warned. He had flown over from his ship to convene with The Commodore.

"That's what I'm banking on," smiled The Commodore.

Hix looked seriously out across the horizon as they flew overland. Spectators had come out of their homes to see the great sky-sailors make their way majestically across the sky. They pointed and shouted in excitement as they too had probably heard that the sky-sailors no longer existed.

Rohan's Reach saw the sun set over the horizon, the warm air decidedly different from what was usual. Intensity spliced the very breeze that rolled in from the hills as the citizens looked out to the skies. Could the rumours be true? Had the so-called 'Galdihar Rebellion' mobilised for an attack against The Celestial Order? Whispers joined the tense breeze – hushed, secretive and cautious as to who might hear them.

"They have sky-sailors... three of them!" whispered a young man to an elf. His thoughts were quite safe – he had known this particular elf for over a century.

"And what source informed you of this information?" the elf scoffed from under her hood. "The Rebellion is nothing but myth and rumours, spread by the fickle and faint-hearted in an attempt to smear The Good Shepherd."

"Hardly!" snapped the young man. "I have legitimate sources for my information, don't you worry about that."

The sound of hobnailed boots and the clanging of armour rattled in the distance and grew nearer. They both ran into a nearby doorway and saw entire battalions of guards and soldiers marching forward. All of them silent, immaculate and in perfect formation. Between the divisions, officers escorted them on horseback.

"A rumour spread by the fickle and faint-hearted?" snorted the young man.

"There, must be some kind of explanation," stammered the elf, her eyes wide open as she watched the hordes of guards.

They made their way to the boundaries of Rohan's Reach, preparing to defend against an enemy that had mostly been dismissed as a myth. The gates were closed and locked down; any citizens making enquiries were told to go home without delay and remain there until further notice.

Vignis paced the walkway of the watchtower that overlooked Rohan's Reach. Hand-crafted armour, custom-made and bespoke to the hilt hung from him. His thoughts thoroughly absorbed his attention as Maybelle hovered alongside, looking rather concerned.

"Do you think they would dare attack us?" asked an uneasy Adelade to Maybelle.

Maybelle looked down on Adelade for a moment before hissing and turning away, leaving the question unanswered.

"The invincible army that we have created for the final solution – how far are they from completion?" Vignis asked quietly, still pacing.

"They are mostly complete, but we need more time to arrange the final preparations," Adelade replied, cutting Maybelle off before she had chance to answer. She hissed at Adelade once more.

"Everything is at risk; we cannot allow news of our solution to travel," said Vignis.

"Master, The Galdihar Rebellion have been crushed to almost nothing. They live every day in fear that we will catch them. They cannot possibly be victorious in battle," replied Maybelle in a soft voice.

"When were the sky-sailors spotted?" asked Vignis.

"Little more than a few hours ago," Adelade replied. "We may be able to prepare the invincible army before their arrival."

Vignis stopped by the observation window and looked out across the clear night sky but saw nothing out of place. He rested a hand upon the handle of his sword, every fibre of his existence itching to engage the Rebellion in battle. It had been a long time since he had engaged an enemy in battle, and how he had missed the skirmish.

The Commodore stared out across the night sky. The three sky-sailors had slowed to enable Hix, The Commodore, Haste and Charlie to draw out an approach.

"Hix, you are to spearhead the attack; sail over the fortification walls as quickly as you can to engage the enemy. Myself and Haste will attack from the east and west respectively in a cross formation," The Commodore explained as he marked his map that had been hastily spread across a table. "We anticipate that they will have a minimum of ten thousand men, a third of them archers with enchanted weapons. Cannons, small arms and other magical items will also be on the agenda, although we do not know how many."

"What about the army they are creating?" asked Charlie, propping up his tired old captain's hat.

"As far as we know, they are not quite ready," said Haste slowly. "Although they may have increased production due to our recent activity."

"They have over one-hundred-thousand guards and soldiers across the realm, why are they only using ten-thousand?" asked Hix.

"They would, if they could. They cannot mobilise them that quickly," explained The Commodore. "That is why it is essential that we head into Rohan's Reach and capture The Good Shepherd and his government."

"What if they aren't there?" asked Charlie.

"They will be. The Good Shepherd cannot be seen to be in hiding when his realm is under attack. It's bad publicity," explained Alwin. Adverse to violence, she had been mostly silent during the negotiations and planning.

"I can provide protection for a short time for the sky-sailors, but I fear it will not be long," said Alwin quietly.

"Anything will be better than nothing," The Commodore said appreciatively.

"What do I need to do?" asked Charlie, realising that he had not been allocated any specific tasks for the attack.

"Stay alive," said the others in unison.

"Once the battle has ended, we will arrange steps to get you home," explained The Commodore.

Charlie looked a little deflated – he missed his younger brother but couldn't bear the idea of returning home just yet.

"But I want to help with rebuilding this world," he replied, rather sad.

The others looked at each other awkwardly. They had not discussed at any point what would happen if they actually won the battle. The next steps had not been outlined yet.

"What would a new governance look like for the Divine world in existence?" asked Hix, scratching his head.

Nobody replied. They looked at each other rather seriously as their minds raced at the possibilities of what could be.

"Well, I think that Charlie should be the chancellor of ice-cream tasting," said Haste with a serious expression.

They all burst into a fit of laughter as Charlie jumped for joy at the prospect.

"I do make a fantastic ice-cream taster, that's for sure!" he laughed with his comrades. He felt a slow sinking sensation in his stomach as he thought about how much he would miss his friends when he returned home. After some time, they looked out across the sky and considered the rising sun and its beauty. As the sun appeared on the horizon, so did Rohan's Reach.

Chapter Seventeen – The Battle of Rohan's Reach

Love borders hatred more finely than you might think. The two concepts of emotion and feeling are practically neighbours in metaphorical terms. Hatred is often driven by a desire to love or be loved. We often consider love to be beautiful and aesthetically pleasing to the eye, mind and heart. Can hatred be beautiful? As beauty is subjective to the individual, why couldn't it be? Be careful with love for you may find yourself absorbed in its closest neighbour.

"Where do you think Charlie is?" asked Christopher from the other side of the vast dinner table. The staff busied around them, cleaning and serving.

He looked blankly at his father, whose mind seemed anywhere but present in their fine dining room. Lord Kingston thought for a few moments and then moved his gaze to Christopher's.

"I don't know," Lord Kingston replied tiredly. He hadn't slept at all for days. "I am sure he is safe and bound to come home soon."

"But that man took him away," Christopher said earnestly.

"I know… we have every constable in town looking for him," Lord Kingston explained.

He looked down at his soup and put his spoon down by the side of the bowl. His appetite had subsided, not only for his supper but for everything. Money, business and politics. He had a hard time explaining to the authorities what had happened to Charlie, but his position had swayed them to be on side and engage in a search.

"The man in the globe took him," piped Christopher between mouthfuls of soup. "I never saw him, but Charlie did. Maybe they were friends?"

Lord Kingston gave a vague nod in agreement, once again distancing himself from the world before him and sinking into his thoughts.

"Friends," sighed Lord Kingston.

He stirred his soup slowly without consuming a single mouthful. He suddenly dropped the spoon against the side of the bowl and looked up at Christopher.

"What was Charlie's friend called?" asked Lord Kingston, rather urgently.

"Who?" asked Christopher.

"Charlie's friend. What was his name?" urged Lord Kingston, impatiently.

"You mean the one you aren't supposed to be aware of?" replied Christopher, blankly.

"The very same," said Lord Kingston, almost pleading for the information he sought.

"Billy. I think. Billy Betts," said Christopher slowly, his eyebrows furrowed in deep concentration.

"Very good, thank you Christopher. Take yourself to bed when you have finished, the staff are on duty and will tend to anything you need," Lord Kingston explained softly. He walked around the table and rested a hand on his shoulder.

"I love you, son," said Lord Kingston, as though he had said it a thousand times before. In fact, it was a very rare occasion these words ever left his mouth, and when they did, vast amounts of liquor were usually a factor.

"Yes, father," replied Christopher awkwardly, not really knowing what to say.

Lord Kingston vacated the dining room and sat by the phone in their vast hallway. He dialled for the operator.

"Connect me to the Himmel residence, please," he barked formally.

"Connecting," the operator droned.

"Who on earth is this calling at this late hour?" a thoroughly angry Thomas Himmel snapped into the phone.

"Excuse me, Thomas, this is Charles Kingston speaking!" Lord Kingston boomed in a rather formidable tone.

"Oh, Mr Kingston, my apologies I did not anticipate a call from you this evening," Thomas stuttered.

"Enough of that, you had in your employment a Mr Betts. Some time ago he was dismissed?" Lord Kingston boomed, slightly louder this time.

The line went quiet for a few moments as Thomas strained his memory – he tended to hire and fire on a regular basis.

"A ginger-haired fellow?" he asked, still stumbling over his words.

"How on earth should I know?" Lord Kingston snapped.

"Anyway, take yourself to the Betts residence and employ the man immediately. We have overlooked some managerial qualifications that he has been accredited with. I want him on the first course to be fast-tracked through the management programme. Make it swift, I will be calling again in two days. If it's not done, you will be replaced," barked Lord Kingston.

"But I don't…" started Thomas in a nervous tone.

Lord Kingston planted the phone back on the receiver before Thomas had chance to answer. Lord Kingston adjusted himself in the chair next to the phone and looked down the hallway. He stared for a few moments and saw that no one was present. Satisfied he was alone, for the moment at least, he wept into his hands, choking and coughing as he tried to mourn Charlie quietly.

The entire civilian population of Rohan's Reach peered at the magnificent sky-sailors as they evacuated their homes and made their way out of their beloved town. Soldiers hammered on doors and ordered everyone to evacuate without any sort of explanation.

They looked on in awe at the beautiful vessels making their way over the morning sun.

Vignis drew his sword as they approached and readied his helmet, standing fast ready to engage his enemy. His guards and soldiers were waiting, poised to strike with an arsenal of weaponry. Bows and arrows, swords and daggers kissed the morning air. Soldiers, Battle Mages and Officers lined the walls, their eyes fixed on the incoming enemy.

"I feel a bit sick," whispered Charlie as they approached Rohan's Reach.

The Commodore glanced at Charlie with a smile from the bow of their sky-sailor.

"Me too," admitted The Commodore. "Always, before every battle, without failure."

The beautiful city of Rohan's Reach came closer as they approached, The Commodore looked to the sky and judged the weather to be fair.

"Hix, take the lead," The Commodore bellowed.

Hix gave a nod, understanding his command.

"Ready the cannons!" shouted Hix as he flew down into the below decks of his sky-sailor. Charlie watched in awe as the huge vessel overtook his own and they stormed forward towards Rohan's Reach.

"Ready the weapons," whispered The Commodore as he leaned in to Charlie.

"Ready the weapons!" Charlie echoed, shouting at the top of his lungs. The crew scrambled as they drew small arms and readied the cannons on each side of the vessel. They loaded enchanted cannonballs, designed to explode on impact and maim any entity within proximity of the blast area. The Commodore drew his pistol and retrieved his watch with the other hand. He flipped open the face of the watch and looked down.

"This is it Domina, no going back," he muttered to the watch low enough for no one else to hear. The second hand began sweeping excitedly around the face of the watch. With a smile, he snapped the face shut and placed her carefully in his pocket. A sense of comfort prevailed over The Commodore. As long as he had the watch, he would never be alone.

"Ready weapons and prepare to engage, we aim to bring down all of the sky-sailors before they can breach the city walls," Maybelle shouted to the guards and soldiers. They all looked on indifferently, they had long since mastered fear.

"Prime the catapults and take aim with arrows and hold!" shouted Vignis, his eyes alive with adrenaline and excitement. The blood in his veins burned as it pulsed around his body.

Hix steered the sky-sailor towards Rohan's Reach, taking the lead as The Commodore and Haste went left and right respectively.

"Fire at will!" Hix shouted to his crew. Burning enchanted cannon-balls exploded simultaneously from the many cannons, sending them hurtling through the air. Screams and yells echoed as some of the enemy soldiers fell. Hix had hoped for a better result, but most of the cannonballs had missed their mark, and only a few causalities were sustained.

"Hold!" bellowed Vignis.

"We should fire now, sir," blurted an officer feverishly from beside him.

"Hold or I'll have your heads!" Vignis screamed, ignoring his colleague.

Small arms fire pelted the readied soldiers and guards; the occasional yell and scream indicated a loss of one of their men.

"Double time on those cannons!" roared Hix, as he drew his sword. "Prepare to breach Rohan's Reach on my order."

More enchanted cannonballs rained down over Rohan's Reach, smashing weapons and fortifications to pieces. Any soldiers that were hit, were obliterated.

"Sir, we must fire now or we will need to retreat!" the officer shouted to Vignis.

He ignored the advisory as more men began to fall. Even one of the vast catapults had suffered a critical blow from their enemy.

Hix sailed the great vessel as fast as the wind would carry them as he almost reached the walls.

"Release the catapult!" Vignis yelled. On his order, the first catapult released, a great whipping sound split the air as it launched its load, a burning ball of phosphorous. Hix held his breath as the great mass hurled through the air, aimed squarely at the sky-sailor. Just before impact, the load exploded but nobody on board came to any harm. Hix looked around, confused, as Alwin fell to her knees.

"I cannot protect them again," she wheezed, panting to regain her strength. At the very same moment, a barrage of arrows struck the sky-sailor that Hix captained. Most of them were absorbed by the undead crew, who didn't so much as make a sound. The arrows sank into them with a sickening thud but they were unmoved and stood straight, awaiting their orders. Hix had crossed the fortifications as they flew over the city. He drew a deep breath to order the crew overboard and into the city, but it never came.

The sound of splintering masonry exploded across the entire city, as did the screams of the crew as they fell to the ground. A load from a catapult had hit them squarely and shattered the rare and beautiful vessel into a thousand pieces. Hix tried to hover but the blast had knocked him off balance. He flailed desperately, trying unsuccessfully to regain control of his flight as he tumbled to the ground.

Vignis turned his attention to the next sky-sailor, making its way from the east. Haste stood at the helm waving gaily to them.

"Have you missed me?" Haste roared to Vignis, his laughter echoing across the sky.

"He's a madman," gasped the officer aside Vignis. He did not reply, once again ignoring his colleague's outburst.

"Alwin, I need more speed. Can you muster some wind behind this old girl?" Haste asked.

All at once, Alwin cast an incantation to the heavens, enabling the winds to blow in the only direction that mattered. Another barrage of arrows made their way through the sky towards Haste and his ship, but the wind had taken the velocity out of them and they simply rattled around the ship.

"Prepare catapults!" screamed Vignis.

"You won't be needing those for me!" roared Haste in return. He gripped the spokes of the wheel and steered them at incredible speed towards Rohan's Reach. Alwin gasped as the crew held on to anything that they could find. Vignis's eyes widened as the vessel hurtled towards them.

He drew his sword and roared as the rest of the guards and soldiers abandoned their positions and made a hasty retreat. Moments later, the sky-sailor collided with the wall, bringing it down and toppling the watchtower with it. The ship had become nothing more than a wreck as they all piled out and stormed the city. The streets were alive with fighting as confused guards and soldiers battled their undead enemy. They struck as hard as they could, but the undead returned blows again and again relentlessly. Kull and San fought savagely together against the soldiers. Kull engaged powerful blows as San fired arrow after arrow at them. Even with limited fighting experience, they were a formidable team. Some of the survivors from Hix's vessel had been cornered in the town square and battled to save themselves. Two of the catapults had been destroyed and those that were operating the others had abandoned their positions, which left The Commodore and Charlie to proceed with far less aggression from the ground.

"Ready the cannons and adjust the masts to take advantage of the wind – and prepare loose cannonballs!" shouted Charlie to his crew.

The Commodore looked on astonished – he hadn't ordered Charlie to do any of those tasks.

"Captain Kingston, why are we readying loose cannonballs?" one of his crew asked.

"Bring them topside and throw them over the side at the enemy. We must provide assistance to Hix and what remains of their crew," Charlie shouted back over the noise. The air had come alive with the sound of tortured metal weapons, screams and explosions.

The Commodore ran to the bow of the ship. Taking careful aim with his pistol, he fired down at the enemy, eliminating as many of them as possible.

Haste scrambled from the wreckage of the ship, in time to hear a battle-cry that could have shattered the eardrums of almost any entity. He jumped out of the way as a sword swished by his head and collided with a piece of wreckage. Vignis lunged back and stood in his warriors' stance; sword poised to kill.

"Good to see you again, Vignis," Haste growled. He put a hand up his sleeve and drew a large katana from within, standing fast against Vignis. His enemy lunged at him once again as they battled along the combined wreckage that was the walls of Rohan's Reach and the once beautiful sky-sailor. Maybelle, particularly skilful with minor magic, engaged Alwin White. Balls of fire made their way towards Alwin at incredible speed as they thumped into the walls and burst in a hot flash.

"Come on, witch! We should have disposed of you when we had the chance!" Maybelle mocked as Alwin climbed to her feet. Alwin steadied herself and brushed down her immaculate gown. She muttered incantations at top speed and engaged Maybelle as they fought for life and limb.

Charlie dropped on to the floor of the deck as a catapult's payload found its target, swiping the sails and some of the bow from existence. Pieces of shattered and splintered timber tumbled to the ground as the sky-sailor groaned and creaked. Some of the undead crew tumbled to the ground without a murmur, only their glazed expressions remained. They tumbled through the air, victims of velocity. They gathered themselves slowly from the ground and began engaging the guards as they did so.

"Abandon ship!" yelled Charlie, climbing to his feet. He kept one hand firmly on his hat to prevent it from blowing away. The Commodore took an arrow to the shoulder – with a roar he pulled it from him and shook a fist at the guards before firing a barrage down at his enemy. The ladder ropes dropped from the side of the ship as the remaining crew scrambled down them and into the skirmish. Arrows and small arms fire screamed past their ears as they descended, missing by mere inches. Charlie, the last to begin the descent, climbed down as quickly as he could. The behemoth sky-sailor began to groan louder as more pieces splintered and fell down into the town. Charlie looked as the ship began to split in half and tumble to the ground. He ran as fast as he could to get away from the ship, but found himself cornered by three guards. He gasped as they approached. They had orders to kill on sight. 'Destroy the Blind boy at all costs'. That was the universal order. Three shots sounded as The Commodore turned them into a mere pile of warm ashes with his pistol.

"Come with me," shouted The Commodore as they ran with their heads down through the battle. Shots rang around their ears as The Commodore unintentionally intercepted another arrow. They watched from behind a felled clocktower as the guards confronted some of the undead warriors. They hacked and fired away at them but they refused to fall, slowly making their way forward and pushing their enemy back.

"We must help Hix!" Charlie shouted above the noise.

"It's too dangerous," The Commodore shouted back.

The Commodore's eyes darted this way and that as they looked for a way out. He held his pistol tightly against his chest as he peered around the remains of the building.

As the hours passed, the sound of screams chased the occasional explosion as the city became little more than ruin. The civilians had been evacuated from the city, leaving their possessions behind in the wreckage.

Hix pressed his back against the wall of the storeroom he had hidden himself in, the sound of the guards thundering up and down the halls echoed as he felt his heart beat louder.

"The Rebellion is falling back!" bellowed one of the guards in passing. "There aren't many of them left... we need to push hard while we can."

Hix felt his heart sink as he slid down the wall. They had prepared for so long for this day. He just needed to get back into the fight.

Vignis led a spearhead with his officers to push back the undead army that had besieged his city. They hacked away at them, taking ten times the effort to yield as one of his own guards. He looked up to see The Commodore and Charlie battling two of his guards behind the undead. His sword rose up as he tried to cut through them as fast as he could. The boy must fall. The prophecy must be stopped. The Commodore fumbled for his watch but the hands stood still and lifeless, their final escape route had been seemingly compromised. He looked at Charlie and smiled slightly in between breaths. 'I must get you home' thought The Commodore, conflicted in his thoughts. The Rebellion had come so far… to abandon them now would reduce their chances of victory considerably.

"Okay, let's get into that building. Go now!" commanded The Commodore. He made to run with Charlie but felt himself fall to the ground. Vignis stood over him, keeping the elusive Commodore pinned to the ground.

"Charlie run!" The Commodore shouted.

Charlie disobeyed, he turned to look at Vignis. Not an ounce of fear flickered in his deep blue eyes as they pierced through Vignis.

"Let us put an end to this prophecy together!" hissed Vignis into The Commodore's ear. He held him pinned and gripped the infamous pistol, still in The Commodore's hand, aiming squarely at Charlie.

"Charlie, run!" yelled The Commodore once more, with fear across his face as he struggled fruitlessly against Vignis and his impossible grip.

"Silly little Blind boy!" sneered Vignis as he took aim.

Charlie looked from the barrel of the gun to the wicked smirk that Vignis wore so boldly. A smile split Charlie's face as his gaze met Vignis's.

"You had better not miss!" remarked Charlie rather casually as he held his captains' hat to his chest. He looked to the sky to catch a glimpse of the sun for one last time. Charlie looked back to The Commodore, gave a nod and closed his eyes, waiting for the inevitable. The shot rang out. Charlie felt a rush as he flew backwards onto the ground. The air had been knocked from his lungs as he felt the cold floor on his hands. Hix met Charlie's eyes as they opened. They were wide open in shock as his mouth hung open, gasping for air.

"What… are… best friends for?" Hix smiled painfully as he clawed gently at Charlie's chest. Hix faded slowly into the inevitable collection of ashes as his final words echoed in Charlie's ears. The Commodore screamed as Hix disappeared from existence and simply ceased to be. An undead ally to the Rebellion fell on to Vignis, knocking the legendary pistol from Vignis's and The Commodore's grip. The three fell to the ground and fought savagely, though Vignis, being an experienced warrior, had the upper hand.

Charlie sifted through the ashes frantically, tears in his eyes as he tried desperately to resurrect his friend from his demise, though his efforts were fruitless.

"Please, please come back," he wept into the ashes as he sifted through them. Arrows and bullets cracked and whipped as the battle reached new heights. He looked around at the carnage that surrounded them. The Celestial Order had the upper hand in numbers and in progress.

"Charlie, run!" The Commodore bellowed from atop Vignis – he had pinned him to the ground and proceeded to beat him as hard as he could, knowing it would not be long before Vignis managed to escape him.

Charlie ran as fast as he could across the battlefield, dodging the engaged warriors of both factions. He swooped down and took hold of a Moorish dagger from a felled soldier and continued to run. Although not a warrior and with little battle experience, it gave him comfort to be armed in such circumstances.

"Charlie…" coughed a voice from the shadows.

Charlie skidded to a halt and looked around. He saw Haste slumped against a destroyed door, his face a bloody

542

mess and an arm wrapped around his midriff, clearly in considerable pain.

"Haste, come on, let's get you out of here." Charlie panicked, looking over his shoulder to make sure no one had seen him.

"I am fine, there is no need for a rescue. I'm just catching my breath," wheezed Haste in between gasps.

"But we must get you out of here. The Rebellion is losing, the battle is almost lost. Hix has been destroyed and The Commodore is still fighting," Charlie explained frantically.

Haste held out a hand and gripped Charlie's arm, pulling him closer. He smiled warmly at Charlie and even managed a small laugh as he considered him.

"My boy, we have shown the world that we exist, that our plight is real and that The Celestial Order are not invincible," whispered Haste. "But there is something more to be done."

"What is it, how do I help?" Charlie pleaded desperately. He ducked down instinctively as a stray arrow missed him by only inches. "What needs to be done, Haste?"

"The world… must know… what The Celestial Order are planning…" Haste coughed. "Remove the veil from The Celestial Order… let the people know what they are planning with the invincible army."

"How can I possibly do that? They will never believe the word of a boy!" Charlie pleaded.

"Show them," coughed Haste. "You must show them. Reveal the army of the invincible to the world – that will be enough to expose their vile plans. The Bank of The Celeste, that is where the invincible army are kept. Expose them to the world! It's up to you now, my boy."

Charlie ducked down once more as a bullet shattered against the wall, showering them both with spent pieces of lead. He looked out and saw guards battling their way towards them – the battle began to enter the final stages.

"Go now!" Haste bawled as loud as he could.

Charlie scrambled across the wreckage and further into the destroyed city, his eyes darting in every direction as he looked for The Bank of The Celeste. He planned his sprints and found himself on part of the railroad. The Celestial Flight sat motionless in the yard, purple clouds of steam billowed out indifferently from under the beast. He climbed the cold metal steps and threw himself into the cab, observing the huge dials and many gauges that controlled the beast. He turned the different valves and jumped as a 'wheesh' of steam shot out from underneath, but the locomotive did not move. Charlie dropped to the floor and wept, having exhausted as many different combinations as he could. He threw his hat against the dials and watched as it dropped down and hooked onto a giant lever, on which was written 'Brake'. With renewed vigour, he jumped to his feet and yanked the lever south. A great thump followed as The Celestial Flight huffed and hawed into life. He took hold of the grab handle and peered outside, looking forward as the locomotive clicked and clacked slowly out of the yard.

His eyes scanned the railroad and saw a sign, spotless and clearly new. 'End of the line, Bank of The Celeste, two miles'. Charlie turned one of the pressure gauges and felt the beast pull harder along the tracks, the speedometer slowly beginning to climb. Thirty, forty, fifty miles per hour. The clickety-clack became louder and louder.

"I'll show 'em. Hix!" Charlie shouted aloud as he hung on to the grab handle, watching as a driver would. "Let's open their eyes! If we are to fall, The Celestial Order will never forget us!"

He pulled at the whistle release, the locomotive whistled loud and gaily across the city, echoing the noise of the engine as it ploughed on forward across the line and onto the viaduct. Many of those engaged in battle, friend and foe, looked up to see the source of the racket. Their mouths dropped open as they watched Charlie waving at them, his hat in his hand as the locomotive ploughed on at full speed.

"Charlie!" shouted The Commodore. He had no hope of him hearing, but didn't know what else to do. He brought his attention back to Vignis and launched another renewed attack upon him, getting the upper hand for the first time since they had engaged.

Steam spewed from the funnel of The Celestial Flight in huge clouds as the wheels slipped intermittently, struggling to put power to the tracks. The huge locomotive reached one-hundred miles per hour as a sonic boom drowned out the sound of battle. Electric-blue beams split and sparked at the front of the behemoth monster – a second later, the locomotive disappeared. After no more than a minute, it re-appeared much further down the track at incredible speed. The immense torque of the steam engine sent the beast hurtling forward without a single hope of stopping.

Charlie pulled the whistle once more and laughed heartily as it blew.

"What an adventure I have had," Charlie laughed to himself.

The Celestial Flight sailed along the tracks at breakneck speed as they approached the end of the line, the final station integrated into The Bank of The Celeste.

Vignis glanced occasionally at the locomotive, wondering what the Blind boy could possibly have been planning. He dealt The Commodore a blow to the back of the head and sent him hurtling to the floor. Vignis had enough time to realise what was happening, but there was nothing he could do.

"End of the line for The Celestial Order!" Charlie bellowed heartily as the locomotive met the final piece of track, and beyond.

The gut-wrenching sound of bending metal and crashing masonry stopped the battle in its tracks as The Celestial Flight concluded its maiden journey. The carriages smashed together, shattering into thousands of pieces, as the building absorbed the impact of the great machine.

"Charlie!" shouted The Commodore as he and Vignis turned in time to witness the destruction of The Celestial Flight. "I'm coming, Charlie!"

The Commodore turned to set off at a sprint when, a moment later, an ear-splitting explosion came from the locomotive. The shockwave overwhelmed The Bank of The Celeste and razed it to the ground. The entire battlefield silenced and looked on as the building imploded, sending a sea of debris and dust into the air in a mushroom-shaped cloud.

The Commodore took hold of Vignis's arm and turned it towards him, forcing Vignis to drop his weapon. With a swift sweep of the legs, he sent Vignis to the ground and reached for his pistol but it wasn't to be found. He turned and saw that it had fallen into a pile of debris. By the time he turned back to Vignis, he had vanished from sight.

"No, oh no..." The Commodore stammered as the dusty cloud made its way skyward, far above the ruin that was Rohan's Reach. He collected his pistol as he ran to find the Blind boy that had shaken The Celestial Order to their very core.

As The Commodore approached the wreckage, he heard a horn blow in the distance. Shortly after came a roaring celebration. The Celestial Order had overcome their enemy and put a halt to the invasion of Rohan's Reach. The Commodore barely acknowledged they had lost the battle, as he looked up at the ruined building.

Evidence of The Celestial Order's unexecuted final solution lay scattered for all to see. Papers and equipment worked as damning evidence of the plans that had been prepared. The invincible army stood motionless and cold – for the first time, they had been uncovered for all to see. The Commodore dug through the wreckage frantically, trying to uncover the locomotive. Alwin White staggered over and began to help, her gown lying in tatters over her burnt flesh.

"Find Charlie!" shouted The Commodore feverishly, without looking over at Alwin.

She collapsed onto the wreckage and began pulling away the debris in an effort to find him.

Vignis raised his sword skyward as his comrades cheered and celebrated their victory all across the city. Rohan's Reach lay in ruin, but it remained under their control. Vignis dropped to his knees exhausted, though fully satisfied. He had quenched his thirst for battle and bloodshed of an enemy, all the more fulfilling as it happened to be The Galdihar Rebellion that he had overcome. Maybelle fluttered over, almost completely untouched. A huge smile split her face as she looked around at the celebrating guards, soldiers and officers. They had lost an incredible number in their effort to keep Rohan's Reach, but this mattered little in the grand scheme of the final solution. Loss of life had never been a concern for Vignis.

"We are victorious!" Maybelle squealed in excitement. "The Galdihar Rebellion are done for!"

Vignis looked up at her as he breathed deeply.

"Do we have Haste, Alwin or The Commodore in custody?" he gasped.

"Haste is presumed expired, but Alwin and The Commodore have been sighted fleeing," she replied.

"That demon, Hix," Vignis wheezed between breaths. "He has been concluded by The Commodore's own hand."

Maybelle cheered and whooped in excitement at the prospect of the demon expiring. Hix had gone, erased from all planes, along with any secrets he may have had about Maybelle.

The Commodore pulled some of the rubble from the top of The Celestial Flight. Water from its boiler was still warm as he got closer. Alwin helped The Commodore move a piece of masonry from the driver's cab. Inside lay Charlie, curled up in the corner. The Commodore reached down and pulled him out, dusting his face off frantically, gasping in panic. On the surface, Charlie had barely even a scratch. Alwin checked his pressure points as The Commodore felt his chest. They both looked at each other as both examinations revealed the horrific truth. Charlie lay cold and very much dead.

The Commodore howled as he held the boy close to him, tears streaming down his filthy face as Alwin looked on helplessly.

"Help him!" The Commodore choked. "Help the boy!"

"I can't" whispered Alwin.

"Yes, you can! I know you can, you know the magic of necromancy!" The Commodore pleaded, holding Charlie out towards her.

"That will only raise his corpse, it will not be Charlie," she explained, trying to calm him. She looked down at the prophecy that lay before them. They had hoped that Charlie would save the Divine world and beyond from the evils of The Celestial Order.

The Commodore looked down and saw a small piece of paper sticking out of Charlie's pocket. He pulled it out carefully and unfolded it. He jumped to his feet with the piece of paper, his eyes filling with tears for the boy he had failed to protect.

"Read it, Alwin! Read it quickly!" The Commodore stammered, forcing the paper on her. She looked down at the incredibly strange writing and looked back to The Commodore. A hopelessness filled Alwin as her shoulders dropped.

Chapter Eighteen – Passing Time By The Mercury Tide

Part I

The night sky embraced an amber glow as the fires raged. What was once regal and majestic had been reduced to rubble and ruin. Those that fled slowly returned and as they did, their eyes were opened for the first time in centuries. The truth had been unmasked, the veil lifted and the rumours put to right. The truth lit the lips of all the souls across the planes and returned a long-lost concept that had almost been forgotten – hope.

The flames that engulfed Rohan's Reach began to fade and settle into perishing embers. The final skirmishing had settled to nothing as silence reigned. The faint crackling and snapping of dying fires gently interrupted the silence.

The receding fires crackled and snapped as they faded, complementing what was otherwise an eery, telling silence.

"What are we to do now?" asked Lovian.

He stood with his hands on his hips as he pondered the burning pile of rubble that used to be his livelihood. The small store had been passed down from generation to generation, providing rarities and enchanted wares to many travellers and residents alike. He hadn't cared much for energy, but instead traded wares for wares, as was traditional.

Lovian's assistant, a small old lady, said nothing, but considered the wreckage also. They watched on as the embers flickered and glowed angrily. More of those that had been forced to flee returned to salvage what they could from the ruined city.

"Hurry along now, there isn't anything to see," ushered a battle-fatigued guard.

"But where are we to go?" piped Lovian.

"That is no business of mine. Orders are to clear citizens from the wreckage," the guard barked, irritably.

"Why?" replied Lovian, stubbornly.

The guard shot Lovian a scornful look, but became more aware of the growing crowd that surrounded them.

"There could be dangerous items remaining and they must be cleared," replied the guard, feverishly. The growing crowd began to become unsettled as whispering and hesitation spread like wildfire.

Eyebrows were raised along with short tempers as they became unsettled. Hushed voices spread amongst them as they refused to be moved on.

The Commodore held Charlie close as the boy became colder and colder. Alwin watched on and tried to comfort The Commodore, but that did little to ease him.

"We cannot stay here," said Alwin gently, placing a hand on The Commodore's shoulder.

"I have lost it all. Once again, I have failed," muttered The Commodore. "What was it all for? What have these decades upon decades been in aid of? I thought that I had found myself and my purpose."

Alwin smiled weakly before looking out across the wreckage that was Rohan's Reach. The guards had become more active and were extending their search for their enemy. Voices grew in volume and were getting closer.

"We must leave," pleaded Alwin.

"Don't move!" came a bawling voice from behind them.

Alwin turned slowly and met the gaze of a guard, badly wounded and struggling to steady himself. His sword was drawn and his intentions were obvious.

"We have no quarrel with you," said Alwin, calmly. "If you open your mind, you will be blessed with the truth about The Celestial Order."

"Lies! All lies!" he spat in reply.

"You have nothing to fear from us," Alwin explained as she glanced awkwardly at The Commodore. "Look across at The Bank of The Celeste and see for yourself."

The soldier looked at Alwin suspiciously, occasionally glancing over his shoulder to see if his comrades had arrived, but they were nowhere to be seen.

"And what do you expect me to see?"

"The truth," Alwin replied, bluntly.

"No tricks now!" the solider barked.

The Commodore stared into the distance as he rocked with Charlie in his arms, unmoved by the soldier's presence.

The soldier looked across the wreckage of The Bank of The Celeste, his eyes darting this way and that until they finally landed upon the invincible army.

"What are they?" gasped the soldier as he lowered his sword slightly.

"They are the invincible army, crafted from the energy gathered by The Celestial Order. They cannot be destroyed and you can see that they are ready and waiting," Alwin explained, grimly.

"But why?" asked the soldier in awe of the monsters that lay in slumber.

"To gain access to the places that The Celestial Order does not control, starting with Sanctuary. They will invade the plane and take control by force. After that, the Blind world and then on to Oblivion," Alwin explained in a friendly manner.

The soldier stared on, unblinking, trying to calculate the deception he had been part of. The sword fell from his hand and clattered to the floor; his helmet followed shortly after as he limped forward to inspect the beasts.

Alwin returned to The Commodore, unravelling the paper she had been handed.

"These are co-ordinates, but I'm not sure what for," said Alwin with a raised eyebrow.

She rotated the piece of paper round and round, checking again and again for a different combination, but none came.

"What do I care for some silly co-ordinates? Of what importance can they possibly be?" snorted The Commodore.

"I'm not sure," replied Alwin, puzzled. "They seem to have been written by an elder."

"An elder?" echoed The Commodore.

"I think so, a very old one at that," said Alwin slowly.

"The Giving Tree," whispered The Commodore. "That's what those co-ordinates are for. Hysterias tried to bargain with them! I threw them away; Charlie must have picked them up!"

The Commodore climbed to his feet and held Charlie with one arm as he checked his watch – the second hand shifted forward and back in a happy fashion.

"Come along, Charlie," soothed The Commodore as he placed the boy's corpse gently on the ground and produced a woe-globe from his pocket. "You'll be safe in here."

A moment later and Charlie had been placed safely inside the woe-globe. The Commodore held out the woe-globe so that Alwin could see. On peering inside, they both saw a small bed with a sleeping child inside.

"Let's go and find 'The Giving Tree'," said The Commodore to the woe-globe.

"But, 'The Giving Tree' is rumoured to be only a myth, a legend. Most deny its existence," Alwin explained, trying to bring The Commodore to a more rounded way of thinking.

The Commodore looked from the woe-globe to Alwin and placed a hand on her shoulder. A kind, friendly smile appeared.

"They said the same of us, my dear Alwin," said The Commodore. "Rumours and myth."

"Indeed, they did," Alwin agreed, amazed at her own contradiction.

The Commodore tightened his belt and adjusted his mostly ruined shirt, before turning back to Alwin.

"Find 'The Giving Tree,' James. I know you will find it," said Alwin as she embraced The Commodore.

"I certainly hope so. Goodbye Alwin," said The Commodore.

The inevitable flash and bang echoed across the ruined city, as The Commodore disappeared in search of 'The Giving Tree'.

The injured guard studied the forged army with childlike curiosity, poking at their hardened faces and then leaping back to see if they moved. Their faces were solemn and expressionless with empty, vacant spaces where eyes would normally be. A hardened version of what looked like porcelain but nothing he nor anyone else had ever seen the likes of before. Along with the wreckage, masses of evidence condemning The Celestial Order lay scattered.

The most heinous of experiments had been completed over centuries to exert the desired outcome and help to create the perfect army. The experiments had been carried out on living and expired subjects alike in secret, until today. The injured guard felt his head spin as he absorbed the information before him, uncovering lie after lie that had been told by The Celestial Order.

"What are you doing?" came a formal request from behind the injured guard.

"Uncovering the truth," he muttered without looking back.

A high-ranking officer of The Celestial Order's army stood with his hands on his hips, eyeing the same evidence that the injured guard had discovered. Two of his colleagues stood the regulatory two metres behind him, on hand to carry out any orders put to them.

"This area is a condemned site and must be vacated in accordance with The Good Shepherd's orders," the officer barked. "Unless you are looting! To which the penalty is eternity in Purgatory."

The injured guard continued to ignore him as he searched further into the wreckage.

"I warn you!" began the officer, wagging a finger.

He was cut short by the arrival of some of the displaced citizens that now had nowhere to go. They gathered together, craning their necks to see what was going on.

"Nothing to see here," barked the officer at the crowd. "Move along."

"To where?" came a voice from deep inside the crowd.

The officer looked around at the solemn faces that surrounded him and his colleagues, they looked lost and condemned. Everything they owned had been destroyed.

"Anywhere but here, there is nothing to see," the officer's voice started to wobble as he spoke – he was clearly nervous.

The injured guard staggered upright and limped slowly towards the crowd, a fistful of papers in his hands.

"The truth can be found in the wreckage; we have been fed a pack of lies and deceived beyond comprehension. If you wish to open your eyes to the truth, take a look for yourself and see."

The injured guard's gauntlets clattered to the ground along with his armoured vest. He gave a brief nod and headed north away from the crowd. They looked awkwardly to each other and back to the smouldering wreckage before them. The officer's eyes began to dart in all directions as he considered what to do.

"Do you deny that the truth can be found in the wreckage?" asked one of the citizens from the crowd.

"There is no truth to be found here… now let's be moving on!" the officer called. He waved his arms to usher them on, but they remained.

The crowd began to whisper feverishly, occasionally pointing at the officer. Eventually a few of them moved forward, past the officer who simply looked on at them, not knowing what to do.

His colleagues looked on indifferently. They had no intention of improvising on the situation, and simply waited for an order that never came.

The Commodore breathed a great sigh as he tightened his belt once more. He looked around at the forest that surrounded him. The huge trees cast vast shadows, even though the sun shone. The forest seemed untarnished and natural, the sound of birds chirping echoed merrily. Peace and calm prevailed as The Commodore made his way forward between the trees, unsure of what 'The Giving Tree' actually looked like.

"Where could it be?" the Commodore muttered aloud.

He studied the inevitable time-piece, staring without blinking so as not to miss a beat… but nothing happened.

What seemed to be hours passed, but the sun remained at the highest point in the sky, beaming down.

The Commodore seated himself on a fallen tree, the mossy bark crunching softly as he sat. A steady calmness emanated from the natural beauty that surrounded him. The forest seemed infinite and went on far into the distance.

"I wonder where we are, Domina," The Commodore whispered to the face of his watch. He stroked the broken face with his thumb as he hoped for an indication of life, but none came. He thought of Charlie, his cheeky smile and hearty laughter. Many fond times had been enjoyed even in the relatively short period he had known the curious Blind boy.

"Could this be the 26th hour?" The Commodore thought aloud. "Wherever we are, it is certainly a curious place."

Had The Commodore arrived under any other circumstance, he would probably have been more cautious.

"But what can they possibly take from me now?" he thought to himself.

With renewed fervour, he started and continued his journey through the bracken and bush to find the mythical tree. The feeling of being observed began to creep over him. He stopped from time to time to see if anything had been following him but saw only the indifferent trees around him.

"You're a long way from home," sneered a silky voice quite suddenly.

The Commodore turned curiously to see who had spoken to him, but no one could be seen. The words had come from right by his ear, as if a thought had become audible. His hand moved slowly down to his pistol as he wrapped his fingers around the grip.

"There won't be any need for that," giggled the voice. "It's been so long since we've had visitors."

"We?" asked The Commodore aloud.

"Quite. We. Plural. More than I," the voice replied as a matter of fact.

The Commodore could not make out if the voice was real, or a thought inside of his own head. Either way, he was certainly not piloting the voice.

"I wish to find 'The Giving Tree'," the Commodore stated, his eyes darting wildly around him.

"You? Ha!" the voice scoffed. "A man of your history doesn't stand a chance of a confrontation with 'The Giving Tree'.

The Commodore scowled angrily as he became more accustomed to hearing the voice within him.

"Do you know where it is?" he asked, a little less than politely.

"We do. We know where everything is here," the voice replied, indifferently.

"Where can I find it?" The Commodore asked.

"What do we owe you, stranger?" the voice replied. "It will only lead you to your conclusion."

"That's for me to worry about, not you," The Commodore snapped, his hand returning to his pistol.

The voice subsided for a few moments. The shadows cast by the trees began to spin across the floor at an accelerated rate as the sun began to set at a remarkable pace. After only a few moments, the sky had become full of stars and a bright shining moon, though they were mostly hidden by the trees.

"Commodore, captain of the high seas," the voice mocked. "You can find 'The Giving Tree' north by thirty degrees. We are not certain you are genuine in your skillset, but you can try to follow the stars for a bearing."

The Commodore rolled his eyes and gave a loud tut. He looked skyward and observed the stars, trying to get a bearing on where he needed to be.

Vignis sat in his wing-backed chair in the meeting room of The Grand Manor. He sipped at a cold beverage and sank deeper into his comfortable smoking jacket. The fire-place crackled merrily and lit the room as rain hammered down outside of the large building. He smiled slightly as he stared into the flames, the smile of a triumphant man.

His staff raced to and fro throughout the building, as did many guards and soldiers as they tried to resolve the current situation.

Hundreds of voices could be heard outside the main doors of the building. Fists hammered the huge doors and windows in a rage.

"We know the truth! We know the truth!" they chanted in unison.

Entities of all kinds had gathered to confront 'The Good Shepherd' and his secrets that had now become very public. The location of The Grand Manor had many secret enchantments, but an intercepted officer and a few torture tactics later, they gained entry to the grounds.

Vignis sat, unmoved by the growing tension outside his own door. He let his head fall back into the chair and studied the vast oil paintings that hung on the wall. They represented the previous leaders of the Divine world, though Vignis had some of them removed simply because he didn't like them or they didn't fit with the décor he had applied.

A guard made his way past the door to the meeting room when Vignis called to him.

"You! Solider!" he barked.

The guard stood to attention by the door, but not daring to take a step over the threshold. Vignis considered the guard, still unmoved and rather chipper about the growing situation.

"Remove the trespassers by any means necessary," Vignis growled, his smile turning sinister.

"Yes sir!" the guard saluted, before he shot off down the hallway at full pelt.

Vignis resettled himself in the chair and felt a grin grow even further across his face as he closed his eyes to an incredible orchestra. Not of strings, brass or wind, but of screams and gunfire. The area outside of the building had become alive with the sound of weapons, screams and groans as the protesters were eliminated.

"What an era this is turning out to be," whispered Vignis to himself as he took another sip form his cold beverage.

The night air had become very cold, and as the trees had blocked most of the night sky, The Commodore saw almost total darkness.

"Are you giving up yet?" mocked the mystery voice.

"You clearly haven't heard of me," The Commodore replied confidently. "I'm The Commodore. The most wanted man across the planes. If you think I'm ready to throw in the towel just yet, you're sorely mistaken."

"Oh, did you hear that?" the voice mocked once more. "We have 'The Commodore'."

The Commodore smiled as he had provoked the response he had intended. The undergrowth cracked and creaked as he made his way through the forest.

"Your mission is quite unclear to us," came the voice with less hostility. "You search for 'The Giving Tree' which will judge your request, and if it is not granted, you will be destroyed from all forms of existence."

"I am aware of the legend," The Commodore replied shortly.

"I do not wish to spoil your quest, but you are certain to be doomed by the tree, as is any request you make by it," the voice replied.

"What detriment is that to you?" asked The Commodore, coldly.

"None," the voice, returned just as frosty.

"Then mind your own business," The Commodore snapped back.

"As you wish," the voice obliged.

Silence prevailed once again from the voice as The Commodore continued his way forward.

The hours and miles passed as The Commodore navigated his way through the forest. Silence reigned as he continued without even a thought of abandoning his mission.

"Oh, you bet. She knows you better than almost anyone else," The Commodore replied with a smile. "I don't think I've ever met a kinder lady of stature, aside from my wife, of course."

"My mother," said Charlie quickly.

"That's right. Lady Kingston," said The Commodore. "It was a great pleasure."

Charlie frowned as he thought about his mother and how his father must be missing him terribly, not to mention Christopher.

"Do you think she is proud of me?" Charlie asked, looking up at The Commodore. His eyes were full of expectation and hope.

"Are you kidding? Of course, she is. Lady Kingston had not a bad word to say about you. What a wonderful mother you have," said The Commodore in complimentary fashion.

"Had," corrected Charlie.

"Have," re-iterated The Commodore. "You will see your mother again, though not for a long time yet, I imagine."

"Death is a grim business," Charlie chipped in. "I'm quite keen not to experience it again for quite some time.

"I wonder who that voice belongs to," The Commodore considered to himself.

"There are things, you are better off not knowing," the mysterious voice explained coldly.

As The Commodore opened his mouth to reply, a clearing in the forest appeared. In the middle of the clearing stood a beautiful blossom tree. Its petals rained from the branches steadily but the branches were never naked. A strange, subtle light seemed to pulse from the tree as he approached, but it didn't look any different from other blossom trees. Just as beautiful, just as indifferent. He approached and stroked the bark, almost as if checking to see if it was real. The Commodore dropped his bag to the floor and sat down to rest, pulling the woe-globe that contained Charlie from his pocket and peering into the glassy dome.

"Here we are," whispered The Commodore in a soothing voice. A loud ticking sound buzzed from his pocket in a panicked fashion. He opened the watch and considered the sweeping second hand.

"Nice of you to join us, Domina," he smiled.

The Commodore placed the woe-globe on the floor and pondered it for a length of time unknown even to himself. A day, a week or a month, he couldn't be sure. The feeling of serenity and contentment that filled the air around the mythical tree was sublime. An inner peace that The Commodore hadn't felt in centuries flowed calmly throughout every fibre of his being.

"Are you going to stay there forever?" asked the voice in his ear.

The Commodore chuckled to himself, no longer afraid of the rude and rather arrogant voice that had kept him company.

"I do not intend to stay here forever; I am merely considering my purpose," The Commodore replied, calmly.

"There's someone who wishes to meet you," said the voice, rather more politely than usual.

At every spoken word, The Commodore tried to figure out if it was familiar. A woman, a man, a child. He could not tell. He wasn't altogether confident that the voice wasn't a severe symptom of insanity. The lines of reality had been blurred somewhat over the past few months, but that wasn't his main concern.

"They wish to meet me, but require my permission?" The Commodore enquired, still considering the woe-globe that contained Charlie.

"That is correct," replied the voice as a matter of fact.

"It all sounds very demonic, asking permission. Are they of Oblivion?" asked The Commodore, curiously.

"Perhaps. They may or may not be of the plane of wickedness and cruelty. Though, most that find themselves amongst the damned have committed atrocities most deserving," the voice thought aloud. "I ask you once more, would you like to meet the one that requests your company?"

"Well, Hymm doesn't wait for an invitation, and today cannot possibly get any worse. I am sat in an unfamiliar land where time has no bearing and I have the corpse of a small boy in a woe-globe," The Commodore replied, cheerfully. "I give permission for the visitor."

"Very well," the voice replied.

The Commodore lifted his head and looked out into the forest; darkness surrounded the glow of 'The Giving Tree'. After a few moments, a figure appeared and walked towards him slowly. The Commodore watched with curiosity as they approached him, without fear or wish to flee. He noticed the figure was a lady, clearly once of high standing. Her long dress flowed serenely and complemented her beauty. Suddenly realising his company approached formally, The Commodore jumped to his feet and began brushing himself down. He breathed on a torn piece of his shirt and brightened his buttons before standing straight in perfect military fashion.

"Good evening, Ma'am," said The Commodore rather formally, but ever so politely.

The lady considered The Commodore curiously, an eyebrow raised and a curl in the corner of her mouth. He considered her in polite return. Her eyes and her smile were familiar but he couldn't quite place them.

"It's a pleasure to meet you finally, James," she replied, holding her hand out. The Commodore absorbed her silky well-spoken voice and stood even straighter. She clearly came from a blue-blooded background or similar.

"My apologies, Ma'am," replied The Commodore, politely, kissing her hand in proper fashion. "I am embarrassed to say I have not met you before."

She stood straight and considered The Commodore once more, with growing curiosity and a wider smile. An air of pleasantry and friendliness surrounded the lady, which made The Commodore feel that bit more awkward.

"My name, is Lady Edith Kingston," she smiled. "I have watched you for quite some time, and though I find your behaviour most… unorthodox, you are certainly interesting."

"Begging your pardon, Ma'am, are you Charlie's mother?" The Commodore asked, stumbling over his words.

"That's right," she replied, her hands together. "You have given an incredible gift to Charlie, one that most have neglected, including my husband."

"Begging your pardon once again, Ma'am, I consider myself to have taken more from Charlie, than given" The Commodore explained, as he tugged awkwardly at his collar.

"You have given my son time – something that has been lacking in his childhood since my departure some years ago," she explained, calmly.

"Are you not a resident of Sanctuary?" The Commodore asked after a moment.

"I am," she replied.

"Is Charlie there with you? Is he happy?" The Commodore asked eagerly.

Lady Kingston's smile faded slightly as she considered The Commodore's question. She moved her gaze away from his.

"There's a lot of curiosity that plagues the planes. Even in Sanctuary. Charlie is not resident in Sanctuary. I am not sure where he is," she explained.

The Commodore began to tremble and opened his mouth to speak, but Lady Kingston raised a hand politely.

"Great things are expected of my son, he is an integral part of an incredible prophecy. I was not pleased to learn this but, alas, it has been decided by higher powers," Lady Kingston explained with only a hint of her sadness. A certain strength could be found within her.

"My lady, many proposed prophecies are proven to be false and are simply myth," The Commodore explained as though it might be of some comfort to her.

"What you have not considered, is that a prophecy can be, and often is, tangibly manipulated. The expected path may become a road, sea or mountain," Lady Kingston explained.

"There are choices for the champion of the prophecy," she concluded. Lady Kingston looked to the floor and spotted the woe-globe. With an eyebrow raised once more, she leaned down and retrieved the enchanted object.

"You are part of the prophecy, James," she explained with her eyes focused tightly on the figure of a small boy sleeping soundly. "It is your choice that will shape the future and the outcome. It's hard to believe my son's lifeless body resides within this otherworldly device."

The Commodore turned to the vast and beautiful Giving Tree and considered the purple blossoms that descended around them. He held out a hand and caught one of the petals as they tumbled to the ground. He pondered it.

"If Charlie is not in Sanctuary, then where is he?" The Commodore asked, his voice cracking with worry.

"Sadly, I do not have an answer," Lady Kingston replied after a moment.

The Commodore rubbed his chin in thought, mostly to distract him from the tears that welled in his eyes.

"You could request anything you want from 'The Giving Tree'," Lady Kingston explained.

"To take back everything that I ever did wrong, back to the night upon 'HMS Fury'," The Commodore dreamed aloud. "I could wish for a mortal lifetime with my family… my wife, my son."

The Commodore considered the petal in his hand once more and smiled as he considered how beautiful his family were. A single tear rolled down his cheek as a slight breeze blew the petal away from his palm and into the abyss.

"You know the consequence of a wish declined, don't you?" asked Lady Kingston, severely.

"I will be concluded – dead across every plane and removed from any kind of relative existence," The Commodore replied casually, unmoved by the prospect of not existing.

"Whatever your choice or request, it was a pleasure to meet you, James," said Lady Kingston, politely.

He felt a warm hand on his arm. He reached to touch it with his own but her hand had disappeared, along with the rest of Lady Kingston. The Commodore looked around and saw that he was alone once more.

"Oh, how exciting, what will the felon choose!" mocked the mysterious voice by his ear. "Condemned, that's what you are, Commodore. All those terrible decisions you made, 'The Giving Tree' will take everything into account."

The Commodore threw back his head in laughter at the mocking tones of the voice, which quickly fell silent.

"Do you think that I fear my own conclusion? At worst, I will be free of my pain," laughed The Commodore as he approached The Giving Tree. He placed a hand upon the smooth bark and took a deep breath.

"Here we go," he whispered with a smile, the woe-globe in hand.

The Commodore moved his hand from 'The Giving Tree' and soon felt a pulling sensation as darkness surrounded him. His eyes began to feel heavy as the energy slowly drained from within him as he embraced the abyss.

"This is it… I guess I'm finished," The Commodore whispered aloud, smiling as he did so.

"I decide who is finished and who is worthy," sneered the mysterious voice. "We reside within 'The Giving Tree' and we have reached our conclusion."

The Commodore smiled and put out his arms as he fell backwards. His stomach filled with butterflies as he fell into a pleasant nothingness.

Part II

The night sky over Rohan's Reach came alive with the sounds of screams and renewed fires as far as the eye could see. The residents protested against the sudden and strict implementation of a curfew, which had come with no explanation. Anyone that resisted was eliminated on the spot or sent for special interrogation at The Grand Manor. The incidents were no longer restricted to just Rohan's Reach – news had spread to every corner of the Divine world. The plans for a war that no citizen wanted had been uncovered. Even the cells of Purgatory raged as inmates whooped and screamed. The bedlam and unrest had made its way to the plane of contemplation. The masters and guards responded by beating the inmates, in an attempt to keep them in line.

Vignis's sponsors and elitist acquaintances had also heard the news, with most of them removing any kind of affiliation with such a person. It was simply bad for business and their reputation.

"The Grand Manor has been locked down, sir," Maybelle reported as she hovered in the doorway to his bedroom.

Vignis sat looking out into the gardens. Once beautiful and well kept, they were now littered with barbed wire and guards.

"Very good," Vignis replied, only half-listening to Maybelle.

"Should I summon Judge Humphrey and Omar Asghari?" she continued.

"Yes. And ensure that Adelade makes an appearance as well," Vignis added.

Maybelle looked awkwardly out into the hallway, checking to see if anyone else was in earshot.

"Sir, Adelade won't be associated with The Celestial Order anymore," she stammered nervously.

"Why ever not? She has information that is crucial to our success," Vignis barked. "Are you a simpleton, Maybelle? Must I spell everything out for you?"

Maybelle ignored his remarks and looked away from his gaze.

"She has been summoned to the inner circles of Oblivion and will not be returning," Maybelle explained, as a matter of fact.

"What? Hymm is an ally to The Celestial Order," Vignis snapped, impatiently.

"She defaulted on the agreement to acquire certain artifacts for Hymm. The deadline for the contract had arrived and he concluded their arrangement."

Vignis reeled at the devastating news and leaned against the mantelpiece to keep himself upright. He considered his plans and how this loss would mark a pivotal change.

"The plane of Oblivion could have been a powerful ally in our plight. We now have another realm to conquer," Vignis muttered, irritably.

"But sir, do not give in. We have come so far and have overcome our most formidable enemy, The Galdihar Rebellion," Maybelle pleaded.

A series of shots could be heard in the grounds of The Grand Manor. A partisan-like group of entities had banded together to try and overthrow The Celestial Order. So far, they had not been successful and suffered heavy losses with each attempt. A brick sailed through the window, sending pieces of glass in every direction. Neither Vignis nor Maybelle so much as flinched as the brick entered their presence.

"Gather the remaining members of The Celestial Order. We will meet and discuss the next steps," Vignis snapped from next to the mantelpiece.

He contemplated his options as Maybelle gave a brief nod and flew away to carry out his orders.

The Commodore felt as though he had slept for a month, a refreshing feeling washed over him as a pleasant warmth touched his face. His eyes remained closed as he heard the sound of the sea, gently washing the shoreline.

"Where have you been?" asked a familiar, ever-so-polite voice.

The Commodore sat bolt upright and opened his eyes. The bright sun stung his eyes as he shielded them and squinted.

"Charlie?" asked The Commodore, half-laughing. "It worked! The Giving Tree, it worked! I wished that you were back and here you are! My boy! My fabulous boy!"

The Commodore leapt to his feet and embraced Charlie, pulling him close and squeezing him tight.

Charlie sat patiently with his legs crossed, looking confused but happy to see The Commodore. The Commodore looked around and saw stunning rolling hills and a silver sea which looked almost like mercury. Looking atop the nearest hill, he noticed a beautiful house that couldn't have been more than a year old.

"My boy, are you alright?" The Commodore asked, trembling.

"Yes, I believe so," Charlie explained.

A tall man with the most fabulous of moustaches casually made his way down from the house beautiful house and approached The Commodore and Charlie.

The three looked at each other, the stranger smiled at the puzzled Commodore and Charlie.

"This is Sanctuary," the stranger smiled.

"Sanctuary?" snorted The Commodore. "Surely not. I am not allowed to enter Sanctuary."

"The circumstances are not usual," he replied casually, staring out on to the mercury sea. "You may enjoy the shoreline for a little while longer. We ask that you escort Charlie back to his timeline and, of course, his father."

"Certainly," replied The Commodore, slowly, still rather suspicious of their surroundings.

The stranger turned to leave, before suddenly stopping in his tracks.

"Oh, James. Please can you refrain from any further visitation to Oblivion?" the stranger asked politely.

"Oblivion? I have never been to Oblivion!" The Commodore retorted.

The stranger smiled a knowing smile.

"The Giving Tree…" said The Commodore slowly, "was in Oblivion…"

The stranger gave a faint nod whilst retaining his smile.

"Very few people have the pleasure of meeting The Giving Tree, let alone surviving its judgement."

The Commodore gave a nod, and the stranger ascended the hill to the beautiful house.

"Do you know him?" asked The Commodore, once the stranger was out of earshot.

"I don't think so. He visited me earlier and said that it wasn't my time and that I shouldn't be here yet. And then said something about building my own house," Charlie continued.

"I am sorry for letting you down, Charlie. I did not mean for anything to happen to you. I wanted to protect you," The Commodore explained. His arms trembled as he embraced him again, as though confirming he was really there.

A faint ticking sound came from the watch in The Commodore's pocket. Without delay, he retrieved it and opened the face, presenting it to Charlie.

"It seems that Domina is happy to see you too!" he cried, happily.

"Hello!" said Charlie, cheerfully, waving at the watch with a big smile on his face.

They both sat and watched the silver tide creep its way in onto the shoreline, enjoying the heat from the sun and the serenity that came with it. For the first time, The Commodore no longer needed to run, hide or look over his shoulder. The Celestial Order would be preoccupied with plenty of other priorities, if only for the day. Charlie watched on, smiling next to The Commodore as he thought about his adventure so far.

"How did you find me?" asked Charlie after some time.

"I didn't. You found me, I believe," said The Commodore slowly, having not really considered their meeting in much detail.

"I met a wonderful lady who had only great things to say about you, Charlie," The Commodore explained as they watched the silver tide.

"And she knew me?" asked Charlie, curiously.

I've heard how death is a kindness and there are fates far worse. But I'm not so sure."

"I asked your mother if you were in Sanctuary, but she informed me you were not. We did not know where you were," explained The Commodore with fascinated curiosity. "Where were you?"

"All I remember is darkness, it was pitch black. I heard voices that were unkind and said the most horrible of things. I would not repeat their wickedness to anyone," Charlie recalled, quite casually. "Then, after what seemed like forever, I ended up here. Shortly after you arrived."

The Commodore scratched at his chin thoughtfully as he considered Charlie's tale. He returned to considering the silver sea as it teased the shoreline in effortless fashion.

"For many years, I thought I knew everything there was to know about the planes – the damned and otherwise. What you have taught me is that every day there are learnings to be had – about oneself, the ever-changing worlds and, most importantly, kindness. My years being on the run had hardened me from feeling anything other than self-importance," The Commodore explained. "Thank you, Charlie."

Charlie smiled at The Commodore for a moment and then looked away as the smile began to fade and sadness began to take its place.

"Whatever's the matter?" asked The Commodore, concerned.

"You're going to take me home now, aren't you?" said Charlie, sadly.

"Yes, it's not safe in the Divine World," The Commodore admitted. "The Celestial Order think you are dead, so they won't come snooping for you. They are preoccupied, to say the least."

"But we have achieved nothing. The Celestial Order were victorious, the invincible army still exists and is poised to attack, and the Rebellion have been defeated. Many of them have probably been captured or killed," Charlie explained, deflated.

The Commodore looked at Charlie admirably, a smile spreading across his face as he observed Charlie's naivety.

"My boy, that is not true," The Commodore explained in a kind tone. "The Celestial Order had spread lies and hid the truth about The Galdihar Rebellion. Most of the world thought that we were a myth and didn't exist. We were never going to win the battle at Rohan's Reach. We were destined to lose the battle from the moment we set sail, but what we achieved is far more important."

Charlie looked at The Commodore confused, not sure of what he meant.

"The world knows that The Galdihar Rebellion is real. They know of the lies and deceit that they have spread so callously. But most importantly, you exposed the invincible army. You opened their eyes to the truth, my boy, and that is why we are victorious," The Commodore explained, bursting with pride. "It is true that we have a lot of work to do, the Divine world is now more dangerous than ever, but we have the truth on our side."

"I see," said Charlie, slowly. "But what will you do now?"

"I will fight, with every fibre of my being. I will do everything I can to battle The Celestial Order and bring peace to the world," The Commodore replied, proudly. "I have real purpose; we could not have done anything without your help."

Charlie beamed up at The Commodore with pride, and embraced him once more.

"It is time for you to go home now," said The Commodore with a sigh. "I am sad that we will no longer be a team, but one day you will be called upon."

"What shall I do until then?" asked Charlie.

"Live, my boy. Live well and be kind," said The Commodore. The watch began to tick once more from The Commodore's pocket.

"It's time for us to go. I'll take you home. Thank you again, Charlie." Charlie wept as The Commodore fiddled with the watch. The familiar bright flash and resounding boom echoed as they shifted back to Charlie's home timeline.

"Ouch!" cried Charlie, rubbing his head. He looked up and saw the vast beauty of Kingston Abbey. The warm summer night came with a complementary breeze as Charlie stood, wondering how long he had been absent. A light graze bled but he hardly seemed to notice. A great sadness began to descend upon him as he thought about the incredible adventure he had taken part in and the friends he had made. He felt a movement in his pocket and reached inside. A woe-globe had made its way into his possession. He silently considered the empty glass globe and the tiny bottle he had acquired from the shroud.

The lights of the hallway illuminated as the heavy locks in the door began to turn and unlock.

Charlie looked out into the night and saw The Commodore looking back. Charlie smiled and waved. The Commodore returned a friendly salute before vanishing into the night with a flash and a bang.

The End

Acknowledgements

As I have stumbled and tripped through life, I have been fortunate enough to meet some incredible people. Some of them are mentioned below, as they helped me first-hand to realise a dream. A dream that seemed at one point or another, impossible.

Deborah J Sills – *My mother, for being incredibly supportive and introducing me to books from an early age.*
Catriona Sproston – *My partner and soul mate, for bringing me endless cups of tea and loving me beyond comprehension.*
Charles Macauley – *The absolute epitome of kindness and selflessness.*
Zachary Birchall – *My brother, for accepting me, supporting me, and for staying. Always.*
Jordan Birchall – *My youngest brother, for being an incredible uncle to my children. You truly are a cherished member of the family.*
Raj Virk – *The creative agitator, whose feedback has not only been critical, but essential.*

Justyna Kowalska – *Fellow petrol-head and book cover designer.*

Adam Kara & Jo Wright – *For showing me how to reach my full potential.*

Hayley Brackley – *For realising my potential and for being a fantastic friend.*

Jack Fielding, John Worsley, Lewis Wilkinson, Jack Hibbert, Jack Knowles – *For laughs, tears and bellyaches.*

Thank you.